Mystery Bor
Borthwick, J. S.
My body lies over the ocean

My Body Lies
Over the Ocean

Also by J. S. Borthwick

My Body Lies Over the Ocean

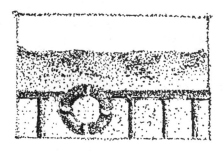

J. S. Borthwick

ST. MARTIN'S PRESS ✖ NEW YORK

The *Queen Victoria,* her crew, her passengers, and the events described on her Atlantic passage are entirely fictitious.

Chapter drawings by Margaret Creighton
Ship diagram by Mac Creighton

Library of Congress Cataloging-in-Publication Data

Borthwick, J. S.
    My body lies over the ocean / J. S. Borthwick. — 1st ed.
      p.   cm.
    ISBN 0-312-19991-0
    I. Title.
    PS3552.0756M9   1999
    813' .54—dc21   98-41754
                                              CIP

First Edition: February 1999

10 9 8 7 6 5 4 3 2 1

To the memory of my mother, Jean Scott Ramsdell, who, on her many Atlantic crossings, had close encounters with the ships *Lusitania*, *Titanic*, and *Andrea Doria* and happily lived to tell the tale.

Acknowledgments

Many thanks are due to my son, Mac, for his medical advice and his rendition of the deck plans of the good ship *Queen Victoria*. Also my gratitude goes to Douglas Hartley who consented to disturb the peace of his transatlantic trip by taking notes on shipboard equipment, procedures, and protocol. Also a thank you to my daughter, Margaret, and granddaughter, Louisa, for lending me their diaries and photographs, and jogging my memory about our shared Atlantic crossing.

Cast of Principal Characters

SARAH DEANE—Teaching Fellow, Bowmouth College, wife of Alex

ALEX MCKENZIE—Physician, husband of Sarah

JULIA CLANCY—Sarah's aunt, owner of High Hope Farm

DEEDEE HERRICK—Wife and partner of Richard Herrick

RICHARD HERRICK—Husband of Deedee, lecturer of "Ships in Peril" lecture series

GERALD HOFSTRA—Manager of the "Ships in Peril" lectures

SAM GREENBANK—Physician, friend of Alex

AUBREY CLYDE SMITH—Passenger on the *Queen Victoria*

VIVIAN SMITH—Passenger and cousin of Aubrey

MARGARET LEE—Passenger and friend of Vivian

EDWARD HOGARTH (TEDDY)—Passenger, Member of British trade commission

LIZA BAUM—Passenger returning to New York

ERIK ANDERSON—Passenger returning to New Hampshire with two grandchildren

ADÈLE AND CHARLOTTE—French passengers visiting the U.S.

CHARLES AND MARCI—American passengers returning home

Crew

FATHER PETER BOTTOMLEY—Church of England chaplain

AMORY FRYE—Assistant to Father Bottomley

MARY MALONE—Stewardess on Deck One

FREDERICK—Waiter in the Windsor Castle Dining Room

Simplified Plan of Queen Victoria

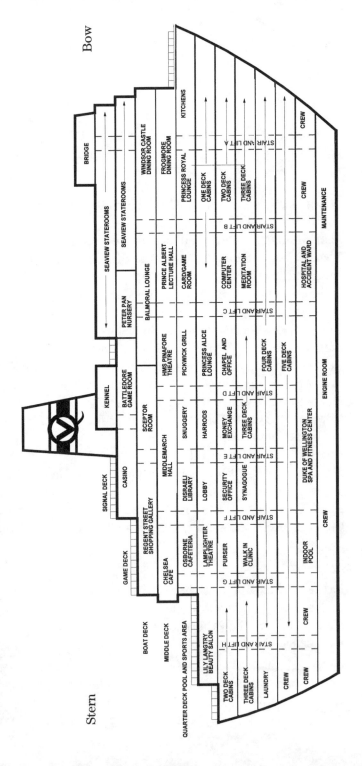

Stern

Bow

BRIDGE

SEAVIEW STATEROOMS

SEAVIEW STATEROOMS

SIGNAL DECK

GAME DECK

BOAT DECK

MIDDLE DECK

QUARTER DECK POOL AND SPORTS AREA

KENNEL

CASINO

REGENT STREET SHOPPING GALLERY

LILY LANGTRY BEAUTY SALON

BATTLEDORE GAME ROOM

SCEPTOR ROOM

MIDDLEMARCH HALL

CHELSEA CAFE

OSBORNE CAFETERIA

LAMPLIGHTER THEATRE

HMS PINAFORE THEATRE

SNUGGERY

DISRAELI LIBRARY

PURSER

TWO DECK CABINS

PICKWICK GRILL

HARRODS

LOBBY

WALK IN CLINIC

THREE DECK CABINS

PRINCESS ALICE LOUNGE

MONEY EXCHANGE

SECURITY OFFICE

SYNAGOGUE

LAUNDRY

CHAPEL AND OFFICE

THREE DECK CABINS

FOUR DECK CABINS

CREW

FIVE DECK CABINS

CREW

DUKE OF WELLINGTON SPA AND FITNESS CENTER

INDOOR POOL

CREW

CREW

ENGINE ROOM

PETER PAN NURSERY

BALMORAL LOUNGE

PRINCE ALBERT LECTURE HALL

CARD/GAME ROOM

COMPUTER CENTER

MEDITATION ROOM

HOSPITAL AND ACCIDENT WARD

WINDSOR CASTLE DINING ROOM

FROGMORE DINING ROOM

PRINCESS ROYAL LOUNGE

ONE DECK CABINS

TWO DECK CABINS

THREE DECK CABINS

KITCHENS

CREW

MAINTENANCE

STAIR AND LIFT A

STAIR AND LIFT B

STAIR AND LIFT C

STAIR AND LIFT D

STAIR AND LIFT E

STAIR AND LIFT F

STAIR AND LIFT G

STAIR AND LIFT H

1

Things are seldom what they seem,
Skim milk masquerades as cream,
High-lows pass as patent leathers,
Jackdaws strut in peacock's feathers.

    —*H. M. S. Pinafore,* W. S. Gilbert and Sir Arthur Sullivan

TRAVELERS of today who embark on an ocean voyage do so for purposes unrelated to getting from here to there with any degree of speed. Some, like Deedee and Richard Herrick, arranged passage on the new British liner, the *Queen Victoria,* for their Atlantic crossing on Wednesday, the twenty-eighth of June, for a very simple reason: because of their onboard lecture series, "Ships in Peril," the trip was almost free.

"It's like being given a great glamorous something for practically nothing," enthused Deedee as she finished her packing.

"Not," said Richard with a meaningful frown, "if you can't stay away from the shops. I've heard there's a Harrods aboard."

"Wonderful!" exclaimed Deedee.

Other passengers, like Aubrey Clyde Smith, hoped to combine business with a certain amount of pleasure, so he had dug out his black studs and cuff links and sent his dinner jacket to be cleaned—he was traveling Balmoral class, the new name for the former and politically incorrect first class. And, Aubrey told himself, there was a chance he would be taking to the dance floor in a sedate way, as befitting his age, with cousin Vivian, or with Vivian's traveling companion, Margaret. Better check out his black patent-leather shoes. No need for seasick pills; Aubrey was a good sailor, having been hardened by service in the Royal Navy for some seventeen years. Last and most important, he must remember to leave a wake-up call at the Ebury Court Hotel desk for his very early A.M. departure for Southampton.

Edward David Hogarth, known to his friends as Teddy, needed the five days at sea to clear his brain and so be able to attend to the demands of his new job. Flop-haired, loose-jointed Teddy, one of the United Kingdom's most notable Good Time Charlies, had recently been booted out of his very junior slot in the Foreign Office, and his father, Colonel Sir Arthur William Hogarth, a man with clout in high places, had managed to attach his son to a quasi-official trade commission that had arranged a confrontation with certain American industrial powers.

Teddy Hogarth—who had private funds supplied by a doting grandmother—had been holed up in the Savoy following his father's orders to stay alcohol-free before embarkation and now felt he deserved a few quick ones in his room and then dinner out on the town. Perhaps run to earth the lovely Liza Baum, who was booked on the same trip although many decks below Teddy, whose income allowed him a cabin on One Deck. But no reason, Teddy argued, that after the *Queen Victoria* turned her nose toward New York, Liza couldn't be sprung from the bowels of the ship and turned into a companion and bunk mate.

A senior member of this same trade commission, one tall, blond athletic specimen, Donald Lyman-Smith, had been quartered at the Savoy at considerable expense by Colonel Hogarth for the sole purpose of keeping an eye on Teddy. Curiously enough, Donald Lyman-Smith also had an interest in bedding the lovely Liza, whom he had met that past Sunday afternoon while watchdogging Teddy. Liza had not appeared to favor

Teddy in any very particular way, so Donald counted on his clear head and physical vigor to outmatch his less stable junior. And since Donald was a handsome and purposeful man who stuck to small intakes of wine, a speculator would certainly have put his money on Donald.

But like horse races, nothing is sure. Both men, having decided on dinner away from the Savoy, left the hotel between seven and seven-thirty. Teddy Hogarth, at ten after seven, walked, a bit unsteadily to be sure, across the street with the clouded idea of hitting a pub before he made his restaurant choice. Plenty of time on shipboard to turn himself into a teetotaler. Donald Lyman-Smith, entirely sober, emerged from the hotel three minutes later, the doorman hailed a taxi, the taxi approached and slowed, Donald Lyman-Smith reached the curb, took a step, stumbled—or was pushed—and found himself plunging forward into the street, his arms reaching wildly into space. A dark vehicle coming up behind the taxi, whose driver was—or was not—aware of Mr. Smith's lurching body, accelerated slightly, swerved, and with his left fender neatly hooked Mr. Smith at hip level. Mr. Smith, now attached to the automobile, continued in a contorted and flailing condition a considerable distance down the street before rolling free.

The driver of the dark car continued his way, then turned and disappeared into traffic, while at the same time the doorman and several passersby hurried to attend the damaged person of Donald Lyman-Smith. Teddy Hogarth, however, now a block away, continued on his muzzy way, only looking up some twelve minutes later when an ambulance, heading toward the Savoy, lights blinking, siren whooping, passed him.

The lovely Liza Baum, who had not made either of the above two gentlemen part of her evening plans, closed her wheeled suitcase, zipped up her briefcase, inspected her passport and traveler's checks for the last time, then reached for the telephone, stabbed in a well-known number. Jean-Philippe, who had been absolutely super last month in Paris, should be over within the hour, and then they could think about interesting ways in which to spend their last evening together.

Sarah Deane, U.S. citizen and teaching fellow at the state

of Maine's Bowmouth College and future Ph.D.—if all went well with her thesis defense next fall—knew that for her the beauty of ocean travel on a large cruise ship lay not in the joy of being a voyager on a floating resort with its promises of luxury unparalleled; it lay in the elementary fact of the vessel being on the water. Not in the sky. Not jetting through the ether at forty thousand feet subject to all the ills that air travel is heir to: turbulence, wind shear, the hijacker, the dreadful conviviality of the seat neighbor who "just loves to fly."

Sarah, her short hair brushed into a shining dark brown cap, wearing her navy T-shirt and tan cotton skirt, sat at the wheel of the rental Ford Escort the morning following the unfortunate accident to Donald Lyman-Smith. Sarah was cheerful; she hummed under her breath, and drove toward the Southampton docks with the increasing sense of satisfaction at not being aloft on Flight One-oh-something-or-other. Beside her sat her husband, Alex McKenzie. He was in a somewhat rumpled condition due to the exertions required in wrestling baggage out of last night's B&B second-floor room in Winchester into the automobile, and then, as a passenger—not a condition he submitted to easily—enduring the crawl through heavy southbound traffic on a day of increasing warmth.

Alex, possessor of dark hair, black brows, and thin slash of a mouth, considered by many friends to be a species of latter-day pirate, was a physician in ordinary life. He had flown to Italy some weeks before for a Lyme disease conference, but had been derailed by untoward events involving his wife and her aunt on the shores of Lake Como. Now he found himself the possessor of six free days and an Atlantic crossing on the new ocean liner called affectionately the *Vicky*. Alex, aware that when he returned to work he would pay in spades those doctors who had covered for him, was prepared to enjoy himself to the fullest. To this end he had laid in a supply of three new paperbacks featuring espionage in its most exotic aspect and armed himself with newly purchased lightweight binoculars. Alex, an ardent bird-watcher, would not be one to neglect a chance of sighting pelagic species.

In the rear seat sat Sarah's aunt, Julia Clancy, her gray

Brillo-like hair ruffled by the open window, and her mind busy with the business aspects of the transatlantic venture. Julia—the prima mobile of the trip, the planner, the gift giver—rummaged through her Welcome Aboard Travel Package with its tickets, color-coded luggage tags, a chart of the vessel, and A Special Message From Your Captain, who, judging from his smiling photograph, could hardly restrain himself from leaping down the gangplank and personally welcoming passengers aboard.

"I hope, Sarah," said Julia Clancy, as the three emerged from their car at the rental agency, "after spending five days bounding around at sea, that this trip will seem worth it, because we could have been home in just a few hours by plane. In our own beds."

Sarah paused in the act of hauling a duffel bag from the boot of the car. "Aunt Julia, if you're going to go around talking about the time we could have saved, I will have nothing to do with you. You can go sulk in a deck chair or you can live it up with us. I don't care if we have fifty-foot waves and fifty-knot winds."

Standing on tiptoe, Sarah stretched her neck and thought she could just make out an expanse of the English Channel. This she viewed with lively satisfaction. Water supported not only aquatic life; it supported—at least for a time if the water was warm enough—live bodies. Persons flung into the water had a fighting—or in this case a swimming—chance. Not like those in a 747 plummeting earthwards. After all, the *Lusitania*, the *Andrea Doria*, and other ill-fated vessels boasted survivors. A certain number of passengers had made it home after the *Titanic* had plunged more than two and a half miles to the bottom of the ocean after slicing into an iceberg. Although, as has been noted at regular intervals in the succeeding years, the first-class passengers on the *Titanic*—especially if female—certainly had the best shot at making it to a lifeboat.

"Even *Titanic* had some survivors," she informed her aunt. "Even in that cold water. And that's because there were a few lifeboats and a few passengers could swim. On a plane all you get are fragments of the fuselage, floating luggage, and, if you're lucky, the black recorder box. So, Aunt Julia, I'll say thank you every morning and every evening and I'll bring you tea and scones and your slippers. As long as you don't go around saying how much happier I'd be flying."

"Now that's enough," said Julia. "To be honest I'm looking forward to the trip. Years ago Tom and I sailed across the Atlantic. It was great fun and I felt like a movie star. Champagne in our cabin and a basket of flowers." She paused, and Sarah, always aware that Julia could become misty-eyed when talking about her dead husband, Irish Tom Clancy, diverted her attention to a taxi looming by the sidewalk.

"Come on, let's grab it. Alex, have you got everything?"

Alex, focused on the impending departure, nodded, seized Julia's old khaki duffel, ran to the curb, and hailed the approaching cab. Usually Julia would have insisted on shouldering her own luggage, but today, stricken with misery from arthritis, she allowed Alex's assistance. And the cabby, hoping to carry rich Americans to a distant destination—possibly as far as London or to a tourist spot in Cornwall—shot his taxi forward and assisted the party to climb in. And then heard the discouraging news that only a few blocks to the Southampton Eastern Docks terminal gate would take care of the trip.

"You could've walked," he observed sourly.

"I am an old woman and I expect you to take us to the *Queen Victoria* dock without complaint or overcharge," said Julia Clancy, reverting to her normal manner—a manner honed to sharpness by years of managing a horse farm and instructing beginning riders to keep their heels down, their heads up, and to pay attention.

Clutching shoulder bag, passport, handbag, and a newly acquired straw hat with a red and black ribbon, Sarah stood at the entrance of an enormous and crowded room. They had been deposited by their annoyed driver in a huge passenger holding tank that masqueraded as an outsize living room. People of all sizes and shapes and ages milled about, opened folders, hailed officials; children ran full tilt pursued by caretakers; babies wailed; and a small number of the infirm inched their wheelchairs and walkers toward what might or might not have been an exit door.

"Those movies," said Sarah with a sigh. She turned to her aunt. "Remember people hanging over the rail waving goodbye? And the crowd on the dock waving back. And the handsome purser—or the first mate—calling out, 'All ashore who's going ashore.'"

Julia sighed. "Those ocean trips with Irene Dunne and Cary Grant. Or was it Charles Boyer and Deborah Kerr? Then meeting at the Empire State Building and being run down and going blind. Or crippled."

"And then Bette Davis and Paul Henreid in *Now, Voyager*," added Sarah, who was a great fan of old movies. "Paul standing by the rail at night lighting two cigarettes for Bette. And movies with people rushing up the gangplank for a last embrace. Or hiding in a lifeboat because their lover was being sent away by Mama and Papa to get over an 'unsuitable attachment.'"

Alex shook his head at his two female companions. "That's exactly why we're being processed," he said. "No one wants people hiding out in lifeboats and passengers rushing off the boat."

Sarah looked at her husband with disfavor. "Alex, you have absolutely no imagination. And 'processed' is right. We're exactly like sausage meat. Pushed from desk A to desk B to inspection C and then divided up into high class and steerage."

"No more steerage," said Alex, the practical. "Just a comfortable cabin five decks below."

Sarah grinned at him. "Where we'll be the first to go. You know that old song, 'Oh they built the ship *Titanic*.'" She pulled out a chair for her aunt and sank into another next to it.

"You can all visit me," said Julia, the possessor of a cabin on One Deck. "Then we can go down together in style. I'm sorry I couldn't manage an outside cabin for you two but the *Vicky* was completely booked."

"It's booked with people who couldn't get on the *QE Two*," put in a voice, and Sarah swiveled to find a small round-faced woman with a mop of curly red hair looking down at her.

"A lifelong dream," said the woman. "Richard and me on the *QE Two*. With our new show."

"Show?" said Sarah.

"Yes, our new maritime series. But we had to settle for the *Vicky* since the *QE Two* was full. But really, we lucked out. Think of it, the *Vicky*'s maiden voyage."

"It is exciting," said Sarah in a repressed voice. She looked back at Julia and Alex, thinking that the three of them weren't ready to be drawn into what promised to be a rather unstable conversation. Time later for shipboard friendships. Now she had to concentrate on keeping a grip on her luggage and her passport.

". . . and still vulnerable," said the woman.

"What?" said Sarah, who had missed the beginning of the sentence.

"All oceangoing vessels. Vulnerable. Richard and I are doing a three-program series on this trip. It's called 'Ships in Peril.' "

"You mean," said Sarah, "you're one of what the brochure calls star attractions on board?"

"I'm not sure about the star part, because it all started as a sort of hobby. Our shows and traveling. First at home in Buffalo—Buffalo, New York, not Wyoming. Then all over. Richard is a wonderful speaker and now we're real professionals. At our age, imagine! We do on-site research, take our pictures or do our filming, dig into the archives, and then put it all together. Gardens and stately homes. Trips down the Rhine, through the fjords. The rain forest. That's why we're on the *Vicky*. We started this winter."

"Started what?" said Sarah, speaking in spite of herself.

"Our shows. Videos and slides and Richard doing the narration with a musical backup. You know, bagpipe music fading into the glen if we're doing Edinburgh or 'Santa Lucia' if we're in Italy. I do props and lighting mostly. And, like I said, the focus is all maritime because Richard's found a manager who has worked out this new format. Sunken ships."

"Sunken what?" demanded Julia, suddenly alert and focusing on the stout little figure. Partridge, Julia decided. A puffed-out partridge. Even her print dress and coat. Brown and white. And the fluffy hair done in the Orphan Annie style, curly russet hair that looked, despite her middle years, absolutely genuine.

"Sunken ships," repeated the woman. She settled down in the empty chair next to Julia. "I'm not that crazy about disasters but they do seem very popular. We do liners and ferries and pirates. The ones who ravaged the coast."

"Coast, which coast?" put in Sarah.

"Any coast. Even the Great Lakes. The Spanish Main. The South Seas. Around the Horn. You name it. Richard's found wonderful old film clips. When we first started out we were small time. Historical societies, museums, social clubs, the Rotary. Elderhostel. Resort hotels. But now we've got this manager, Gerald Hofstra, and he's organized our show around the sea. He says since there are lots of older people going on cruises or who do the Atlantic crossings, well, they simply devour maritime disasters because they were the right age in the twenties and thirties for traveling by ocean liner. But I do think some of the shows are a little on the gruesome side. Anyway, we're excited and you wouldn't believe the clothes I've had to buy. Evening dresses and afternoon suits. Richard has a linen jacket he got in London and a new tux."

The woman paused and took a breath while Sarah and Alex, and even Julia, stunned into silence, stared at her.

Then, getting her second wind, the woman extended a hand to Julia. It was time apparently for social rapport. "I'm Deedee Herrick," she said. "Dorothy, actually. Mrs. Richard Herrick if you want to be formal. But let's make it Deedee. After all, we'll be shipmates."

"You mean," said Sarah reverting to topic A, "that you and your husband do pirates and sunken ships? And the *Titanic*?"

"The *Titanic*, of course, is the big one. And Gerald and Richard really run the program. When Richard and I started it was the 'The Dick and Deedee Show' and later, after we'd done the Greek islands and an African safari, we called it 'Adventure Travel,' but now it's 'Ships in Peril.' Gerald says people on boats like to hear about danger at sea. Experience it. You know, virtual reality."

Alex joined in. "You mean you travel on cruise ships to get new footage, hoping that the seams will open up or a boiler will burst? Or a gang of thugs will board the ship?"

"Oh, no," said the woman. "You haven't been listening. It's the ambiance. Gerald wants to make people *feel* a disaster."

"Gracious," said Julia for lack of anything else to say. And then she turned to her companions. "They're waving our section forward. We have to go past that desk and have our passports checked. Then I'll probably be sent on another route because I have yellow tags on my things."

"And we peasants with purple tags go where?" asked Sarah.

"Purple tags?" interrupted Deedee Herrick. "Yes, that's Five Deck. They used to call it third class but now I'm told it's all very nice. Chocolates under your pillow and TV. Gerald and Richard and I will be on One Deck. And you are?" She hesitated.

Sarah pulled herself together. "My aunt, Julia Clancy. And my husband, Alex McKenzie. I'm Sarah. Sarah Deane."

Alex shook the outstretched hand of Mrs. Herrick and Julia nodded. "We're looking forward," she said, "to five days of rest."

"You mean," said Deedee, looking at the three with a bright inquisitive eye, "you don't want to think about disasters. But Gerald says it's the history that gets to people. How something happened. Why someone didn't notice a big wave. Or read telegraph warnings, smell smoke, see the strange ship with the black flag. And, after all, the *Vicky* is safe as a church and brand new. Gerald says we passengers can have our cake and eat it, too."

"I understand," said Sarah. "We can wallow in the details of ships going down and still be all cozy and snug in our bunks."

"That's what Gerald claims," said Deedee, and Sarah heard a slight note of doubt in Deedee's voice with each mention of the manager's name. It suggested that the lady's heart was not perhaps one hundred percent in the showing of sea disasters.

But now Deedee jumped to her feet. "There's Richard." She pointed at a bespectacled man with a head of receding gray-brown hair who was bustling in her direction. "We'll see each other soon," said Deedee. "We're giving our first show in the

H. M. S. Pinafore Theatre. I hope you three can come." Here Deedee cupped her hand to her mouth and let out a yodel. "Yoo-hoo, Richard, I'm coming." And she pushed her way through a throng and disappeared into the thickening crowd.

"I think," said Julia, standing up and gathering her handbag to her breast, "that we can give Deedee and Richard a miss. Who in God's name wants to hear all the ghastly details about people being chopped up with cutlasses and clinging to rafts?"

Alex smiled down at Julia. "You'd rather read Dick Francis describing maimed horses and mutilated jockeys? Or," he added with a side glance at Sarah, who was a fan of Brother Cadfael and his felonious associates in thirteenth-century Shrewsbury, "entertain yourself with poisoned yeomen and decapitated monks?"

"Oh, don't be so logical, Alex," said Julia. "It's a very annoying habit you have. Look, everyone is moving along. Now, when I'm settled—it's cabin ten-forty-five on the starboard side—I'll come by and collect you for lunch. I'll knock three times to show I'm family, because we certainly don't want Deedee and Richard around our necks. At least not yet." And Julia draped her raincoat over her arm, activated her cane, and marched off in the direction of the moving stream of passengers.

Sarah and Alex followed, Alex shaking his head. "I don't think," he said, "that your Aunt Julia is going to walk off with the Miss Congeniality award."

Sarah nodded. "What Aunt Julia needs on board is some mighty distraction. Since we can hardly come up with a horse, let's hope for a man. A man who's crazy about horses."

"Who is attracted to difficult older women," added Alex.

2

SARAH could only think of what followed as the swallowing process by a monstrous whale of hundreds of Jonahs. The passport presentation, the transfer of the tagged luggage to designated cabins, the movement through a series of dreary departure buildings and up the gangplank—this sheltered from public view by high side walls. No chance to flutter a handkerchief at Cary Grant on the dock or to blow a kiss to Fred Astaire, who leaned elegantly against a bollard. Or, once on board—to bring the scene up to date—no Tom Hanks or Ralph Fiennes lurking in the shadow of a lifeboat. These present-day passengers had only the dubious experience of being photographed—for a "photo-memory"—in a bedraggled condition as they pressed forward and up the gangplank. It would not be, thought Sarah, brushing a limp wisp of hair from her forehead, the sort of picture proudly displayed on a family mantelpiece.

Finally, after presenting evidence to the purser's henchmen that they were not indigent and could present viable credit cards at the various onboard shops, Sarah and Alex found themselves in the lower reaches of the *Victoria* facing cabin 5023—this marked in dark purple on the ship's chart and reached after a descent by elevator and stairway and a trek through an endless corridor of blank walls punctuated by cabin doors.

"It's like going down to the bottom of a mine," said Sarah, inserting the key into the lock of the door. She dropped her shoulder bag to her feet and walked over to the lower bunk.

"Aha," she said, eyeing the small nightstand. "We do have chocolate mints—one for each."

"A shower in the head," announced Alex, ducking in and out of the lavatory. Alex was a sailing type who, once aboard any vessel, instantly reverted to the proper terminology. Already, he had begun to speak familiarly of aft and forward and starboard and port and trod the deck, not the floor.

"Lots of literature," said Sarah, burrowing into a sheaf of pamphlets and booklets. She turned to examine the walls. Or bulkheads, as Alex called them. "Where's the porthole?"

"Inside cabin," said Alex. "Not a room with a view."

"What!" exclaimed Sarah. "Why, that's like being in a coffin. Are we below the waterline?"

"You prefer a seven-forty-seven?" asked Alex. "United, American? Or British Airways?" He reached for his duffel and shoved it into a small clothes locker.

"Seriously, isn't there a porthole?"

"Julia said she was sorry there weren't any outside cabins. Remember, she's giving us the tickets, so don't go and bite the hand that's paying the fare and then complain about portholes."

But Sarah had turned to a television set and was flipping switches. And immediately came up with the announcement that the *Victoria*, by means of a camera fixed on the bow, would soon transmit a constant view of the ocean.

"A secondhand view," Sarah announced.

"You have views on the brain," said Alex. "We won't be living down here. We'll be up on the deck playing shuffleboard or in the Throne Room doing the cha-cha."

"Is there a Throne Room?"

Alex consulted a diagram. "Make that the Scepter Room. Besides, we can hang out in Julia's cabin. It'll have a porthole."

*   *   *

Julia Clancy was not a woman given to premonitions of disaster. She had made her way briskly to One Deck, found her stateroom, and viewed with satisfaction the two oval portholes and the peach and blue furnishings, the framed reproductions of Windsor Great Park and the Crystal Palace over her bed, and the makings of tea on a small table. Then, unexpectedly, she found herself prey to a slight unease. A sense of gastric distress and a slight giddiness. She paused in her tour of inspection and grasped the back of an armchair. In the next few minutes the undefined symptoms, shooting between her head and her stomach, intensified, and Julia took several deep, unhappy breaths. She knew what it was: that apricot tart taken on top of the poached salmon and the caper sauce eaten last night at dinner. Fresh air was the answer. For Julia, who shunned medical remedies except for her horses, this was always the answer. She walked slowly to her cabin door, closed it behind her, and, stepping less briskly now, headed for a section of the ship that offered the greatest degree of open space and, if she were lucky, some privacy. Here, feeling more feeble every minute, she chose a section of the rail on the side of the vessel which did not overlook the embarkation tunnel. Then, feeling another wave of faintness, hung herself head down over the top rail and closed her eyes and tried to breathe slowly through her nose.

But if her last night's dinner had caused Julia to seek fresh air, the blow to the back of her neck, the clenching sensation around her waist, and the lifting of her body halfway up and across the rail could hardly be blamed on the dinner. Her head spinning, she opened her eyes to a terrifying view of black water miles below the deck. But then, at the soft sound of a door closing behind her, she felt the sudden unceremonious loosening of a tight grip around her torso so that she fell in a crumpled heap to the deck. And heard—or thought she heard—the sounds of disappearing feet. But somehow they didn't seem to matter, nothing seemed to matter. Gasping for breath, she was overcome by a great urge to stay unmoving and tightly curled beside a heavy stanchion.

It was an urge she fought. Julia Clancy, although arthritic and seventy years old, was not going to give in to vapors or manhandling. She struggled on shaking legs to a standing position, found her handbag beside her, intact and apparently unopened, took several tremulous breaths, and, walking with uncertain steps back to the ship's interior, she fumbled her way back to her cabin. It had been a moment of pure panic, and for a little while she sat collapsed in the peach-covered armchair, her pulse racing, her breath still coming in ragged gasps.

Then, breathing more steadily, she considered two unpleasant possibilities. First—the most unbelievable—that she had been the subject of a random attack by some mad person who had it in for an unknown elderly woman. Second, it was—she hated to admit—entirely possible that she had had some sort of hallucinatory fit. The discomfort in her cabin, the dizziness, the sense of being unwell, stumbling topside, hanging over the rail. Then a sort of seizure, a seizure involving a sense of being squeezed and lifted. And dropped. Perhaps she had simply fallen forward, overcome by vertigo. But those steps? The ones she thought she had heard? Probably someone on the deck above. Or part of the fit, which may have included sound effects. What had that Herrick woman said—virtual reality. Oh, dear. Oh, damn! Well, face it. These things happen to the aged no matter how splendid their health, how combative their spirit. All things considered, Julia decided not to bring the matter up with her shipboard companions. Not now, anyway. They mustn't think they were saddled with someone subject to staggers—Julia tended to think in terms of equine ailments. After all, there had been enough sticky moments in Italy this past month to last the three of them for a year. But all that was behind them; the doers of the fell deeds had been safely hauled off and locked up and could not possibly be aboard the ship ready to exact vengeance. So why, she asked herself, choosing an apt metaphor, rock the boat? For now, stand up, brace shoulders, and stay alert.

And open the small traveling supply of whiskey and toss a good snort down her throat. Perhaps hit the library and read up on some of the grimmer neurological conditions involving vertigo and hallucination which lie in wait for the senior citizen. And wait and see. An ocean voyage was always said to be beneficial to one's health; Julia hoped she was no exception to this rule.

Thus, forty-five minutes after this disturbing event—or non-event—Julia gave a smart triple rap on the door of number 5023.

Alex opened the door and Julia stepped into the cabin, accompanied by a faint cloud of whiskey not entirely masked by a breath mint. "I've had a quick drink," she said, "because I was feeling a bit wobbly. No, Alex,"—as Alex looked up alertly—"you don't have to check my blood pressure. It's that blasted apricot tart last night. I knew I should have stuck to the sorbet. Anyway, I'm fine now and I'm here to check your quarters. I have a lovely cabin. Flowers, an apple, shower gel, and everything in peach and blue." She looked about with disapproval. "This looks like a seagoing coffin."

"Certainly not. It's very nice and has everything we need," said Sarah stoutly.

"Absolutely," said Alex. "And we also have shower gel and soap and a large collection of towels with a monogram. Everything Bristol fashion."

"Or shipshape," added Sarah.

For a moment Julia viewed the space with pursed lips.

"We're close to the laundry," offered Sarah. "Maybe we'll get clean sheets faster than you will."

"Umm-hmm," said Julia again. "We shall see. I've heard of a passenger who didn't make it aboard on my deck. At least so far. There's been a call for him. Someone called Smith. Or Smythe. Maybe there'll be a cabin available."

"Nonsense," said Sarah. "We're perfectly happy. And we have a splendid view of the ocean from the TV."

For a moment Julia stared at the television view of the ship's bow and the busy harbor and then examined the framed portrait of the late Queen Victoria that hung above the clothes locker door. It showed the profile of the queen in old age complete with crown and scepter. Then she marched to the cabin door. "Come on," she announced. "Let's go topside. Watch the ship leave. The white cliffs of Dover. The Isle of Wight. Wave good-bye to Humphrey Bogart and Charles Boyer."

"You can wave to those," said Alex. "I'll be waving to Sandra Bullock and meeting Gwyneth Paltrow later in the Balmoral Room."

Ten minutes later they stood leaning on the rail of the Boat Deck. Far below on the dock a brass band had assembled and the music of "Rule Britannia" sounded as if played on toy trumpets.

"Tom," said Julia, peering down at the dock, "could not stand that song. Whenever he heard it he sang 'Cockles and Mussels' or 'Danny Boy' until it was over. Tom never took kindly to the idea of Rule Britannia."

"Irishmen generally don't," said Alex.

"Why, hello," said a bright voice close behind them. It was Deedee. Flanked by the bespectacled Richard, whose balding head was now framed in a tweed cap.

"Imagine bumping into you so soon," exclaimed Deedee, now in a flowing lime-green dress with a wide chiffon scarf thrown around her neck, and waving a hand heavy with chunky gold bracelets at the figures on the dock below. And Richard, inclining slightly, gave a semimilitary salute in the same direction.

"I believe in ceremony," said Deedee. "I love hearing 'Rule Britannia.' "

"At least it's not 'Nearer My God to Thee,' " observed Sarah.

"Aha," said Richard. He advanced one step and confronted Sarah. "I'm Richard Herrick," he announced. "Deedee's my better half."

He waited and Sarah gave the obligatory smile, Alex made a noise in his throat, and Julia emitted a low growl.

"You've made a common mistake about that hymn," said Richard. "No one is sure exactly what the orchestra was playing on the *Titanic*. A good example of how a possibility turns into legend. Has Deedee told you what we do on these trips?"

"Sunken ships," said Julia in a disapproving voice.

Richard ignored Julia's tone of voice and beamed at her. "Now let me set you straight, my dear."

Julia frowned. No stranger called her "dear" without peril.

"The orchestra," went on Richard in a relentless voice, "on

the *Titanic* at the beginning of the alarm was playing popular numbers. Survivors have remembered 'Alexander's Ragtime Band' and then the 'Autumn Song.' "

"Probably not the Episcopal hymn," put in Deedee. "A popular music-hall thing called 'Songe d'Autumne.' "

"Fascinating," said Julia.

"Now, Mrs. Clancy," said Richard, "you should know that our shows don't dwell on the terrible things, just the how and why. And who. Think about all those vacation advertising programs that wallow in violence. Murder mystery weekends. Playacting about some strangler or serial killer. We show real life in a maritime history setting. Gerald Hofstra, our manager, has convinced me people are fascinated by accidents and danger if they happened in the past. Particularly if the show is tastefully done."

"It still comes out to the same thing, doesn't it?" said Alex.

"Sudden death no matter how you slice it," said Julia inelegantly.

"Now," said Richard, "you're being morbid. We are never morbid."

"You needn't worry about the *Victoria*," added Deedee. "Plenty of lifeboats and a boat drill tomorrow. The *Titanic* taught everyone a lesson. This is going to be a wonderful trip and Richard and I hope to see you again. Shipboard friendships are such fun."

"Are they?" said Julia, turning away.

Sarah poked her aunt in the ribs. "Behave, Aunt Julia, or we'll throw you in the brig. In irons."

"It's all right," said Deedee. "I know how anxious older people can be at the beginning of a trip. Mrs. Clancy will feel better later."

Alex took Julia by the shoulder and rotated her toward the *Victoria*'s bow. "We're casting off, Julia," he said in a firm voice. "I know you'll want to watch everything." He pointed down at the dock, where ropes like overgrown pythons were lifted from the huge bollards. "I think I see Walter Pidgeon down there with Greer Garson. They seem to be looking at you."

*   *   *

Pressed against the rail in a crowd of fellow passengers—but now free of Deedee and Richard—Sarah, Alex, and Julia watched as the *Queen Victoria* slipped through the Southampton Water, entered the Solent, left the Isle of Wight to starboard, and with a small flotilla of sailboats circling like pilot fish began the traverse of the English Channel toward Cherbourg to take on a second installment of New York–bound passengers. Together they watched the headlands of England slide by, diminish, and become part of the horizon.

Julia turned away from the rail. "I seem to be over my spell of indigestion, because I'm starving and it's way past two. Unless I find a luncheon plate in front of me in the next ten minutes I will be obliged to take a bite out of one of my fellow passengers."

"Raw meat," said Alex. "Even you, Julia, wouldn't like it."

"Alex?" said a voice behind him. "Alex McKenzie? The scourge of the Atlantic?"

Sarah turned. A shaggy-haired man with brown beard, a pointed nose, and very blue eyes. He had a familiar look, but then, she decided, half the passengers looked like someone she had met somewhere before.

And now Alex was peering at the man. "Sam?" he said. "Sam Greenbank? With a beard. Med school! A hundred years ago."

The man grinned. "Feels more like two hundred, and I won't say small world because I've already seen a pair of my mother's cousins I'd like to avoid. But yes, I'm Sam, and I remember when you threw a raw egg on Halloween night and hit the dean of the med school right between the eyes. At the time I assumed you had a death wish."

Here followed introductions and hand-shakings, and then Alex moved over next to Sam Greenbank and both began to fill in the years between as well as explaining their present appearance aboard the *Queen Victoria*. Sam, it appeared, had been talked into the ocean crossing by one of the ship's doctors—an old friend—and was returning to New York after attending the very conference on Lyme disease in Bologna that Alex had regrettably missed.

"Good," said Sarah to Julia. "Alex will find out that he missed nothing by not going to Bologna, and I can stop feeling guilty about mixing him into our little affair."

"Not so little," Julia said tartly. "A garden tour run amuck, a homicide, an attempted drowning, and a spectacular fall down a flight of stone stairs. But I am glad Alex's found a medical buddy, so let's hope this Sam is a reasonable human. And," she added, frowning, "that any so-called loved ones he's traveling with are also reasonable. You meet so many decent singles and find they're attached to perfect horrors."

"Aunt Julia," said Sarah, "ease up. Mellow out. Look around and remember we're on an ocean crossing. We are privileged people. Days and days of relaxing ahead. Deck chairs, steamer rugs, soothing novels, and slot machines. I saw a whole casino in there. We can win our way across the Atlantic."

"Fat chance," said Julia. "And speaking of fat, I'm still starving. Raw meat or not, I must have food."

It was agreed by the company, now enlarged by the presence of Sam Greenbank, that if they didn't hasten toward some sort of food service it would be time for tea and dancing in the Scepter Room.

"Are you first class or Balmoral Class or whatever they call it now?" asked Sam as they pushed their way through the railside passengers and headed in the direction of the ship's interior.

"That's Aunt Julia—our founder—and she's on One Deck," said Sarah, who had studied the *Victoria*'s prospectus. "She eats in the Windsor Castle Room. Very exclusive. And we're down below on Deck Five with purple luggage tickets. We can relax in the Princess Royal Lounge and eat in the Frogmore Dining Room."

"Frogmore, isn't that where they buried Prince Albert?" asked Alex. "I seem to remember something about it. 'Frogmore' seems the right name for a subterranean dining room."

"Prince Albert is with us still," announced Julia. They had arrived in a long, richly carpeted hall lined with chairs covered in a floral pattern which faced wide windows opening out on the ocean expanse. She pointed to double doors leading to the interior. "See, there's the Prince Albert Lecture Hall." She pointed to a gold-lettered sign decorated with the profile of Her Britannic Majesty's late husband.

"Food," said Sarah. "Before we all faint. The Osborne Cafeteria. It's back—I mean aft—by the swimming pool. The brochure says they serve until midnight."

"The decorators have gone berserk on Victorian," said Julia. "I've been reading the pamphlets. Victorian England. Dickens and Lily Langtry. And a Disraeli Library and the Duke of Wellington Spa and Gym."

"But probably not a Newgate Room or the Workhouse Restaurant or a Marshalsea Cafeteria," said Sarah.

"As to cabins, I lucked out and got myself moved topside," said Sam Greenbank. "There was a sudden vacancy. A passenger didn't make it. It was on the morning news. Apparently some government type, name of Donald Something-Smith. Smith, if you can believe the name. Obviously a spy. Reputed to be on his way to New York for a trade meeting and then gets himself mugged in London. Or run down. Or went crazy and ran into the street. In front of the Savoy, no less. At night just as he was about to climb into a taxi."

"So you have his cabin?" asked Sarah.

"It seems so. There's a bottle of a not very exciting Beaujolais in a basket and 'Have a wonderful trip, Donald dear,' from 'Mother' on a tag and a bottle of schnapps with a note saying, 'Let's make it a trip—Liza.' "

"But he's okay, this spy Donald Smith?" persisted Sarah.

"No," said Sam. "Actually, he's not. Died on the way to the hospital. I suppose it only made the headlines because this trade conference has been in the news. Loosely connected to the European Common Market and those messy Euro-U.S.A. industrial negotiations."

"Well," said Julia, "let's hope this Smith doesn't choose to haunt the Atlantic Ocean."

"More likely to haunt the Savoy," said Sam. The quartet made their way rather soberly to a long table laden with foods of all possible color, shape, and texture, presided over by baskets of flowers and a massive ice sculpture of a dolphin rampant.

Settled at a table overlooking the afterdeck with its swimming pool, its badminton court, and a phalanx of deck chairs, soothed by the sight of a tranquil ocean and the liner's white foaming wake, the four forgot the deceased Donald Something-Smith and attacked their plates with a certain ferocity. Then Julia put down her fork and looked regretfully at her unfinished lobster salad.

"I overdid," she said. "It's feeling woozy earlier and then much better and having all this wonderful food and wanting to get my money's worth." She turned to Sam Greenbank, who had finished for Alex's benefit a drawing on a scrap of paper of the dorsal view of the European sheep tick, *Ixodes ricinus*, featured at the Bologna Lyme disease conference. "Do you suppose there are other vacancies?"

"Probably," said Sam, "there are a lot of no-shows. With hundreds of passengers you're bound to have accidents. Or people change their minds, something comes up, they get sick—lots of older citizens on these trips. After all, that's why people take out trip cancellation insurance."

"Or there's an emergency, a horse colics and you don't dare leave home," said Julia.

"We are hoping," said Alex to Sam, "to find a suitable fox-trot partner for Julia and let her dance the night away."

Julia pushed her lobster salad aside and confronted a slice of melon. "My dark view of life," she said with a certain asperity, "had been created by my association with Ms. Sarah Deane, who attracts trouble like flies on a hot day. It's making me imagine things that probably never happened."

Sarah turned to Sam. "Don't listen to a word this woman says. We've already begun the social whirl. We've met a couple who specialize in shipwrecks, Deedee and Richard Herrick."

Sam put down his fork with a clatter. "Deedee and Richard Herrick! Oh, my God, those two are my mother's cousins. The ones I'm trying to keep clear of. Apparently Mother let them know I'd be on the ship, and I decided that I could do the right thing with one gala dinner and then duck out of sight. I've even been thinking that you three would be good protection."

"Not to worry," said Alex. "We just bumped into them before boarding. I'm sure they have other friends."

"Listen, those two live to collect people. And most people love to be collected. Their early shows were pretty popular. You know, stuff like 'Tulip Time in Holland' or 'Down the Nile in a Felucca.' Deedee plays the part of the friendly helper, and Richard Herrick is one of those faceless people who get turned on when they're in front of an audience."

"Turned on?" asked Sarah.

"I mean Richard's good. Can do voices, accents. Sort of a chameleon. A deadbeat personality when you meet him, but an Oscar winner when he's doing his thing. Women's voices, even little girls. Pigs and dogs. The type that should have been on vaudeville in the old days."

"And now," said Alex, "they're doing shipwrecks."

"Oh, that's Gerald. Gerald Hofstra, their manager. He's taken over the whole act, jazzed it up and gone for blood and guts. Or in this case, gunpowder and pillaging and foundering. Captain Kidd and Henry Morgan and passenger ships like the *Eastland, Lusitania,* and, natch, *Titanic.* Deedee and Dick— as people—are harmless enough, but I think the new subject matter and this Gerald are, as the kids say, positively toxic."

"Speaking of toxic," said Julia, "here they come."

Here followed more rejoicing, with Deedee adding further remarks on the shrinking size of the world, and how the more people one meets the more people find they've already met and that everyone is a friend of a friend.

At which Julia remarked that as far as she was concerned her circle of friends was exactly the right size.

Fortunately Deedee had turned to Sam Greenbank and was exchanging family news and Richard was frowning over a small notebook.

"Aunt Julia," said Sarah, leaning forward so that her face was two inches away from her aunt's, "you cool it. I promise we're not going to spend the whole trip embracing the Herricks, so you promise to be a sweet old lady who loves—"

"Not loves," corrected Julia.

"Tolerates the occasional incursion of alien persons into her personal space," finished Sarah. "Besides, you've just had a wonderful lunch, the lobster was out of this world, and I'm looking forward to that fluffy white dessert with the almonds on top I saw on the buffet table. I'll bring you one. Sweeten you up."

"No, thank you, Sarah," said Julia. "It's that little bit of feeling faint. No," as Sarah began to speak, "I'm perfectly fine now so no more about it. And I'll try very hard to behave and pull in my horns."

"Well, you'd jolly well better," said Sarah over her shoulder as she headed for the dessert display.

But now Deedee Herrick was leaning over Julia and patting her shoulder. "I'll bet you feel a lot better now you've eaten. It makes all the difference with us older folk."

"I am not an . . ." began Julia. Then throttled her remark. "Yes," she said, "everything was delicious."

"Oh, you can trust these ocean liners," said Richard. "Every meal is something else. I'm taking double the number of my digestive enzymes and extra lactobacillus just to cope with the richness."

"You'll want to know," announced Deedee, "that Richard and I are scheduled for Thursday afternoon. A family show. 'Pirates and Plunder.' In the H. M. S. Pinafore Theatre. The cruise director has been wonderful and Gerald will have the stage all ready."

"With our pirate lecture," put in Richard, "we aim at families and the children. We keep it short and action-packed. For the next, 'Disasters at Sea,' we cover several unusual sinkings. Then we finish Saturday night with the *Titanic*."

"Is that going to be popular aboard the *Vicky*?" asked Sarah, returning with a dish heaped with a diaphanous white pyramid topped with slivered almonds and sliced strawberries. "I'd think sinking ocean liners was a subject to be avoided like the plague."

"No problem," said Richard. "*Titanic* was a White Star ship, and there isn't a White Star Line anymore. And you can't buck popularity. The *Titanic* disaster has everything. Look at that movie. Everyone is still talking about it. And the musical, all those books. As Gerald says, it really gets to people. And after the show the *Vicky*'s captain is going to give a short talk on all the safety improvements made since the disaster."

But now Deedee had spied another couple across a forest of glass-topped tables.

"Why, it's the Cohens!" she cried. "From Buffalo," she explained to the group. "Shirley and Joe. You know, Richard. That big house on Chapin Parkway. And Karen Adam. You know, Richard, she's Albert's daughter. My goodness, it *is* a small world." And the two Herricks, stepping nimbly, twisted their way through the tables to greet their friends.

Sam Greenbank, who had watched the retreat of his older cousins with ill-concealed relief, stood up and announced he was headed down to check out the gym. He'd join them later for a serious drink if that was okay.

"I," said Julia, "since I've been designated an 'older folk,' am going to put my feet up in my cabin and read. I'll meet you all for tea. The Balmoral Lounge. Tea or whiskey. Four-thirty."

"Are persons with purple luggage tags allowed in the Balmoral Lounge?" asked Sarah.

"You're my guests," said Julia. "I dare them to throw you out." And Julia departed in the direction of her cabin and found it occupied.

A stout, pleasant-faced woman with neatly netted gray hair was in the act of placing a tray holding a carafe and a glass on Julia's bedside table. She wore a blue and white striped uniform with a *QV* embroidered on a pocket.

"Why, hello," said Julia, stepping into the room.

"Hello," said the woman. "I'm Mary Malone and you are Mrs. Clancy. I'm your stewardess for the trip." She walked over to the porthole and drew back the curtains. "Anything you need, anything at all," she said, "just push the room service button."

Julia hesitated, but the woman with her slight Irish accent looked so kindly, so, well, motherly, that even Julia, probably twenty years her senior, felt a sense of comfort. "I'm wondering about seeing the ship's doctor. I'm traveling with a physician, but I don't want to bother him. You see, I've had a little . . . a sort of a spell, and I thought that if I had it again I might want to talk to someone. Or," she added, finding the words marching out of her mouth, "I might have been bumped by someone going by." And then, why she could not explain, she found herself describing what had happened and ended saying that it sounded crazy but perhaps, just perhaps, she'd been mugged. "Not exactly mugged—hit and grabbed and pushed half over the rail and then dropped. And I thought I heard footsteps."

Mary Malone regarded her with a serious expression. "Did you see someone? Someone you could identify again? Was someone standing near you? Or came at you from behind? Did you hear a voice?"

"No," said Julia. "It happened all at once and I was feeling peculiar at the time anyway, so I wasn't certain how much was my—" Here Julia halted, boggling at the word "hallucination," and ended lamely, "My imagination."

"So you're not really sure about it?" asked Mary in her soft Irish voice. She shook her head at Julia. "I'm afraid it's the excitement. It happens a lot. Particularly with older people. All that rushing about to get packed and trying to remember your passport and not having a proper breakfast at all. Then hurrying to make it on board on time. Why don't you have a nice lie-down. Put your feet up."

"Oh, no need for that," protested Julia. "But thank you."

"And," said the woman, turning to go and then looking back, "if it would make you feel more comfortable, don't go out on deck by yourself. These days, well, you never know. Even on this ship there are some rough types. Someone may have had too much to drink. And you're an older single woman. Just a word of advice."

Julia drew herself up. She knew a challenge when she heard one. "I'm a perfectly healthy single woman, and I always do things by myself. But thank you, Mary Malone, for your concern."

And Mary Malone became formal. "Certainly, madam. And I hope you have a pleasant trip and no more trouble."

After Mary had closed the stateroom door behind her, Julia

sank back on her bed, stretched full length, and placed her feet—still in their shoes—firmly on the peach comforter. Really, she thought, you'd think I was planning to go creeping around the London docks at midnight. Or, she added unhappily to herself, maybe Mary Malone has seen another passenger have a seizure. Or being mugged as she hung over the rail and knows whereof she speaks. Julia yawned. It certainly bore thinking about.

But not now. She closed her eyes.

3

WITH an hour or so to go before the tea or cocktail festivities, Sarah and Alex prepared for a tour of the ship. A ship, as Sarah remarked, dedicated to the establishment of a seagoing Victorian world—a world considerably better furnished and far more comfortable than the genuine article.

It was a labyrinthine world—one of thick floral carpets, dark furniture with carved curls and scrolls, hanging chandeliers dripping with crystal, and wall sconce lamps fashioned like gaslights. "Or," suggested Alex, as they pushed the door open on a paneled and heavily draped cul-de-sac in the middle of the Quarter Deck titled by its brass plate, SNUGGERY, "maybe they really are gaslights. I'll bet the decorators rifled the contents of half the old houses in England. All we need is the fog rolling in and Holmes and Watson to come round the corner."

"Even the art," said Sarah, pausing to examine a framed copy of the sketch of Dickens in his study at Gad's Hill that hung on one red brocade wall and faced rather incongruously Landseer's painting of a stag, "Monarch of the Glen," hanging on the opposite wall. "And look," she added, pointing to a nearby mahogany table with claw feet. "All the magazines. Reproductions, I suppose. *Punch* of 1891 and copies of *All the*

Year Round. Household Words, 1857, volume sixteen. Plus a folder of pictures of the Diamond Jubilee."

There was a sudden snapping of a newspaper. "Welcome to the Snuggery," said a voice. "A place to be snug in. Away from the hurly-burly. I recommend it. Everyone else is hanging over the rail, drinking at the bar, or feeding at the buffet trough. This is the place for peace on sailing day."

Sarah and Alex looked around and found in a dim corner a gentleman fixed in a leather wing chair and peering at them from the top of his open newspaper. Not a nineteenth-century one, Sarah noted, but an up-to-date copy of *The Observer* with headlines featuring a labor strike in France.

"We didn't mean to barge in and interrupt," said Sarah. "We didn't see you." She shook her head. "This whole Victorian thing is a bit much."

"Nostalgia is big business—a yearning for a time that never was. No one points out how hellishly inconvenient and unsanitary and very grim a great deal of the nineteenth century was." The man was a smooth-faced, nondescript, gray-haired specimen who, in his dark suit and somber tie, looked like a schoolmaster in a lesser English public school, one who spoke with the measured sort of speech often heard on the BBC's educational programs.

"You haven't interrupted me," the man went on. "I'm simply having an interval of quiet before I brave the hordes. Wait a minute. I've turned down my hearing aid." The man reached up and twirled something plastic and flesh colored in his ear. "There, that's better. The décor doesn't bother me. In fact it reminds me of my grandmother's house. Only not so moldy." He lowered his newspaper, folded it carefully, and laid it on his knees. "Actually, I'm meeting someone," he said, his voice taking on a confidential ring. "My cousin. We haven't seen each other in years, so I told her I'd be in the Snuggery between three and four. She's going to New York on a business trip—she works for a publisher. Traveling with a friend whom I've never met. And since I was booked aboard for the same crossing we thought we should get together but might not know each other by sight. So she said she'd be wearing a tartan skirt and a plum-colored jacket with white buttons. Plum or was it raspberry? A fruit, anyway."

"An assignation," said Sarah. "Right out of Sherlock Holmes. Or Trollope."

"Exactly," said the man. "Or Dickens or Wilkie Collins. I've always rather fancied myself as a Wilkie Collins character." He gave a tentative smile. His was the sort of bland face in which no single feature dominated the whole. It was, thought Sarah, always alive to the possibilities of mystery, the sort of face one could never identify if called on to do so. In fact, the face had something in common with that of their new friend, Richard Herrick—another noncommittal facade.

"Of course," the man went on, "it would be more interesting if Vivian were not my cousin. A mysterious Hungarian widow who has a coded message sewn into the hem of her skirt."

"And," said Alex, getting into the spirit of the thing, "a poison ring filled with cyanide."

"And a maid who follows her everywhere carrying a small locked ebony box," added Sarah. Then, thinking that the time had come for further civilities, she introduced herself and Alex, adding that they were traveling back to the States with their aunt.

"My name is Smith. Aubrey Clyde Smith. The Clyde part came from the river. I was born a month ahead of time almost on the banks of the Clyde. Smith isn't a name to remember, because I suppose there must be at least a hundred Smiths aboard."

Sarah nodded, frowning slightly. "I think I heard somewhere that a Mr. Smith didn't make it aboard. An accident." She paused, feeling somehow that the rest of the story should not be public property.

A slight cloud passed over Mr. Aubrey Clyde Smith's face and he nodded soberly. "Yes, I did hear something about it last night on the late news. Very unfortunate." He paused and smiled again. "And now if either of you see anyone in plum or raspberry with another female in tow, send them along. Fond as I am of the Snuggery, I don't wish to spend the entire day here."

"What's Vivian's last name in case we bump into her?"

asked Sarah, amused at the arrangement. It sounded more and more like a Victorian spy story.

"Smith. Vivian Smith. Another Smith. We are legion. Her friend is Margaret. An American, and her name is Lee. She's from South Carolina. I'm told Lee is a popular name in that part of the country. From Robert E. Lee, I suppose. Apparently Margaret is winding up her very first trip away from the States. And I'm told she's quite deaf. As I am, so I hope she's wearing a hearing aid. So good to have met you. Perhaps we'll see each other here again and catch up on the news of the nineteenth century. Find out if the Reform Act has passed or whether Disraeli is speaking to Gladstone."

Alex told Mr. Smith that they'd keep an eye out for Vivian and he and Sarah backed out of the Snuggery and headed topside.

"I have the sense," said Sarah as they made their way up and aft in the general direction of fresh air, "that we were ever so gently dismissed. As my grandmother would say, given our congé."

"It was the Snuggery," said Alex. "The atmosphere is suggestive and you're always looking for subplots. The sea air will do you good. You'll start trusting people again. And I certainly didn't want to spend any more time down there. Too claustrophobic. If I'm on the ocean I like to see it. Which is one reason I'll spend as little time in our cabin as possible."

"The Snuggery is very snug," agreed Sarah, "but that's Victorian for you. Snug as hell. And dark as a pocket. If I'm visiting in one of those houses where the owner has gone mad with the Victorian 'look,' I want to open windows and snatch down the curtains and the velvet draperies and the bellpulls and the plush tablecloths and throw a few teapots around. Now let's track down Julia and Sam and prepare to pour something down the hatch."

The late afternoon tea and/or cocktail meeting concluded, Sam Greenbank disappeared to look up his physician friend in the ship's hospital. Sarah and Alex partook of a light dinner at a partly filled table in the Frogmore Dining Room while Julia chose to have hot soup and toast in her stateroom—her heavy lunch was still with her. Now it was nine-fifteen in the evening, and in the interest of overseeing the departure from Cherbourg the three travelers stood at the rail in one of the less crowded sections of what the ship's diagram referred to as the Quarter Deck. "Which I thought," remarked Sarah, "was the captain's turf. For him to pace around in."

Their chosen lookout point gave them a bird's-eye view of a small band of musicians who stood bunched with their brass instruments on the Cherbourg dock, and now as the lines were cast off, the band launched into their final selection, and for the second time that day the *Vicky* had her departure serenaded.

The music floated up, its notes almost indistinguishable.

"I am just not sure but I do think I sang that in sixth grade," said a tall, willowy, bottle-blond woman in a strong southern accent. She was standing next to Julia and waving a slim white hand with bright red nails at the band. "I think it has a million verses all about sheep getting lost."

Julia inclined her ear. "It sounds military," she announced.

"No," corrected Sarah. "I think it's that funeral march. 'Marche Funèbre.' Only they're playing it too fast."

"Wrong, all of you," said a man's voice by Sarah's elbow. "The French are terribly complex about ceremonies. They wouldn't play something so obvious as a funeral march. Listen. It's a children's song. *'Malbrough s'en va-t'en guerre.'* All about Malbrough being killed and then buried."

"I just knew it was a children's song," said the woman.

"We meet again," said the man. It was Mr. Aubrey Clyde Smith, late of the Snuggery. "I decided to see the ship off. *Faire mes adieux.*"

Sarah looked up at the man, surprised to see that, standing, he was almost up to Alex's six feet, something his slouched posture in the wing chair had not suggested. Then, seeing the blond woman step up and place herself at the side of Aubrey Clyde Smith, Sarah was about to ask if the cousins had found each other in good time when she stopped. No tartan skirt and no fruit-colored jacket. The woman was dressed in a cotton suit in a pattern of black and white checks, and Sarah decided that hers was the sort of face and build that could handle black and white checks—as thin as a wand and with strong cheekbones, wide lipsticked mouth, arched eyebrows, and blond hair pulled tightly back and wound with a black scarf. Barely noticeable was the pink tip of a hearing aid in each of her ears. All in all, quite a dish, Sarah decided. Middle-aged, yes, but still a dish.

Aubrey Smith followed Sarah's gaze and shook his head. "No, not my cousin. This is her friend, Margaret. Margaret Lee. We had a bit of a mix-up. My cousin was given the wrong key to her cabin, and by the time it was straightened out I gave up and managed to track down Margaret."

"I just knew Aubrey right away," said Margaret. "Vivian said he looked just exactly like that British actor, I forget his name. The one who plays village clergymen and the hero's father."

"Not a very distinguished presence, I'm afraid," said Aubrey. "I'm always being taken for someone's uncle."

"And his cousin Vivian is always taken for someone's aunt," said Margaret. She spoke with an accent that indicated residence south of the Mason-Dixon line, but it was an accent slightly modified by residence elsewhere in the States.

Introductions to Julia were made and remarks passed on the beauty of the evening, the softness of the sea air, and the joys of transatlantic travel.

"I declare it's the truth," said Margaret, "that I didn't know how tired I was until I saw my cabin and that lovely bedspread and pillow just waiting for me to fling myself right down on it. Isn't this what doctors always recommended in those old novels? Ocean travel? A sea voyage?" She turned to Alex. "And you're a doctor, aren't you? So do you recommend ocean trips to restore health?"

"Of course," said Alex lightly. "Ovaltine at night, cod liver oil in the morning, and twenty deep breaths every half hour."

"We'll see you again, no doubt," said Aubrey Smith. "Now I really must find Vivian and see about changing our dining room seating time. They had us down for seven, not eight. Come along, Margaret."

And Margaret was taken by the arm and gently urged to the rear and toward a door opening to the interior. In fact, so quickly did the couple retreat that Margaret had only time to twist her head about and say, "How very nice it was to meet . . ." before she was hustled away.

"Hmmm," said Sarah. "Another dismissal."

"Nonsense," said Julia. "We weren't dismissed, Margaret was."

"We were dismissed back in the Snuggery," said Sarah. "Gently but firmly."

"Sarah," explained Alex, "is still operating under the delusion that we are still in Italy surrounded by malefactors. She's the one who needs cod liver oil and twenty deep breaths."

"All right, all right," said Sarah. "But I'm not imagining that she called Alex a doctor. I didn't introduce him as a physician. I never do." She turned to Julia. "Did you mention it?"

"No," said Julia. "Of course not. Why would I?"

"Alex?"

"Don't be ridiculous. I don't go around sticking out my hand and saying I'm Dr. Alex like someone in *General Hospital.* In fact, for complete peace on this trip I'd like everyone to forget it or I'll find strangers opening their jaws and asking me to look inside or talking about their triple bypass and beta blockers."

"So how did Margaret know?" demanded Sarah.

"Maybe she can read brain waves, or it came up when you met that Smith man in the Snuggery," suggested Julia.

"No mention of medicine in the Snuggery," said Sarah firmly. "But once Margaret said it, Alex didn't deny it. So the secret's out."

Alex shrugged. "No reason to make an issue of it. Then, or as a matter of fact, now. And my dearest Sarah has promised nothing but healthy thoughts on this trip. I think Margaret may have detected a medical aura surrounding me, or I have a residual stink of carbolic acid or formaldehyde."

"Okay," said Sarah. "I have reformed but I do have an explanation. Our new friend, Aubrey Clyde Smith, or cousin Vivian or friend Margaret have been sneaking looks at the passenger list—if it's available—and seen Alex's name. Or asked someone in the know about what high-profile types are aboard. Some people do that, you know. Nosy people who aren't satisfied until they find out if movie stars or gangsters are making the trip."

"A humble MD hardly qualifies for high profile," said Alex.

But Julia wasn't listening. "Does it seem to you," she said in a meditative voice, "at all odd that the name Smith has cropped up three times in our lives today?"

Sarah stamped on the deck. "Talk about being suspicious. No, it is not odd. As Aubrey Smith himself said, there are at least two hundred Smiths on board and they run the full gamut from cabinet minister to scullery maid. And probably a couple hundred Clancys and fifty or sixty McKenzies. Not to mention multiple Sam Greenbanks and Deedees and Richards."

"Break it up, ladies," said Alex. "It's time to sleep."

"In the cradle of the deep," said Sarah and reached over to give her Aunt Julia a steadying arm.

Sarah woke in the dark of her first night aboard ship, and by habit fumbled across her bed in the direction of her alarm clock but encountered only the edge of her bunk. She sat up, turned toward what should have been a sleeping Alex only to find a bulkhead. She remembered. Double bunks. One on top of the other. To save space, no doubt, but a little unfriendly to the interests of love and desire. But what time was it and what sort of a day? If it was day. She pulled herself to the floor—no, the deck—of the cabin and reached blindly for curtains. But she had forgotten. No sea view. Fumbling, she found the television set on top of a built-in bureau and remembered. The view. She pushed the volume number all the way down and then by dint of pressing several numbers and skipping past assorted news and entertainment features she found the bow of the *Vicky*. The ship seemed to be plunging comfortably along, leaving a shelf of foam to each side of her bow, and if one could judge from the television screen, it promised a fairly clear day with only a few clouds on the horizon.

And Sarah was hungry. What time was it? She sat back on her bunk, switched on her bedside light, and reached for her watch. Six o'clock. But no, it wasn't. There was that sign hung by the door reminding passengers to "retard" their clocks one hour each evening, so it was really five. Moving quietly, aware that Alex above her might be sleeping and wouldn't care to be rousted out without due cause, she reached for the "Welcome Aboard Queen Victoria" pamphlet complete with a colorful insert of the *Vicky* next to one of a smiling Captain Stuart Mitchie on the bridge, his hand holding some sort of lever. Well, he looked capable enough, Sarah decided, and turned over the page to see a list of all the marvels available to passengers. My God, she thought, it is a resort. Swimming lessons, fitness training, computer learning, dynamic demos of how to handle wayward or flabby flesh, gentlemen escorts ready to dance with lonely ladies, food stations every fifty feet, gambling by machine or croupier, movies, magic shows, and meals eaten with the "piano stylings" of Morty Mountain and vocals by Tracy Laramie.

Sarah moved from this menu of delights to "Passenger Emergency Procedure" and discovered that an emergency boat drill would be held in the first twenty-four hours. Another lesson from *Titanic*. The instructions were in five languages and offered assistance to the puzzled. Passengers were urged to locate their life jackets and study the proper way of wearing them. Okay, thought Sarah. That'll keep me busy and then it's breakfast.

"Are you abandoning ship?" queried a voice from above. Sarah had just finished tying and strapping herself into her life jacket over her nightgown and was holding a map of the ship to see how Deck Five people worked their way up a series of elevators and stairways to the Boat Deck in time to be considered for rescue.

"Just practicing," said Sarah. "Listen, I'm starving. I've looked up the chart and we can hit the Osborne Cafeteria for breakfast. It's next to the Quarter Deck pool and so—" She stopped abruptly, aware of a tattoo of muffled thuds on the cabin door. Puzzled, she went to the door, pulled it open, and was immediately and violently elbowed aside by a fast-moving lime-green sweatshirt.

"Help!" said the sweatshirt. "Let me close the door, will you?" She—the sweatshirt enclosed a female form—pushed the door behind her and leaned against it, facing Sarah. And an astonished Alex, who was hanging over the side of his top bunk.

"Oh, shit," said the person. Then, "Hey, I'm sorry. But let me stay. For a few minutes. Until I'm sure he's gone."

"He?" said Sarah, reaching for the main cabin light. The woman was a tousled honey-haired female who could only be described as a thing of great beauty. Slender, tall, packed into her sweatshirt with swelling curves in the appropriate places, becomingly flushed of face, hazel of eye, a few random freckles scattered across the bridge of her slightly tilted nose, she was the sort of presence that prompt other women to turn their mirrors to the wall, order treadmills, and plan trips to diet spas. She had evidently been running hard because her perfect lips were open and her breath came in gasps.

"He?" repeated Sarah, overcome by visions of molesters pounding up and down the hall. And overcome also, it must be confessed, by the presence of a goddess in the cabin, one who diminished early-rising, rather scruffy mortals: Alex, bleary-eyed from sleep, wrapped in his sheet, toga style—he slept in the buff—and she with unbrushed spikes of hair sticking from the crown of her head and still tied into her bulky orange life jacket.

The woman eyed Sarah and giggled. "Is the boat sinking? That would take care of him, all right, but with my luck I'd end up in the same lifeboat."

"He?" said Sarah for the third time. "Who's he? And, by the way, who are *you?*"

But the woman had turned, reopened the cabin door the space of two inches, peered out, and slammed it shut.

"Shit," she said.

"You said that," Sarah reminded her. "So please try to tell us what you think you're doing or I'll call the steward. Or someone," she ended rather lamely.

"Yes," said Alex from above. "Sit down and explain. If someone's after you, we'll be glad to send up rockets and get rid of him."

The woman heaved an enormous breath, shook her head, and collapsed on a chair by the small chest of drawers; collapsed on Alex's shirt and trousers, neatly laid ready the night before.

"Okay," said the woman. "I guess I owe you this. My name is Liza. Liza Baum—you know, like L. Frank Baum, who invented Oz. Actually I think he's kind of a sixteenth cousin twenty times removed. And I'm going from London to New York, back from a business trip. I work for a documentary movie outfit—you know, authentic background research stuff—and I'm trying to dodge a hungover Brit called Teddy Hogarth. Of course Teddy's okay when he isn't drinking up a storm. Anyway I opened my cabin door and saw him coming down the corridor—chasing me down here—Teddy's in first class—and judging from what I saw he's not in shape to do more than say hello. If that."

"He's tracking you?" said Sarah, trying to boil down Liza's message to its essentials. "You mean stalking?"

Liza giggled again. " 'Stalking' is a bit much for what Teddy does. Right now he's sort of weaving after me. And I don't think he's got rape in mind. Or assault. Actually, he tries to get me in this big smelly hug like some sort of a Newfoundland puppy, only not half so cute. Call it harassment. Anyway, I'll hang in here just another minute and then sneak out. And thanks for being great and not calling the cops or whoever this ship has for policemen and having them throw me over the side."

But Sarah had relaxed and began to unbuckle her life jacket. "Oh, what the hell. Any sixteenth cousin of L. Frank Baum's is a friend of mine," she announced. "And I certainly don't like drunks, especially before breakfast."

Liza stood up, leaving the soft imprint of her shapely bottom on Alex's shirt. "I really was sort of hoping that Donald would neutralize Teddy. Donald Lyman-Smith, that is. I thought we could make a trio. Donald's part of the trade commission thing Teddy's working with, but he seems to have disappeared. You see Donald was going to nursemaid Teddy until we hit New York because this was supposed to be Teddy's big chance to rehab himself and grow up."

But Alex and Sarah had come to at the same time. "Hey, wait a minute," said Alex. "What was that name?"

"Yes, hold it," said Sarah. "Did you say Donald Lyman-Smith?"

4

LIZA looked puzzled. "Yeah, Donald Lyman-Smith. You know him? You probably do. I mean if you've hit the London party scene. Donald gets around, and when he was appointed Teddy's nanny it meant he went everywhere because Teddy goes everywhere. Tall, good-looking guy with yellow hair. Serious type."

Sarah shrugged. "We don't know him, but . . ." She hesitated, looked up at Alex, who was leaning over from the top bunk and seemed to be fixed on the television picture of the *Vicky*'s bow cleaving the waters. No help from that quarter. Alex probably wanted Liza to leave so he could have his shower and get dressed. "We don't know Donald but we've heard about him," she said. "Secondhand information. That he didn't make the boat."

"What do you mean?" Liza exclaimed. "Of course he made the boat. He had to. He's number two on this trade commission thing. And he's supposed to be hanging on to Teddy's leash."

"Probably another Smith," offered Alex. "Lots of them around."

Liza frowned. "Another Donald Lyman-Smith?"

"You could probably check with the purser," Sarah said. "Or maybe this Teddy of yours . . ."

Liza shook her head vigorously. "Not my Teddy, not by a long shot. In fact, without Donald I don't know if I can put up with Teddy. I had this idea that the three of us might balance each other out. Donald to keep Teddy on the wagon and Teddy keeping Donald from being too dreary. I've always wanted to go transatlantic and this seemed like a great opportunity, and it's more fun when you know people. We talked about doing New York when the two guys got off evenings. The rest of the commission is flying to New York next week. Anyway, I've got to find Donald."

"The Purser's Office," repeated Sarah. "Or one of the cruise staff people. Try one of those."

"Good idea. I'll hit them after breakfast." Liza turned to the door, thrust her head into the crack, and pulled it back. "Okay, the coast is clear. But if I can't find Donald, can I come back and ask where you heard about his missing the boat?"

Alex looked doubtful but Sarah nodded. "If you come up empty we'll put you in touch with the man who told us about Mr. Smith."

"Lyman-Smith," corrected Liza, and she slid out through the open cabin door and closed it behind her.

"I won't say small world," said Sarah.

"Then don't," said Alex. "Say things like hot breakfast and over the bounding main and the wind following free or whatever that poem was. We can pace the deck and shoot the stars and forget about this Smith character."

"Lyman-Smith."

"Whoever. Come on, time and tide wait for no woman. Get thyself dressed."

Sarah peered into the mirror and ran her hand ruefully through her short-cropped dark hair. "Later on I'm going to hunt down the hairdressing establishment. Liza makes me feel like something that came in on the tide. I'm going to be retooled. Highlighted or have a butch and wear long earrings. A ravishing new look and to hell with the Smith tribe."

"How about a wig?" said Alex helpfully. "Life as a blond."

Sarah made a face. "Breakfast first, exercise next, and then beauty. You can spend the time dodging Liza Baum."

"What makes you think I want to dodge the lady?" said Alex, and ducked away from a well-aimed pillow.

The Osborne Cafeteria was a huge semicircular room whose many windows opened to a view of the Quarter Deck pool and beyond that the ship's wake. Between windows hung pictures of buildings and views from the Isle of Wight as it must have been seen by Victoria and her Albert: Osborne House itself in the style of an Italian villa, sailboats on the Solent, the royal children's Swiss Cottage, a view of the garden from the queen's sitting room balcony.

Breakfast in the Osborne Cafeteria was, in Sarah's words, staggering. Certainly not a simple continental offering. Fruits and juices and eggs and meats and fowls and fish and muffins and cakes and cereals cold and porridges hot. Coffee of sixty different flavors and strengths and teas from the seven seas.

Julia Clancy joined her party midmeal and settled for juice, kippers, toast, and black coffee. "I need to be disciplined," she announced, "or I'll end up looking like Queen Victoria."

Sarah smiled. "As well as acting like her."

"Age and arthritis hath their privileges," said Julia, "and one of them is the leeway to be a little ornery from time to time. Now, how did you sleep in that compartment of yours?"

"Just fine," said Sarah. "And we had a morning visitor." She described the visitation of Liza Baum. "She was avoiding someone called Teddy and hunting for Donald Lyman-Smith. And Liza is a beautiful lady," she added. "So I'm going to have my hair done. She has provoked me into it."

Julia put down her coffee cup. "I may sound like Sarah," she said, "and I suppose it's a coincidence, but everyone we've met seems to know everyone else. There's Dr. Greenbank, who has this Lyman-Smith's cabin, and the Herricks, who are related to Sam Greenbank and also seem to know half the ship's passengers."

"Not surprising," said Alex. "Those two are in show business so they'd make it a point to meet people and steer them in the direction of their 'Ships in Peril' lectures."

"You're saying," put in Sarah, "that Liza Baum looking for Lyman-Smith is just one of those things."

"One of those crazy things," hummed Julia, who, fortified by protein and stimulated by caffeine, was now in high good humor.

"Right," said Alex. "I'm going to start marching around the deck and work off a few calories. Sarah? Julia?"

Sarah nodded and Julia picked up her cane. "I'll march a lap or so and then hit the library before someone checks out all the good new mysteries. And then put my feet up for a bit. Let my wonderful stewardess bring me my elevenses. Eat little but often, that's my rule."

"You have a wonderful stewardess?" asked Sarah. "We haven't even met ours. Just a note saying welcome and anything she can do."

"Mary Malone. The old-fashioned kind who really cares. You know, motherly without overdoing it and turning soppy. Or bossy. Very comforting when I had this little dizzy spell. Which I am now completely over. Mary Malone pointed out how many older people have what she calls 'a turn,' what with the stress of packing and making the ship on time."

"Aunt Julia," protested Sarah, "things like that have never made you turn a hair. You're the woman who handles stress by taking some sixteen-hand monster horse over five-foot fences."

"That's exactly the point," said Julia triumphantly. "I didn't have a natural outlet so the tension was bottled up. Mary Malone is what the British call a 'real luv.' I'm lucky to have her."

Sarah nodded. "So, hurrah for Mary Malone. All right, let's hit the deck."

Julia dropped out after the first lap and a half and Sarah slowed to a firm march, but Alex, exhilarated by sea air and the slight roll of the deck under his running shoes, moved into a solid, fast jog. And so it was that when a series of short rings followed by a long ring and a blast from the ship's whistle announced the boat drill, the Clancy party was split into separate units.

Julia, resting comfortably with the latest Inspector Morse mystery—someone had beaten her to the new Dick Francis—

heard the alarm bells with complacency. After all, her cabin was on the One Deck and she didn't have to do much more than to collect a sweater and scarf—the emergency instructions asked for warm clothing and a head covering—fasten on her life jacket, and, following the green arrows, make her way in a leisurely fashion up the two flights of stairs to her assigned muster station.

The alarm bells found Alex visiting the Wellington Spa and Fitness Center with an eye to a later workout. Alex, being an organized type who knew at all times exactly in what part of the ship he stood, turned and made his way without error to his cabin on Five Deck, opened the clothes locker, grabbed a sweatshirt, tied on his life jacket, noted that Sarah had beaten him to it—hers was gone—and returned by way of stairway C to the Pickwick Grill, up a short flight of stairs, through the Prince Albert Lecture Hall, aft to stair D, and thence to his muster station in the Balmoral Lounge, which overlooked the boat deck. There he joined his fellow Deck Five company and found that Sarah had not yet turned up.

Sarah, who had been searching for the Lily Langtry Beauty Salon, heard the bells and had promptly taken several wrong turns despite the attentions of ship's personnel standing on the stairways. At the last landing, in cabin 5023, she found her life jacket missing. A period of frantic scrabbling followed, and then, remembering that after Liza Baum's visit she had kicked it under her bunk, she reached for it and hastily tied it in place.

She returned and after frequent consultation with the ship's diagram she managed to arrive at her muster station in the glassed-in anteroom of the Balmoral Lounge.

"Oops," she said to Alex as she slid into the line of life-jacketed passengers. "I got mixed up on the way up, so I hope all the lifeboats haven't been lowered."

"We," Alex pointed out, "have now missed being saved because they won't lower a lifeboat until the passengers for the whole boat have turned up. Where on earth have you been?"

But the question went unanswered with the panting arrival of Margaret Lee, who thrust herself in behind Sarah. "I am so sorry," she told anyone within earshot. "But I joined the wrong cabin group going up the wrong stairs and had to start right over from the very beginning." Margaret, whose southern accent seemed to have thickened overnight, took a deep breath, tugged at the straps of her life jacket, and ran a bejeweled finger over her golden hair as if to see that every strand was in place. She needn't have worried, Sarah thought. Her hair seemed to have been firmly lacquered into shape without a wrinkle or stray lock.

She turned to Sarah and Alex as if happy to find familiar faces. "If I have to be in a lifeboat I surely like to be in with someone I've met before because it would make all that time on the ocean so much easier."

"Well, it's only a practice," Sarah pointed out. "I don't think we're going anywhere."

"But we have to pretend, don't we? I've read that 'Passenger Emergency Procedure Card,' which is in Spanish, German, French, Italian, and I think it's Japanese—which certainly discriminates against all those other countries. Anyway, the instructions ask for warm clothing and a head covering—in German it's *warme Kleidung und Kopfbedeckung* as well as my *Schwimmweste*, which, goodness knows, in German sounds like putting on body armor. And this at the end of June. Anyway." Here Margaret smiled brightly at the crew member and her accent descended into the lower reaches of Mississippi. "Offissah, Ah do apologize with all mah heart for causing y'all any trouble, and Ah thank you for your patience and understanding but Ah have absolutely no sense of direction."

The crew member nodded and began checking cabin numbers and names on a clipboard.

"I thought you were traveling with Mr. Smith's cousin," said Sarah, twisting about and confronting a flushed Margaret.

"Heavens, no. Vivian and I just could not bear the idea of sleeping in the same cabin because I toss and turn and she makes little mouse noises when she's asleep. So I took a cabin on Five Deck, which is much cheaper, and Vivian's spending an absolute fortune going Balmoral Class. But at least we're not keeping each other up at night, and I don't mind one little bit being down in the bilge."

Conversation now ceased and the muster station groups from Deck Five stood en masse and respectfully quiet while an officer went over the finer points of the boat drill and what would happen next if a real emergency . . .

Sarah found her mind drifting. The sea beyond the glass doors leading to the Boat Deck was slightly more agitated than it had been the day before. Small ruffles appeared on its shifting green surface and the color of the sky had taken on a pale washed blue with thin cloud feathers trailing above the horizon. Sarah became aware of a barely discernible motion underneath her feet and wondered if she would be seasick if the weather turned heavier. It was one thing to know that you didn't get queasy on a fourteen-foot sailboat with the wind in your face, another to wonder what the effect of dining and sleeping away from fresh air would have on one's equilibrium.

She pushed these negative thoughts away from her and decided to concentrate on the boat drill. It was fairly obvious that if this had been a real emergency the passengers in the completed muster stations must enter the boats and be lowered first. And if you happened to be on one of the decks close to the Boat Deck, wouldn't you get into a lifeboat and away from the sinking ship faster than those good folk on the lower decks? Of course, there was no help for it. Someone had to be first. Money talks; money gets you not only a view of the ocean and the pleasures of the Balmoral Lounge, it jolly well gets you out of trouble faster.

Or did the crew lower all the boats at once, each crew member waiting until each complement was ready? She looked around at the serried ranks of orange-jacketed passengers and thought that the costume reduced their individual humanity into troops of so many anonymous quilted lumps—lumps looking very much like strange crustaceans. She tried to remember movies dealing with abandoning ship, words like "Lower one, lower five, lower ten," with lifeboats being lowered as soon as they filled. Of course, in the *Titanic* some boats went off almost empty, but even if they had all been full there hadn't been enough of them. The *Titanic* song again came drifting back, that line about the "rich not having to associate with the poor so they put them all below where they'd be the first to go, oh it was sad, so sad . . ."

"Come to, Sarah," said Alex. "You don't have to stand there all day waiting for the ship to sink. It's over. We can take off our life jackets and start living the good life."

Sarah blinked and retreated from visions of darkening oceans and hulking ice and tilting decks.

But they were not dismissed. A ship's officer, spick-and-span in his summer white uniform, came forward and mumbled something into the ear of their boat crew chief, who nodded and held up a hand. "We've been asked to keep you here a bit longer. Nothing serious. Just a question about one of the passengers from One Deck."

It is a well-known fact that as soon as a group of people are informed that they will be held in a place beyond the expected time and that "nothing serious" has taken place, there is an immediate sense that something entirely too serious has occurred. Reaction is quick. In fact, if there had been a roving health aide equipped with a sphygmomanometer he might have found in most of the assembly a notable rise in blood pressure.

The assembled life-jacketed passengers began to move slightly out of their neat lines to confront each other. A murmur rose somewhere near the ship's bow and like a wave gathered momentum and volume. It reached Sarah and Alex as an audible rustle and hum. A man in an adjacent line said something about an illness. A sudden illness. A heart attack. Or a fall. An injury. The doctor had been called. Or a crewman. Or a stewardess. Someone was being taken to sick bay. The words "IV," "oxygen," "stretcher," "CPR" were bandied about.

And then in front of them an officer—was it the purser? Sarah wondered. She had seen him before.

"Thank you for your patience," said the man in his clipped and controlled British accent. "We're asking you to return to your cabins and place your life jackets back in your clothes lockers where you found them. And we're also asking all of you to please use the aft stairways and lifts because we are, for the moment, cordoning off a midship section of One Deck and the Stair C lift. A passenger, an elderly man, has been taken ill and we must be able to get him comfortably below to the ship's hospital without the disturbance of an audience." The man smiled and added, "I know you'll understand and we thank you for your cooperation."

A brief silence and then the ranks of life-jacketed passengers broke up and began flowing aft toward the elevators, the stairs, the library, the gymnasiums, all the shipboard activity stations. But with the departure came a louder hum of speculation. What had happened? What had *really* happened?

"Well, of course things do happen," said Margaret to Sarah as they both headed for the Osborne Cafeteria and Stairway G, which led to the *Vicky*'s entrails on Five Deck.

Sarah slowed up and waited for Margaret while Alex, always impatient at loitering, bounded ahead of them and toward the stairway. "Meet you at the swimming pool," he called over his shoulder to Sarah.

Sarah, suspended between curiosity and a desire to dump Margaret and grab her bathing suit, hesitated. Curiosity won. "What do you mean, things happen?" she demanded.

"You know. People falling down. Getting sick. Goodness me, half the population on the *Vicky* are tottering. Wheelchairs, walkers, canes. Or taking their last trip. I met a couple who are taking their son—he looks very ill—on a sort of last voyage. And there's another man who's at least a hundred years old."

" 'Sans teeth, sans eyes . . .' " murmured Sarah.

" 'Sans taste, sans everything'—but a bad temper," finished Margaret, to Sarah's surprise. Margaret had not seemed the literary type. "It's just like a busy city street," Margaret went on. "Things happen, people fall apart, the center . . ." She stopped at the landing that marked One Deck. "Gracious, I do declare I forgot. I'm meeting Vivian after the boat drill. Sarah, we'll surely see you again, you and Alex." With that Margaret, still in her life vest, whisked through a door, down a passage, and disappeared.

Sarah, released from Margaret's presence, turned to continue her descent. And bumped directly into Aubrey Clyde Smith emerging from the lift at the Two Deck stairway area. He was out of his life jacket, moving quickly, gave Sarah a hasty nod in recognition, and disappeared in the direction taken by Margaret.

Sarah looked after him and was immediately overtaken by another woman, a short gray-haired woman clad in a tartan skirt and a raspberry cotton jacket. She, decided Sarah, by her costume must be the last member of the triumvirate, cousin Vivian Smith. The woman was certainly in a hurry; life jacket over her arm, she bustled past Sarah and vanished after Margaret Lee and Aubrey Smith.

Sarah continued her way down to Five Deck, marched down the long passageway, and unlocked the cabin door, took off her life jacket, replaced it in the clothes locker, secured her bathing suit and bathing bag, and filled it with the necessaries for outdoor ocean life—sunglasses, sun lotion, and her just-purchased Barbara Kingsolver novel. But as her hands busied themselves, her mind remained elsewhere. Why was the Aubrey Clyde Smith party in such a hurry to meet with each other? Were they simply moving efficiently, having made plans to meet after the boat drill? To plan their day? To talk over family news? Or perhaps the "accident," the sudden "sickness" on One Deck had something to do with one of them. An older man, the officer had said. Perhaps an ancient uncle, a cousin with a cardiac condition.

Oh, give it a rest, Sarah ordered her brain. The whole ship's company, like most closely packed communities, was a rumor factory, and in the fullness of time the "accident" or "sickness" on One Deck would be revealed—accurately or inaccurately. She, Sarah, had a date with a swimming pool and a deck chair. Later with some skilled hairdresser who would recreate her as Audrey Hepburn or Sandra Bullock. But now she should check up on Aunt Julia. Julia was a notable proficient of a nineteenth-century form of the sidestroke and might like to join Alex and herself for a few pool laps.

But Julia's cabin when called, did not answer, and Sarah arrived at the Quarter Deck Pool to find the area packed with children, families, and bronzed singles in bikinis. But no Alex. No Julia. Never mind. Sarah pulled a chair off to one side into partial shade on the port side of the boat and fixed her eyes on the wake of the good ship *Victoria*. It was absolutely mesmerizing, the moving water, the white foam, and the faintest of rocking motions. Sarah fell asleep, her book opened and unread on her lap.

"Lunch?" said a voice. Alex.

Alex not in a bathing suit. Dressed in a blue striped shirt, khaki trousers. The outfit in which he had begun the day.

Sarah opened her eyes and yawned. "I've been dozing away and haven't even gotten in the pool. You went swimming without me?" Then she looked again. Alex's hair was dry and he had his bathing suit—dry—in one hand.

"Oh," said Alex, "I ran into Sam. We went off into a medical cloud. Shop talk and all that."

At which Sam Greenbank appeared behind Alex. "Swim time, then lunch," he announced. "Alex and I have been chewing the fat. You know, the good old days."

"Where's Julia?" asked Alex. "I always look forward to seeing her sidestroke. I think she could cross the Atlantic doing it."

But Sarah wasn't listening. Her eye was fixed on Sam Greenbank. He was wearing a tan denim jacket over a yellow polo shirt, but around his neck she could see the telltale strings of a face mask, the top of which she could make out under the open collar of the polo shirt.

5

SARAH stared at Sam with such intensity that Sam looked down at his chest, fingered his neck, found the strings, reached around, untied the mask, and slipped it into his jacket pocket. He gave Sarah a rueful smile. "Playing doctor," he said. "Ran into someone who had a sore throat so I took a look."

Sarah's eyebrows rose. "You travel with face masks?"

"You never know," said Sam. "Actually it was a kid with the throat. In the cabin next door. The family knows I'm a doctor."

"And I'm Clara Barton," said Sarah. "So why don't you start at the beginning. Maybe when that person—whoever it was—on One Deck had the 'accident.'"

"No connection," said Sam with an attempt at severity.

"So make one," said Sarah. "But not some kid with a sore throat. You've either set up a practice on board, or, since you're a pal of the ship's doctor, he might, just for the hell of it, have called you in for a little consultation."

"Well," Sam admitted, "you're not too far off base. Let's have a swim and then find a private nook for lunch and I'll tell you what I can. Alex knows."

"And what Alex knows, I usually find out," said Sarah.

"We care and share," said Alex. "I feel her pain and she feels mine. And if I don't she leaches it out of me anyway."

"He never talks about his patients," Sarah put in. "Tight-lipped and a model practitioner. But some of our extracurricular activities have had a lethal side to them and he's been around to do the medical examiner bit."

"I've told Sam all about my life as a sometime medical examiner and he knows I don't do forensics," Alex said. "That's for a proper pathologist. Me, I just look at a body and say things like, golly, he's dead and he's got a bump on his head. Or he seems to have been shot, or look, she's fallen off a cliff."

"An important function," said Sam. "So we'll just say that I'll tell you what I can, Sarah, and what I don't tell you has to do with a patient's privacy. For now, anyway."

"And what Dr. Greenbank won't tell you," said a voice from behind, "perhaps I can."

Aunt Julia. Julia in a navy-blue taffeta bathing costume circa 1936, the costume completed by white rubber bathing shoes with a starfish design and a white terry-cloth robe over her shoulders. Her rough gray hair was tousled and short wet strands stuck to the tanned and wrinkled sides of her cheeks.

"I've just had a quick swim," she announced. "But the pool was alive with children. They kept bumping into me so that it was very hard to do my laps."

"You were saying," prompted Sarah.

"Later," said Julia. "When I'm dressed and decent."

"Mrs. Clancy," said Sam Greenbank, "if you saw something or know something that would be useful to the ship's hospital personnel, I think you should go and tell them about it."

"Not useful. Just the impressions of a bystander. My cabin is—what's the expression—at the scene."

"The scene!" exclaimed Sarah. "What scene?"

"Not," said Alex sternly, "the scene of a crime. Most probably an accident. As I think you've been told. Now for a quick swim and then say we meet at twelve-thirty in the Snuggery. The place ought to be empty because no one will want to be huddled down there on a beautiful day like this."

"An accident?" repeated Sarah.

Sam Greenbank nodded. "Like the man said."

Sarah, as she rotated around the swimming pool, considered the word "accident." "Accident" covered a multitude of sins. The abrupt onset of illness, poisoning, trauma, sudden death: these are rarely expected, and even, she thought, if the event occurs through the diabolical agency of man, the victim might describe his event—if he were able—as an accident. But, she told herself, climbing out of the pool, there were now two accidents connected with the voyage of the *Vicky*.

At twelve-thirty, per arrangement, Julia Clancy, much diminished by her choice of the Snuggery's largest wing chair, told her story. Hearing the boat drill signals and fastened into her life jacket, she had been about to depart for her muster station when untoward activity across the passageway three cabins away had attracted her attention. A life spent dealing with unpredictable horses and pigheaded riders had made Julia especially alert to accidents, and this disturbance, she decided, came under such a heading. Perhaps a fall, one which had now been followed by discovery of the injured one. She had stepped back inside her cabin but left her door slightly ajar so as to give her a view of the goings-on. After all, since she was only two stairways away from the Boat Deck, she had a few minutes in which to linger. The proddings of an unwholesome curiosity are always hard to resist. Julia had not resisted.

From her six-inch viewing slot she had watched the opening and closing of the stateroom door, observed a steward hurrying away, saw the arrival of a ship's officer and the subsequent appearance of a woman in blue scrubs, followed by a covey of persons pushing wheeled boxes with dials, IV tubes, and plastic bags. The mystery cabin door opened, swallowed the group, and closed. And opened again to admit the man who might be one of the ship's doctors, Julia had decided, noting the uniform, the stethoscope, and the small briefcase-sized bag. There then followed muffled sounds, perhaps chairs being shoved back against a wall, then the arrival of a stretcher and two more crew members. Julia had hesitated, looked at her watch. The boat drill had now become an imperative. She must not be one of those confused elderly persons who have to be rousted out of their cabin and reminded that today was Thursday, June twenty-eighth, that her name was Clancy, and that she was due at her muster station.

So Julia had hurried down the passageway to her assigned place, but not before she had caught a brief look at their new friend, Sam Greenbank, hastening toward the mystery cabin. Was he excused from the boat drill? Had some friend been stricken and called his name, or was a second medical opinion desired? Julia had frowned, tightened the ties of her life vest, and stepped into line at her muster station.

Here she had found herself in the company of Aubrey Clyde Smith and a troop of strangers all bundled into their life jackets. Her station filled rather quickly, and Julia had been relieved to see that Deedee and Richard were not among those present. It would have been, she thought, quite tedious to have the two of them bobbing about in the same lifeboat while they rattled on about notable sinkings. But where were Cousin Vivian and her buddy, Margaret? Surely they were on the same deck as Aubrey Smith. Julia, pushing the scene she had just witnessed from her mind, tried to settle herself by scanning the horizon seen past the glass doors of the Balmoral Lounge. Just a watery vastness and not an iceberg in sight. The calming effect of the sea view had then been disturbed by a bump into her right shoulder. She had turned about and found a young man with dark tousled hair hanging over a flushed face wearing an incompletely tied life jacket stumbling into place behind her. And panting so hard that she felt enfolded by a cloud of whiskey-laden air. Julia had ceased breathing through her nose and fixed the man with the Clancy look—a look renowned for turning her riding students into lumps of clay.

The young man received the message, blinked, backed up a step, and mumbled something about being sorry. And was answered by the man immediately behind him upon whose toes he had trod. "Mind your feet," said the man.

"Sorry," Teddy Hogarth had answered, for it was indeed Teddy, turned out of the bar by the alarm bells and the orders of the bar tender. Teddy, without Donald Lyman-Smith as his guardian angel, had decided that very morning to stay entirely sober and had celebrated this decision by knocking off a post-breakfast double Scotch on the rocks.

Now he eyed Julia, gave her up as a source of interesting information, and accosted the man behind him. "Have you," asked Teddy, "by any wild chance run into a woman called Liza Baum? Friend of mine, but I can't seem to find her."

The man declared his ignorance of such a person and backed away from Teddy's breath, the officer in charge called them to attention, and the boat drill ran its course.

All this Julia related in the entirely too tight snugness of the Snuggery. Even cold drinks and a bowl of pretzels did nothing to ease the sense that this room should be reserved only for after-dinner winter nights or cold rainstorms.

But Julia's tale was sufficiently compelling to keep the three listeners in their seats—seats of a plum velvety velour, a cloth in keeping with the Victorian ambiance but unwelcome, even with air-conditioning flowing from beneath a settee, on a summer's day.

Sam Greenbank stared at Julia with undisguised admiration. "I've always said—excuse the language, Mrs. Clancy—that what can be fucked up will be fucked up. You know when you try to keep the lid on, all creation is there to take notes."

"But I didn't really see anything," protested Julia. "Just people going into the cabin and then noises. But it doesn't take Miss Marple to guess that something funny—or not so funny—is going on." She looked over at Alex and then to Sam. "So out with it. What happened?"

"Right," said Sarah. "Just give us a rough idea. We don't want to hear state secrets or names if it's some prime minister or an important tribal chief, but a few hints might be in order. If you want to keep Aunt Julia quiet you'll have to work at it." She looked over at Alex, who shrugged and nodded to Sam.

"Okay, my turn," said Sam. "But this much and no more."

It had not been a pleasant sight, Sam told them. He had been discreetly tapped on the shoulder by a crew member just as the final members of his boat station had settled themselves in line. Still in his life jacket, he had followed the man out of the Balmoral Lounge, through the Prince Albert Lecture Hall, and down the stairs to the starboard side on Deck One to cabin 1042, and walked in on a scene of emergency-room activity.

On the crimson patterned carpet sprawled a sticklike figure. A man. Half dressed. Blue striped pajamas, bottoms pulled low over thin shanks, the top yanked off and shoved crumpled to one side. Bare feet. Face up. Face a mess: steel-gray skin streaked with blood that had dribbled from a wound into white wispy hair.

A man in a white summer uniform—open-neck shirt, shoulder boards—stood over the figure, and a woman in blue scrubs knelt to one side and disengaged a stethoscope from her ears while a second man, also in scrubs, stood looking down at the victim's chest and holding an unused IV bag in his right hand.

The man in the uniform looked up and saw Sam. "Good, they found you. Here, have a look. He was on the carpet when the steward found him. We were called and made it here in double time, but he was stone cold and flat-line on the monitor, so there was no point in trying anything else."

Sam in his turn knelt down and went through the motions of examining the body, although there was little point to the effort; death had long since set its seal of approval on the man.

"So what happened, Grant? Was he mugged?" demanded Sam, standing up and stepping back.

The man—the ship's principal medical officer, Grant Rosenthal—got to his feet. He was a short, wiry, dark-haired man with intense gray eyes and heavy brows that met in the middle, giving him a ferocious look. For a moment he gazed soberly at the body on the floor. Then he shrugged. "Not mugged, unless a doorframe can mug you. See over there by the door to the bathroom? He may have lost his footing or felt dizzy and went down like a tree. Slammed directly into the doorframe. You can see bits of hair and blood about three feet above the carpet."

Sam frowned. "Was he traveling alone? He looks to be about eighty. I'd say if you breathed on him he'd topple."

"He's listed as Brigadier General Keith Fletcher Gordon. Retired. Don't know anything else about him. Oh yes, he had an attendant. A valet. A man traveling with him. He's listed as being on Five Deck and was probably at the boat drill. We're tracking him now and we've let the captain and the purser know. They can take it from there. Family notification. All that."

"Are you treating it like an accident, then?" asked Sam.

"I'm only saying that the man is dead. We'll let the ship's security people take care of the details. Seal the room, photograph and document the condition of the cabin, take an inventory, diagram the position of the body and take it off to the ship's morgue."

"In case it isn't an accident?"

"It's out of my hands. I'll make a report of what I've found and what might have been the cause of death, and if the security people want an autopsy they'll call ahead to New York. Any problems, we can borrow one of the New York forensic wizards."

"Or have one flown in from the U.K. to meet you," suggested Sam.

"That, too," agreed Dr. Rosenthal. "So thanks, Sam. I wouldn't have bothered you if I'd known how completely dead the general was. But first report suggested heroic efforts might be needed."

"And this caretaker, the general's man Jeeves? He might know if there were any medical problems."

Grant Rosenthal shrugged. "Most men of eighty have medical problems."

"So," said Sam, leaning back in his chair in the Snuggery and surveying his audience. "That's the story. Now you know almost as much as I know. The ship's people want to keep the whole thing quiet. At least let the general's family—if he has one—know before it becomes general gossip and passengers start speculating about some thug sneaking around. Shipboard is a great breeding ground for rumors. And it did look like the sort of accident an elderly guy might have. Felt dizzy, lost his balance, and over he goes head first right into a solid doorframe."

"How about a stroke or a heart attack?" asked Sarah.

"Well, sure," said Sam. "Anything's possible. He might have

been overcome by heat or cold or an attack of cholera. You name it. The autopsy, when and if they get to it, will settle that. And this Jeeves character, when they track him down, will probably tell us that the old boy's been at death's door for years."

"But why all the hush-hush?" demanded Julia. "I mean keeping it quiet after the family knows. After all, this attendant will probably talk, and the general won't be turning up for dinner."

"It seems," said Sam with some hesitancy, "that there's a quirky little connection that may mean zip. I bumped into the purser and my friend Grant after I finished my quick swim. He told me the cabin has been locked up, and Jeeves has been located—actually his name is Jasper something; he started as the general's batman and just hung in. He'll be debriefed this afternoon."

"And?" prompted Sarah.

"And," said Sam, "it seems that this General Fletcher Gordon was one of the senior members of that trade commission."

Sarah opened her eyes wide and sat up. "You mean the one the Donald Smith person was supposed to be part of, only he was a hit-and-run victim in London."

"Lyman-Smith," corrected Sam.

"You're suggesting," said Julia, "that trade commission people are targets?"

"Aunt Julia," said Sarah, "you always say that I leap into space without a parachute, and listen to you."

Alex looked up. He had been thumbing through one of the large blue and gold bound copies of *Mr. Punch's Victorian Era* and had been particularly caught by a cartoon of Lord Randolph Churchill in Roman armor brandishing a sword at a three-headed army-navy-civil-service monster. He held the cartoon up for general admiration. "Nothing has changed in a hundred years," he said. "And as for leaping, Sarah leaps, Julia leaps, but Sam and I keep our feet on the ground and we say—"

"Say what?" demanded Sarah.

"That the unexpected removal of two members of a group

might smell a little fishy to the amateur mind, but to the professional mind—Sam and yours truly—the collapse onto a doorway by an eighty-year-old man isn't much of a surprise."

"In fact," said Sam, "it was almost to be expected."

"You and Sam," said Sarah crisply, "are coldhearted medical creeps. I'm sorry for this general. Dying like that. Alone in his stateroom in the middle of the Atlantic Ocean."

"Wait a minute," said Julia. "That Teddy person—the one you told me about at breakfast—the one who was chasing after the blond princess from Oz who turned up in your cabin."

"Well, what about him?" demanded Sarah, standing up.

"Didn't you tell me—or his girlfriend told you—that he was a member of the trade commission? Don't you think someone should keep an eye on the man?"

Alex held the Snuggery door open for Julia and wagged his finger at her. "Julia, I've heard the rest of the commission is flying in next week to New York, and yes, this Teddy is the sole survivor on board so feel free to warn the ship security people, but count me out. If you think that I'm going to waste one minute on watching over a drunken young twit who from Liza's description will probably botch whatever the trade commission thinks it's trying to accomplish, well, think again."

"Do you say that to all your alcoholic patients?" said Sarah sweetly as the four reached the elaborately curled and curving grand staircase—a staircase that unhappily reminded her of a certain doomed liner lying on the bottom of the ocean.

"When I see my alcoholic patients in my office or in the hospital I am the very model of understanding. But not aboard an ocean liner in the middle of a vacation. Forget this Teddy. He sounds like bad news. Come on, let's have a glamorous lunch and then wander the decks and see what the *Vicky* has to offer."

"More than you can do in a week," said Sarah as they climbed the stairs. She pulled a folder from her pocket. "Let's see, we already missed half the Morning Excitements—they print everything in caps. There was the Computer Lecture, the Guess the Mileage Contest—cash prizes yet—and a demo on

Fitness, Hair Style, and Beauty in that order in the Wellington Spa. And at eleven-thirty a choice: Favorite Cocktail Melodies with Pierre on the Beckstein or Square Dancing for All Ages, *Especially the Young at Heart*—that in italics—with Jo-Jo of the Cruise Staff, whoever he is."

"Or she," said Julia. "Or them."

"My God," said Alex.

"You could have had Him, too," put in Sam as they reached the Osborne Cafeteria. "Holy Mass at nine in the Lamplighter Theatre."

"Don't look now," said Alex, "but we're about to have Dee-dee and Richard."

Julia whirled about, ready to sidle out of sight, but then clasped her hands thankfully. "They're not interested in us. It's that Mr. Smith over there."

"Aubrey Clyde Smith from the Snuggery," said Sarah, peering past her aunt's shoulders. "And he's hustling them to a table as cozy as all get out. I wouldn't have said that he was their type—or they his."

"Gets me off the hook for lunch," said Sam, as he began heaping his plate with an indiscriminate pile of salad, lobster, roast beef, and a pale green molded affair built on the lines of St. Paul's Cathedral. "I'll snag a table with a view," he told them. "We can stuff ourselves and watch old man ocean rolling along. Actually, he is rolling just a bit. Enough to rock us to sleep tonight."

Settled at a far corner on the port side of the Osborne Room, Sarah, Julia, and Alex, all with plates loaded with a happy disregard for saturated fat and cholesterol and displaying a notable absence of dietary fibers attacked their lunch. At last Sam sighed deeply, put down his fork, and nodded. "At some point I've got to play the family card and at least turn up for one of their shows or dear Mama will never forgive me." He glanced up and lowered his voice. "Oops, spoke too soon. Here comes Deedee."

But Deedee's brow was slightly creased, her manner not quite as bright as before. She nodded briefly to Sarah, told Alex and Sam not to get up, and then rather hurriedly informed her cousin that there was a problem and had he seen Gerald. And then when Sam hesitated, she rushed on.

"You know him, Sam. Gerald. Gerald Hofstra. Our manager. You met him at that party your mother had this spring. I know you'll remember because you had a big argument with him about our starting the 'Ships in Peril' series."

Sam nodded. "Yeah, I know. Short guy like a jockey. Hooked nose, bald on top, a black fringe all the way round, and three strands he combs over. Have you lost him?"

"He was supposed to turn up after the lifeboat drill to go over technical details, coordinate the music, things like that. We knocked on Gerald's cabin door, but no answer."

"You've paged him?" asked Sam.

"Well, no. We didn't want to make a fuss. It's bad publicity. But we have a show this afternoon at four in the H. M. S. Pinafore Theatre. Richard wanted to do a quick run-through."

Sam looked at his watch. "It's just past one-thirty. Lots of time. Have you tried the Casino? He may be trying to beat the house."

Deedee brightened. "What a good idea. Gerald is a real gambler and he just about lives at Vegas when he's on holiday."

"There you are," said Sam, attacking the remains of the green molded cathedral and watching it jiggle under his fork.

"And how are all of you?" said Deedee, now apparently feeling free to recognize the other members of the party. "I see you know Sam. He's my cousin, or rather his mother is."

"Kissing cousins," said Sam, smiling at her. Then, with an unexpected show of gallantry, he rose from his seat and pecked Deedee on the cheek, a gesture she seemed to take as her due. "Not to worry, Deedee. Gamblers have nine lives. He'll show."

But he didn't.

6

SAM Greenbank left the Osborne Cafeteria saying he had promised his friend Dr. Rosenthal to stop by the ship's hospital to see if anything new had been learned about General Gordon's injuries. The Sarah-Alex-Julia trio had planned to dedicate their afternoon to investigation of the *Vicky*'s delights: Sarah off to the Lily Langtry Beauty Salon to nail down a hair retooling appointment for the following day and then to simply drift from deck to deck, from Harrods to the Wellington Spa, to the Disraeli Library, with frequent intervals of lounging and reading on the aft sundeck. Alex opted for bird-watching mixed with vigorous deck walking, while Julia, admitting that she, too, might drop in at Harrods, announced that what she really needed was a temporary disconnection from anyone younger than sixty but that she might—or might not—meet them all later for tea. Or a good stiff drink.

But somehow the idea of the vanished Gerald Hofstra acted as an irritant which followed each person as he or she traversed the *Vicky*. In fact, it became difficult to shake free of the cloud, because just as Sarah, for instance, had settled on a claret-colored scarf of gossamer texture in the Harrods shop, she was tapped on the shoulder by Richard Herrick—he in a banana-yellow sports shirt and a jaunty straw hat with a black ribbon reading "The Jolly Roger"—and queried about the missing Gerald Hofstra.

"Not," said Richard firmly, "that we can't perfectly well handle the video and sound system by ourselves. Deedee and I always used to do the whole thing. But it's been handy having Gerald."

Sarah shook her head. "I've never seen the man but I have tried to notice any man as short as a jockey with a black hair fringe. But," she added, "have you tried the Casino?"

"He's not there," said Richard irritably and then, remembering that Sarah was a potential member of his audience, he smiled and told her not to forget their show, "Pirates and Plunder." "I think it will start the series off with a bang. Great props, too, a real cutlass and dirk and a cat-o'-nine-tails."

"Terrific," said Sarah, who was determined not to commit herself for the sacred hour of tea.

After Richard had departed, Sarah paid for her scarf and fled in the opposite direction toward open air and a sea view, but much as she would have liked to forget Gerald Hofstra, she found herself scrutinizing all small men with scarce black hair and at the same time finding this effort an annoying distraction. Most certainly she would skip the pirate lecture. Enough was enough.

"Hello there," said a voice. "Are you taking in the pirate lecture at four o'clock? Because I've had the most interesting chat with Mr. Herrick."

It was Aubrey Clyde Smith, natty in a navy blazer with an open blue shirt and light gray trousers, his impassive face rosy with a slight sunburn.

"Actually," said Sarah, "I'm thinking of skipping the show."

"He and his wife—her name is Deedee, as in Dorothy— seem to be quite put out by their manager being missing. Stubby fellow, partially bald and short like a—"

"I know," said Sarah crossly, "like a jockey."

"Right. Well, if you see anyone fitting the description it would make those two very happy. They're a cheerful couple. And while we're on the subject of missing persons, there's a chap called Teddy Hogarth—I know his father, was at school with him and all that. Teddy's a bit of a party boy, but he claims that he's pulling himself together and he's running around like a dog that's lost its tail looking for a lovely lady called Liza. So if you happen to run into her—"

"I've met Liza," interrupted Sarah, "and as of this morning she didn't want to be found by Teddy. In fact, she ducked into our cabin when he was chasing after her."

"Well, I'm just acting the family friend. Or what do you call it, a facilitator."

Sarah grinned at him. "I'll bet you can think of another word for it."

An answering smile. "I hope you weren't going to call me a pander or a pimp. No, the boy has been adrift. Too much money and party-going has been very bad for him. But his father has great hopes that he'll—as the Bard has it—suffer a sea change."

"Into something rich and strange?" said Sarah, picking up the quotation.

"We can hardly hope for that, can we? Just into a sober, hardworking fellow who lets his father settle into a peaceful old age."

They parted, and Sarah after a period of wandering found herself on the edge of the Quarter Deck's volleyball court, faced with Liza Baum doing stretch exercises. Liza, fair hair damp from exertion, was fetching in her white shorts and black tank top.

She hailed Sarah. "Listen, I've heard that one of my buddies, you know, Donald Lyman-Smith, the one I was asking you about, walked into a taxi before he could even get down to Southampton. I called from the ship to a pal in London about him to see what happened, and she said the early news had said 'seriously injured' but now she's heard he's dead. Just like that. My God, that really hit me, because even if he wasn't Mr. Personality, Donald was a pretty nice guy and he didn't deserve this. I mean, what a lousy thing to happen. I feel awful. I've been to the health spa and I've done laps to take my mind off the whole damn thing because thinking about it makes me want to puke. I mean, poor Donald. Jesus."

"I'm sorry," said Sarah, feeling helpless. Then, thinking that the death of Donald Lyman-Smith and Liza's being distracted by the news had left her in peril of being found, she added, "Have you managed to stay clear of Teddy Hogarth?"

Liza shook her head. "I haven't seen him, but then I don't think Teddy's thing is hanging around the health spa or swimming. Actually, I'm feeling a little guilty about the guy. I think I'll try to sneak up on him and if he happens to be sober, I might give him another chance. Tell him what happened to Donald and have dinner with him, nothing too cozy, if you know what I mean."

Sarah said she knew what Liza meant and that Teddy had a champion. A friend of Teddy's father . . .

Liza broke in. "I don't know who the friend would be, but I know Teddy's dad. Colonel Sir Arthur William Hogarth, KCB. Not a bad old freak, like something out of a nineteenth-century cartoon—*Punch*, maybe. I do a lot of nineteenth-century U.K. research for my boss, and believe me, those retired military types are still clumping about in big moldering houses. Anyway, if you see Teddy—did I tell you what he looks like? Tall, floppy dark hair, good-looking but sort of gone to seed—tell him I'll hang out by that Pinafore Theatre. There's a pirate show thing at four o'clock. Anyway, what I'm saying is Teddy's heart, if it hasn't been entirely pickled, is probably in the right place. Besides I need to talk to someone who knew Donald."

Sarah listened without much enthusiasm. The Teddy and Liza relationship was not a compelling subject. She turned to leave but was hailed back.

"Hey, Sarah, have you heard about this other old military character? General Somebody? Dead, only nobody's supposed to know. But I keep my ear to the ground. Hit his head on the bathroom door or the edge of his bunk. Something like that. I guess they've got a regular morgue down in the bilge, but it's not something the cruise ship people feature. You know, there's nothing in the brochures telling passengers they can take comfort in a well-maintained morgue. Two people dead. I tell you, Christ, nobody's safe. Okay, Sarah, I need to work off my miseries and try not to think about Donald. See you around, and listen, you take care." And Liza, spying two approaching volleyball types in shorts and sneakers, gave Sarah a parting wave and hastened to meet them.

Damnation, thought Sarah. Now I'll be looking for Gerald Hofstra and Teddy Hogarth even if I don't want to, so I'd better keep my own head down before someone else puts a finger on me.

The finger was put on Sarah within ten minutes of her dragging a deck chair into the shadows of a nook on the port side of the Quarter Deck, well away from the social nexus of pool and sundeck.

The finger belonged to Margaret Lee. She stood over Sarah wearing what could only be described as a playsuit for the mature woman—a one-piece white cotton number with a striped blue sailor collar and a perky red tie. Her golden head, carefully wrapped in what appeared to be a turban, completed the shipboard look.

"Sarah, what are you doing in a dark corner on this gorgeous day? Don't say it, I know, you're in hiding from the likes of me. Well, I have been all over the whole of the *Vicky*, listened to a string quartet, did aerobics with the 'young in heart,' and lost twenty dollars at the roulette table, and I am done in and I've been looking for a friendly face and a chair so I could sit down and have a friendly chat. Not more than five minutes, I promise, cross my heart. Well, have you heard the latest ship news?"

Sarah wanted to say she was sick of ship news and let's talk about something else. The election, perhaps. Any election. Or the situation in Pakistan, in Egypt, in Cuba. Anywhere but news on the *Vicky*. But there was no hope for it. Her silence was taken as assent and Margaret launched forth. The search for the missing Gerald Hofstra, the demise of General Gordon, the request to look out for this Teddy person for someone called Liza she had bumped into. Whom had Sarah seen? What had she heard?

Sarah sighed and said not much. Nothing more than Margaret knew already but wasn't the food amazing? So many choices.

But Margaret was not to be derailed. She pulled a deck chair over next to Sarah and settled into it. "From what I've heard, this General Gordon was quite a piece of work. One of those ramrod characters who absolutely knew he was from the upper reaches of society and could hardly bend his neck down to see anyone else. And a real temper. Stamped around switching at things with a sort of riding crop. You know, like an officer in one of those old army movies where some poor corporal is mistreated, goes berserk, and cuts the officer's head off with a bayonet."

"Is that what you think happened to General Gordon?" Sarah asked, giving up any attempt at diversion.

"Well, it could be a revenge thing, couldn't it?" said Margaret. "It certainly is more interesting than having him lose his balance and hitting his head on something. I mean he could have been shoved or doped so he would fall. There are so many possibilities. I tell you it pays to read murder mysteries because then you're alert for these things in real life."

"I thought," said Sarah repressively, "that General Gordon's death was being kept quiet. I only found out by accident."

"You can't keep things like that quiet. It was much too public with the emergency team and all that rescue paraphernalia being wheeled into the cabin. And that man, Jepson or Jasper, who took care of him. Well, Jasper's been very vocal about it all until someone told him to be quiet. It seems that Jasper was once—what do they call it, a batman or something—anyway, a sort of army servant, and he was struck all of a piece, as my sainted mother used to say, by the general's being dead. And then there's this Hofstra person gone missing."

"He may not be still missing," protested Sarah. "Let's give the man the benefit of the doubt. He's probably taking bridge lessons or signed up for a massage. But no, I haven't seen him."

"But you are going to this lecture, aren't you?" asked Margaret. "Aubrey Smith and Vivian have met the Herricks and say the shows sounds wonderful."

"Tea," said Sarah. "I never miss tea. Or a stiff drink with Aunt Julia and Alex. It's a tradition. But I hope you enjoy it."

Margaret shook her head. "Try to change your mind. The

Herrick shows are one of the major features of this trip." She pushed away from her deck chair and struggled to her feet. "I'm getting too old to stay sitting in one place," she complained. "But at least the activities keep you moving. And lots of new friends. A ton of fun, as my Aunt Bessie used to say."

"I guess," said Sarah doubtfully.

"Take my advice," said Margaret. "Just all of you stir your-selves and get over to the pirate show. You won't regret it, from what I hear."

And so Sarah, propelled by familiar forces—a nasty mix of curiosity and a regrettable tendency to go with the flow—found herself at the Pinafore Theatre at five minutes before four. She had headed originally for the Balmoral Lounge hoping that she wouldn't look like a denizen of Five Deck and that Aunt Julia's sheltering first-class ticket would permit her and Alex to join her relative for the tea hour. Instead she found Alex and Sam heading for the stairs that led directly to the Pinafore Theatre. Curiosity, or as Sam put it, centripetal force, had stimulated the move from the peace of the lounge to the stream of passengers headed for "Pirates and Plunder."

Julia Clancy arrived by another route. After a satisfying pur-chase of gloves at Harrods and a walk on the Boat Deck, she had settled contentedly in a deck chair with her half-finished needlepoint canvas and her mystery novel. The needlepoint, now rather crumpled from travel and general neglect, featured a fox-hunting scene depicting several leaping horses at the in-teresting moment of dumping their riders in ditches and bram-bles. Julia unrolled the canvas, smoothed the little woolen stitches, and was pleased with what she saw. One distinctive horse, clearing an enormous fence with grace, its top-hatted female rider in sidesaddle habit, had been altered so that the horse resembled Julia's favorite steed, Duffie, and the rider, slightly shortened and broadened, represented herself.

Julia picked up a length of red wool—the color known in hunting circles as "pink"—threaded her needle, and inserted it into the shoulder of a fallen rider.

And then a voice. "That's marvelous. May I see?"

Annoyed, Julia looked up to see a large gray-haired man

with intense blue eyes and ruddy face peering at the canvas scene.

"Do you do needlepoint?" she growled, thinking that might cool the gentleman, although she had several male friends who did wonderful work and turned out pillows and wall hangings in quantity.

"No," said a cheerful deep voice, "but I have a flea-bitten gray like that one on the horizon"—he pointed to the canvas—"and he's dumped me more times than I can count."

It is a truism that sooner or later like finds like, and, in particular, one horse addict finds another. And undoubtedly for both these persons, there was a dearth of equine-related subjects featured on the *Queen Victoria*, and they were both needy. The man's name was Anderson. "Erik Anderson," said the man. "From Norway by way of my grandfather and now from the wilds of New Hampshire. Do you have a stable? A horse you ride now?"

Julia indicated an adjacent deck chair, and the man—he was broad shouldered, long-armed, built for felling trees—sat down and the two went at it. Julia spoke of her farm; her old thoroughbred, Mickey Mantle, now long gone to earth; her husband, Tom Clancy, also departed; of his perfect eye for a useful stallion; her problems of riding and jumping the seventeen-hand Duffie when she was in her arthritic mode. "I need something smaller. I'm seventy and though I hate to say it, I should probably look for a large pony."

"Well, I have just the beast," said Erik Anderson. "I've been over to the north countries, taking my grandchildren on a trip to meet some cousins, and I think I'm going for the Norwegian Fjord."

"Oh," said Julia, her voice squeaking with excitement. "I have thought about the Fjord. I have a friend with a wonderful animal called Loki and he can do anything and is strong as a bull."

"And they're smart," added Mr. Anderson. "Let me tell you . . ."

And so, in utter contentment, the two plunged into the heaven of a totally horse-centered discussion until, just as they had reached a complete agreement on the management of bowed tendons, Erik looked at his watch. "Good God, it's almost four o'clock!"

"Does something happen at four?" said Julia, who was reluctant to cut off the conversation.

"The kids," explained Mr. Anderson. "My granddaughter, Kirsten, she's nine, and my grandson, Brian, who's eleven. I stashed them at some sort of kids' center and said I'd meet them at the pirate lecture. Why don't you come? We can have a drink together after because I want to tell you about a problem I've had with ringbone."

And so it was that Erik Anderson and Julia Clancy joined the hustle of passengers pushing into the Pinafore Theatre, located the two grandchildren—a boy with a buzz cut and a girl with a long blond braid—and found tenth-row seats.

"Thank God for air-conditioning," said Mr. Anderson as he settled into his seat.

Julia nodded absently. She had just remembered saying something about meeting Sarah and the two men for tea or drinks and was prey to a slight spasm of guilt, a spasm easily quelled. After all, the young—or the almost middle-aged, as Alex insisted he now was, being well into his thirties—didn't need ancient Auntie around its necks. Then, turning to check the house, she caught sight of these very persons: Alex, Sam, Sarah, two rows in front on a side aisle. Well, so much for meeting at the cocktail hour. She, Julia, was glad she had taken charge of her own entertainment and was not again going to feel guilty. Besides, she told herself, loving as was Sarah, helpful and friendly as were Alex and Sam Greenbank, not one of the three knew squat about horses.

These reflections were cut short by the sudden eruption onstage of three men in sailor costume who leaned toward the mike and let out with a synchronized hum that jumped into that old seagoing favorite, "Blow the Man Down."

"It's the Merry Times," said Erik's grandson, Brian. "Their name is a sort of joke for 'maritime.' Gramp, do you get it? Mrs. Clancy, do you get it? Merry and maritime."

Julia and Erik both said they "got it" and leaned back to

listen. They were very good, Julia thought. Good harmony, a good sense of rhythm. And, smiling to herself, she let her thoughts take her far away, take her flying on Duffie over fence after fence and then go galloping off toward the horizon.

Sarah, in her eighth-row seat, found that she could close her eyes on the vision of the three men on the stage in their ersatz sailor suits and be transported to the nineteenth century. Keeping the beat of the music with one fist she pictured royals and topgallant sails and flying jibs and a ship plunging through the scudding foam and let the words of the shanty wash over her.

Then "Blow the Man Down" gave way to a rollicking tune called "Hanging Johnny," a song most appropriate for the upcoming lecture.

> *O! they call me Hanging Johnny, hooray!*
> *Because I hang for money, so hang, boys, hang!*
> *O first I hung my mother*
> *And then I hung my brother,*
> *O, hang and haul together*
> *O, hang for better weather.*

And as the last note died away, Richard Herrick stepped to the apron of the stage.

"Yo ho, me hearties," called Richard.

And Sarah's eyes bugged out of her head, and a quick side-wise glance at Alex showed him equally affected.

Richard, that gray presence, that dullard husband, that man with a face as bland as a cream doughnut, turned into a buccaneer before their eyes. The doughnut face proved to be made of rubber; the voice, hitherto a mild tenor, traveled up and down, baritone to countertenor, the accent from Wales to Devon, as Richard became first the marauding Sir Henry Morgan, sacking the city of Portobello; stamped across the stage as one of Morgan's hands, who sliced his way across the foredeck with a raised cutlass; next transformed himself into Blackbeard, shouting, "Damnation seize my soul if I give you quarter," and then, to the children's delight, became a menacing Captain

Hook, waving a rapier at an imaginary Peter Pan and calling vengeance on the waiting crocodile.

Through it all Deedee acted the part of the stooge. She waved the black flag with the skull and crossbones; trotted off- and onstage with piratical props, the whip, the eye patch, the dirk; and at one point submitted to the placement on her head of a rakish black hat as the female pirate, Mary Read, who had spent an active and hazardous life as a cross-dressing soldier and buccaneer.

Between her comings and goings Deedee was somehow able to change slides and oversee a short video sequence of an imagined boarding of one of Her Majesty's privateers. But Sarah, always interested in the odd detail, thought Deedee was not really into it. Somehow her dogged expression, her per- functory distribution of props, spoke more of the reluctant drudge than the glad helpmate.

"Busy as a bird dog," observed Sarah. "But not as happy. I can see why a manager is needed. Deedee is about wiped out."

Alex nodded, folded his program, and stuffed it in his pocket. "They're winding up," he said, as Richard plucked off his bandanna and handed what looked like a seagoing claymore to his wife.

But Richard was not quite done. He stepped forward, looked serious, and switching to a documentary narrator's voice touched on the differences between the pirate and the privateer, regretted that the program had only touched the tip of the iceberg (ha ha) of piracy on the high seas, and then began a hype of the next two programs. Tomorrow, Friday at four, they would present the thrilling tale of two shipwrecks and the treasure found fathoms deep on the ocean floor. Then, Saturday evening, the saga of *Titanic* . . . Richard paused as if waiting for a mass intake of breath.

"He's going to say 'ill-fated,' " groaned Sarah.

"On her ill-fated maiden voyage," intoned Richard, lowering his voice to give a somber emphasis.

There was an excited rustle and a turning of program pages, and on the screen loomed an artist's rendering of the sinking ship: night sky background, the vessel lit fore and aft, her bow down into the waves as half-empty lifeboats hovered in the distance.

"Hasn't everyone about had it up to here with the *Titanic*?" demanded Alex as he rose to leave. "My God, why don't they let the poor ship rest in peace now? Enough is enough. There must be families around, third and fourth generations of people who drowned, who don't think of the sinking as just another version of *Jurassic Park*."

"Yes," agreed Sarah. "But, as Deedee said yesterday, it's the big one and apparently this manager of theirs—the one that no one can find—got the booking on the *Vicky* partly because a *Titanic* show was part of the series."

"I'm with Alex," announced a familiar voice. Julia Clancy stood in the aisle. "Why, my mother's Uncle Harry went down with the ship and left five children and a wife who went out of her head afterwards."

"You can't get away from it," Sarah said. "The *Titanic* is a musical, a raft of movies including The Movie. Plus at least sixty books."

"I know," grumbled Julia, "and it proves my point. I almost wish that anyone in the audience who sits oohing over people drowning could go straight down to Davy Jones's locker. And that includes this manager Hofstra who is putting the whole thing on."

"And," said Sarah, "they'd make a movie out of that. And an 'as told to' eyewitness account best-seller. You can't win."

"What can't you win?" asked a voice. It was Deedee, flushed from her exertions.

"We are talking about the morbid fascination some people seem to have with other people drowning," said Julia.

But Deedee was in too frazzled a state to take in the meaning. She simply looked puzzled. "You didn't like the show?" she queried.

"Everyone seemed to eat it up," said Sarah, taking the peacemaker route. "Kids love pirates and Richard does a terrific job, all those voices."

Deedee smiled a weary smile. "Yes, Richard is something else. But now we've got to find Gerald. I can't do the lights and videos and keep running around like a rabbit up there on the stage. After all, I'm getting on."

"You certainly are," said Julia, but happily Deedee had turned to receive further congratulations, and Sarah was able to land a sharp crack to her aunt's ribs.

"Drinks," said Alex. "Especially for you, Julia. A tot of rum and a flagon of grog."

"As a matter of fact," said Julia complacently, "I have a previous engagement." She turned and waved at the tall, gray-haired man emerging from the crowd. "His name is Erik Anderson from New Hampshire and he has a breeding farm and is importing several Norwegian Fjord ponies. Stay here and I'll bring him over and introduce him."

Sarah and Alex watched Julia's retreat with amazement, and then Sarah spoke for both of them. "I said Julia needed a companion who loved horses but I didn't think even this ship could produce one."

"Now," Alex returned, "you can believe the brochures. The *Vicky* does have everything."

7

INTRODUCTIONS to Mr. Anderson were hastily made, and his two grandchildren were produced and, after prodding, offered limp hands and then were sent packing to a showing of *Treasure Island* in the Lamplighter Theatre. Sarah, turning to Julia, asked if she would be eating with them. "You can join us in the Frogmore Dining Room, but we can't come to you because of being on Deck Five."

"You'll eat with me," said Julia firmly. "Eight o'clock and none of this upstairs-downstairs nonsense."

"Class is class," said Sarah, "and we don't qualify. There'd be a nasty scene and we'd be tossed out of your fancy-pants Windsor Castle Dining Room before we could sit down."

Julia frowned. "I'll have a chat with the powers that be."

"Don't worry about us," said Sarah. "We're just fine. The food is great wherever you are and we can meet for coffee afterwards." Privately, Sarah thought that dinner without Aunt Julia, even if they had to eat from the floor of the ship's engine room, might be something of a blessing.

But Julia wasn't listening. "I'll knock on your stateroom door just after seven. I should be able to straighten things out by then."

"Oh, God," said Sarah, watching her aunt and Erik Anderson depart in the direction of the Scepter Room. "I hope she isn't going to bribe someone and try to move us. I hate people who flourish rolls of dollars . . . or pound notes."

"Actually," said Alex, "that isn't Julia's style. She uses the power of persuasion. She's willing to pay, but never a cent more than necessary. And since I really miss having a porthole I won't object to having an outside stateroom forced on me."

Which is what happened. Julia, flushed with triumph and probably several tots of rum taken with Erik Anderson, arrived at their stateroom door at a few minutes after seven with a sheaf of papers and yellow tags and slapped them down on Sarah's bunk. "It worked like a charm. I became the helpless old lady who needed her loved ones at twenty-four-hour beck and call, and it happened that a stateroom had just been released by a young man who prefers true love on Five Deck to the comforts of One Deck. He'll take your cabin and has gone off to find his lady and tell her the good news. A steward on One Deck is making up his cabin for you and you can move in after dinner. All is arranged and paid for. Don't thank me, because I'll get my pound of flesh sooner or later. Besides, I hate eating alone."

"You wouldn't have eaten alone," Sarah pointed out. "There'll be all sorts of people at your table. Possibly other curmudgeons."

Julia gave a small chuckle. "I'd hate to spend time with other Julias. Mr. Anderson asked me to join him, but he has those two grandchildren with him, and how can one talk comfortably about artificial insemination and viable sperm counts and a mare being in heat with those two hanging on every word?"

"They probably know more than you do," interrupted Sarah.

"What I'm trying to tell you," Julia went on, "is that my seating—and yours now—is at eight. Sarah, have you an evening dress? Because you have to dress in first class. If you don't, go buy one. Right now. The Regent Street Shopping Gallery on the Boat Deck. Here's my credit card so charge it to me."

"Are you saying I have to find a dinner jacket?" asked Alex.

"A dark suit with a sober tie and white shirt and you can pass muster," said Julia. "Now I need to put my feet up and think about buying a Fjord."

"A what!" exclaimed Sarah.

"Large pony. For the old lady. Erik Anderson has been telling me about them. It's an important decision. They have special gaits and very thick necks and a wonderful temperament. I'll see you later." And Julia vanished in the direction of the staircase.

"Good," said Sarah as the cabin door shut behind her aunt. "Julia has a new horse to occupy her mind and a possible boyfriend. That should keep her out of trouble. Me, I'm going to buy that dress before she regrets the offer. What do you think, a black drape on the shoulder with sewn-on sequins, or just something fluffy? And some pointy shoes. How about something for you? A sexy-looking bathing suit, you know, a black thong, and maybe some hair oil to give you a Latin look. I can't have my life's partner always looking like something out of the L. L. Bean catalog."

Alex bent down and kissed the back of her neck. "I'll look for a pirate suit and come to bed with a dirk and a scimitar in my teeth. We can have a kinky time with sharp instruments. And now I'm going to hunt up Sam and see if he has any news from the morgue."

"You," said Sarah, "are hopeless and you don't deserve an adventurous wife. I'll find a dress fit to kill for." She shook her head and departed for the Regent Street Shopping Gallery, which lay aft below the casino. Her route lay through the Sceptor Room, a space dedicated to cruise staff displays and a snack and drink bar. There, in the far reaches of the long room, she saw a drooping figure sitting at a small table, a brandy glass set in front of him. And something about the person reminded her of someone described as important. Or necessary. Or something. She frowned, staring at the man, who, not drinking, was gazing with a despairing expression at the glossy table surface in front of him.

Balding, with dark hair in a monk's fringe, prominent teeth, jutting chin. His posture, his whole gestalt, suggested a bookie who has had a particularly unsuccessful day at the track and is now awaiting a reckoning with the boss of the Mob.

The man's name was hovering about in the lower reaches of her brain, but now her mission was a dress. A slinky, dangerous, woman-of-the-wicked-world dress. So Sarah continued on her way and in short order found herself staring at a rack of slinky, dangerous, wicked dresses. Sleeveless, one sleeve, wrapped, flounced, tight, loose, open bust, slit leg, slit stomach, dresses of brocade, gold, magenta, peach, ivory, heavy, thin, see-through fabrics. And judging from the price on little tags hiding modestly from the important-sounding labels, each garment could probably feed a family of ten for several years. Even with her social conscience on hold, Sarah felt uneasy, and after a period of pawing through the dresses and fending off the attentions of a sales clerk with purple hair and matching lipstick, she took a deep breath and settled for a long black skirt—marked down—and white silk blouse together with a junk-jewelry necklace at half price, a number of scarves in various hues plus a cherry colored shawl, all of which could be arranged around one's body to give the impression of multiple costumes. Thus, with a compromise reached between the prickings of conscience and fashion, Sarah clutched her purchases and walked back amidships. And as she reentered the Scepter Room it came to her. Of course. Where had her brain gone? That dreary man with the brandy glass—he was the missing manager. Gerald what's-his-name—Hofstra? The mastermind of the "Ships in Peril" productions. And if this were so, why in hell was he sitting in a corner brooding over brandy instead of supporting the Herricks?

She paused at the door, peered about the room, and there he was. Same place. Same expression, same slump, still looking like a soul newly sprung from some inferno. Well, never mind that he'd chosen to have a nervous breakdown, Deedee and Richard needed him. Sarah advanced and planted herself in front of his table.

"Hello," she said. "My name's Sarah Deane and I'm a friend—well, not exactly a friend—but I've met Deedee and

Richard and they have the whole ship looking for you. They had to do the show without you and I thought Deedee would die of exhaustion." Here, Sarah paused and, seeing no immediate response, thought, okay, that's enough. I've done my good deed. He can take it from here. I'll tell one of the ship's officers where he is and that's that.

But as she turned to go, a mournful voice stopped her in her tracks. "Hey, wait up. Yeah, I know I've missed the show. Couldn't help it. Sick as a cat. Threw up all over the place. I've been down in the ship's hospital or infirmary—whatever they call it. Some sort of bug. Or poison, because I have these allergies. It hit me like dynamite. And now what if this goddamn boat starts to roll around? I've heard there might be a storm coming, and I'm a lousy sailor. If I had the energy I'd throw myself overboard."

"You're sick," said Sarah, latching on to what seemed to be the heart of Gerald Hofstra's statement.

"Was sick. Like I said." Gerald raised his head and Sarah saw dark circled eyes and the slightly open mouth as if he had to gasp for air. "But," he added, "I'm pretty much over the stomach business, but I didn't have the strength to help with the show."

"If you feel okay now," said Sarah firmly, "you should check in with the Herricks. They've been so worried."

"Okay," said Gerald Hofstra. "Will do." He gave a long, heavy sigh that seemed to come from the pit of what was undoubtedly an empty stomach. "How was the show? How'd it go over? I chose the pirate thing for starters because it's got something for everyone. Richard, the man has talent. He could have been big time if he hadn't spent all those years in harness with Deedee on stuff like 'Our Visit to a Persian Garden.' Crap like that."

Sarah, who privately thought she might have preferred a visit to a Persian garden to sinking ships, told Gerald Hofstra that Richard was amazing, a real mimic with a rubber face, and that the audience seemed to eat it up.

"Good," said Gerald, who appeared to be reviving. "That

first show, those two could handle it without me. I'll be there for the big stuff. Especially *Titanic*. That's the crème de la crème. Takes a lot of finesse and special effects to pull it off. You know, the iceberg ripping along the hull, the sound of the water rushing in. After all, everyone and his mother has read about it, or seen the musical or the damn movie, or bought the video, so we have to work against that."

"So why do it?" asked Sarah. It seemed a sensible question.

"Hey," said Gerald, becoming positively animated, "it's the setting. On the *Vicky*. Her maiden voyage. We're all on this big mother of an ocean liner with all this old-fashioned décor and furniture and turn-of-the-century details. Listen, for me it's a dream come true, like we're all *on* the *Titanic*."

Sarah said she could understand the attraction and now she had to go but perhaps she'd see him at dinner or afterwards.

Gerald shook his head. "Think I'll skip dinner. Maybe some soup. A cracker or something."

"Chicken broth," said Sarah. "It never fails. Ginger ale. Coca-Cola. Tea. And fresh air. Go out on the deck. The ocean is beautiful and the air will make you forget to be sick."

"I don't think," said Gerald mournfully, "that my stomach will forget to be sick."

"Don't you have a sedative, seasick pills? Something to take?"

Gerald brightened. "Yes. I told them down in the infirmary that besides this stomach bug, I always got seasick, too, and they gave me some pills. I'll take one now." He reached for his glass.

"Actually," said Sarah, feeling like a visiting nurse, "I'd skip the brandy. It doesn't mix with most medicines." I sound just like Alex, she thought. Sensible and practical. It's contagious.

Gerald pushed the glass away. "You're right. I'm not think-ing straight. I think I'll get some tea and go sit on the deck."

"After you've found the Herricks," Sarah reminded him.

"Yeah, I'll do that. Thanks. And listen, babe, who are you, anyway? I mean who is Sarah Deane? Are you on the ship's staff?"

Sarah grinned. "Just a passing stranger who hates to see people throw up. And who's been told at least sixty times by sixty different people to look for Gerald Hofstra."

Back on Five Deck in cabin 5023, Sarah exhibited her purchases to Alex, who said as far as being sexy went she might just as well put on the habit of a Benedictine nun.

"Never mind," she said. "I can wear the outfit to faculty dinners without one of those drunken tenured types trying to grope me. And the skirt was on sale. Aunt Julia ought to appreciate my care of her bank account. Besides, I think I'll be one of those women who look chaste but have fires smoldering inside."

"We have just time," said Alex, consulting his watch, "to check out those fires. Come here and let's give cabin five-oh-two-three a night to remember."

"I don't like the reference and it isn't night, but why not?" And Sarah took a step toward the bunk and Alex only to hear a sharp triple knock on the cabin door.

"Hell," she said. "It's the story of our lives. What's all this jazz about shipboard romance, anyway?"

"Christ," added Alex with feeling as he went to open the door.

It was Liza Baum. Flaxen hair tousled, cheeks pink, glowing. "Hey there, you guys," she said. "Guess what?"

"What?" asked Sarah without enthusiasm.

"You remember I was looking all over the blessed ship for Teddy? You know, Teddy Hogarth?"

"Yes," said Sarah. "You told me about Teddy Hogarth."

"Well, he's gone all noble and self-sacrificing on me. I bumped into him at the gym this afternoon after my volleyball and he was nearly sober and said he was trying for a cabin on Five Deck—to be near me—and that I was the strong sort of support he needed because if he was going to quit drinking he'd need someone like me since we'd lost Donald. All of which frankly I question."

Alex shook his head. "You bought the story?"

"No, not really. It may be a bunch of bull. But if he's willing to come down to Lower Slobovia after lushing it up on One Deck, well, I suppose I can walk the extra mile and eat with the poor fish and work out with him in the gym. You should have seen him this afternoon. Sweating pure scotch and shaking like a willow tree but . . . well, what the hell. If he's too much of a pain in the ass or he starts in with the hard stuff, I'll just lock my cabin door and let him get on with ruining himself."

"All of which means," said Sarah, "that Teddy's coming into this cabin and we're moving up to his."

Liza grinned. "You got it. And we're having an early—well, early for us—dinner in the Frogmore Dining Room—don't you love the name? Actually, I worked on a documentary on the royal family and Albert dying of typhoid and being buried in the mausoleum. Anyway, after dinner we'll do something deadly like go to the library or listen to a lecture on Victorian architecture. I don't think Teddy's up for dancing because it might make him thirsty."

Alex, feeling that enough was enough, moved away from his bunk and indicated a packed duffel bag and backpack. "Tell Teddy he can have the place now if he wants. I'll ask the steward to haul our stuff up to his cabin."

"One thing," said Liza. "I mean, you're a doctor, aren't you?"

"Yes," said Alex, with a familiar sinking sensation.

"It's only that if Teddy starts to come apart at the seams, or goes slightly crazy, could you give him something to sort of calm him down? A sedative maybe. I mean he's been doing the drinking scene for so long that quitting in one day may make him go completely ape."

"I can't prescribe on a British ship. I'm just a passenger, and there's a perfectly good medical staff down in the ship's hospital," said Alex in a repressed voice.

"But Teddy doesn't want to go officially. Somehow it would get back to some of those stiff-necked creeps on the trade commission. They're sure Teddy's going to help botch the meeting and they're just waiting for him to fall apart."

"Sam. Sam Greenbank," murmured Sarah. "Couldn't he work it through his pals in the ship's hospital?"

Alex blew through his cheeks, studied Liza's face, her eyes

wide, chewing her lower lip. "All right," he said. "I'll ask a friend to make an appointment after regular clinic hours. Frankly I think this Teddy sounds like trouble. For himself and you. But I'll see what I can do. Okay?"

Liza looked relieved. "Great. Just some stuff to help keep Teddy's lid on. I can bring him down to the sick bay anytime."

And Liza departed, leaving Alex and Sarah, who, after looking first at their watches and then regretfully at the inviting lower bunk, scrambled the rest of their packing into their bags and hurried to meet Julia for dinner.

Dinner at eight in the nineteenth-century splendor of the Windsor Castle Dining Room—a place of blue brocade and elaborate chandeliers—was, in Julia's words, "worth every penny." Julia, Alex, and Sarah sat at a table set for seven, but since two of their fellow diners—elderly females in silk vests, one black, one plum, and long gray silk skirts—spoke only to each other in rapid French, they could for the moment be disregarded. An exchange of "Good evenings" and *"Bon soir"* had taken place, and then the two ladies—sisters surely, with dark birdlike eyes, matching beaked noses, and thin lips—had put their heads together and begun a nonstop chatter which, judging from their angry tones, was directed at some undesirable person and recent event. Expressions like *"maigre"* and *"trop malin," "formidable et incroyable"* surfaced from time to time.

Sarah, regarding the two, found the word "harpy" floating into her consciousness. What was a "harpy" anyway? Some sort of predatory female? Certainly nothing very nice, but there really was something unholy about those two women. Then, banishing such uncharitable thoughts, she turned and regarded the other two diners.

These were a young couple, she a tangle-haired blond in a rose dress, he, a round-faced man with his brown hair in a buzz cut wearing a sky-blue dinner jacket and a frilled shirt, both so enchanted with each other—hands clasped, leaning close— that for all practical purposes they were absent.

Thus, Julia and her party to a great degree had the conversation to themselves. Sarah rather regretted this; she had always heard that one met fascinating people at shipboard dinners and began to blame their isolation on the splendor of being in the Balmoral-class dining room. Perhaps the Frogmore Dining Room fed more lively down-to-earth types.

But Julia, who preferred the company of a select group of familiars, was content. She ordered Cornish hen with wild rice and a game sauce and looked about with a satisfied air. She wore her best all-purpose evening costume of a paisley dress topped by a black silk jacket and a gold necklace fitted with garnets.

"I approve your skirt," she told Sarah. "You can wear it into old age. I thought you'd go for more glamour. Gold lamé or satin."

Sarah shook her head. "Centuries of frugal ancestors spoke and I had no choice. But I think Alex should spring for a real dinner outfit." She pointed at Alex in his navy blazer and a sober tie. "He looks like the ship's detective."

"Well, I haven't been asked to leave yet," remarked Alex, who was performing delicate surgery on a grilled salmon fillet served with *herb beurre blanc*.

"At least Deedee and Richard aren't at our table," said Julia.

"I forgot to tell you," said Sarah. "Their manager is back, although he's a little worse for wear. Upset by a stomach bug and afraid of getting seasick. But he claims he's going to make it at least for the *Titanic* show. Major visuals and sound effects."

"And that," said Julia. "is one event I will skip."

"Hello, hello," said a voice. It was Sam Greenbank, followed by a waiter holding a gilt chair.

"I've talked the people into letting me wedge into your table. I could eat with the hospital staff, but that's too much like work. These tables are designed for eight at a pinch. Excuse me, please," he said to the most dour of the two women as he settled in next to her elbow. She frowned and whispered in French to her sister—Sarah had concluded that they must indeed be sisters.

"Well, then, *bon soir* to you both, *mesdames*," said Sam, beaming at the two ladies. "And good evening to you," he added to the lovebirds, who looked up, startled.

"Ah, good," said Julia. "You're most welcome, Dr. Green-bank—Sam—because you can bring us up to date about the morgue and the dead general. *Le général qui est mort*," she added for the benefit of the two French women.

At which all four strangers reared their heads and stared at Julia.

"*Mon Dieu*," said the black-vested Frenchwoman.

"*What* did you say?" exclaimed the female lovebird, a tangle-haired blonde with inch-deep mascara and a receding chin.

"I think Mrs. Clancy misspoke herself, didn't you, Aunt Julia?" said Sarah.

"Oh, all right," said Julia, returning to her Cornish hen, which was proving to be a slippery item, scooting about her plate. "But if we can't talk about the general, what's the point of Sam joining us?"

"I couldn't have put it better myself," said Sam. "But frankly I'm not allowed to say more than there's no news, which happens to be true. Now, tell me about the pirate show. Did Richard pull it off without their manager?"

"He was," admitted Sarah, "amazing. Alec Guinness, Peter Sellers, and Lon Chaney have nothing on Richard Herrick. A hundred faces and twice as many voices."

"And Deedee perspiring like Gunga Din," said Julia.

"Who?" said the blond lovebird, still wide-eyed.

Julia looked at her. "Ancient poetry. Kipling. India. Gunga Din carried water to the British soldiers." Julia put down her fork, closed her eyes, a wicked expression creeping over her weathered face.

> " 'E lifted up my 'ead,
> An' he plugged me where I bled,
> An' 'e guv me 'arf-a-pint o' water green:
> It was crawlin' and it stunk,

But of all the drinks I've drunk,
I'm gratefullest to one from Gunga Din.
It was 'Din! Din! Din!'
'Ere's a beggar with a bullet through 'is spleen . . ."

Here Julia paused and looked about the table. "Shall I finish the whole thing?"

The blond woman gulped, said "No," and returned to a plate of veal cordon bleu while her male companion glowered at Julia.

"We're having dinner," he said in a reproachful voice.

Alex stifled a laugh, Sarah tried to look severe, and Sam chortled. "My father could recite the whole thing. He learned it in fifth grade instead of 'Ode to a Grecian Urn' and got two days' detention."

For the next few minutes attention was paid to the food in front of all eight diners, even the French sisters giving up whispering to deal with the intricacies of stuffed lamb. Then, in the short pause between the clearing of plates and the presentation of the dessert, Sarah took the time to look about the dining room. Almost immediately, only two tables away, she saw Vivian Smith. Vivian sat not with cousin Aubrey Clyde Smith but with five other persons—persons unknown to her, if one could judge from the fact that Vivian, not speaking, sat with head bent, attending to her meal while the other five chatted as an animated group of friends.

And why, Sarah asked herself, was not Cousin Vivian sitting with Aubrey? After their reunion had they had a falling out? Had the dining room staff not accommodated their seating requests? But look at Sam Greenbank, sitting where he damned pleased. Puzzled, she shifted her gaze across the circles of snowy tablecloths, the passengers in evening clothes—lots of women in pale tight satin, pink silk, and mauve chiffon, whose bodies would have been better served in a dark fabric—and discovered Aubrey himself. He sat next to Deedee Herrick, smiling and laughing as if Deedee was the most amusing conversationalist in the world. Most peculiar. And adding to this apparent rift between the cousins was the fact that Vivian's particular friend and traveling companion, Margaret, was undoubtedly having her dinner in the Frogmore Dining Room.

"Alex," said Sarah, as an apricot sorbet swathed in meringue was slipped in front of her, "why isn't Aubrey Smith eating with his cousin? They're at different tables altogether and Vivian doesn't look like she knows anyone with her. Look over there. She hasn't said a word since I started watching her."

Alex turned his head slightly, examined the indicated table, and shrugged. "Maybe those two see enough of each other in the daytime. Or Vivian wanted a separate table, wanted to meet new friends. A new man? A new woman?"

"Sarah," said Julia in a forbidding voice, "are you looking for trouble?"

"I'm looking over the passing scene," said Sarah.

"Fine," said Julia. "But don't try to make sense out of human relations on shipboard. People do odd things because they know that in a few days they won't see each other again. I mean why would anyone want to sit next to Deedee Herrick, who is a good woman, but quite dull? But there she is surrounded by gallant gentlemen."

"Aubrey Smith," said Sarah, "seems to be following her around. And tonight he's all over her like a rug. Chatter, chatter."

"An excuse," said Alex, "to get away from Vivian. He's found out that after all these years Vivian's a bit of a bore."

"So he chooses Deedee," said Sarah.

"That's enough," said Julia. "We don't want to start heating up Sarah's imagination. Sarah, concentrate on General Gordon. Perhaps an asp was slipped into his cabin, and after he was bitten, he swooned into the door, and when they do the autopsy they'll find he was done in by the, the venom . . ." Julia paused.

"The neurotoxic venom of a black mamba," said Sam Greenbank. "Colonel Gordon has been trailed for sixty years by a secret tribe of Afghanis who were attacked by the general's regiment on the Khyber Pass and they have sworn to bring his scalp—"

"Not scalp," said Alex. "Wrong trophy. Perhaps bring back his left thumb, or a recognizable piece of his liver. Or his . . ."

"*Ah, mon foi,*" said the sister in the plum vest. She turned to her sister. "*Une autre table pour le demain?*"

"*Certainement, ma cherie,*" said the black vest.

"Oh, do shut up, Alex," said Sarah. "You, too, Sam. See what you've done. Those two are disgusted and I don't blame them. Gunga Din and pieces of liver and severed thumbs." She turned to the sisters and said in her struggling French, "*Excusez-moi, s'il vous plaît, mes amis sont espèces d'idiots.*" She glowered at her friends. "And you *are* idiots," she said, stood up, and flung the end of her new shawl around her neck. "I for one am going to skip coffee and leave these people in peace." She inclined her head in the direction of the sisters. "*Bonne nuit, mesdames. Nous sommes enchantées de vous voir.*"

"Nice exit," said Sam Greenbank, following Sarah as she swept toward the doorway. "The Windsor Castle Dining Room should be proud to feed you."

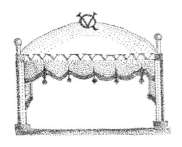

8

SARAH stood with Alex at the stern rail of the Boat Deck and inhaled the salt air. A small breeze had come up and now blew softly, and in the dim evening light beyond the churned wake she could see the dark moving waters extending toward a darker horizon.

Alex, beside her, breathed deeply. "Now we've got some space. Fresh air. That dining room scene is a bit much."

"You don't like floating hotels," Sarah pointed out. "You can't adapt to the niceties."

"Don't want to adapt," said Alex. "And neither do you. Only you won't admit it."

"I like a change, something totally different, so for a few days I can stand a little elegance. Even Aunt Julia is lapping it up. Tonight she looked like the dowager duchess of something. We love each other dearly but we all need space. She's having coffee with this Anderson man so I hope she's found a soul mate. Now, let's get moving. I feel very healthy and I could almost climb the shrouds and man the topgallant royals or whatever they're called."

And together the two set off, keeping their steps in rhythm, dodging clusters of passengers who were scattered here and there, leaning over the rail, laughing under bulkhead lights. But as they rounded the stern for the second time and made the turn toward the bow Sarah found directly in their path three familiar figures, the two women in evening dress, the man in a dinner jacket. The man held a small flashlight over an open piece of paper and was pointing at its center. Sarah came to an abrupt halt and dragged at Alex's arm.

"Wait up, I think it's Aubrey Smith. And his ladies."

"So?"

"But they didn't have dinner together. Remember I told you."

"So now they want to see each other. Make up for lost time."

"Don't be dense," Sarah hissed in his ear. "That's not the point. I mean why didn't they eat together? I didn't get it then and I don't now. Aubrey Clyde Smith and his long-lost cousin. And why is dear friend Margaret down on Five Deck eating by herself? I know she said she couldn't afford Balmoral class, but it seems weird. And now look at them, acting like spies looking over a map."

"It's probably a chart of the ship and they're trying to figure out where the library is. Or that concert tonight. Didn't you read your program? Schubert and Brahms in the Lamplighter Theatre. And movies and the Casino and God knows what all."

But now the three had discovered the two possibly sinister shapes of Sarah and Alex hovering in the distance. The flashlight snapped off and Aubrey Smith approached them. "Good evening, Ms. Deane. Dr. McKenzie. We don't mean to hold you up from your walk. We're just out enjoying fresh air and deciding whether it's to be the concert, which might just put us to sleep—all those slow movements—or one of the movies. A hard choice. *Wuthering Heights* with Laurence Olivier and Merle Oberon or *Disraeli* with George Arliss in 1929."

"I suppose there's something for everyone," remarked Sarah. "You all could go your separate ways and report later." To herself she said, You don't eat together, so why play together?

At which Cousin Vivian, who with Margaret had come forward, threw her head back and laughed. "We could turn that into a plot for a thirties movie. The long-separated cousins and the dear friend go sneaking about on their own searching for clues. What sinister plans are being hatched? Are they agents for Icelandic mining interests? Members of an international gambling syndicate?"

"Or passing messages to the Argentinean secret police," put in Aubrey Smith with a chuckle.

Sarah found herself speechless for at least six seconds.

"You took the words right out of her mouth," said Alex.

"Sarah's probably like me; she's seen too many spy movies," said Margaret. "As for me, I vote for Laurence Olivier on the moors. That man, he just makes my little old heart beat faster."

"*Disraeli* for me," said Aubrey Smith. "You?" He turned to Sarah and Alex. "Want to join in the fun? What's your poison?"

"Actually," said Sarah, recovered from the shock of having her mind read, "I'm going to take a long hot bath and go to bed with my good novel."

"And I," said Alex, "am going to stomp around the deck for a couple of circuits and hit the hay."

"Y'all are just party poopers," said Margaret, and the three waved a farewell and took off down the deck.

"I hope you are properly chastened," said Alex.

"They were awfully quick on the draw," admitted Sarah.

"And you think they were prepared for remarks about doing things alone and had an alibi ready?"

"No alibi. They just laughed at us. And not one of them said anything about why they weren't eating together."

"And why should they? It's absolutely none of our business. Come on, let's get moving. You need some air to blow some of that fluff out of your head."

"For once, Alex, you're absolutely right. I don't care whether they ever see each other again."

"Good, so come on." And Alex strode off in the direction of the bow, Sarah following and full of resolution about not letting her mind become overloaded by the harmless behavior of a trio of not very interesting passengers. In fact, she had purified her brain to such a state of blankness that when Margaret Lee—who should have been at the movies sighing over Heathcliff—appeared in the distance in the close company of a ship's officer, she simply sent the fact into one of her mental files labeled "Scrap."

Julia Clancy had spent an enjoyable evening with Erik Anderson. His two grandchildren had taken themselves off for some youth activity based on the recently seen ship's movie, *Treasure Island*, and Erik and Julia were free to pursue their favorite subject in peace over coffee and brandy in the Balmoral Lounge. Then, as the ship's clock struck ten—or, to be more accurate, four bells—the two children returned, chattering about treasure hunts, and Julia, after making a tentative date to try her luck at the Casino the next afternoon with Erik Anderson, headed for her stateroom. Even after a tiring day, Julia was in a singularly benevolent mood. Erik had suggested a visit to his New Hampshire farm in August for the horse trials to be held there, and Julia thought how pleasant it was to have met someone her own age with such sensible interests.

Opening her cabin door, she found her stewardess, Mary Malone, engaged in folding down her bed and placing the de rigueur silver-wrapped chocolate mint on the snowy pillowcase.

"Good evening, Mary. Doesn't my bed look inviting," said Julia.

"Have you had an enjoyable day, Mrs. Clancy?"

"Yes, indeed I have," said Julia. "And how do you manage to remember my name with all the people you have to take care of? And staying up until all hours waiting for passengers who want you to do something special for them." Such was Julia's good humor that, tired as she was, she stopped to consider that the woman now folding the counterpane led an arduous life centered on the needs of transient and often inconsiderate strangers.

Mary smiled and adjusted the peach comforter that covered the foot of the bed. "It's my job, Mrs. Clancy, and besides, I don't remember everyone's name—not at first, mind you—but I remember Clancy. It's an Irish name and my brother married a Clancy."

"Yes," said Julia. "My husband Tom came from Ireland and we went back as often as possible to see his family."

"Ah, that was nice," said Mary, and then she busied herself with a pile of towels monogrammed with a *QV*, and, these disposed of in the bathroom, turned to leave. Then stopped. "Did you, by any chance, Mrs. Clancy, see the show tonight? The pirate one? I've heard that it's very well done. Many of the crew are hoping to see one of the shows."

"Yes, it was well done," Julia said. "Mr. Herrick is amazing. The kind of man that can do anything with his voice. And his face. And the slides and film were very colorful."

"And the next show is to be something about several shipwrecks. And then the last one, they tell me, will be *Titanic*."

"I," said Julia with great firmness, "will probably skip the rest of the shows. I can do very nicely without hearing about ships being blown up or hitting rocks and icebergs. My mother lost a dear uncle on the *Titanic*. He stayed aboard with the other men, so I have no intention of sitting comfortably in a theater watching fourteen hundred people drown."

Mary Malone took a step toward the door and stopped. "Fifteen hundred, I think it was. Or more than that, some say. As many as fifteen hundred and seventeen. Lost, I mean, and most of them those poor souls who died down in steerage. I've read that book on the sinking and gone to that movie, you see."

"One lost person," said Julia, "would have been one too many."

"Oh, I agree," said Mary. "A terrible thing it was. Good night, Mrs. Clancy. I hope you have a fine night's rest. They say we may be in for a little bit of a wind tomorrow."

"Thank you, Mary," said Julia. "I think I could sleep through a hurricane."

Julia busied herself with a hot bath, and crawled into bed feeling the weight of double seventy years on her limbs. And just before she fell asleep she thought of Mary Malone's last remarks. She's as bad as the rest of them, Julia told herself sleepily. She's dying to go to the Herrick shows and reads books about the Titanic sinking and she knows how many victims there were. And Julia drifted off into an uneasy dream in which horses cavorted in pastures that rolled and heaved like a disturbed ocean.

Sarah had her long hot soak, luxuriating in the fact of a real bathtub, while Alex, arriving fresh from his circuits of the deck, took his turn in the shower and then gathered his wife to his bed and into his arms for the loving interlude interrupted earlier by the arrival of Liza Baum down in their Five Deck cabin. Then, lulled by the gentle movement of the ship, Sarah fell asleep in Alex's bed, her head pillowed by Alex's arm.

And woke up. Was suddenly completely awake and alert. She opened her eyes and, without moving her head, searched the darkness. Nothing. Not a sound. Had she heard something, something like a tiny click? The cabin door? The porthole being closed in some miraculous manner? A bathroom water tap left on? She stared over at the dim silhouette of her own empty bed, divided from Alex's by the bedside table.

It was nothing. The result of a muddled dream or footsteps in the passageway. Sarah resolutely closed her eyes. And then froze. It was the faintest of rustles. The sort of sound that might be made by something brushing against a piece of cloth. She held her breath and opened her eyes again and stared at the twin bed only five feet away. A shape. The cabin was dark but this was a blacker shape, and now it loomed over the empty bed. A human shape—man or woman, it was impossible to tell. Now it bent over the bed, its dark arms reaching along the edge of the bed, hands feeling their way along the comforter, over to the pillow. The shape standing up, slowly, as if being pulled by a string. Pausing, then reaching again.

Sarah took a long silent breath, held it, and then slowly let the air out. Should she wake Alex, who would undoubtedly spring into vigorous and possibly foolish action? Dangerous, anyway. Because what if the man—or woman—had a gun? Maybe playing dead was the way to go. The figure was now pawing at the headboard and under the pillow. She kept her body rigid, her mind racing with questions. Had they locked their cabin door properly? Because this might just be some passenger who had found his way into their cabin by accident. A drunk in the wrong cabin.

And then she remembered. Teddy. Teddy Hogarth. Liza's drunken boyfriend. This had been his cabin on One Deck. He'd been drinking. Of course, no surprise there. And Teddy had forgotten that he was turning over a new leaf, moving to Deck Five to be near his support person, Liza. And here he was invading their cabin, pawing at the bed, thinking he still slept here. Well, goddamn it.

Sarah reared up and yelled. "Goddamn it, get out of here, Teddy Hogarth! You get the hell out of here!"

"What!" shouted Alex, rising out of the bedclothes.

And the dark shape rose, wheeled, took a step, stumbled, grabbed at a chair, then charged at the cabin door, yanked it open, slammed it shut, and was gone.

"I'll get him!" yelled Alex, getting to his feet and striding toward the door.

Sarah grabbed him by the elbow. "No. Let him go, damn him. It's Teddy Hogarth, drunk as a skunk, forgetting that he's switched cabins with us."

Alex paused, then, shaking her off, reached the cabin door, pulled it open, and disappeared. Sarah, after grabbing a raincoat as being more suitable for pursuit than a see-through shortie nightgown, stepped out in the passageway. And met Alex returning, shaking his head.

"The bugger's gone, and I can't chase him all over the ship. And I don't want to call Security and make a big deal out of this."

Sarah walked over to the bedside table and switched on the light. "We can tell the steward in the morning and he can take it from there."

Alex sank down on his rumpled bed. "I locked the cabin door. I'm sure I did. But maybe I didn't shoot the bolt."

"And guess who probably still has his key to this cabin?"

Alex groaned. "Oh, God. Okay, we'll have to frisk him tomorrow. Or have the locks changed. I thought Teddy was going to be trouble and that Liza had taken on more than she could handle. Drinkers don't usually quit just like that without back-sliding a few times. And I don't think a resort ocean liner with bars at every turn is the ideal drying-out tank."

Sarah drew several deep breaths. "So let's lock up. Key and the bolt. Do you think we should call Liza and warn her that Teddy's on the loose?"

Alex considered, then shook his head. "No, let her get her sleep. She'll find out soon enough that he's fallen off the wagon. And she said she'd lock her cabin if he started drinking again. She also thinks he's harmless—drunk or sober. After all, he didn't do anything violent just now, did he?"

"No," said Sarah. "Actually, for a drunk he was pretty quiet. Obviously he'd forgotten where the light switch was and so was just pawing around to find the bed, fumbling with the blankets. And then, when I figured out who it must be, I yelled my head off."

"You can say that again," said Alex. "Remind me never to slip silently into our bedroom and fumble at the blankets. Now let's try bed again."

"Yes," said Sarah, suddenly overcome with drowsiness. "And damn Teddy Hogarth. Think of that poor trade commission with him in their midst."

"Not to worry," said Alex. "The British know how to get rid of undesirables. He'll be packaged and flown home ten minutes after he hits New York." And Alex, who had not been party to the alleged invasion of Teddy Hogarth, closed his eyes and slept undisturbed, breathing deeply the salt air pouring in from the partly opened porthole.

But the rest of Sarah's night was not peaceful. The intrusion had left its imprint on her dreaming brain, and she tossed and worried in her own twin bed for more than an hour before falling into a muddled dream of being engaged in a pillow fight with a large number of dark anonymous figures with multiple arms.

Both Alex and Sarah woke on Friday morning, the thirtieth of June, in a state of ravenous hunger and the certain knowledge that because of the nightly clock setback it was only six in the morning, when their stomachs were certain that it was eight.

"We can eat at the Osborne Cafeteria again," said Sarah. "A glamour breakfast. Finnan haddie and kippers."

"You don't like finnan haddie and kippers," Alex reminded her. He was emerging from his early morning washup and shave and had been humming sea chanties.

"They're just symbols for a big spread," said Sarah. "You're right, I hate fish in the morning, but I like the setting for that sort of thing. The groaning sideboard, the chafing dishes, the spirit kettle, the footman handing around dishes of this and that, the maid with the silver toast rack and the Cooper's Oxford Marmalade. The master of the house arriving in his tweeds and opening the *Times* and the mistress in her cashmere twin set slitting open the day's letters and young master Algernon in his Guard's uniform . . ."

"Dream on," said Alex. "And while you're dreaming let's zip up topside and see if we can locate a bowl of raisin bran and some hot coffee."

Sarah pulled on her blue linen jacket and began brushing her dark hair into something resembling flatness—the disturbed night had left her short brown hair in something of a bird's nest. "Thank heavens for my hair appointment," she said. "And I do think our beloved *Vicky* is rolling ever so slightly. I looked out the porthole and the ocean was moving around."

"Good. I like to know I'm on the Atlantic, not a millpond. I'll take our key and we can have a talk with the Security Office about changing locks."

"Wait a minute," said Sarah. She stared at her feet. It was a green plastic something now partly hidden by the skirt of her twin bed. She reached down, pulled it out, held it up for inspection. A common green plastic shopping bag with a drawstring at its neck. She smoothed it out so that the golden letters clearly spelled "Harrods Knightsbridge" and then felt inside.

"Empty," she announced.

"Well, you've been shopping in the Harrods store," said Alex.

"I bought a scarf—I always seem to buy scarves," said

Sarah. "But it was wrapped in paper. This is a plastic bag. And my fancy evening things from the Regent Street Shopping Gallery came in a white bag."

"Maybe Julia left it," suggested Alex. He was, Sarah thought, looking particularly nautical that morning, with his dark hair, his black eyebrows, his slight sunburn, his white turtleneck shirt and the cotton sweater pulled over an ancient pair of khaki trousers.

"You look like a crew member," said Sarah with approval. "Not on this ship but on a Hollywood fishing boat. And Julia only bought a pair of gloves at Harrods, and she didn't come down here with them in a big Harrods bag."

"So, Dr. Watson, we must reach the conclusion that our visitor last night—the suspect Teddy Hogarth—was shopping at Harrods."

"Drinking up a storm and hiding the liquor bottle in a shopping bag so Liza wouldn't see it," said Sarah. "Listen, it's useful. Someone probably needs an extra green plastic bag."

"You don't want to test for fingerprints?"

"I don't need fingerprints because today Detective S. Deane is going to wrap up her last case."

"Which is?"

"The chewing out of Mr. Hogarth. If I can find him. And having a word with Liza to let her know what her buddy is up to."

"Breakfast first," said Alex. "Then you can loose yourself on our nighttime prowler. I'll stand by with a cat-o'-nine-tails."

Sarah and Alex arrived in the Osborne Cafeteria, busied themselves with choosing juice and cereal and a selection of buns, croissants, and scones, and so laden they made their way to one of the glass-topped tables that ringed the room. And were immediately joined by Liza Baum. She in her yellow sweatpants topped by a red sweatshirt featuring Donald Duck.

"Top of the morning," announced Liza. "I hear there's going to be a little wind kicking up. I love bad weather. Keeps the crowds down and then there's no big hassle getting breakfast. When the weather's good the place is a zoo. Just look around." Liza waved an arm at the lines circling the long buffet tables.

"Sit with us," Sarah said. "I've got some questions. My over-worked bump of curiosity."

"Her long nose," said Alex. "And for once a genuine event."

"You've got my attention," said Liza. She put down her tray—Liza apparently intended to eat the breakfast of a well-grown elephant.

"You eat," commanded Sarah. "And we'll tell."

"Oh boy, a genuine mystery," said Liza, sinking her teeth into a plate-sized chunk of apple pastry.

"I don't think it's either genuine or a mystery," said Sarah, "but here goes." And in detail she described the events of the night. The opening of the cabin door, the dark figure feeling the bed, the sudden realization that Teddy Hogarth—undoubtedly drunk as a skunk—had forgotten where his new cabin was. Sarah's yelling and telling him to get out, the aborted pursuit, his disappearance. And for good measure, the appearance of the green plastic Harrods shopping bag.

Through the recitation Liza remained quite still but with an increasingly puzzled frown on her face, and by the time Sarah had begun sketching in the picture of Teddy stumbling out of the darkened cabin she began an emphatic head shaking.

"No way," said Liza. "Hey, it makes a great little story, and I grant you it's just the sort of stupid thing Teddy might have done, but the only problem is he didn't."

But Sarah shook her head in turn. "Of course he did. I mean who else could be drinking too much and running around with our cabin key and forgetting where he was supposed to be sleeping?"

Liza took a long swallow of her coffee, looked displeased, and ladled a huge spoonful of sugar into the cup. Then, a second and more agreeable drink having gone down, she put down the cup and faced Sarah. "Now hear this. Teddy Hogarth has been under surveillance—mine—since I last talked to you about getting some pills for him. Which I did. Dr. Greenbank"—here Liza looked over at Alex—"was great and got Teddy shooed into an examining room, and the ship's doctor went over him, checked his heart, his blood pressure, poked his liver, looked in his throat, hit his knee with a rubber hammer to see if he had any reflexes left, peered into his eyes, and for good measure sucked some blood to see if he was anemic. Which he was. Anyway, they gave him two doses of sedatives and told him to come back tomorrow."

"Well, okay," said Sarah. "But then what happened? He hit the bar scene."

"You're not listening," said Liza. "You've made your mind up, haven't you? Teddy broke into your cabin and that's that."

"I think," said Alex mildly, "we'd better listen to the lady."

"Okay, here's how it goes. I take charge of the sedatives and I'm planning to give him one at bedtime because even if he only has two doses I don't trust him to remember whether he's had the first dose. Anyway, Teddy's feeling pretty rotten, but I haul him off to that *Disraeli* movie, which I'm sure will quiet him down because it's not what you call a thriller, and by the end of the movie he's almost a zombie, so I see it's time to zap him with the sedative. And I think, damn, I'd better keep an eye on this guy, so I get him to his cabin—the one that used to be your cabin with the double bunk—and I stuff the pill down his throat and help undress and dump him in the lower bunk like I'm a real Florence Nightingale. And I spend the night on the upper bunk to keep an eye on him."

"And he was there all night," said Alex.

"Yeah. Sure. I slept like a log and he did, too. The medicine did its job. He was completely zonked when I got up this morning to do my run on the deck. Anyway, Teddy's probably still there."

"But," persisted Sarah, loyalty to preconceived ideas being a strong point, "he could have gotten up—after you fell asleep—left the cabin, hit the bar, drunk so much that he couldn't remember what cabin he was supposed to be in. And then when we chased him out he remembered and went on back to the Deck Five cabin, fell into bed, and that's where you found him this morning."

Liza nodded. "And I thought I was stubborn. You don't give up, do you? Listen, I grant you it's a lot nicer to think that old Teddy bear was bumbling around in your cabin than some serial rapist or steward gone mad. But Teddy spent the night with me.

I locked and bolted the cabin, put the key under my pillow, and, for good measure, tucked a chair under the doorknob. And another chair upside-down on the floor where if he got up, he'd fall over it and I'd hear him."

"Have you considered going into the law, Liza?" asked Alex. "You'd make a good defense attorney."

Liza nodded. "Well, this is an open-and-shut case, and the prosecutor had better throw in the sponge. Right, Sarah?"

But Sarah only sniffed and tugged a piece of toast into two pieces and reached for the raspberry jam.

Liza finished her coffee and turned to Alex. "How about it, Doctor? Can Teddy do normal activities, or should I keep dragging him to the movies and Bingo games? I mean, should he work out in the gym or would he have cardiac arrest or liver failure?"

"Why don't you see how he feels this morning and then check in with the medical officer," said Alex, loath to even put a finger into the care and management of Teddy Hogarth.

"If you're talking about me," said a voice, "I've felt better. But I've felt a hell of a lot worse."

Liza waved a croissant and Sarah and Alex swiveled around. Teddy Hogarth in gray shorts and a T-shirt with "Edinburgh Festival" written large across the chest. He certainly did not look like a picture of health: shadowed eyes, sallow skin, limp dark hair falling across his brow all suggested a long sojourn in a cave or a life spent in a bar. But he also appeared sober and in marginally better shape than Sarah had expected.

"I woke up," said Teddy, "in this strange cabin and then I remembered. I'd switched to Five Deck and Liza had put me to bed. Drugged me and tucked me in. Thanks, Liza."

"You see," said Liza to Sarah and Alex.

"See what?" said Teddy, reaching over to Liza's plate and helping himself to a cinnamon bun.

"Mistaken identity. Sarah and Alex, meet Teddy Hogarth. Sarah thinks you broke into their cabin last night because you thought you still lived there."

"I may have been a little pickled yesterday afternoon," said Teddy, "but not that pickled. I turned my old key in to the Steward's Office yesterday, and they gave me the one to the cabin on Deck Five. To be near Liza, who is going to hound me day and night to behave myself. So that I'll be in shape to hound her."

Teddy, thought Alex, was not only sober but making a small approach to something like humor. He looked over at Sarah and saw a determined set to her jaw.

"Hello, Teddy," she said. "I've heard a lot about you, and I have a question. Have you shopped at Harrods recently?"

"Have I *what?*"

"Shopped at Harrods."

"Well, yes. Last month, I think. A birthday. My sister's. Penelope. We call her Pelly. I bought her a red cashmere sweater which cost the earth. And she didn't like the color."

"And on shipboard? There's a Harrods aboard ship."

"You're joking. No, I see you're not. Well, I've done those things I ought not to have done, and left undone those things I ought to have done, but I haven't been shopping at Harrods."

"And," said Sarah, grasping at last straws, "you don't carry things, a Thermos, a camera, something, around in a Harrods bag?"

Teddy Hogarth stared at her. "No. I do not." But then he brightened. "You've lost something? In a Harrods bag. And you think I might have nicked it in a drunken stupor? Right?"

"Wrong," said Sarah. "I haven't lost a Harrods bag, I've found one. An empty one."

She looked at Alex as Liza got up to leave and Teddy followed her. "I think," she said regretfully, "that I have successfully established myself as a fit candidate for a straitjacket."

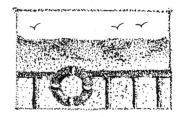

9

SARAH and Alex watched as Liza and Teddy Hogarth left the cafeteria, Liza pulling Teddy's sleeve and propelling him forward.

"Liza has missed her calling," observed Alex, watching the two disappear toward the stairs leading to the Boat Deck, presumably for a period of strenuous walking. "I think some armored division could use her. I wouldn't want to take Teddy on as a project."

"Liza is full of the milk of human kindness," retorted Sarah.

"And I'm not?"

"Not as far as Teddy is concerned."

"Look, beloved. Let's worry about something closer to the bone. Teddy is in good hands, and if he arrives in New York sober, well and good. I will congratulate Liza on her rehab efforts. Besides, despite her protestations to the contrary, I think she actually likes the guy. Meanwhile what we have had is someone who is *not* Teddy Hogarth sneaking into our stateroom using what must have been the correct key."

Sarah grimaced. "That's a problem. Where do we report it?"

"Our steward—his name is Thomas Petrovski. Whom we haven't met yet although our beds were nicely turned down and the mints were in place."

Sarah shook her head. "Don't report to a steward. Nor to a maid, nor to the head steward, if there is such a person."

"Why not? They're in charge of the staterooms."

Sarah put down her teacup with a thump, managing to create a small wave of tea that washed over the rim and soaked into her croissant. "Listen, Alex, stewards—and housekeeping types—are the ones who have keys. Master keys for all cabins."

"And you think the good ship *Queen Vicky* has employed a bunch of sneaks? Sarah, be real. The personnel on these big babies probably have the kind of clearance that diplomats get when they're posted to Israel. These ships depend on, they survive on, the trustiness of their staff. Forget stewards."

"Then forget the purser and the doctors and the fitness center people and the captain and the librarian. Forget the whole crew. Because now you're talking passengers with keys in their pocket?"

"Exactly."

"Passengers who have lifted master keys from trusting or careless stewards? Or from careless passengers?"

"Correct. I suppose if you and I really put our minds to it we could swipe some passenger's key. And"—Alex smiled the smile of one who can come up with an unbeatable argument—"who would be more careless of his key to his former stateroom than our unsteady friend, Teddy Hogarth?"

"He just told us he'd turned in his key."

"Hell, Sarah, he probably had two of them. Maybe three."

A shadow loomed over their table. "You two," said a now familiar voice, "seem to be into heavy argument. Shall I go away or shall we have a spot of breakfast together? Catch up on the news. What do you think of this marvelous weather? But I hear the wind's going to change. Then we'll see who has sea legs."

It was Aubrey Clyde Smith, natty as usual in his open shirt, linen blazer, and flannels. He held a tray burdened with a plate of scrambled eggs and a carafe of coffee.

"We're about finished with our spot of breakfast," began Alex, but Sarah interrupted.

"Sit down, Mr. Smith. We're having an argument about who can sneak into someone else's cabin."

Aubrey Smith put down his tray carefully, arranged his plate of eggs to the left of the coffee, and eased himself into the chair, a wrought-iron number with a straight back. "These chairs are built to encourage you to get out of them," he complained. "Now, into what cabin do you two wish to sneak?"

And Sarah for the third time in less than an hour went through the night appearance of what she now called the "bed fumbler" and concluded with the finding of the plastic Harrods shopping bag.

Aubrey Smith listened with close attention.

"I think," said Alex, who was growing very tired of the whole affair, "we can skip the Harrods bag as just one of those things that turn up. Everyone and his brother is probably shopping at Harrods and leaving bags around."

"So what do you plan to do about it?" asked Aubrey.

"Well," explained Sarah, "as I said, the real suspect, Teddy Hogarth, was under wraps last night, so we're trying to decide whom to tell. I'm sure there's a security office somewhere."

"I suppose that the house staff has keys and also many of the officers," said Aubrey Clyde Smith. "I suggest you finish breakfast and then go over to Security. It's on Two Deck next to the Purser's Office. You'll probably be issued new keys and your cabin lock will be changed."

"Mr. Smith," said Sarah, a small seed of suspicion beginning to root itself, "you sound as if you've been involved with lost keys or have had midnight visiting strangers."

"Please call me Aubrey. And yes, I've made a lot of Atlantic crossings because I'm not a flying enthusiast, and when I come aboard I check the chart for the locations of the various offices."

"And the Harrods bag?" persisted Sarah.

Aubrey Smith shook his head. "I'm inclined to agree with Dr. McKenzie—whom I shall call Alex since we're shipmates, aren't we?"

"For better or for worse," said Sarah a little grimly.

"Let's hope for the better. What I'm saying is I think you can forget the Harrods bag. But you know, I would love to have one. I have so many oddments, shaving tackle, medicines, a shoe kit. I packed in rather a hurry, and you would be doing me a great favor if you gave it to me. I could certainly use it, and I'm not about to go to Harrods and buy some overpriced gadget or Shetland steamer rug for the sake of one of their nice bags."

Sarah, rather startled at the suggestion, looked hard at Aubrey, but he sat there calmly, expectantly, simply loading his fork with scrambled eggs.

Alex spoke up. "Take the bag. It's in our cabin. Come on down in an hour. We'll be back from Security by then."

Sarah, who had been wrestling with her suspicious and a desire not to seem like a total fool, finally came down on the side of the fool. "Fingerprints," she said. "Wouldn't the security people like to test the bag for fingerprints?"

Aubrey Smith threw back his head and laughed. A good hearty laugh that made Sarah blush to her eyebrows. "I suppose," he said, "that you are a great fan of murder mysteries. Agatha and Dorothy and P. D. James—my wife lives by those ladies."

"And so my brain has been affected," said Sarah, making a face. "Okay, never mind the fingerprints. The bag is yours."

"I'll be at your stateroom door," said Aubrey. "What was the number? Ten-twenty-seven? I'll just jot that down. I have a memory like a sieve." And, suiting action to word, he whipped out a small notebook from his blazer pocket and made a note.

"Okay," said Alex. "We're off to the Security Office like good responsible citizens."

"I think you'll find," remarked Aubrey as Sarah got to her feet, "that the *Queen Vicky* people will almost guarantee no more nocturnal visits."

"Now how does he know that?" demanded Sarah as she and Alex worked their way past the other breakfast tables.

"He said he crosses back and forth," Alex reminded her. "Maybe he has stock in the shipping company. Come on, we have to go down two levels. I hope we won't be snarled up in a lot of red tape and filling out forms."

Alex proved a prophet. Ahead of them several passengers stood in line. One anxious woman wanted to get into her safety deposit box but had lost her key; an elderly gentleman wished to complain of a purloined deck chair—someone had claimed the one he had been assigned, and then when his back was turned, the damn thing had vanished. "Probably overboard," grumbled the man, who with his hanging mustache resembled a disgruntled walrus.

Sarah and Alex were at last ushered into a little cubicle marked SECURITY OFFICE. Here a white-uniformed officer, a telephone receiver to the ear, waved them to a pair of chairs.

"I see," said the officer. "Yes, I think so. Quite right. Johnny on the spot, I'd say. Yes, we'll be right here waiting. Thanks again, Mr. Smith. Keep in touch."

Sarah sat up straight. "Did you say 'Smith'?"

The officer smiled. "One of a host of Smiths. I don't have the exact total, but with almost two thousand souls aboard there are bound to be quite a number of Smiths, not to mention the hyphenated Smiths. And Browns and—what's the other popular name? Miller. Quite a few Millers. Now, how may I assist you?"

And Sarah and Alex again recited their story—a tale that was beginning to sound even to their ears tattered and wholly unbelievable.

But the security officer, a Mr. Harper, was sympathetic, took notes, stopped the story midway, and called in another uniformed man identified as the assistant purser. "I want him to hear this," said Mr. Harper. "It's a security matter, but the purser's office always wants to know about these things. Could you start from the beginning?"

Alex began again and under his guidance the tale became coherent, neatly packaged, factual, and brief. Sarah, now sick to death of the affair, remained silent until they were about to leave. Standing up, shaking hands, she mentioned the Harrods bag and waited for general laughter. But Mr. Harper made a note and assured her that if anyone came to Lost & Found looking for such a thing, the claimant would be asked a few questions. "Now don't worry about giving away the one you found," he told her. "Those bags are all over the place. It may have blown in when the cabin door was open after Mr. Hogarth moved to Five Deck."

"Smith!" exclaimed Sarah when they reached their cabin. "Another Smith. On the telephone to the Security Office. You don't suppose our dear friend Aubrey . . ." She let the name hang.

"Sarah, Sarah. Cool it. Ease off. Avast and belay. You heard what the man said. Smiths are like fleas. All over the place."

"And you think I'm crazy to go on about the Harrods bag?"

"Frankly, yes. Let it rest. We'll go back on deck as soon as our own favorite Smith shows up."

Which he did within the minute. Accepted the plastic bag with thanks, admired their view from the porthole, the slow rising and falling of the horizon, and then suggested a glass of something stimulating in the Snuggery. "Perhaps Vivian and Margaret can join us. Say six o'clock. And, Sarah, ask your aunt to come. She certainly adds spice to the party. And many thanks for my Harrods bag. It will give a great deal of class to my luggage."

"Aunt Julia adds more than spice," Sarah said when Aubrey Smith had gone. "But now that she's got a boyfriend we may never see her again. And Alex, for the absolutely last time—"

Alex cut in. "No, I do not think that damn green bag is on a par with a kilo of cocaine or a bloodstained dagger or a spent cartridge. I say forget it. Now and forever more."

Sarah closed her mouth. And made a resolution. From now on, by God, she would keep her own counsel, keep her doubts about last night's incident to herself. She would pursue the subject by stealth and in silence. To hell with Alex, to hell with Liza Baum and Teddy and Alex and the assistant purser. And Aubrey Smith. And for that matter to hell with the Herricks and manager Gerald Hofstra and Cousin Vivian and friend Margaret down there on Five Deck. Something smelled, something was out of whack. Something nattered and nibbled at the back of her brain and itched at her fingers and curled her toes, but yes, she was going to keep her mouth shut. She, Sarah, was not going to share a single qualm with anyone else. So there. Bugger off, the whole lot of you.

And in this bracing mood Sarah marched out of the stateroom and, taking long strides, led Alex upward toward the Boat Deck and into the bright and breezy air. And the breeze blew a bright clear new thought into her head. Yes. Yes! Of course. Why hadn't she seen it? She turned without thinking to speak to Alex, who was standing by the rail, an expression of great pleasure on his face.

And then she turned back. No, dammit, remember her promise. She had been laughed at enough for one day. This was her idea and she was not going to have it flattened by her nearest and dearest. She would button her lips and keep them closed.

Julia Clancy rose late that Friday and took an approving look out her porthole. Then she lifted the phone and ordered a substantial breakfast to be brought to her stateroom. For once in her life she would enjoy luxury. Enjoy the fact that she didn't have to pull on her farm boots and go shivering down into the barn and supervise the feeding and turning into pastures of her equine children. She would not have to argue with Patrick about reducing the grain for a pregnant mare, or disagree with her farrier about bar shoes for her school pony, Gingersnap. Or meet with her farm supplier to complain about the quality of last month's hay. No, she would have breakfast, find her way to her deck chair, and prepare to enjoy the summer's day. Perhaps see Mr. Erik Anderson in time for a preluncheon whiskey. And then, all in good time, hunt up Sarah and Alex and see how they were doing without her guidance.

Breakfast was splendid. Grapefruit, kippers, and muffins slathered with marmalade, all sluiced down with strong milky coffee. The fact of a slightly increased ocean movement had no effect on the Clancy digestive system. As one of her seasick friends had remarked on an earlier Atlantic crossing, all those years Julia had spent thundering around on horses, galloping over uneven ground, jumping logs and coops and timber, had apparently numbed her balance system and made her body indifferent to the ills of normal mortals.

Breakfast concluded, a hot shower taken, Julia pulled on her gray twill slacks, a long-sleeved cotton shirt, and her ground-gripping sneakers. First a deck prowl, followed by a contemplative period in her deck chair. Julia needed to think. She was beginning to have misgivings about Erik Anderson. Was she perhaps too much attracted to a man who, for all she knew, was a card shark, a sought-after footpad, or—what was that word used by nineteenth-century novelists—an adventurer? Wasn't she a perfect target, an elderly widow whose only protection was the intermittent presence of her niece and her niece's husband? She would have been seen as having enough money to afford Balmoral-class passage and had already described her horse farm in Maine to him in some detail. True, Erik Anderson—if that was really his name—was traveling with grandchildren—even Julia's imagination, which at times rivaled Sarah's, couldn't convert the two children into criminal adjuncts—but all that talk about horses, about Fjords? Wasn't it the sort of information anyone with fraud on his mind would load into his brain? He could probably talk knowledgeably about yachts, raising Labrador retrievers, the opera at Glynbourne, skiing in Aspen, bird-watching in the Everglades.

Julia braced her shoulders. Forewarned is forearmed. Not that she'd been actually warned, but it was all too pat. She would sound him out. See if he was equally enthusiastic on all subjects she dragged into the conversation. If he were a true adventurer he would have many subjects at his fingertips. She would try him on music and dogs—subjects Julia could handle on an amateur basis since she played the piano and had raised English setters. Bird-watching she could deal with, but not skiing. And sometime soon she would phone home to Patrick and find out if there really was a New Hampshire farm owned by an Erik Anderson.

Julia pocketed her cabin key, and opened the door into the corridor. And then remembered her wallet with her *Vicky* credit card. After all, she had planned to meet with Erik Anderson at the Casino that afternoon. And perhaps later look around the shopping gallery. She turned and faced the outside of her cabin door. And, as she turned, she noticed that a few inches above the upper hinge was a tiny red thread. Or a minute strip of plastic. Something alien, anyway. Hardly noticeable but certainly out of place. The doors of the staterooms were each marked with a number—Julia's being 1045—the numbers in raised black set into the center of the door. Otherwise the doors were perfectly plain.

Julia collected her wallet, stuffed it in her trousers pocket, and then, interest aroused, made her way slowly along the starboard passageway toward the exit to the outer deck. The illumination was not strong—discreet lights had been centered and inset along the ceiling—but by squinting, Julia decided that there were no other little colored threads pasted against the door hinges. Except Alex and Sarah's stateroom, 1027, which showed a green thread identical to hers but for the color. She turned back and worked her way down to the notorious 1042, where General Gordon had met his end. The sign "No Admittance" was still fastened above the door handle, but alongside the topmost hinge Julia thought she saw a shred of color. But because she was only five foot three inches tall, close examination of this shred without the use of a stepladder was impossible. She returned to her own door. The little red piece was less than a quarter of an inch wide. Back to General Gordon's and, standing on her toes and craning her neck, with difficulty she again made out a sliver, more like a hair, really. Not red, but green. Two greens, one red.

Curious, thought Julia, staring at the door.

"May I help you, Mrs. Clancy? Are you all right?"

Julia jumped. And wheeled around. And then relaxed. It was Mary Malone, starched and proper in her blue and white striped uniform, her gray hair in its tidy net, with a neat stack of bath towels over her arm.

"You frightened me," Julia accused her. Better to be on the attack or Mary would be escorting her to the ship's psychiatric unit—or, more likely, to the Security Office—for gazing at forbidden doors.

"I'm sorry, Mrs. Clancy. Have your forgotten your cabin number? May I take you there?"

Julia swallowed hard and opted for the truth. "You see, Mary," she said, "I noticed this tiny red sticker next to my door hinge, and since I have this horrible bump of curiosity—as bad as my niece Sarah, whom I hope you meet pretty soon, she's always sticking her nose into things—anyway, I saw this red strip above my door hinge and wanted to see if anyone else, any other door, had it. And no one did until I saw a green one on my niece's door and another green one on General Gordon's door."

Mary Malone gave Julia a forgiving smile. "It's a code, you see. We, the housekeeping staff, use it to let each other know which cabins are due a complete wash-up. Sanitizing. We do them at least twice a week. Your red sticker says your stateroom's just been done. The green marks say the rooms are still to be done. The Security Office gave us permission to wash the general's room. Put it back in perfect shape ready for debarkation in New York. I'm sorry if all these bothered you, Mrs. Clancy."

"I wasn't bothered," Julia protested. Honestly, too much was being made over absolutely nothing. "I was just wondering. But," she added, puzzled, "why would you clean the general's room if it could be a police case?"

"Well, they don't know that, do they?" said Mary. "He was an old man and very tottery, if I do say so. And the security people have gone over the whole cabin, taken their photographs and samples, and so it's time to be cleaning it. And a very real mess it is. I've been in and looked about. Bloodstains are difficult—pardon me if I mention something not pleasant—so the maintenance people will be laying a new carpet when we come into New York."

"I see," said Julia, now anxious to be about her day.

"Is everything in your stateroom quite to your satisfaction, Mrs. Clancy?" said Mary.

"Perfectly," said Julia. "And I love having a bathtub. I almost used the whole of the little bottle of bath gel."

"I'll replace that," said Mary, "and be sure and have a lovely day. There's a bit of a roll to the ship this morning."

"I've hardly noticed it," said Julia, who then walked quickly in the direction of the passage stairway and began her careful ascent to the Boat Deck.

It was not until almost an hour later, her walk finished, and now stretched out in her deck chair, that a thought pricked Julia's peace of mind. Why in God's name were cleaning people allowed in the stateroom of someone who had died—or been killed—in a yet-to-be-determined manner? Wasn't there some sort of scene-of-the-crime protocol—in case it was a crime—to be followed? For a few minutes Julia puzzled over this oddity and then reverted to topic A: the questionable presence on shipboard of that most agreeable gentleman and avowed horse fancier, Mr. Erik Anderson.

10

IN the first hours after boarding the *Vicky* on that Wednesday, Deedee Herrick told herself that she had never had so much fun. But by the time Thursday had dawned—the day of their "Pirates and Plunder" show—a certain pinching uneasiness had begun to trouble her. She identified this feeling as created by the person of their manager, Gerald Hofstra, and although she had energetically searched for him when he had gone missing, at the same time she did not entirely regret his absence. The show had gone well, and even if she had been almost wiped out at its end, why, it was almost like old times, she and Richard running the whole affair. On Gerald's return on the Friday morning of June thirtieth, she had begun to wish that he had remained missing; she had never really taken to the man.

Now she and Richard sat together at a corner table of the Osborne Cafeteria hunched over a stack of notes and a pile of video cassettes and a box of slides. From time to time passengers, single or in groups, with and without children, came up to congratulate the pair. Such a wonderful show! So realistic. All those effects and the lighting going off and on. And the scary sound track. And you, Mr. Herrick. A real genius, just like that man in the old movies with all the faces. What was his name?

And your different voices, like, you know, someone with a multiple personality disorder. Oh, Mr. Herrick, we all think you should be on the stage.

At which Richard tried to point out that in a way he was on the stage, but thank you very much. And he hoped they'd come to this afternoon's show, "Disasters at Sea." And Deedee nodded and said in a repressed voice, yes, Richard was a real magician.

And through the congratulatory flow, leaning back and huddled in his chair, a brooding and unhappy presence, sat the returned manager Gerald Hofstra. He was wearing a black T-shirt and a black cotton jacket, neither of which did much to give him a healthy look. His face was the color of gray clay and his brow wet with perspiration so that he had to mop it from time to time with a handkerchief imprinted with the image of the Eiffel Tower.

At one point, when the stream of visitors had thinned, Deedee spoke to Gerald in a voice of concern. Deedee was a kind-hearted soul, and even if she didn't like the man, she felt concern for his obvious ill health, although underlying the concern was the fear that Gerald would improve sufficiently to resume management of the shows and impose on them a morbid emphasis—one unacceptable to Deedee but eagerly seized by Richard.

"I'm going to ask Sam Greenback for some medicine for you," she told Gerald. "Not just seasick pills but something that will hold you together. But you should take it easy. I'm sure Richard and I can manage alone tonight. The pirate show yesterday was a real success."

"I'm beyond help," complained Gerald in a husky voice. He wiped his brow again and squared his shoulders. "If I had any more pills, I'd fall on my face. Listen, I'm not going to let you two down. I'll be there for the *Titanic* show. But maybe for today's show, I'll sorta lie low. Be around but not hands-on. The work's all done. I've sorted out the sequence of tapes, and I think you hafta sock the audience smack in the eye with the first one. You got all those hyper kids squirming in their seats sitting with parents who'd rather be having a stiff drink somewhere else. Gotta hook 'em right off the bat."

"But not anything too gruesome in the beginning," pleaded Deedee. "Not one of those shipwrecks where the passengers or the sailors wash up on some island and have to eat each other. Let's just settle for an adventure."

"You're not hearing me, Deedee baby," said Gerald. "Jolt 'em, zap 'em, knock their socks off. Or you lose 'em. Listen, I've been in this business a long time and I know what I'm talkin' about."

Deedee felt she had to protest even if being called "Deedee baby" made her truly a show biz personality. "What I'm saying is, Gerald, skip the cannibal scenes, especially that one where the survivors eat the little slave boy. We can do wrecks and people washing up on the rocks and miraculous survivals. Maybe that French Canadian shipwreck, because Richard does such a good French accent."

"You're not hearing me, babe. Small-time stuff, it's not where it's at," Gerald reminded her. "Listen, I think the one with the captain whose head was chopped off and put into a tub of brine is a terrific lead-off number, and then follow with a couple of the everyday wrecks, and end up with a real bang. Now I'm going to my cabin and try to rest, so I'll meet you here after lunch and we can do a quick run-through." And the manager pulled himself laboriously to his feet and in a hunched-over condition and moving with great care from table to table worked his way out of the Osborne Cafeteria.

"You know," said Deedee to her husband, "Gerald just plain gives me the creeps. I don't know if I want to be big-time if it means giving all these terrible shows that he's so excited about. I'd rather be back showing slides of our visit at Howarth to the Knox County Ladies Club. The Brontës were almost wholesome by comparison. And I'm simply dreading the *Titanic*."

Richard looked up from his notepad. "Gerald tells me it's the way to go if we want to have any share in the tour market. He thinks he can slot us into some major cruise schedules. Cape Breton and the Gaspé next month, then the winter circuit. The British Virgins and a chance at Hawaii after that. Then maybe another crossing on the *Vicky*. Cunard if we're lucky, because he says even the *QE Two* isn't beyond our reach."

Deedee inhaled and then blew out a long breath. "Some of it still sets my teeth on edge. All those bodies when we have children in the audience watching."

"Gerald put up a notice in the bulletin saying 'Parental Guidance Advised.' He really cares and he doesn't want to scare little kids any more than you do. But the teenagers will eat it up. Think of the stuff they've seen. *Jurassic Park, Anaconda, Godzilla,* not to mention all those *Godfather* films and *Reservoir Dogs.*"

"All right, all right," said Deedee. "But sometimes I think we're in the hands of—what's that man's name that manipulated people? Rasputin? Svengali? I think Gerald's sort of a Svengali."

"Deedee, look, he's a nice guy and he's got a heart. And we're on the edge of making it. Money coming in and not having to worry about where our next free dinner is coming from."

"Which brings me," said Deedee with asperity, "back to castaways eating people. What I say is, just dump . . ." But then a trio of blue-haired ladies in pastel travel suits came hesitantly forward, programs in hand. Would the Herricks just sign their names? Such a wonderful show. So exciting. And the music, the sound effects, why it was almost like being on shipboard and being asked to walk the plank.

Deedee gave up, reached for her pen, but inside her a sense of desperation was building. She had to get away—which was no problem as Richard was busy with his notations, music cues, costume changes, video sequences. She pulled her pink nylon windbreaker down over her hips, tied her canvas hat under her chin, and walked out of the Osborne Cafeteria aft to the Quarter Deck pool and past the busy recreation area toward the stern.

There, in a secluded corner, staring out to sea at the ship's churning wake, she found Sarah. And somehow the sight of someone she actually knew stimulated Deedee into a sudden desire to unload. To explain how she felt about what had become an almost distasteful "Ships in Peril" series.

Sarah, wrestling with her own demons, her anxiety about her sudden insight into last night's cabin invasion, was not pleased to be discovered by Deedee Herrick. She had escaped from Alex—it would have been too easy to break her promise to herself and burden him with her idea of what had actually happened in their stateroom the past night and what she feared might happen again. But she had stood firm, told him she needed some time to herself, and found her way to an area which she hoped would be sparsely populated. And now, Deedee.

"Sarah!" exclaimed Deedee. "I'm so glad to see you. A friend. At least I hope we're going to be friends. I need someone to talk to. It's about our lectures, because I'm really upset about the ones coming up, and Alex, or was it Sam Greenbank, anyway someone, said you were an English teacher, so maybe you can give me the proper perspective. I mean an objective view. You see," Deedee rushed on, seeing a frown deepening on Sarah's face, "I do hate blood all over the screen and parts of drowned bodies, some of them children, but it all seemed so glamorous at first. You know, a big international audience and the maiden trip of the *Vicky* and the free passage . . . all those things."

Sarah braced herself. Deedee was under a full head of steam and it really seemed that the kindest thing to do was to let her get it all out. So Sarah made an encouraging sound and settled her face into what she hoped was an understanding expression.

And Deedee relaxed. Here was someone who might be an ally, who might share her feelings. "You see," she explained, "I've just been listening to Gerald and his plan to shock the next audience with something that would glue them in their seats."

"You mean a really exciting shipwreck?"

"If it was only that," sighed Deedee. "The pirates and Captain Kidd and treasure hunting were okay because people think of those things happening in almost the Dark Ages. You know, the costumes and the big sailing ships. But Gerald wants to start off in modern times with perfectly ordinary people being wrecked or drowned or dying of starvation. With lots of horrible details, and Richard—he adores acting, it's something he should have been doing all along instead of insurance adjusting—well, Richard is just eating out of Gerald's hand and—"

"Wait up," said Sarah, who found herself agreeing all along the line with Deedee. "Don't you have a say in this? After all, you're half the act."

"I'm the stooge. It's always been more Richard's production, but now it's Gerald's. Gerald calls the shots and Richard goes for it. But now the whole thing is getting to me, upsetting my stomach, and even taking Pepto-Bismol doesn't help. And you know, I did overhear someone say something about the *Titanic* show, about how it was in bad taste. I think it was Mrs. Clancy."

Sarah was sure it was Mrs. Clancy but only murmured that the sinking of *Titanic* seemed to be one of those events that was impossible to escape, but if the sinking was told as straight and tragic history and not as some kind of glitzy celebrity adventure with sexy movie stars, well, she supposed that was all right.

"But," groaned Deedee, "I think that's exactly what it's going to be. A hyped-up affair with all the things everyone saw in the movie anyway. You know, husbands being brave and wives clinging to their husbands, third-class people being trampled, babies being washed away, and lifeboats going off empty. And Gerald has this sound track with the kind of music they did in *Jaws*. And Richard is doing everyone's part—he's even got a uniform jacket and hat so he can be the captain and go down with the ship."

"Oh, God," said Sarah with feeling.

"You see. It's going to be a circus and I want out."

Sarah considered. Derailing an already planned program seemed an impossible idea. But it could be modified. "Why don't you talk to one of those social directors? Maybe they can cool things, go for the documentary approach."

Deedee brightened. "That's a good idea. I should have thought of it, but Richard will think I'm going behind his back."

"Well, you are," said Sarah. "And more power to you."

"And he'll be furious." Deedee's worried brow smoothed. A furious Richard seemed all at once an appealing idea.

"Let him have a fit," said Sarah. "Listen, Richard can't throw you overboard just because you want a little restraint."

"I suppose not," said Deedee. Then bravely, "The man I

want to throw overboard is that Gerald Hofstra. He's made Richard forget all about decent values. He's a . . . what's the word?"

"A sleaze," offered Sarah.

"No. I'd say he's pathetic with this dream of the big time. I don't want the big time anymore, and I'm sorry you found him."

"But since he is found, maybe you can put a knot in his tail."

"A spoke in his wheel, take the wind out of his sails," said Deedee. "And blister his balls," she added with a giggle. And she stomped off down the deck, leaving Sarah with her mouth open.

There is a lot more to Deedee than meets the eye, Sarah told herself. At least my eye. Maybe Aubrey Smith was right when he sought her company at dinner. You could never tell about little ladies in flowered dresses and pink jackets. And then, dismissing the matter of gory maritime shows from her mind, she returned to the problem of Teddy Hogarth and the Bed Fumbler. Or, more ominously, the Night Visitor.

And somehow, hanging over the deck, watching the spinning, foaming wake, the slow rising and falling of the waves, Sarah found her resolution of being a Lone Ranger beginning to waver. Well, not exactly waver, but she felt the need to expound, to test out her ideas on someone. But who? Certainly not Alex. Nor Julia. She didn't need Julia's sarcasm. And not Deedee, despite their recent exchange of sympathy. Deedee had enough on her plate.

Who, then? Oddly enough the voice and face of Aubrey Smith floated across her mind. He might have been a possibility except for his sometimes rather strange behavior, his staying away from his cousin and her friend, and then huddling with them in odd corners of the ship—these actions argued against any revelations. So who was left? For a moment she toyed with the idea of Sam Greenbank, but he was too much Alex's friend and she didn't need the two of them chortling over her.

And that left only one person. One person with the background to understand what she was talking about. A person with no ax to grind and who probably wouldn't think she had gone off her rocker. Liza Baum. Liza seemed to have her feet on the ground. Even with her questionable liking for Teddy Hogarth, she seemed to be pretty solid. Okay, Liza it was. Now if she could only find Liza *without* Teddy in attendance.

Sarah wiped salty moisture from her cheeks, pushed her damp hair away from her forehead, and went in search.

Hustling from the afterdeck along the reaches of the Boat Deck, striking out in the Balmoral Lounge, the two theaters, the Card and Game Room, the Frogmore Dining Room, and the Disraeli Library, Sarah caught up with Liza Baum leaving the gym. Liza, in a glowing condition, explained she had just finished a forty-five-minute workout and had a sauna and plunge in the Duke of Wellington Spa.

"I dragged Teddy for two laps around the Boat Deck, got him a Carl Hiaasen mystery from the library, and left him on his bunk breathing hard."

"You *think* you left him, you mean," amended Sarah.

"Hey, I go so far and no farther. Or is it further? Who said that? I can tolerate being his rottweiler up to a point, for a few days, anyway. But if he wants to screw up he's on his own. So what's on your mind now that you found that Teddy wasn't crawling around in your cabin last night?"

"Let's go somewhere we can talk, where there aren't hordes of happy passengers."

"No problem. The Chapel. It's just opposite the Computer Learning Centre. If anyone comes into the Chapel they'll steer clear of us and do their own thing, light candles, pray, whatever. Us, we're just a pair of devout passengers saying our prayers."

Sarah, confirmed in her choice of a resourceful confidante, nodded, and the two set off at a trot along the passageway, up the carpet—deep-pile claret with twined roses—of Stairway C and, reaching Two Deck, found the Chapel empty of visitors. Sarah led the way to a pew halfway down to the altar, sat down, turned and confronted Liza.

"I wanted to talk to you because I'm damned if I'm going to have everyone else holding their sides laughing at me. Besides, this really concerns you—in a secondary way. It's about Teddy."

Liza frowned. "I thought we'd cleared all this up. Now what?"

"Teddy's a member of this U.K. or Euro trade commission thing, isn't he?"

"Like I told you. If he doesn't get bounced in New York."

"But officially he still is?"

"Yeah, I guess so. Junior member without portfolio. But what's that got to do with anything?"

"And the Donald who got hit by a car?"

"Donald Lyman-Smith," prompted Liza.

"He was a member of the trade commission. And was Teddy's watchdog, you said."

"Supposed to have been, yes. Poor Donald, being a sober and responsible citizen, was one of the senior members of the trade group. And," Liza added wistfully, "I wish to hell he was here. He could share Teddy and take me dancing."

"And," continued Sarah, "General Gordon was a senior member, too, wasn't he? The dead General Gordon."

"Where's all this going?" said Liza uneasily.

"Just sit tight. Donald Lyman-Smith is run down in London, General Gordon is dead, and Teddy Hogarth switched cabins— with Alex and me. He moved from One Deck to our cabin on Five Deck."

"So big deal. What are you getting at?"

"Well, no one made a great public announcement about our switching. No calls on the loudspeaker saying Teddy Hogarth will now take up residence on Deck Five to be near his beloved, and that two low-life Americans on Deck Five will be promoted to Deck One thanks to the generosity of Aunt Julia Clancy."

Liza looked mildly exasperated. "No, for God's sake. It wasn't one of the day's special events, if that's what you're driving at. The Purser's Office okayed it, the housekeeping people made up the beds, and we switched. End of story."

"Not quite. How many other members of the trade commission are on board?"

"You know. Only those three. The rest are flying over on Monday. General Gordon apparently didn't like to fly and Teddy was using the time to rehab himself and Donald was stuck as his keeper. By request of Daddy, Colonel Sir Arthur David Hogarth, upon whom the sun never sets and who keeps Teddy in cash."

"And two of those men are dead, and I'm saying that someone—someone who had got his mitts on Teddy's old cabin key; Teddy's probably pretty careless and left one around—and thinking Teddy was still in residence, and possibly drunk and out of it, came in to take care of him."

Liza stared at Sarah. "How do you mean 'take care of'? You mean kill him?"

"That's what I've been trying to tell you. Someone came in, maybe someone who knew that Teddy slept in the bed nearest the door, and began feeling around. As if he—or she—expected to find someone in it."

"But didn't and left. As you said."

"After I yelled at him, calling him Teddy. And get this, he—we'll call it a he for now—dropped the Harrods bag."

"You and that blasted Harrods bag. So someone went shopping."

"Maybe so. But what else can you do with a nicely made plastic bag with a convenient drawstring around its top? Isn't that a handy item if you're planning to do in a man lying in a drunken stupor? Get in the cabin, feel around to see if the guy is really out of it—and you're pretty sure he will be because he's been drinking since he came on board—and slip that nice, perfectly head-sized bag over Teddy's head, pull the string tight, sit on him in case of struggle, perhaps remove the bag when it's all over, and go on your way. Mission accomplished."

Liza was now wide-eyed and nodding vehemently. "But mission wasn't accomplished, you yelled, the man drops the bag as he scrambles to get the hell out of there. And you and Alex, convinced you've sent Teddy back to Deck Five where he belongs, settle down for the rest of the night. My God, Sarah, I hate to say it, but I agree right down the line. Donald, General Gordon, Teddy. But why, in God's name? That trade commission isn't anything weird. I mean it's not like it's a nuclear weapons treaty group or a European antiterrorist organization. For Christ's sake, it's trade. Donald said they were going to talk about protective commerce policies between the U.S. and the U.K. Not about trading with Cuba. Or Iran or Iraq. Probably just going to argue whether more Land Rovers can come into the States or more Jeeps can be shipped to England. Dull. Bor-ring."

"How about all that as a cover? A cover for something really covert or sinister? Plutonium supplies, bomb capabilities, germ warfare. Something like that."

Liza considered and then shook her head. "I'd believe anything of either government. They wouldn't be beyond using the Girl Guides, the Boy Scouts, or the Boston Symphony as a cover. But no government in its right mind would tack on Teddy Hogarth even as a junior member if there was any stealth stuff behind it. Teddy had a reputation in London. Everyone knew he was one drink away from the DT's and only Daddy Hogarth made it possible for him to go over to New York. In a job where he could do as little harm as possible."

But Sarah had started up from her seat. "Teddy!" she shouted, frightening a kneeling man in the pew opposite, someone who had just arrived as Liza was talking.

"God, keep it down," said Liza, looking around and pointing out their new companion.

"Teddy," repeated Sarah in a lowered voice. "He's alone, isn't he? In our cabin. I mean his cabin. And that's no secret now."

But Liza was already on her feet and heading for the door. Sarah followed, tripped over a fallen hymn book, picked it up, and restored it to the pew, but just as she turned to follow Liza she became aware of a familiar face watching her. The pious gentleman kneeling turned his head, and she saw the interested face of her friend, Aubrey Clyde Smith. And at the door, hesitating, Cousin Vivian Smith in a navy jogging suit, followed by dear friend Margaret in a teal cotton suit, looking like a cutout from *Vogue*.

"Oh, Christ," said Sarah aloud as she bolted out of the door.

"Amen to you, too," called Margaret, waving a braceleted hand.

11

WITH Liza ahead, Sarah behind, the two women hurled them-selves down the two flights of Stairway C and into the long passageway on Five Deck. Liza fumbled in her shorts pocket for the key to cabin 5023 and pushed the door open and walked in. But Sarah halted outside in the passage in case Teddy was in the nude or on the toilet or otherwise not ready to receive strangers. After all, she reasoned, if he'd been attacked and was lying strangled or bloody she'd hear soon enough. But no shrieks from Liza announced such an event, and in another sec-ond Liza reappeared, grabbed her arm, and dragged her over the threshold.

Teddy Hogarth was sitting on the edge of the lower bunk and for a moment Sarah thought their worst fears had been realized. Teddy was nothing short of a mess. His face looked like a raw piece of hamburger, and spatters of blood dotted the front of a gray T-shirt.

He gave her a haggard look and then turned back to Liza. "Do you think you could find me an electric razor? After all, there must an ordinary shop somewhere on board. I tried to use my regular razor but I think I've lost a pint of blood shav-ing." He looked over at Sarah and grimaced. "It's lucky I'm on

Five Deck; they wouldn't want me around to scare passengers in the Balmoral Lounge."

Liza shook her head at him. "Believe me, Teddy, you're not going to be allowed anywhere looking the way you do. You'd ruin the ship's image. And you don't have to worry about the trade commission people seeing you, because Donald and General Gordon are both dead. What you have to worry about is you. Sarah, tell him."

And Sarah told him.

And Teddy, who had been holding a wet towel against his damaged face, listened without interrupting. And then, "But that's absolutely crazy. Why would anyone bother with me? My head isn't worth putting a bag over. And I'm only on the fringe of the commission, which isn't anything tremendous anyway."

"I thought the trade thing might be a cover," said Sarah.

Teddy gave a sort of throttled guffaw. "You think General Gordon would be put on anything even smelling like a clandestine operation? My father told me that he was sent as a sort of acknowledgment for past efforts in Her Majesty's service. Not because he was likely to be an effective negotiator. Which makes two of us, doesn't it?"

"You'll be effective if you stay off the sauce, shave properly, and start reading all those papers they sent along with you," said Liza. "But in the meantime, consider yourself my prisoner until we can clear up about this cabin sneak and the Harrods bag business."

Teddy grinned ruefully, rubbed his chin, winced, removed a bloodied hand, and applied the towel. Then he looked up. "There was that nursery rhyme and a play about ten little Indians. They were eliminated one after the other until then there were none. Am I supposed to be number three?"

"It's not funny," said Liza. "Poor old Donald being run down in London. And I suppose someone loved General Gordon."

"The point is, Teddy," said Sarah sternly, "we both think someone tried to kill you, so try to keep your head down and don't fling your cabin key around. Okay? Liza, I need to go. But thanks for listening."

"Thanks for telling," said Liza. She paused, and then, "You don't suppose we should toss this ball over to Security?"

Sarah stopped by the door. "Security already knows someone got in our cabin. What can they do at this point?"

"Nothing," said Teddy, "unless we can come up with something to make them sit up. Like another General Gordon affair. General Gordon, even if he was past his prime, was what is called a man of consequence. But Donald Lyman-Smith, nice guy and all, wasn't one of the world's movers and shakers, and I'm no great prize alive or dead. Why would anyone bother with Donald or me? So how can anyone think these things are connected?"

"You're saying," retorted Liza, "that these are random events because with all these hundreds of people aboard, shit happens. For all we know the hospital morgue may be stuffed to the gills. And breaking and entering and falling into doors are run-of-the-mill events. And I suppose everyone thinks Donald should have looked where he was going. And the trade commission isn't a connection, it's just a coincidence. You might as well say that the victims all had tickets on One Deck. Or are citizens of the U.K. Or males over the age of twenty. Or were born under the sign of Capricorn."

"Accidents, just accidents," said Teddy. He turned to Sarah. "But seriously, thanks. I'll keep looking over my shoulder . . ."

"And Liza," said Liza, "will be riding shotgun, so I dare anyone to break and enter when I'm around."

And with that Sarah had to be content, although she did pause to wonder if Liza kept a shotgun—a collapsible one—somewhere around her person. She wouldn't put it past her. But now she had other fish to fry. She walked quickly to Stairway C, took the stairs at a run, and headed for the Chapel. It had occurred to her that it might be interesting, even informative, if she found that irregular trio, Aubrey Smith, Cousin Vivian, and friend Margaret, still at their devotions.

But she was only a step away from the dark oak door with its CHAPEL—ALL ARE WELCOME in black letters when the door opened and the three trooped out one after the other, each looking, Sarah thought, as if butter wouldn't melt in their respective mouths.

They were so glad to see her. Twice in one morning. And at the Chapel. A good omen for the start of the day. Margaret smiled broadly and said in her soft southern voice that at least in the Chapel surely there was not a first or second or third class, and she did so like a peaceful moment, you know, to sort things out for the day. Margaret was looking particularly . . . the only expression Sarah could think was well cared for, soignée. Fawn knit slacks, fawn knit jacket, flowing tie of russet silk, fawn makeup with a wisp of blush on the cheeks and darkened lashes lowering and rising, and a strong whiff of Amarige de Givenchy. Really, Margaret put Vivian to shame. Vivian with her square-cut graying hair, her faded blue eyes and sandy brows, and her sensible navy cotton suit looked like a retired high school Latin teacher. Then Sarah became aware that Margaret in her soft voice had been speaking at some length.

". . . that naughty old wind is going to come right up and make us all wish we were on solid ground. Ah do not know if Ah am a good sailor."

Cousin Vivian Smith then asked Sarah if she had observed the four little panels in the chapel. "Very nicely done, quite professional. For Wales, England, Scotland, and Ireland—Saint David, Saint George, Saint Andrew, and Saint Patrick, which I think is just a little chauvinistic, don't you? Think of all the neglected ones like Saint Ladislas of Hungary or Hyacinth of Krakow. And how about the Buddha and Mohammed and Lao Tse and Kali and Shiva?"

"Now, Vivian," said Margaret. "Father Somebody holds Mass in one of the theater rooms, and there's a synagogue and a meditation room down on Three Deck, so I think the *Vicky* has covered her bases. Sarah, a little bird told me you had a visitor in the middle of the night. Now that's just too frightening for words, so I hope you've reported to the security people?"

"What little bird?" demanded Sarah. "But yes, Alex and I reported it this morning and our locks are being changed."

"I'm afraid I'm the little bird," said Aubrey Smith. "Or rather the large bird. What would you say? I rather fancy the wood pigeon—or the stool pigeon. I told Vivian and Margaret because I think we should all be a little careful about our cabin keys. After all, not every passenger aboard is entirely honest."

Margaret shrugged. "Sarah, honey, you know how it is on shipboard. Like the poor general falling in his cabin. Accidents like that get around, they surely do. Even if Aubrey hadn't told us. I'll just guess you talked about it at breakfast. Waiters have big ears. After all, wouldn't it be boring for the poor things if they couldn't hear a little gossip?"

But Sarah, half listening, asked herself why Margaret hadn't acknowledged Aubrey as her source, instead of going on about a little bird. But now Aubrey was reminding her of their date. "The Snuggery at six. For drinks. I've left a message for Mrs. Clancy."

And with that the three took their leave, and Sarah watched with interest as Margaret headed in the direction of the Computer Learning Center—was she a traveler on the World Wide Web?—Vivian took the stairs up to the next deck, while Aubrey started down Stairway C. And Sarah, keeping her distance, followed. She couldn't follow all three of them, but somehow Aubrey Smith seemed to be going in the least likely direction—toward the hospital and the Wellington Spa and the gym on Six Deck. Somehow Aubrey's comfortable figure and slight middle-aged slouch didn't suggest workouts and saunas. But you never knew.

Sarah kept well back, and fortunately the stairway curved at the four landings so that she could see Aubrey's head with its thinning gray hair moving in a spiral below her. And then on Six Deck he turned toward the ship's hospital and reached for the door.

But before he opened it, Aubrey rotated his body a quarter turn, lifted his head, and gave her a cheerful wave. A wave that could only be directed at Sarah; no one else was in sight on Stairway C.

Furious, Sarah climbed rapidly back four tiers of stairs and, breathless, found herself facing the Chapel door. Time to think.

And regroup. Damn that man. Well, no, damn S. Deane. Inspector Clouseau could have done a better job.

With no particular object in mind besides escape into a quiet place, Sarah slipped into the Chapel. It was no longer empty. Two figures sitting in the pews, one to the rear, one to the side, but neither person looked to be a threat to thought—or, more appropriately perhaps, to prayer. She walked quietly down the crimson carpet of the short aisle flanked by polished oak pews and slipped into one on the right—or starboard side. She wondered if port and starboard held true for seagoing chapels. Or did they revert to land terms? The phrase "In my Father's house": did it suggest a land base? Or a heavenly sky one? Certainly not a houseboat. But then there was Noah.

Stop it, she told herself. Keep your mind on what you're supposed to be thinking about. Aubrey Smith and his concubines. First huddling in the chapel, then off, again going their separate ways. And why was Aubrey visiting the hospital? He hadn't looked ill or seasick, but who knew what ailed anyone else? It might just be a matter of those ailments beloved of early evening television, bad breath or irregularity or hemorrhoids. Perhaps it was just a matter of his blood pressure; it needed checking.

Folding her arms over the smooth oak roll of the pew bench ahead of her, she put her head down on her arms—a posture she hoped would be considered as one indicating piety. Could any of those three have been the one who entered their cabin last night? Yes, possibly, given that one of them had a key to the room. Nothing strenuous had happened, no trial of arms or feats of strength that might rule any of the three out. How about the size of the intruder? Impossible to tell, since Sarah had only the dim idea that it—he—or she—had not been extremely small or large.

Go back, she ordered herself, to the trade commission. Aubrey Smith, hadn't he said that he knew Teddy Hogarth's father? Was that a connection? Could Aubrey be working for what was called in old-fashioned novels a "foreign power"? But he seemed entirely British. But so had Burgess and MacLean and

Kim Philby. And Anthony Blunt. How about some sort of spy or agent-provocateur from one of the British trade unions? Or a Tory bent on revenge on Tony Blair's new Labor government and trying to wreck any trade agreements reached? Was it as Teddy had suggested, ten little Indian boys? Two gone and one—Teddy—in jeopardy and then there would be—how many were there in all? Would the rest of the commission be dealt with when they arrived in New York? Was Aubrey working alone, or was it a three-man wrecking crew?

All of this speculation—Alex and Julia would have called it wild and unfounded—was making Sarah's head ache. She sat up and looked around, hoping perhaps that the reverent atmosphere would shine some light into her clouded brain. Instead she found herself staring at two stained-glass windows fixed into one side of the chapel wall and two on the opposite wall. Four chapel windows in all and soft overhead lights, giving the illusion of sun striking different pieces of colored glass. The designs were simple ones, and none showed the livid reds and harsh purples and poison greens seen in all too many church windows. All in all they were quite entrancing. She remembered Vivian—it had been Vivian, hadn't it?—talking about the little panels. Well, these weren't so little, almost five feet long. What else had Vivian said? Wales, Ireland, Scotland, England? And their patron saints.

Sarah straightened in her seat. These windows weren't exactly panels, were they? And they didn't show saints. Wasn't Saint George always shown with a dragon? And Saint Patrick doing something about snakes? She didn't know anything about Andrew, except the cross shaped like an ✗, and David, who might or might not have anything to do with leeks.

Her eyes fixed on the first window. Noah. Could there be a doubt? An ark floating on a light blue sea with assorted animal heads sticking out of it and a dove flying off the bow. The next window must be Moses—a baby, anyway—in a woven basket floating in a tangle of bulrushes. And on the other side, Jesus and loaves and fishes, and a man—Peter perhaps—with a net and a watery background. And last, the figure of a man, one hand raised in blessing, the other holding a small but fully rigged ship. Mystified, Sarah got to her feet and confronted Noah. A small brass plaque under the window settled the matter: *"And the waters increased, and bare up the ark, and it was lift up above the earth."* She inspected the other three windows and their plaques, the last window of all being identified as a rendering of Saint Anselm, whose symbol was a ship. All the windows were water or ship centered. Most appropriate. But where in holy—here Sarah caught herself—where in heaven were Vivian Smith's saints? Could she have mistaken Noah's ark for Saint George? Stuff and nonsense! Could Vivian have been remembering last night's colorful dream? Or was she lying like a rug?

Sarah, walking slowly around the Chapel, halted in front of the lectern at a small wooden carving, wonderfully intricate, of yet another saint. Saint Christopher with his staff and the Child on his shoulders.

"Rather fetching, isn't it?" said a voice next to her shoulder.

Sarah jumped, fell forward, and had her elbow grasped.

"Easy does it. Did I startle you? But I came in a few minutes ago to get ready for the eleven o'clock prayer meeting and saw you studying our windows. And our carved Saint Christopher. I like him because his expression shows he's a little anxious about getting wet. We've been lucky with our artists. And having a chapel, too. It's a quiet place in the midst of all the Victorian whirligig. We were going to have a dedication ceremony yesterday—this being the first crossing—but now it's going to be Sunday. Because, I ask you, how can we compete with the 'Ships in Peril' productions?" This last said in a tone of mixed resignation and humor.

Sarah, during this recitation, had time to close her mouth, settle her thoughts, and try to look like a sensible visitor. Her companion was now in full flow—he must have had few visitors, she decided, or perhaps he was simply such an amiable enthusiast that any pair of secular ears would do. He was a tall angular man with a mane of graying hair and a large chiseled face dominated by overhanging black bushy eyebrows. He wore what Sarah presumed was a regulation white collar and a black cassock, from the bottom of which stuck out a startling pair of two-tone running shoes, black and white with silver inserts.

"How do you do? My name is Peter Bottomley," said the man. "I'm the ship's chaplain. At your service. Or at our services." Peter Bottomley chuckled at his little joke. "And," he went on, "visitors are always welcome. I'm usually about or my assistant is, that's Mr. Frye. And please look around the Chapel. We have tried for a maritime atmosphere."

"You certainly have," said Sarah, now back in balance. "But I ran into someone who mentioned windows, or a series of panels. In the Chapel, she said. Saint Andrew and Saint George and—"

"Saint Patrick and Saint David. But they're not in the Chapel."

"Oh," said Sarah. "Is there another chapel?"

"The *Vicky* has a synagogue, a place for Mass, and a meditation room for persons of all faiths, but not another chapel."

"So my friend was mistaken?"

"Not at all. She must have been in my office. Quite a few passengers find a need to talk to me or to Mr. Frye. I think the whole holiday ambiance, the setting, the programs are a bit much for some people. They're overwhelmed. The Chapel, by itself, does well for services and prayer, but not for private counseling. Comfort and reassurance. The listening ear. That's our game." He looked down at Sarah—the man stood at least six foot three and spoke in a deep and, yes, comforting voice. Surely she'd heard him on *Masterpiece Theatre*—an elderly king, an ancient prophet, a humorous statesman. She might take him up on the listening-ear idea if things went on as they had been.

But Father Bottomley had returned to the subject at hand. "Well, now, would you like to see our saints?"

Sarah admitted that she had a great desire to see these particular saints and was led behind the altar through a door into a small room fitted with a desk, bookshelves, four leather armchairs, and a long cushioned bench under a porthole.

"There they are." Father Bottomley waved at a space between the door and the bookcase.

And there they were. Not stained-glass windows—had Vivian said windows? No, she'd mentioned panels. These were four painted panels. Colorful, simply done, well executed. Saint George with the red cross on his chest, sword arm upraised, and expiring dragon curled at his feet; Saint Patrick brandishing a crosier at several fleeing snakes; Saint David holding a leek; and Saint Andrew centered in a reverent posture against his blue ✕ cross.

"We really don't know very much about Saint David or Saint Andrew," said Father Bottomley, "so the artist went along with the symbols. After all, what is Saint George without his dragon? I suppose, though, I should do a spot of research and find out about leeks. They may have magical properties. Anyway, it's really the idea, isn't it? The four parts of Britain."

But Sarah had moved on to her own concerns. "They're lovely," she said, "but do you ever have whole groups in here? For counseling, I mean."

Father Bottomley took this switch of subject in his stride. Perhaps, Sarah thought, he'd decided that she had a group of troubled souls under her wing.

"Group counseling can be arranged. We sometimes have several members of a family in at the same time. But not often on an Atlantic crossing; it's such a short period of time. Not like a thirty-day cruise or an around-the-world trip. Then we're called on quite often. People start getting on each other's nerves, too long away from their roots and having doubts."

"But today? This morning? That friend of mine . . ." Sarah stumbled on, "the one who mentioned seeing the saints, she said she was troubled, so I thought she might have come back here. Perhaps to have another look at the panels."

Father Bottomley, apparently used to incoherent persons in distress, nodded sympathetically. "Yes, I was asked to reserve my office for a group earlier this morning, but I wasn't here. A request came down for a private place, and I left my office key with the purser for the group to use. And since I had duties elsewhere, from the Seaview Staterooms to Five Deck, communion and conversation—I try to take the stairs to keep myself in shape—I had just returned when you saw me. And Mr. Frye has been down in the hospital for a list to see who should be visited."

"Thank you so much, Father Bottomley. I've taken up too much of your time." Sarah extended her hand and shook Peter Bottomley's hand vigorously.

"I can give you a card listing our times of service," he said. "Or perhaps"—this said almost wistfully—"you would like to bring your troubled friend in for—shall we say—conversation?"

"That," said Sarah, "is a wonderful idea."

And she turned smartly, left the office, walked quickly down the aisle, out the door, and smack into Vivian Smith. Who looked for a moment as if she'd stepped on an asp. Then, showing great talent in pulling herself together, Vivian exclaimed with pleasure, "Oh, Sarah. How lucky. I was hoping I'd bump into you again, but I didn't know where you'd gone off to. I gave you wrong information. Those panels aren't in the Chapel at all."

"They aren't?" said Sarah sweetly. "I was just in there looking. I thought there must be a mistake."

"Yes, I don't know what I was thinking about. The Chapel has stained-glass windows. Noah and Moses and Jesus. And Saint Somebody with a ship."

"And where *are* Saint George and his friends?" asked Sarah, fixing her expression to that of an interested crocodile.

"Somewhere else on the ship. I know I've seen them but I do get mixed up. There's so much to see on the *Vicky*. It's a floating museum. The Disraeli Library with all those *Punch* cartoons, the Pinafore Theatre and the D'Oyly Carte posters, and the Balmoral Lounge has authentic tartan furnishings and the etchings of the queen and Prince Albert and all the children and that gillie, what was his name?"

"John Brown?" suggested Sarah.

"Yes, the one standing around with the white pony. But you know what I mean. This ship is simply so stuffed, all those

Victorian ruffles and flourishes, that I cannot remember where I saw what."

You, Vivian, are overdoing it, Sarah said to herself. Aloud, she said, "Don't worry. I'll find Saint George somewhere. And I do understand. It's so hard to say what you mean and not say what you don't mean. Isn't it? And we'll be meeting you for drinks, the Snuggery, wasn't it? Or was it the Card Room?"

Vivian eyed Sarah with narrowed eyes. "The Snuggery," she said.

"So I'll see you later," said Sarah. She turned and with great dignity walked past Stairway C over to the lift door, pushed the button, the door opened, and she stepped inside. The last glance of Vivian showed that person with a frown on her face and both hands rolled into fists.

12

WHILE Sarah, after her recent encounter with Cousin Vivian Smith, was finding her suspicions solidifying about what she now labeled the Gang of Three, Julia Clancy was on her way back to her cabin. Julia had had a stimulating morning sounding out Mr. Erik Anderson on a variety of subjects that might prove that he was an "adventurer" or just possibly the real thing: an amiable horse lover traveling with his grandchildren. He had withstood what only could be called a minor inquisition with good humor, and they had confirmed their date to try their luck at the Casino after lunch.

But, Julia scolded herself, there is no fool like an old fool, and she must not find this man too pleasant because think where it could end. At which idea she found herself smiling and then shook herself and decided on a cold shower.

And Julia, intent on her thoughts, inserted the key into her stateroom door, swung it open, and was halfway across the room before she saw she had visitors. Or one visitor at least.

Mary Malone, her faithful stewardess, stood by the porthole holding a small plastic carrying case of cleaning supplies. Standing next to her, a broad-shouldered man with a turned-up nose, freckles, a wide mouth, and a mop of russet hair. He was dressed soberly in gray flannels, a white polo shirt, and a navy cotton windbreaker. The arrival of Julia seemed to have startled him because his head jerked up and he stepped back away from Mary.

"Who," said Julia, using the her best teacher-of-the-incompetent-riding-student voice, "are you?"

"Mrs. Clancy, you did give us a start," said Mary Malone, putting down her cleaning box. "This is Mr. Frye."

"And who," demanded Julia, "is Mr. Frye?"

But Mr. Frye had regrouped and advanced with an open hand. "I'm so sorry to startle you, Mrs. Clancy. I'm Amory Frye. I'm the assistant to the ship's chaplain, Father Bottomley. I've been distributing pamphlets to all the staterooms. To tell passengers about the Chapel and the times of services. And that Father Bottomley—and I—are always available should anyone wish to visit or talk. Or pray," he added, although his doubtful expression announced his understanding that Julia probably would not wish to do either of the first two and certainly not the last.

Julia extended her hand and allowed Mr. Frye the middle three fingers. "Are you a priest?" she said, dropping her hand back to her side.

"No, I'm just a lay assistant, but I'm hoping to go to theological school next year."

"What school is that?"

"Well, I'm still working on my applications, Mrs. Clancy. But this is a wonderful experience, working with Father Bottomley."

"I assume Father Bottomley is either Roman Catholic or Anglican," said Julia, "so I suppose you are one or the other."

"Well, yes, yes, I am. Anglican or maybe Episcopalian."

"You don't sound too sure, young man," said Julia. "You'd better make up your mind. And now if you'll excuse me, I want to get ready for lunch." And Julia turned on her heel, leaving Mr. Frye holding out a folded pamphlet, made for her bathroom, and closed the door firmly behind her.

When she emerged some ten minutes later she found Mary Malone hovering. "Oh, Mrs. Clancy, I hope you'll forgive him.

This is his first time on an ocean crossing and for sure he doesn't know he can't be treating the whole ship like his home parish. He's a good lad and he means well. An American, he says, but lives in England."

"If he means well he should be staying out of passengers' staterooms. We don't need pamphlets and we all have diagrams of the ship and can find the Chapel if we want to." Then, seeing Mary's flushed face, Julia softened. "Now, Mary, it's not your fault."

"Ah, but I shouldn't have been letting him in the way I did. I can see that now. But some passengers welcome that sort of thing."

"Please forget it. And if my niece Sarah Deane turns up, or Dr. McKenzie, say I'll be having my lunch in the Osborne Cafeteria and then take a walk on deck."

"Now do be careful, Mrs. Clancy," cautioned Mary. "They do say the wind is coming on to blow and the deck will be rolling a bit so it won't be so easy to keep your balance."

Julia smiled, good humor restored by the idea of her approaching lunch. "Thank you, Mary, but they haven't built the storm that can upset Old Lady Clancy."

But as she worked her way up toward the aft section of the ship and onto the Quarter Deck, she understood what Mary had meant. The once softly undulating ocean had broken into small waves, and a strong breeze disordered her hair and tugged at her jacket. And Julia discovered with her first steps that the combination of her arthritis and a definitely enhanced movement underfoot was going to be a challenge. Perhaps she should reactivate her cane; nothing would be more annoying than a bad fall and finding herself in a cast and trapped in the ship's sick bay. But for now she would be cautious and conservative. And with this resolve she stepped gingerly toward the rail, found the deck had sunk slightly below her foot, and tottered forward.

Forward into the arms of Dr. Sam Greenbank.

"Whoa there, Mrs. Clancy," said Sam, pulling Julia straight and setting her back on her feet.

"Julia, are you trying for a trip to the hospital?" said Alex, who was standing just behind Sam.

"No," said Julia crossly. "I hadn't realized that the deck was so unstable."

"The deck is fine," said Sam. "It's us folk who have to adapt."

"How about lunch?" said Alex. "We're heading that way. And have you seen Sarah?"

"Not hide nor hair," said Julia.

"She's in a snit because I told her to cool it on some of her untoward suspicions. I think she believes the trade commission people are the target of a shipboard hit team."

"And well they may be," said Sam, who had listened to Alex's tale of the night prowler. "But on the other hand, why? Can you think of a more useless group of people? Heading off to New York to engage in futile economic discussions, probably at the lowest possible level. Subcommittees from Washington, lobby outfits from New Hampshire, and product manager groups from Iowa."

"As for Sarah," said Alex, "I'm sure she wants some time free of all of us, so I won't go hunting. Let her enjoy a little sovereignty to pursue whatever nefarious ideas she has."

"In the past," remarked Julia, "her nefarious ideas have led directly to nefarious goings-on."

"Aren't you all the worrywarts," said Sam. "Me, food comes first. Then bring on the gangs and the gangsters. Or even the lamentable Mr. Gerald Hofstra and his sinking ships. Another show at four this afternoon. Are you coming?"

"I," said Julia with asperity, "am skipping the 'Ships in Peril' series. After lunch I'm going to walk the deck, gamble at the Casino, and then listen to some good music. There's a string quartet in the Princess Royal Lounge at four. A Beethoven program. And later a showing of *Kind Hearts and Coronets*."

"What you need, Julia, is some rock music," said Alex. "Loosen you up. And I'm supposed to remind you we have a date in the Snuggery with Aubrey Smith and his ladies at six. For drinks and what-have-you. Sarah seems to think those three are at the center of the trade commission destructo team."

"Which means we can count on Sarah turning up," said Sam. And the three friends, adjusting their stride and balance to the moving deck, found their way into the Osborne Cafeteria and its loaded banquet table.

Sarah, now that she had caught Vivian Smith in some sort of truth twisting, wasn't sure what to do next. Concealing knowledge of where one had seen a collection of painted saints didn't exactly equal dangerous behavior. And the fact that Margaret knew Alex was a doctor didn't mean she'd been reading the files in the Purser's Office. She could have overheard some medical reference to him anytime. And Aubrey Smith's visit to the hospital probably meant he was loading up on seasick pills. After all, with the increase in the ship's motion it was likely that a large portion of the ship's population would be doing likewise.

One thing was certain. What *not* to do was to unload her suspicions on her fellow travelers. So, squelching an impulse to join those very people for lunch, Sarah decided that her next step was to simply latch onto one of the trio and become the new friend who was ready with an open and sympathetic ear— if not an open mind. Or, failing that, to follow him or her at a distance—not too difficult on a crowded and busy ship. Not exactly as she might have planned the afternoon but, to borrow from the great man, the game was afoot. Or in this case, afloat. But first food. No one could be expected to conduct a campaign on an empty stomach.

The Osborne Cafeteria with its grand luncheon spread and tables should have been Sarah's choice, but the possible presence of the familiar scoffers ruled it out unless all of her chosen three were lunching there.

She was in luck. Sarah, hanging off to the side of the big double doors leading to the Osborne Cafeteria, was able to mark Aubrey Smith joining Deedee Herrick at the salad section of the buffet table and then from the corner of her eye caught sight of Cousin Vivian walking with a determined step forward toward the Disraeli Library. Sarah followed and found herself walking past the library directly toward the Snuggery.

Her heart sank. She didn't think she could come sneaking into the Snuggery as if by accident and settle down in that small space with a Victorian periodical while Vivian Smith—already suspicious—sat two feet away from her. Then, to her vast relief, Vivian ignored the door of the Snuggery and headed directly for the Pickwick Grill—a vast feeding operation amidships that catered to those who liked homely food served without a flourish: the pizza, the fish and chips, the hamburger, the ploughman's lunch, the barbecued ribs, the sausages and mash, the Coke, the tankard of ale. Here the dress was informal and the surrounding walls lively with characters from *The Pickwick Papers*: Sam Weller, Tracy Tupman, Mr. Snodgrass, Mrs. Bardell, and the rest of that wonderful company. The population here ran definitely to the young side—teenagers and the under-twenty-five crowd, although here and there Sarah spotted a head of white hair or a bald pate.

It was easy to tag behind some dozen persons trailing Vivian, and Sarah watched with interest as Vivian first stood scanning the room and then settled herself down at a long table of what might be thought of as young executives—men and women in sweatsuits or tennis shorts or bathing suit coveralls. Sarah quickly sat down at a small table next to a window overlooking the starboard horizon—a horizon that had certainly increased its upward and downward dip. Then, after almost absentmindedly ordering the fish and chips special from a waitress tricked out as a pert nineteenth-century tavern maid with mobcap and apron, and keeping a potted geranium between her and Vivian, Sarah settled back to observe the goings-on.

The first puzzle was why on earth Vivian had chosen a table already filled. There were several smaller empty tables around and quite a few with only a single diner or a couple seated at them. And judging from puzzled expressions and some head bobbings, Vivian was among strangers and busy asking if they minded and then introducing herself. What was the woman up to? Was she so alienated from her cousin Aubrey and her friend Margaret that she sought strange company? And yet this very evening they all planned to meet together in the Snuggery, one happy band of travelers.

The Pickwick Grill was doing its best to make passengers

pleased with their choice of restaurant. A small brass quartet played and, despite the chatter of diners, it was possible from time to time to pick out selections from Gilbert and Sullivan and bits and shreds from *Sergeant Pepper's Lonely Hearts Club Band*, from Elton John, from the Spice Girls. At another time Sarah might have enjoyed the cheerful good humor of those around her, but now she clamped her teeth down on her fish, chomped her chips, swigged her Coke, and took very little pleasure from her food. Because, God, she was probably wasting her time when she could have been having scallops supreme with her nearest and dearest. And then she became aware of her waitress offering her the dessert menu, and as she was wavering between gooseberry tart and rice pudding she saw that Vivian was on the move. Up, off, and away. And out the far door.

Sarah sprang to her feet. "Oh damn!"

"I beg your pardon," said the waitress.

"Oh, not you. But oh damn. Here," and Sarah unrolled four one-pound notes, pushed them at the startled woman, and began her pursuit. Not an easy task, because the place was now jammed with late arrivals in search of a table.

Vivian was, of course, nowhere to be seen. Forward of the Pickwick Grill lay Stairway C and many choices. The Chapel—was Vivian going to make another tour of Saint George and his fellow saints? Or would she head topside to the Balmoral Lounge? Or aft to the Scepter Room, a space used, Sarah remembered, for tea and dancing? Sarah opted for the Balmoral Lounge, but after a quick circuit on the rim of that elegant space with its Highland murals and tartan accessories, she drew a blank. She retreated below to the entrance of the Frogmore Dining Room and was rewarded, not with Vivian, but with friend Margaret Lee, who was in the act of taking leave of fellow diners at a distant table.

Okay, as quarry, Margaret could sub for Vivian. Sarah slipped into an open door, found herself in a small room filled with dining room supplies, napery, folding tables, and stacks of menus, and from this excellent vantage point saw Margaret leave the dining room and cross Stairway B. Sarah followed at a distance. Margaret certainly knew where she was going, because after a quick look at her watch she walked directly into the Prince Albert Lecture Hall. Sarah, well behind her, checked her own watch. Five minutes to two.

It was with a sense of doom that Sarah saw the large red and blue poster announcing that one Professor Clarissa Clayton would lecture at two o'clock on "Some Aspects of the Victorian World." Well, it might have been worse, Sarah told herself; it might have been a seminar on isotopes or a group dedicated to getting in touch with their fetal memories. She found a seat in the rear of the hall and was interested to note that Margaret, like friend Vivian, did not choose to sit alone but cozied up to a third-row group and began a conversation. She saw again nodding heads, Margaret's hand extended and grasping another hand.

Sarah added it up. Three so-called friends still avoiding each other and spending their time seeking new friends in disparate places. In God's name, why? Were they so constantly in need of new companions that they must embrace packs of total strangers—assuming these *were* strangers? They certainly seemed to be. Of course, Aubrey Smith seemed to be courting Deedee Herrick—whom by now he knew—but also he seemed glad to mix it up with the passengers and all the fans of the "Pirates and Plunder" show who buzzed like bees around Deedee and Richard.

Sarah leaned back in her seat and to her surprise found herself listening. Professor Clayton spoke clearly and had the sense not to sink her audience with some of the more labyrinthine goings-on in nineteenth-century British history. She brushed over the Second Reform Bill and the Poor Laws, choosing to lecture by anecdotes laced with often humorous references to Her Majesty the Queen and the domestic trials and tribulations of her reign.

And then the professor paused and raised her voice. "I wonder if the person in the rear row would like to move closer. Join the rest of the audience. I fear she cannot hear."

Sarah jumped in her seat, looked up, and saw the speaker's eye upon her.

"Yes," encouraged Professor Clayton. "Do come up and join us."

There was no help for it. Sarah was the only soul in the last four rows—apparently "Some Aspects of the Victorian World" was not a hot item—and so she rose and reluctantly walked forward, watched by the audience and only too aware of Margaret's welcoming smile and her hand patting the empty seat on her right.

The rest of the lecture passed for Sarah in a blurred haze. She listened without listening to descriptions of Victoria's loss of Melbourne, the antics of the Prince of Wales, the death of Prince Albert, Victoria's distaste for Gladstone, the flattery of Disraeli, and to a scattering of references to the disgrace of the children in mines, the workhouse and crossing sweepers, problems in the Punjab, the Diamond Jubilee, the Boer War, and Victoria's troublesome grandson, Kaiser Willie.

Sarah came to when the audience began to clap, and when she rose to leave the theater she found Margaret at her shoulder.

"My goodness, Queen Victoria was surely something, wasn't she?" said Margaret. "But what is so nice about these lectures is I find new friends wherever I go, and isn't that what cruising is all about?" She turned to the knot of people behind her. "This is my friend Sarah Deane. This is Janice from Iowa, and Monsieur de la Courte from Marseilles, and here are Mr. and Mrs. Pajoli from Manhattan." And Sarah found herself shaking hands, telling them, yes, she was from the States, Maine in fact. And yes, it was a beautiful state, and no, she didn't live near Kennebunkport and had never run into former President and Mrs. Bush.

For a moment the group bubbled indecisively about Sarah and Margaret and then moved off to whatever shipboard delights were being offered in the three o'clock slot.

For Margaret it meant the "Your Body and Your Health" seminar.

"A demo and hands-on practice," said Margaret, her voice moving into its extreme southern cadence. "Ah want to catch up with all those new herbal remedies, and then at the end there's going to be a completely honest talk about the new liposuction. And y'all know, dear, Ah am simply intrigued at the idea of beautiful thighs because being in a bathing suit scares me right to death."

The idea of the seminar scared Sarah right to death, and with no reluctance whatsoever, she abandoned Margaret to the stream of women descending the stairway and heading for the Lily Langtry Beauty Salon. But as she turned to go she was struck by the fact that Margaret had moved into the stream and was greeting and introducing herself to a whole new set of passengers.

Sarah shook her head and without any particular plan beyond avoiding the health and beauty session found herself descending to One Deck, poking into Princess Alice Lounge, and then stepping through the Harrods shop, completely immune to the tempting stacks of leather and cashmere and Shetland wool. Then, with a muddled sense of covering the rest of the public rooms, she noted that the Lamplighter Theatre was showing the movie of *Lassie Come Home* to a noisy group of children, turned and climbed to the next deck and waved at Richard Herrick and manager Gerald Hofstra, who were fussing with a string of lights in the H. M. S. Pinafore Theatre. Then back down through the Card and Game Room, where she found Aubrey Smith with a circle of passengers having a bridge lesson. A woman with a pointer was tapping on a screen, showing a deal and describing in elementary terms what was needed for an opening bid. Was Aubrey taking up bridge at an advanced age? she wondered. Or was it part of a getting-to-know-you scheme? From the Card Room Sarah worked her way back up to the Regent Street Shopping Gallery and headed down the outside stairs to the Quarter Deck. She wouldn't give up her surveillance job, but she would move it into the open, where sea air might go far in giving her a sense of being on a healthy holiday. On the starboard sports area she was immediately rewarded by finding Vivian Smith in a terry-cloth jumpsuit, frazzled and puffing, playing volleyball with a group of persons half her age, including a vigorous Liza Baum and a lackluster Teddy Hogarth, who looked to Sarah's critical eye as if what he really wanted— if not a drink—was a bunk with a blanket to pull over his head.

Sarah waved, refused an invitation to join in, and took herself off to the rail to consider her next move. Okay, it would be possible to watch and at the same time enjoy the ocean world. A deck chair and a book perhaps, because walking on the increasingly moving deck was becoming a challenge and even the volleyball players were beginning to stumble, lose their balance, and ricochet off each other. Yes, she could watch nicely from a deck chair. Sooner or later the others of her prey—one at least—was bound to come along to sit in a chair or lean over the rail to gaze at the gathering waves. After all, it was what one assuredly did on shipboard, liposuction and Victorian trivia notwithstanding.

But before she settled she had to go to her cabin and find a jacket because the wind had certainly increased. Before long there would be whitecaps. And she should choose a book to fit the occasion. A mystery, something that wouldn't require too much concentration. She had a stack of new paperbacks. Perhaps one of those with New Orleans gangsters or Chicago undercover cops, and it was just possible that in reading around in different settings she could extrapolate, fasten on something that made sense in the present context. It was almost scary, Sarah told herself, this compulsion of the three persons to mingle with an ever-changing group of strangers. It went beyond being simply needy. Perhaps they were on some kind of therapy cruise. The three were victims of a pathological shyness, an inability to talk to strangers, and the cure demanded that they join group after group of strangers and force conversation and friendship upon them. P. G. Wodehouse had a story about two stutterers ordered to travel and talk to whomever they met. Maybe that was it. The trio was more to be pitied than wondered at. But liposuction! For Margaret, who had the slender build of a willow branch.

Arriving on One Deck, Sarah began the trek down the starboard passageway toward her cabin, but when she was still fifty yards away she saw a familiar figure standing motionless ahead of her. Aubrey Smith, one hand on his hip, standing before one of the cabin doors. In fact, if Sarah had to guess, it might just be the cabin in which the late General Gordon had met his end. She stopped and moved back against the wall—or was it called a bulkhead? Alex's penchant for proper naval terminology could be most annoying. And distracting. She shook herself and focused on Aubrey Smith. What was he looking at? But as she asked herself this, he reached into a trouser pocket and removed what must be a key—she could only make out a small object—and inserted it into the cabin door. And as he did this, Sarah, feeling that some sort of definitive moment had arrived, took a step backward and found to her delight that the door at her back opened inward. She twisted her neck about and saw a small area and the outline of a vacuum cleaner. A utility closet. Excellent. A fine hiding hole. The one by the dining room had served her and so would this. She backed in, keeping an eye on Aubrey Smith, who seemed to be having some trouble with the lock. He pulled the key out of the lock, looked at it, and then pushed it again and turned it sharply.

An awful thought occurred to Sarah. Aubrey Smith might be entering his own stateroom, not that of General Gordon. What was the general's cabin number, anyway? Had it ever been mentioned? Sarah, with a mighty effort of recall, closed her eyes and tried to think. And then opened them. A watcher doesn't let her mind wander. But now Aubrey succeeded. The door moved inward and he disappeared. The door closed. And Sarah, running like a hare beset by hounds, sped down the passageway, noted the cabin number—1042—whirled around, and ran back to her closet, checking before she entered that no stray passenger had appeared in the long hallway. Nor a steward nor a cleaning person who might resent passengers in among the equipment.

Cabin 1042. Whether this belonged to General Gordon, Sarah could not remember. No matter; in good time she would find out, and if it was indeed the general's cabin, well, that was certainly a nasty piece of the puzzle. Sarah found that by fixing her eye to a small crack she could keep the questionable cabin in view and she settled down for a long wait. But now along the corridor came steps, voices. Two women's voices murmuring in French. Passengers, no doubt. Next she saw a black shirt and red shorts disappear into a nearby cabin and then the blue and white stripped uniform of one of the maids. The white shoes and uniform of a ship's officer. The dark trousers and black shoes of . . . well, almost anyone.

Damn. Now the whole passageway was thronged and she could no longer see the entrance to what she thought of as THE cabin. Then silence. Another sound of footsteps. These slower, more purposeful. Heavy. And then softer ones. Steps pausing by the closet. Steps stopping at the closet. Her closet.

Thankful for the darkness, Sarah pressed herself back against what must have been a wet mop. But no sound of departing feet.

Instead the sudden forceful push of the closet door. Snap. Closed. A lock clicking into place. What sounded like a woman's voice. The sound immediately squelched. And then a muffled voice, a man's this time. Then the woman's voice, also lowered and indistinct. Then silence. A long silence.

And Sarah, pressed against her mop, the wet seeping into the back of her shirt, her shoulder pushed into the hard metal handle of the vacuum cleaner, had never felt so completely alone.

You HaVE Till

TEn to-Night

13

WHEN and if one is suddenly enclosed in a dark space—be it
a cave, the trunk of a car, or a utility closet—the first impulse
is likely to be a beating with futile fists on the offending door
and a yelling of, "Let me out of here!" Sarah responded as expected, but just as she raised her arms, clenched her hands, she
stopped, fists in midair. And lowered them.

"Oh, shit," she whispered. Did she want to be found skulk-
ing in the utility closet as a victim of a sudden attack of paranoia
or, worse, an idiot incapable of telling a stateroom from a
closet? And if her rescuer happened to be Aubrey Smith, how
could she explain herself: Hello, Aubrey. I've been keeping an
eye on you and your friends and I wondered whose cabin you
were sneaking into because I thought you three weirdos just
might be members of a hit team trying to destroy the British
trade commission, so, you see, I nipped into this closet to watch
you break and enter General Gordon's stateroom. Oh? It isn't
General Gordon's stateroom, it's yours? Goodness gracious,
sakes alive, what a stupid mistake.

Balls, Sarah told herself. But what in hell to do—profanity
was rising as her situation became clear. She was locked in a
closet sometime late in the afternoon on Deck One, and prob-

ably all the cabin cleaning had been finished for the day. Was there any other equipment in the place besides cleaning equipment? Blankets and bed linen might mean the return anytime now by one of the maids or the stewards. What she needed now was a light. With luck there was an interior light system as well as an outside switch. She hoped they weren't on the same circuit and the person who had locked the door hadn't flipped off the switch. She began to grope around in the dark, identified the wet mop, accidentally kicked a pail, which by the dull thud it made proclaimed it of heavy-duty plastic. Then, taking a backward step, she bumbled into a tall object that just might have been an ironing board. Another mop, a dry one, a broom, a dustpan, a large circular container, probably a trash bin of some sort. And a small stepladder. A wooden one. Next to that a number of shelves which held, judging by size, shape, and smell, bottles and tins of cleansing fluids and powders. And then luck was with her. As her fingers crawled over what felt like a stack of folded cloths, they met a rectangular object of smooth plastic and glass. She fumbled for a switch and was rewarded with a bloom of light from a small battery lantern.

Not a great light, but even this limited glow was a hopeful development. And should this fail her, Sarah saw now a row of larger battery-powered lanterns on a shelf with the sign "Emergency Use Only." Well and good. However, she now saw that the other shelves held only cleaning materials but no blankets, no linen, no collection of mints, fragrant soaps, bath gels, and shower caps with the familiar *QV* imprint. She was truly held in a utility prison, not a luxury one.

And unless someone came by in need of a mop for a quick cleanup, she might well be here for some hours. Perhaps even overnight.

Sarah spared a few seconds for picturing the newly acquired stateroom on One Deck with its beautiful twin beds covered by the inviting blue and rose comforter. And pictured Alex climbing into bed alone. Alone and quite possibly thinking, if Sarah wants to play her little spy games and go prowling around all night, I certainly won't spoil her fun.

Sarah didn't care for that scenario. Obviously she had to

get out. She needed a plan. A short-range plan for now—heaven forbid that a long-range plan concerning food and breathable air might have to be considered. Fortunately the lantern had revealed a double sink on one side of the little room, so water would be available. The short-range plan—if no one came within the hour—involved making a scene, a rousing noise; the only question being when to make it. She settled herself down on a rubber kneeling pad and checked her watch. Ten minutes to four. Aubrey Smith, no matter what cabin he was inhabiting, would soon be making ready, along with Vivian and Margaret, to meet Alex and Julia and herself in the Snuggery for tea or drinks. Okay, if she couldn't escape through her own efforts, she would wait until twenty minutes after four and then on hearing the first passing footsteps she would bang the door and yell like hell. And hope like hell that her rescuer was not Aubrey, Cousin Vivian, or Margaret Lee. And certainly not Dr. Alexander McKenzie or Mrs. Thomas Clancy.

In the meantime she should take stock of her surroundings. Wasn't that what prisoners were supposed to do? Develop escape strategies and get out on their own? In her case, getting loose through her own efforts would prevent undesirable questions and tidbits of gossip for everyone to chew on. An ocean liner was indeed like a very small town; it had fed on General Gordon's death for more than a day and was probably ready for new meat.

Okay, inventory. Nothing remarkable. The usual collection of materials and tools needed for keeping the staterooms spick-and-span and aseptic. Water? Okay, the sink. Food? None visible. Space under the door for fresh air? Only a sliver. She'd better move slowly, use her oxygen wisely. Keep the screaming to a minimum.

Okay, thirty minutes to get out on her own. She rose to her feet and faced the door. Metal. One lock. One keyhole. First, see if there was an extra key hung on a hook or sitting on a shelf. Because, she thought, since it's remarkably easy to get locked in it's a wonder it doesn't happen every day.

No extra key. Nothing, not even a screwdriver, that might work or break the lock. How about a fire alarm? Sarah rather liked the notion of setting the thing off and sending the entire complement of passengers and crew to their boat stations and even into the lifeboats. She searched the walls and shelves. No fire alarm. A fire extinguisher, yes, but Sarah was unable to see what use that would be. All in all, a boring space, no allowances made for someone who might want to escape, unseen, unheard.

In some desperation she reached over for the large trash container and extracted a soiled mop head, a torn cleaning cloth, and several pieces of crumpled paper towels. And a wadded piece of paper with one side colored black. This curious object, cut in a rough circle, Sarah smoothed and stared at. Printing on one side, black on the other. She sniffed it. Crayola crayon—that delicious waxy smell beloved of children. For a few seconds Sarah stared at the thing, trying to fit it into any of her scenarios, and then, before she had a chance to puzzle out the printing, she caught the sound of distant voices and quickly crushed the paper and tossed it back into the wastebasket.

The voices grew slightly louder—speaking French. Footsteps came down the passageway. Paused. Stopped. The same whispery voices—an indistinguishable Gallic mutter-mutter. Sarah gave up on an unreasonable hope she had been nursing that Liza Baum—Liza the unflappable—would somehow be one of those voices. Or even Teddy. He had undoubtedly been tossed into holding tanks not unlike a utility closet and might know some effective escape strategies.

But now the French voices died away, footsteps receded, and new steps approached and slowed so that now Sarah made out an occasional distinguishable word. Two people. Male and female. The man's voice, a deep chesty voice with—if Sarah had to guess—a south of England voice—all those heavy consonants. "What's the matter?" it demanded. "What's going on? Come on now, this isn't a party." The female mumbled, a set of footsteps retreated and became faint, and then someone walking quickly. Another voice, decisive, a voice used to taking charge. Accent, northeastern American.

"Christ Almighty, whatever do you think you're doing?" it said. "You're not supposed to be here standing around, they'll be right on your neck. You know what they're like." And the woman's, "Oh, don't I now. But come away and let me explain." And then, clear and crisp, the name "Clancy" followed by a long murmuring mumbling and then, just possibly, the name "Hogarth." Or was Sarah just waiting for that name? Hogarth was the sort of name that sounded like someone clearing his throat of phlegm. Then mumble, mumble, and the woman, "Mind now, you'll have to be taking my word for it." And the man, "Jesus keep your voice down," and the woman, "There's surely no one around, it's almost teatime. No one will be missing their tea or their cocktail now, will they? So be off with you and let me get back to work and then . . ." and the voice sank and Sarah lost the rest.

Then, receding footsteps. Silence. And Sarah was alone again. Alone and free to consider what, if anything, she had heard. And where she had heard the woman's voice with its special rhythm, and the first man's voice. And why the word "Clancy"? A name that lit up the conversation like a skyrocket.

Sarah settled back on her rubber kneeling pad and hugged her knees. Did Aubrey Smith have a deep male voice? Yes, she thought he had, but not quite so basso. Of course she hadn't paid that much attention to voices. The thing was that when one had all the visual clues—face, expression, body language—the voice was only one factor in an identification. In the closet it was voice only and one paid attention. And how about the second man, the American, the one who talked about "they"? No one she had ever heard.

Sarah checked her watch. Almost quarter to four. The closet was beginning to feel too warm, and although she had no confirmation in such a small space she had a sense that the ship was rolling more noticeably. She sat up straight. If the wind continued to increase, the ship would deepen her roll and pitch, and it must follow as the night the day that passengers would feel uneasy. Be nauseated. Throw up. Barf. Vomit. And someone would come for the mop, the sponge, the cleaning fluid. Hallelujah. Except.

Except Sarah still did not care to be found ignominiously among the brooms and the pails. She reexamined her cell. Perhaps she could hide in one of the corners. There might be room behind the ironing board. She pictured the scene, reviewed the action. The key in the door. The ceiling light on. Enter maid about to take on distasteful task. Maid would seize pail, fill it at the sink, grab the mop, some rags, and a cleaning solution. And make off. If Sarah was lucky the maid would not linger to look around. Haste was necessary. Passengers would not like to find vomit on the stairs, the deck, anywhere. Maid would not lock closet. Why would she? She would be coming back with her cleaning supplies and would lock up then. Lock up an empty utility closet from whence Sarah had fled. End of scene.

Back to the name Clancy. How many Clancys were there on board? Probably several. What did it mean? And if Hogarth had been mentioned, there could be no possible connection with Clancy unless it related to Sarah and Alex's cabin switch with Teddy, the move paid for by Julia. Oh, hell and damnation. No, be calm. Practice her yoga breathing. She would wait an hour or so for the maid and the mop scene to play itself out. And then if that failed, it would be the shriek and beating fists. Sarah leaned back against the ironing board, folded her arms. And waited.

Sarah's Aunt Julia, unaware that the name of Clancy had been sounded in ambiguous circumstances, had spent a pleasant afternoon in the company of Erik Anderson. She had not been able to trap him into making strange claims or showing an eager interest in her income, her farm, or anything really personal. But there was a downside to the man. There were times when his rather overwhelming presence made her feel small, pinched, almost helpless—an unfamiliar sensation. His voice boomed, he seized and pushed chairs forward for her comfort, he insisted on guiding her through doors and in and out of lounges, up and down stairways. He demanded the sudden appearance of drinks and clapped his hands at waiters and stewards and ordered in a voice more suitable for use in the mead halls of the Norse thanes than in the genteel Victorian ambiance of the Scepter Room, where he had steered her after their meeting in the Casino. As planned, they had tried their skill at the gaming board—roulette—and given some time to the slot machines. Julia was gratified; she was thirty dollars ahead and Erik Anderson some five dollars in arrears, an imbalance that made up somewhat for the way that he seemed to be taking charge.

From the start of their acquaintance Erik had urged her to call him Erik and for a while a cautionary fiber in Julia had resisted; she wanted companionship, entertainment, but not intimacy. Only last year Julia had escaped from a certain retired colonel, who, despite protestations of undying devotion, had turned out to be looking for a large farm owned by a widow—any widow. And he had found one who was not Julia. It was a close escape and Julia had determined thenceforth to play with caution. But Erik called her Julia, would correct himself with a laugh, and do it again. She gave up. They were on a first-name basis by midafternoon.

The two had left the Casino and had just finished two brisk tours on deck, tours made more exciting by the increasing heave of the ship and the necessity of Erik Anderson having to steady Julia from time to time with the firm grip of a very large hand. They came to a halt by the starboard rails of the after-deck, Julia breathing hard—she had insisted on the second circuit. She would show him she was no fragile senior citizen. For a moment they both stood at the rail, Erik regaling Julia with a torrent of technical information about the *Vicky*, the weight of her ballasts, measured in over four thousand tons, her cruising speed of twenty-seven knots, and the apparently fascinating—to Erik—fact that her rudder was made by the Norwegian firm A/S Strommens Vaerksted. Julia, not listening, scanned the rolling waves, noted the increasing number of whitecaps, and announced in the middle of Erik's description of the bow thrusters that she had postcards to write and a book waiting. Not for a minute would she admit to serious fatigue and that what she really had in mind was a hot bath and a nap.

Erik abandoned the bow thrusters and looked concerned. "Hey, now, Julia, how about that lecture, 'Disasters at Sea,' I think they said it was? Look, I promised Brian and Kirsten. They're drooling over the idea of ships being blown up or hitting ledges. They've made a couple of friends and are into some

Treasure Island game that probably involves hanging from the yardarm."

It was time to show her independence. "I'm not going near the lecture. I've had it with disaster shows. I'm going to read in my cabin and then I've heard there's a string quartet in one of the lounges. Besides, I really should look around for my niece Sarah."

"Is she missing?"

"Oh, no. She likes to be off on her own now and then, but sometimes she has strange ideas and goes off the deep end."

"Like?"

Julia grew cautious. It was still possible that Erik was not the simple hearty soul he seemed. And also possible that Sarah might be on the track of something really untoward. "Oh, she worries about this and that. She's the intense type. Nervy."

"Well, an ocean crossing ought to settle her down," said Erik. "Does wonders for worrywarts."

Julia allowed Erik to call Sarah a worrywart but pointed out that she, Julia, had been trying not to interfere with her niece's free time. "You know, the ancient aunt trotting behind her. Now, I've had a lovely afternoon. Enjoy your lecture." And Julia waved a hand, turned on her heel, and stepped briskly into the door leading into the Regent Street Shopping Gallery and from there—steadying herself on the banister—to the stairway leading down to One Deck, her cabin, and a welcoming bed. Somehow she had become all too used to the idea of that little afternoon nap even though at home she was up at dawn and worked through the day and evening, finishing only after the final stable check at ten o'clock. New men were tiring; one had to prove one could not only keep up but that one could outdo. And keeping up with Erik Anderson was a job that called for heroic womanhood. That second circuit around the deck she could have done without.

She found Mary Malone in the passageway, and Mary, who seemed to be reading her mind, said she would draw the water for her bath and bring her a nice cup of tea and some biscuits.

And Julia, suddenly bitten by what must be, she decided, the familial bug, stopped short at her stateroom door. "Oh,

Mary, that would be wonderful. But I've forgotten my book. I must have left it on deck. No, I need to look for myself. If you would just draw my bath I'll be back in no time."

And before Mary Malone could dissuade her, Julia took off down the long starboard corridor heading forward, and then when she was sure Mary had disappeared into the cabin to deal with the bath, she slowed her steps. She rechecked the stickers, hers red, the general's green, and now, look at that, Sarah and Alex's green sticker now replaced by a thinner red one. Then she hastened on down the passageway, and as she went by each doorway she looked for red and green stickers. None. Not one. Wearily she made her way around to the port set of cabins, worked her way aft, climbed down the stairs to Two Deck, walked the length of the ship, port and starboard, descended to Three Deck, repeated her journey, and then, aching in every joint and muscle, took the lift back to One Deck and the waiting bath.

Mary was hustling down the corridor with a small tray covered with a white cloth. "Did you find your book now, Mrs. Clancy?"

"Book," repeated Julia stupidly.

"The one you went to find, remember?"

Julia regrouped. "My book. Oh, yes. No, I tried all over. Never mind. It will turn up."

"You could telephone Lost and Found," suggested Mary, holding open the stateroom door.

Julia, who was approaching physical collapse, held herself together. Barely. "I will do that," she said. "And here's my tea. Thank you so much." This said in the firm voice of dismissal.

And seven minutes later, Julia, a teacup settled on the toilet seat, sank deep into the steaming bathwater and tried to force her tired brain into contemplating a system of cabin cleaning in which only three cabins were honored with colored stickers.

Alex McKenzie had spent a busy afternoon. After finishing lunch he had devoted fifty minutes to a book and then hit the gym, worked on the treadmill, then went topside to the Quarter Deck pool, the level of which had been lowered slightly in response to the increasing ship's motion. The water was refreshing but the number of surging teenagers led to his early removal. Suddenly feeling old—a man from a different country than those splashing youngsters—he toweled off, dressed, and considered hunting for Sarah. After all, he had left her in peace for almost the entire day. Now the afternoon was advanced and he felt like sitting with her up on deck away from the artificial resort goings-on and talk of neutral matters such as the rising wind and the now briskly breaking waves and the glory of being at sea. Perhaps catch sight of a few pelagic birds skimming the water. With this picture in mind, Alex betook himself to the Boat Deck, the Game Deck, looked in at the Battledore Game Room, and, finding no Sarah, scoured the library, Harrods, the shopping gallery, interrupted a string quartet practice, a children's party in the Peter Pan Nursery, a group sing-along, and finally in exasperation poked his head into the Lily Langtry Beauty Salon because hadn't Sarah had an appointment to do something about her hair? He left hearing that Ms. Deane had missed her appointment, but that they had her cabin number for the charge. In between these incursions, he checked back at their stateroom, heard from Mary Malone that Mrs. Clancy had had her bath and was having "a nice lie-down," and no, she, Mary, had not seen Mrs. Clancy's niece.

Alex, his annoyance now flavored with the slightest tincture of apprehension, returned to the Quarter Deck and found Liza Baum belting a volleyball at a ragged-looking Teddy Hogarth and heard her deny any recent sighting of Sarah.

He settled himself on a deck chair that overlooked the badminton court and acknowledged once again that Sarah was an independent entity who had been annoyed at her husband's lack of interest in her theory of conspiracy at sea, and, therefore, it was natural for her to keep away from her traveling party. When Alex had first met Sarah on a long-ago trip to the Texas border, Sarah, understandingly enough after the accidental death of one lover and murder of another, was something of a nervous wreck. And as a wreck she had lacked confidence and stability and had harbored a sense that she was the sort of person who caused fatalities to her companions. But much water had passed under the bridge and now Sarah was not only steady on her feet, but had in the last few years gone charging into highly questionable situations and several times had participated in some hair-raising scenes with assorted rascals, felons, thugs, and bona fide killers. And now, for all Alex knew, she had closed her ears again to his wise advice and was at it again.

Alex snapped closed the book that he had been unable to read and got to his feet, finding that something like anger had successfully overwhelmed worry. Let her waste this beautiful ocean day on creeping around the bowels of the ship after phantom suspects like that decent Aubrey Smith, Cousin Vivian, and that southern belle, Margaret. A more harmless trio Alex had never seen. Now if she had been focused on the unsavory Gerald Hofstra or Richard Herrick, he might have been interested. Two men so dedicated to scenes of blood and sudden death must have something to hide. Alex got to his feet and headed for his stateroom. Time for a shower and then off to the Snuggery for drinks with Sarah's designated villains; this was certainly one meeting from which she most assuredly would not absent herself.

But as sometimes happens in the affairs of married persons, the husband was wrong.

14

SARAH had waited with what she considered extraordinary patience for the maid to come in for her mop and pail, or better yet, for the door to be miraculously opened by some unseen hand. But nothing happened. She checked her watch. Almost four-thirty. Time to make a scene. Or hang on for another fifteen minutes? Yes, what was fifteen more minutes? However, she had grown increasingly stiff sitting hunched up on the rubber kneeling pad, and comfort now became an issue. She stood up, stretched, and then took a pile of cleaning cloths from a shelf, spread them on the floor, rolled up the kneeling pad to serve as a pillow, and settled herself in a reclining position.

It seemed to be getting even warmer in the closet. Was that miserable little crack under the door sending in enough oxygen? Having read too many thrillers in which the victim is locked in a small space, she knew that the thing to do was to stay quiet and douse the light. She rose to her knees, reached for the switch on the battery lantern, and pushed it to OFF. Then, sinking back to the floor in the darkness, she told herself that it was simply a matter of being calm. Calm for fifteen minutes. And then action stations.

Sarah closed her eyes and tried to think of something that

would occupy her mind for those fifteen minutes. She considered poetry recitation, but that was perhaps too demanding; counting to ten thousand was boring. Finally, she settled on running through the alphabet and trying to find an American city to begin with each letter, the reward for arriving at Z for Zion, Pennsylvania, being the wonderful release from the utility closet.

She closed her eyes. Albany, New York. Butte, Montana. Carson City, Nevada. Denver, Colorado. Evanston, Illinois. Was Evanston a proper city or just a town? she asked herself sleepily. Next, F for Fargo, North Dakota. G for Gotham City—no, that was where Batman did his stuff, wasn't it? Were fictional cities allowed? H for Happy Valley. Was there a Happy Valley somewhere? Well, there should be. Better than Silicon Valley any day. How about Hollywood? Was that any more real than Happy Valley? Sarah yawned, mumbled, "I for Istanbul," and drifted away.

And slept. Exhausted from a day of clandestine pursuit and from the tension resulting from being holed up in a closet, she was drawn into a series of confused half dreams featuring buckets and mops and lifeboats and the surprising presence of Patsy, her Irish wolfhound, who should be safe at Aunt Julia's farm. Patsy was scratching at the door. Wanting to be let in. Scratch, scratch. Click, click, went his paws as he scrabbled at the door.

Click, click. Sarah sat up with a jerk. No Patsy. But where was she? Oh yes, the closet. The damned closet. But she had turned off the lantern and yet a tiny sliver of yellow light outlined the frame of the door. The door! It was open. Sarah jumped to her feet, missed knocking the pail over for the second time by inches, and was about to shout when she stopped cold. Was someone standing just outside waiting for her? Someone who had so obligingly opened the door and now stood ready for her? But ready to do what? If only she had not quit her karate class after six lessons. Or carried a can of Mace or at the very least thought to wear a whistle.

She stood still and listened. Not a sound. Cautiously she inched closer to the door, reached for the door handle, pulled it open so that the crack of light increased by two inches, and waited. Not a sound. No heavy breathing. No shadow across the beam of light. Then footsteps, several footsteps, and Sarah saw through her enlarged slit two persons rustle by. A man and a woman hurrying somewhere. Both in evening dress, he in dinner jacket and she in floating red and silver. The two swept past the door, and Sarah, seizing her chance, slipped out after them, closing the closet door behind her. Surely no one would attack her with passengers around. But as she followed the progress of the diminishing couple she was glad to see the long corridor ahead was empty. She swung around and searched the corridor behind. Empty. No one fore. No one aft. No one lurking with a blunt instrument or a cloth saturated with chloroform. She returned to the closet and turned the door handle. The door yielded. Not locked. Had it been unlocked for most of the afternoon and she hadn't bothered to try it after the first frantic push and shove?

Oh, for Christ's sake, how dumb could she be? She deserved to have stayed there all night as penalty for stupidity. And what had happened to that fifteen minutes she had allotted to herself before she made a scene, and what time was it, anyway? She lifted her wrist, scowled at the dial. Eight-thirty! Oh God, she'd missed tea and the drinks in the Snuggery with Aubrey Smith and his accomplices and now was good and late for the eight o'clock seating in the Windsor Castle Dining Room.

She flew in the direction of her stateroom. She had to change because evening dress was required for the Windsor Castle set. Hell and damnation. She inserted her key in the lock and pushed open the door. Alex's sweatshirt and a pair of shorts hung over a chair. Of course, he would have changed and dressed and was undoubtedly making merry with his dinner companions. Sarah plunged into the bathroom, saw her dark hair tousled, her face smudged—the rubber kneeling pad as a pillow left a lot to be desired in the cleanliness department. She sluiced her face, dragged a comb through her hair, wiggled out of her khaki jeans, zipped up her new black skirt, and buttoned up a soft white cotton cardigan—a present intended for her mother—over a dusty T-shirt that proclaimed her a friend of the loggerhead turtle. Then she slammed the cabin door shut and headed for the dining room, knowing that her nails were dark from grubbing around in the closet and that she probably smelled of sweat and cleaning fluid and general grunge.

Sarah's absence had been noticed; by Julia with only minor interest, Julia's mind being much taken up with Erik Anderson's suggestion of a nightcap and visit to the afterdeck to look at the stars. As for Alex, he vacillated between the resolution to let Sarah alone and let her call her own shots and an increasing sense that it was unlike Sarah to miss the major meal of the day without telling someone—their waiter, Frederick, for one, because the shipboard brochure had made it clear that dining room staff should be informed if passengers were planning to be elsewhere for dinner.

Sarah slipped into place between Julia and Sam Greenbank, said she hadn't known it was so late, please ignore her, she wouldn't hold them up by ordering, perhaps some soup, she wasn't very hungry.

The French sisters—they had obviously not found another table—merely looked up from the remains of their *filet de boeuf au poivre* and said something about *les americains*, and returned to their meal. Julia said, of course, you're hungry, don't be ridiculous, and waved a napkin at a hovering Frederick. Sam Greenbank said, hey, they missed her, and Alex, throttling his irritation, said he was glad she had thought to join them.

Frederick, all solicitude, opened a menu in front of her, suggested the *chicken à l'anglaise* as an entrée that could appear in minutes, and would she prefer the Graves? Or a Chablis?

But it was the young lovers who eased the situation. They had both apparently overcome their early shyness and seemed now to be on a first-name basis with all the diners, although the French sisters had made it clear that neither had any intention of saying a word to their fellow diners—a fact that escaped the lovers. They were both in the grip of social excitement and, judging from empty wineglasses, alcohol had eased the way.

"Well, hello, Sarah! Where have you been?" cried the blond young woman dressed in diaphanous layers of saffron and white and hung about with chains of crystal beads. Sarah bobbed her head, desperately trying to remember if the woman

163

had a name. But in this she was helped. "Did I tell you our names last night? Like sometimes I forget because there's so much to think about, crossing the Atlantic Ocean for the first time. This is Charlie and I'm Marci spelled with an *i*. Just like *'merci'* in French only without the *e*. *'Merci'* means thank you, which is about all I can remember from tenth-grade French." Here Marci gave a dazzling toothbrush smile to the sisters. "Adèle and Charlotte will forgive me because I'm just one more stupid American, isn't that what you think? Don't deny it." Here Marci wagged a finger at the two. "I heard you say something about *bêtise*, and doesn't that mean stupid? Never mind, Americans love France, and Charlie and I had a terrific time in Paris and spent days and days at the Louvre."

Here Marci paused for a long breath and, seeing her listeners stunned into silence, or simply busy with their dinner, turned back to Sarah. "You missed the whole first course. The oysters were fabulous, and so was the pâté. Charlie gave me a taste," this with a fond look at her dinner partner, the young man with a buzz cut, who was busy cutting his pasta into bite-size lumps. Was Charlie her husband, Sarah wondered, or her lover, or just a recent pickup at the Louvre?

There followed a gap in the conversation, Julia abstracted, Alex frowning, the sisters munching, and Sarah, still breathless, sipping water and trying to settle her wits.

Into this void stepped Sam Greenbank, apparently with the idea of keeping Marci talking up a storm so that no one need pay attention to anything but his or her food.

"Marci," said Sam, "was telling us all about Richard Herrick and his 'Disasters at Sea' lecture when you came in. Why don't you go on, Marci?" he invited.

"Well, I don't know. I mean, Dr. Greenbank—Sam—you were there, too, and maybe you heard some details we didn't."

"I'm sure I didn't," said Sam. "And I know Sarah would like to hear all about it."

Marci twisted about to Sarah. "You weren't at the lecture?"

"No," said Sarah. "I couldn't fit it in, there's so much to do on shipboard." Right, she said to herself, mops to count and cleaning cloths to spread out and keyholes to listen to.

"Okay," said Marci, "here goes." Then she paused and looked anxiously at Julia, and it was apparent that the Clancy tongue had already sounded off on the subject of the "Ships in Peril" lecture series.

But Julia, her head bent over a length of fish with a caper sauce, remained entirely silent.

"Well," said Marci, "it was really great. I mean the shipwrecks weren't great; they were pretty awful. People drowning or hanging on to floating chairs or on . . . what's that word?"

"Flotsam?" suggested Sam.

"That's it. Flotsam. Flotsam and jetsam. Anyway, Richard Herrick was terrific. He did the captain's and the crew's voices, and even the women's parts, you know, shouting in the water or groaning about losing their children."

Julia looked up briefly from her fish. "You could spare us the details," she said.

"Oh, I will, because it was a little on the gruesome side, but Mr. Herrick did quite a few wrecks, British navy ones and American ones, whaling ones and ordinary ones in fishing boats and overturned ferryboats in a typhoon. There was one in which a whole bunch of British transports jampacked with troops went wham right into this Egg Island in Quebec and the French celebrated because so many English soldiers and sailors and even wives and children drowned and the town—whatever it was— was saved."

One of the sisters—Adèle, Sarah thought, smiled a thin smile. *"Grâce au bon Dieu,"* she said, and reached across Marci for a pat of butter.

"Perfidious Albion," said Sam.

Marci frowned, and then, looking about the table and finding her audience not entirely engaged, ground to a halt. "Anyway," she ended, "the whole thing was something else, and at the end that manager, what's his name, Hoffa? No, that's not right, it's Hofstra. The one who looks like a sort of ghost story illustration, dark and sort of scary, got up and told us that the *Titanic* is on for tomorrow evening. After dinner at nine because it's not all that suitable for small children."

"You mean the special effects," said Sam. "Why the fuss?

After all, the kiddies have just had two afternoons of drownings."

"Mr. Hofstra promised special audiovisuals—you know, the band playing and the radio operators calling for help. But Mrs. Herrick wasn't mentioned, and I didn't even see her this afternoon."

"For which," said Julia, "she is to be commended."

"But she's part of the team, isn't she?" asked Marci in a puzzled voice.

"I think," said Sarah carefully, "that she helps with the lighting and the props, but isn't crazy about some of the gritty aspects of the lectures. That's Mr. Hofstra's specialty and he's working directly with Mr. Herrick."

But Marci had ceased to listen, and a strange, dazed expression had overcome her face. She put down her fork, ran her tongue over her lips, and reached for her glass of water.

"Is the ocean getting rougher?" she asked in a thick voice.

"You noticed?" said Sam cheerfully. "I think we are in for some wind and things are rolling a bit. Are you feeling a little queasy? You can get pills, you know, down at the Walk-in clinic."

But Marci did not reply. For a moment she stared bug-eyed at her plate, swallowed with difficulty, then rose unsteadily, cupped her hand over her mouth, and, clutching her napkin in the other, fled the dining room, followed by her companion.

Julia looked up with interest. "Early casualty," she said.

"Won't be the last," said Sam cheerfully. "I think if any of you have a leaning toward seasickness you should collect some medication in case things get really rough. And try ginger. There's a big bowl of it outside the dining room." He turned to the sisters. *"Et vous, mesdames? Avez-vous le mal de mer quand vous faites une voyage?"* Sam's accent and grip on French grammar sounded to Sarah as if it had not been much exercised since high school, but the sisters, with identical expressions of disdain, said simultaneously, *"Jamais,"* and returned to their plates with increased attention.

"Madam would care to see the dessert menu?"

It was Frederick bending over Julia, Frederick having early

decided that this was the senior power of the table and the first person to be addressed in all things.

But Sarah, who had been thinking what with the roll of the ship increasing that a sorbet would perhaps be the better part of valor, suddenly came to attention. Frederick's voice. That accent. She frowned, trying to concentrate. The voice, the accent. South of England. Cornwall, maybe. Or Devon. Sarah had no real ear for the nuances of British dialect, so maybe it was the pitch. She did have a fair ear for the pitch of voices.

"Dessert," said Alex.

Sarah jerked her head around. "What?"

"Dessert. Do you want to order something?"

"What about the *mousse au chocolat* with the Grand Marnier sauce?" suggested Frederick. "It's very popular."

Sarah dragged herself back. "Ice cream," she said. "No, I mean sorbet."

"We have raspberry and lemon," said Frederick, placing the menu in front of her.

"Oh, anything. Any of those."

"Choose," said Alex.

"Lemon. Yes, lemon. That sounds very nice," and Sarah returned to Cornwall and began wrestling with memories of *Poldark*.

The French sisters ordered the mousse, Julia settled for a sliced apple and Stilton with biscuits, and then Charlie returned, sat down heavily, asked for apple tart, and apologized.

"Sorry about that, but you know how it is with seasick people. Marci gets sick if she sits in the backseat of a car. It's a wonder she lasted this long. She's taken a pill and I called the stewardess to keep an eye on her." He smiled at the table. "Of course, Marci's completely bummed because we're paying a mint for the trip and she wants her money's worth."

"So do we all," said Sam affably.

But Charlie, hitherto the silent partner, was now in the mood for chat. He detailed their day, the casino, a workout in the gym, lunch on deck, the meeting of many people.

"We think it's neat to meet people from everywhere in the world. Marci's making a game of it, asking people where they're from. We're seeing how many countries we can count and how many states in the U.S. and provinces in Canada, and counties in England. So far we've even got someone from Tibet and a missionary from Tanzania. Marci's entering it all in our trip journal."

Julia stared at him. "You mean you're actually going around asking everyone where they're from?"

"Not exactly. Not right off the bat. We get into conversation and they tell us. Most people are dying to tell us where they're from. We don't push it. We get friendly and it comes out. We don't even have to ask."

Sarah looked up from her sorbet. "Do you have Massachusetts? Alex was born there and so was I."

"Too bad," said Charlie. "We've already got it. What we really need are states like Wyoming and North Dakota."

Sarah put down her spoon. "How about the British counties? How are you doing with those?"

"We're filling them in. We got Norfolk and Gloucestershire yesterday and Yorkshire and Dorset and Aberdeenshire and Invernesshire today, but I haven't asked Frederick here." He waved at Frederick, who was approaching with a silver coffeepot. "Where do you hail from, Frederick? I hope it's a place we don't have."

"Cornwall," said Frederick. "St. Mawes. But I haven't lived there in years. Been all over the world. Different jobs and different ships."

Charlie grinned. "Good. We didn't have Cornwall. What about you, Mrs. Clancy? Don't tell me you're Irish because I won't believe it."

Sarah bit her lip, waiting for Julia to chop Charlie into small pieces, but Julia, as was her occasional wont, had lapsed into a state of amiability, a state assisted by her third glass of chardonnay.

"I'm not Irish, but my husband was. But you can't guess me by my voice because I was born away from home. My mother was visiting relatives in Tennessee and I came three weeks early."

"That counts for Tennessee, which we didn't have," said

Charlie. "I'm pretty good at accents, but I have trouble with some of the southern ones. They sound like stage actresses taking a part in *Dallas*. Have you met that Margaret Lee? She's so southern it's scary. Listen, it's been fun, but I'd better get back to Marci and see if she's settling down. G'night, all."

And Sarah, hearing the "G'night," wondered briefly about Charlie's early childhood. Australia, perhaps, and then a move to the States. But, as the coffee was passed around, she returned to a closer problem. Had Frederick, now established as a native of Cornwall, been the first male voice she had heard from the utility closet? His voice matched the tone and pitch, but how many males aboard had spent years in Cornwall and had deep voices?

Sarah, her coffee untouched, looked around the dining room hoping that some glint of explanation might bounce off the walls and bring light. She saw that Aubrey Smith lingered in discussion at another table made up with two ships' officers and three stout women of middle age. No sign of other known females, although if precedent meant anything, Margaret had eaten in the Frogmore Dining Room and Liza was sheepdogging Teddy into some safe pen like the billiard room. Of Cousin Vivian there was no sign. Looking around again, she realized that the dining room had tilted unnaturally, waiters moved with caution, and diners, after leaving their tables, walked awkwardly, arms stretched out from their sides, as if not sure if their next step was going to meet solid ground.

Sarah turned to Alex, thinking that she might now unburden herself of the afternoon's events, but found that he had pushed back his chair and had launched into an argument with Sam on the management of something called lupus vulgaris. And Julia? Only a glimpse of that aggravating person as she vanished through the dining room doors. Okay, Sarah told herself, to the deck. Clear the brain and try to make some sense out of something. Anything.

Outside on the Boat Deck, even in the dark of early night, the sea showed itself a troubled expanse with whitecaps visible in every direction, while the deck itself slowly tilted toward the disturbed ocean and then slowly rolled back to a marginally even keel. And here Sarah found Margaret Lee. Margaret languished—there was no other word for it—on a deck chair, her azure chiffon evening dress wrapped in a lacy black shawl, her hands folded tightly around a beaded handbag.

"Sarah, dahling. Ah am so happy to see you . . . but Ah am not so well as Ah should properly be. But y'all do sit down just for a tiny minute and keep me company. Take mah mind off the way this naughty old ship is upsettin' mah little old stomach."

Sarah, feeling that she had wandered onto the set of *Gone with the Wind*, sat herself down on the edge of a neighboring deck chair and nodded sympathetically. Margaret's face, even in the evening light of a bulkhead lamp, did have a greenish cast.

"Ah could not take mah dinner," continued Margaret in a tremulous voice. "Even with a little old pill, Ah declare Ah am not just one hundred percent. Vivian says Ah should be in hospital because Ah am simply all to pieces. Mah hair is a bird's nest, mah mascara has run fit to kill, and Ah have ladders in both mah stockin's."

"If you went to your stateroom to lie down?" suggested Sarah.

"Now, Sarah deah, y'all know fresh air is the very thing for seasickness. But Ah don't want to keep you from your evenin' plans. That would not be fair on you. So y'all just skedaddle along."

"I'll keep an eye on Margaret," said a voice. Vivian Smith, packed into a shimmering green evening dress, looking strangely like an middleaged mermaid. Vivian was followed by Aubrey Smith, impeccable in his white linen dinner jacket and black tie.

"We'll see that she gets safely to bed," Aubrey assured her. "I'm afraid," he added, "that we may be in for a fairly stiff blow. It should be a good test of our sea legs."

"But, Aubrey, dahling," said Margaret, "Ah do not want to test mah sea legs."

"Good night, Sarah," said Aubrey. "Time for all land creatures to be in their bunks. Or indoors at any rate. You never know," he said with a slight chuckle, "what lurks out here on deck in the dark. What is hiding in a lifeboat."

And Sarah, once more with the irritating feeling of being dismissed, rose, said good night, and moved away in the direction of what promised to be a fairly deserted part of the afterdeck. And as she walked, and at times staggered, reaching for support along the cabin bulkheads, she was sure of two things. The first was that Aubrey's half-joking warning, despite the light tone and almost condescending manner, was just that: a warning. And second, Sarah knew that she had nailed Margaret Lee. Margaret was about as much a faded southern belle as she, Sarah, was. And added to that, she was—or had been at some formative time of her life—a daughter of Britannia.

15

WORKING her way aft along the rail, sometimes hanging on to stanchions for support, Sarah found that she was not surprised. Everything about Margaret now seemed false. Not only her overblown southern accent, her mixing it up with total strangers, and, for God's sake, liposuction! Margaret, tall and probably not weighing more than one hundred twenty-five pounds dripping wet, talking about the joys of having fat sucked out her thighs. And what about her so-called friendship with Vivian-the-liar Smith—as devious a female as ever crossed the ocean.

As for Aubrey Smith, Aubrey with his table-hopping, glad-handing, chatting it up with all comers—Aubrey always seemed to be acting against type. When they had met that first day in the Snuggery, Aubrey had struck her as low key. Ironic, possibly whimsical, but not what anyone would call the chamber of commerce type.

Sarah, climbing cautiously down the stairs to the aft Quarter Deck, paused to observe the scene—a scene lit by a little ring of lantern-shaped lights fastened to the bulkhead and dimly illuminating the semicircle of the afterdeck. It had grown darker, with a few slate gray clouds moving across a hazy moon, the roiled ocean dimly seen as a heaving broken carpet of water, and the wind sustaining a soft but insistent whistle. Along the rim of the deck a few figures here and there huddled in chairs. Several people leaned against the rail while one or two couples walked unsteadily back and forth, arm and arm, all either proving to themselves that the sea was the real part of the crossing, something that must be experienced foul weather or fair, or, more likely, trying to beat back an incipient bout of seasickness.

But why was she, Sarah, here?

She had told herself that it was to sort things out. But people and events remained resistant to sorting, contradictory, signifying nothing—or almost nothing. Now in the brisk night air the actions of the Aubrey Smith trio might seem strange, but not necessarily stranger than those of any other group of three. As for a member of a British trade commission being knocked down by a taxi, how many other people had been hit by a car that night in London? As for another commission member, an aged general dying in his cabin by tripping, from vertigo, from an unsuspected cardiac condition, or, most unlikely, from a blow from an assailant: didn't such an event come under that useful category, coincidence? This was a ship with over a thousand passengers, and, as Liza had suggested, the morgue might by now be packed with deceased passengers.

Then what about Aunt Julia's report that she had experienced a sense of being pushed over a rail? More probably she had been—as she herself said—dizzy and been overcome by a panicky sense of falling. Certainly Julia had reported nothing untoward since then. And true, her own and Alex's new stateroom—formerly Teddy Hogarth's—had been entered in the middle of the night by an unknown visitor, someone drunk or disoriented, but she had heard of no other unlawful stateroom entries—although if there had been any, no one would have told her. She thought that the *Vicky*'s security people commonly had a number of like incidents on file, since, as a matter of routine, they would be keeping a wary eye out for dubious passengers, card sharks, dope runners, and run-of-the-mill molesters and con men.

It all added up to a number of questionable but not necessarily dangerous happenings. Wasn't it time to move on? Start living a normal shipboard life? Make new friends, work out in the gym, and finally get her hair completely restyled. And try to keep Aunt Julia from alienating half the passenger list and at the same time maybe take a hard look at this Erik Anderson to judge if he was on the prowl for elderly ladies.

"It's Sarah Deane, isn't it?" said a voice behind her.

She whirled around and made out a deck chair drawn close to the rail and on it a dark muffled shape, a shape with a large square head.

"Who?" she spluttered.

"Me. You remember." The figure reared up into a sitting position and pulled the blanket from his shoulders. "It's Gerald Hofstra. I'm following your advice. Being kind to my stomach, fighting seasickness because I'm such a lousy sailor. Remember, you told me to stay out on deck, and I think it works. I've taken some pills and I'm going to spend the night out here. Only come in to put tomorrow's show together. Did you see the one this afternoon? Went over big. Richard was terrific, and the audience, they ate it up. I still need to do a little work with the spots, but it's going good, I tell you."

"I missed it," said Sarah. "I was busy all afternoon."

"Aw, too bad. We had a little trouble with the props because Deedee got on her high horse and went on about not being—what the hell'd she say?—the show not being responsible or affirming, something like that. Walked right off the stage. But she'll come round tomorrow. I mean it's the *Titanic*. Even Deedee won't dump the *Titanic*. And talk about affirming, I mean look at all those scenes, people saying good-bye and giving away life jackets. It's got a hell of a lot more heart than some movie like *Casino* or all that Rambo gangster stuff."

Sarah walked over to the deck chair and looked down at Mr. Hofstra. "Wouldn't you say that maybe *Titanic* has been done once too often? Think of the millions of people who've seen the movie. Now it's being used for cheap thrills?"

"Now, Ms. Deane, I get your point and I like you being open with me. But, honest, we don't reenact actual drownings. That *would* be cheap. And *Titanic*, she's part of our heritage. The

White Star wonder ship proved nothing is perfect. That people are only human and technology falls on its nose. Icebergs turn up and bolts break. The whole thing is moral. Entertaining, exciting, and goddamned moral."

"The moral part," said Sarah heatedly, "ought to include a lot of people being strung up by their thumbs for letting it happen."

"Listen to you, babe," said Gerald, giving her a triumphant look. "Look who's asking for violence. Hey, it's history. And people learned a lesson. You have to have a train wreck before someone puts up a crossing light and a car smash up before anyone puts up a stop sign. Me and Richard, we're not into blaming, we're not listing names of people who maybe shouldn't have been in a lifeboat. We show what happened, see it now, you are there. This is what happened almost a hundred years ago. It's like Lindbergh, or climbing Everest, Amelia Earhart disappearing. Now me, I don't do gangs and drugs. I stay away from war and the atomic bomb. Someday I might even do a show about Mother Teresa—who knows? But the *Titanic*'s a powerhouse story, and we've got an audience of real live passengers sitting in a big ocean liner making her own maiden voyage across the same damn ocean, and maybe some folks they begin thinking, hey, it could happen again. It won't, but for a while when the show's on we got 'em by the balls, if you'll excuse the expression."

Sarah sighed. No point in arguing. And, to be honest, she had to admit that she herself had gobbled up Walter Lord's *A Night to Remember* and sat without protest through the movie and several documentaries on the subject.

But Gerald Hofstra wasn't finished. "You know Mrs. Clancy, don't you? I mean I've seen you together."

Sarah admitted that indeed she did know Mrs. Clancy. "My aunt," she explained. "Has she been after you?"

"You could put it that way. Like I have this bulldog pulling at my pants. Your aunt wants me to can the whole act. Some kind of relative of hers went down in the ship. I mean that's very sad, but lots of people have sad things happen, and they still go and see shows like the *Titanic*. Only worse sometimes."

This was such an accurate statement that Sarah remained

silent. Gerald Hofstra, the elfish shape with the square head and the big jaw, wrapped in his blanket, looked like a kind of unhappy gargoyle that had ended up in a deck chair when where he really belonged was a hundred feet up on the Cathedral of Notre Dame.

"So do you think you could ask your aunt to take it easy?" persisted Gerald. "I mean she's turning people off."

"That," said Sarah, "is Aunt Julia's specialty. But I don't think you need worry. People seem to love your stuff."

"Yeah, you're right. The only other guy who's giving me a hard time is that assistant minister. Or chaplain's helper. Came barging into my cabin and began storming about depressing passengers and not being sensitive to loss."

Sarah, who had been about to turn and leave, stopped in her tracks. "What assistant chaplain?"

"Name's Frye. Amory Frye. Bending my ear about the whole series, but mostly about the *Titanic*. He'd probably still be there if the stewardess hadn't moved him out."

"The stewardess? Got rid of the chaplain's assistant?"

"Yeah. She came in like someone's mad grandmother and said something like, 'Amory, that's enough now.' Like a nanny. Told him he was wanted somewhere else, and he said he'd finished his visitations—something like that—and she said, 'Go along with you now' in this Irish accent of hers."

"Irish? You mean Aunt Julia's stewardess, Mary Malone?"

"I don't know her name. She's not my stewardess, and I suppose there's a bunch of Irishwomen aboard."

But Sarah, with new fodder to chew, waved a hand at Gerald, wished him good sleeping on deck, and moved on toward the extreme after section of the Quarter Deck's sports area. Here the deck ended in a wide curve, a popular spot in daytime and in good weather a place to watch the churning wake of the great ship.

But now, the area was almost deserted except for a distant couple along the port rail and a man sitting up on a deck chair reading a book with the assistance of a battery lantern. Another seasick victim, Sarah thought, but then, seeing him closer, she saw it was Teddy Hogarth. Honestly, she told herself, with the multitudes aboard why did she keep bumping into undesira-bles? The only person she wanted to meet was Julia's friend, Erik Anderson, and try to get a sense of the man. But no, here was Teddy. He shot his flashlight briefly in her face and then heaved himself into a more erect posture. "Hi," said Teddy.

"Hi," said Sarah without enthusiasm. And then, "Where's Liza?"

"How about 'Hello, Teddy. How are you?' Not just 'Where's Liza?' We're not twins. In fact, I think she's fed up with me. If I'm drunk, I'm a project. If I'm sober, well, what's the point?"

"And you're fed up with Nurse Baum?"

"Not a bit of it. But I'm detecting signs of restlessness in Nurse Baum. She knows there's more to shipboard life than keeping an eye on Teddy Hogarth."

"You can say that again." It was Liza, Liza in a short black skirt, a silver T-shirt, and glitter sneakers, her face a master-piece of makeup and eyeliner. "I hope Teddy hasn't been prey-ing on your sympathy. I went off to find a stash of seasick pills. For me. Just in case. And for Teddy, if he wants. I told him that he can't just huddle out here on deck for the whole storm. Life goes on, and if he can't walk past the café or the bar without reaching for a pint, well, screw him. I mean that's half the battle. So come on, Ted, you old souse. Shake a leg."

"Actually," said Teddy, "I like it out here. Why don't you go on and find out what the beautiful people are doing. Then I can see if I can attract the guy who walked into my cabin—my former cabin. If someone really wants to throttle me or toss me overboard, it will be easier out here on deck. And if you don't think I'm a target, look what came in the mail—actually, under my cabin door." And Teddy fumbled around in his jacket pocket and produced a small folded piece of paper. Which he opened up, revealing its circular shape and its blackened surface.

"Let me see that," said Liza, and without waiting she snatched it up, examined it, turned it over. "It's a message," she announced. "Or a threat. It says, 'You have till ten to-night.' "

"I don't think it's Miss Universe wanting me, so I suppose it's a kid's joke," said Teddy. "It's the sort of thing kids do."

"Except," said Liza slowly, "why choose you?"

"Or you," said Teddy. "We've been cohabiting."

"Officially," Liza reminded him, "you are the occupant of that cabin. And this time, there's no mix-up with Sarah and Alex. Unless—" She turned to Sarah. "Have you had something like this?"

Sarah, who through the exchange had been paying strict attention, nodded vehemently. "I found one like it in a trash bin. Crumpled up. I threw it away." There seemed no point in mentioning the utility closet and why she had been going through a trash bin.

Liza appeared to consider the matter. Then she reached for Teddy and yanked at his jacket. "On your feet. This paper doesn't mean a blessed thing. It's some lover boy marking his trail. And speaking of the cabin switch, I've decided Alex and Sarah were the targets for that break-and-enter scene. Someone wanted to roll them for good American dollars. Also I have a theory about General Gordon. He was killed because he was a real bastard, always acting like one of those British officers in a movie about the Khyber Rifles. I'd say his valet killed him but the guy's apparently in the clear for the death time. I heard that from one of the hospital aides."

Teddy struggled to his feet and for a moment stood, listing to one side, his feet splayed out for balance. "Real storm heating up," he said. "I think I'll take one of those pills."

"Then," said Liza, "if you take liquor on top of a pill you'll be dead. That ought to put the fear of God into you. But things are getting mighty unsteady. I saw Gerald Hofstra back there and I don't think he's long for this world, and some people have been barfing in corners and the crew is running around with mops and deodorants. Okay, see you around, Sarah, and look out for funny paper circles colored black."

And Sarah watched the two of them move cautiously along the rail and disappear though one of the lighted doorways.

But something that Liza had said stuck in her brain like a burr. The Khyber Rifles? Hadn't she just heard someone mentioning the Khyber Pass? What was the name of that old movie, *The King of the Khyber Rifles*? At home Sarah belonged to a film club and met regularly with other fans to watch the likes of Douglas Fairbanks and Ronald Colman and Janet Gaynor do their stuff. Now she sat down on the end of the deck chair Teddy had vacated and began to search her brain while at the same time realizing that her resolve to abandon the hunt was faltering.

Okay, British officer roles. There was Ronald Colman—a favorite, particularly when hitched with Greer Garson. But not useful in the *Vicky* shipboard context. Something to do with one of the passengers had struck a spark. How about David Niven? Errol Flynn? No help there. Charlie Chaplin? No. Claude Rains? Well, Claude in unwholesome makeup was not unlike Gerald Hofstra. But did old British movie types have anything to do with her favorite suspect, Aubrey Smith?

Sarah pushed herself away from the deck chair and moved restlessly over to the after rail and scowled at the dark heaving waters. Diagnosis by old movie? Her brain wouldn't stop trying to fit people and events into cinematic formats. *King of the Khyber Rifles, The Count of Monte Cristo, Mutiny on the Bounty?* Charles Laughton, *Wee Willie Winkie* with Shirley Temple—was she trying to remember a general like the late lamented General Gordon? She considered Gordons. Kitchener and Khartoum. The Mahdi. Several Gordons survived the *Titanic.* How about colonels? Teddy's father was a colonel. Who played colonels in the old movies? Or grandfathers? A British version of Lionel Barrymore. The actor with the white hair, those thick eyebrows, and the angular jaw. C. Aubrey Smith.

Yes! Yes! C. Aubrey Smith. Aubrey C. Smith. Aubrey Clyde Smith. Ha! Except. Except the actor didn't look a bit like this Aubrey Smith; her Aubrey Smith had an anonymous face, a face more like George Smiley as played by Alec Guinness. So was the name a coincidence? As everyone had been saying, the number of Smiths aboard would boggle the mind. And Clyde was a common enough English name. Oh God, was she ever reaching on this one.

Now if Sarah had truly had the soul of an undercover agent, she would have gone into action. She would have somehow stolen a maid's uniform and found her way by stealth into Aubrey's cabin. Would have conducted a swift search of that cabin and of Margaret's and Cousin Vivian's and perhaps even Gerald Hofstra's as well as several other shipboard worthies. But Sarah now recalled that she had forsworn snooping, the hour was late, the flesh was weak, her stateroom bed beckoned, and besides, what evil character would choose C. Aubrey Smith—colonel of the regiment and beloved grandfather to the likes of Shirley Temple and Freddie Bartholomew—as a name to hide behind? Lon Chaney or Peter Lorre would be more like it. Or, since there was nothing left remarkable under the visiting moon—or was it the sun?—she might eventually find out that C. Aubrey Smith, the actor, had fathered or uncled her own Aubrey Clyde Smith.

No ambiguous figures impeded her progress to her stateroom, and there she found Alex in a relaxed and amiable mood. He hoped she'd had a wonderful day on her own, and he did not refer to her late and breathless entrance at dinner nor her no-show at the Snuggery cocktail event.

"After all," said Sarah, "the invitation was informal. I think it was meant that we could take it or leave it."

"Okay, so you chose to leave it. And Frederick, our handsome waiter, took it in his stride. A ship's staff train for years to act as if nothing, absolutely nothing, is unusual."

Sarah grinned. "A slightly tardy passenger is nothing compared to bar scenes and people puking on the Oriental rugs, or even to finding bodies of generals on the first day out."

Alex yawned and stretched. "You are still thinking about General Gordon? The interest hasn't faded?"

"As a matter of fact, I've been trying hard to decide in favor of normality. General Gordon is a past event. As for a midnight visitor to a cabin? Probably some drinking buddy Teddy picked up and who decided to visit him in the middle of the night. Relieve him of cash. That's what happens to people like Teddy."

"I agree. And since you've given up nosing around, you won't mind my asking where you were all afternoon and evening?"

Suddenly Sarah lost her temper. "Damn you, Alex McKenzie. I was locked up in a utility closet—or maybe not even locked up but had the door closed on me and it was probably due to my own stupidity."

"I see. Just an everyday event?"

"Right," said Sarah defiantly. "And I don't want to talk about it."

Alex reached down and began untying his shoes. "Okay. Fine by me. I'm sorry it happened to you, but here you are, safe and sound, so you can tell me about it when you're ready. It's bedtime, and I think this wind is going to keep it up and toss us around at least for the next twelve or fourteen hours, so let's hit the hay and sleep through some of it."

Sarah relaxed and let out a long deep breath. There was to be no grilling. No probing. No third degree and unseemly laughter. She took hold of Alex by the shoulder, rotated his head, and kissed him. "I like being tossed in a blanket," she said.

"That," said Alex, "we can arrange."

Sarah woke only once, sometime around dawn, found herself on the edge of her bed, and noticed the stateroom seemed to be undulating slowly but with great determination. But somehow, the increased motion was tolerable, even pleasant, and she slipped back in sleep, to be wakened by Alex's usual morning shower and shaving commotion. The scene from the porthole presented a gray sky, a gray ocean of peaks and valleys, and a horizon which moved up and down like some giant window shade. Her stomach spent a moment deciding whether it was unbalanced or merely hungry and then settled for hunger. She swung her feet to the floor—no, the deck—and prepared for action. And action she got. A loud thumping on the stateroom door.

Sarah looked at her watch. Eight o'clock. Except it was really seven because of setting the clocks back. She reached for her raincoat, an object that doubled as a dressing gown, and shuffled to the door.

It was Deedee Herrick. Deedee, disheveled, in rumpled pale-blue sweats, her feet shoved into clogs, her curly red hair sticking out in all directions, her Orphan Annie face troubled.

"Sarah, can I come in? I need your help. I bumped into your Aunt Julia in the passageway, and she said you simply live to do things like this." She hesitated, and added belatedly, "I hope I didn't wake you up."

Sarah pulled Deedee into the room, shouted to alert Alex

to the presence of a visitor, and reached for her jeans. "Do things like what?" she demanded.

"Look for things. People. Find out about what's going on. It's Gerald. Gerald Hofstra. He's disappeared."

Sarah tugged a T-shirt down over her head, added a sweater, and began fumbling in the bureau drawer for socks.

"What do you mean disappeared?"

"He's not in his stateroom. At least I don't think he is. I knocked and knocked and no answer. I thought about asking the steward to open it, but I didn't want to make a scene."

Sarah stopped in the act of tying a sneaker lace and looked up at Deedee. "Have you tried the deck? I saw Gerald last night up on the Quarter Deck, and he said he was feeling queasy and thought he'd spend the night there. In a deck chair."

Deedee opened her mouth, closed it, then shook her head. "I feel like a fool. Well, I'm glad I didn't break into Gerald's cabin. You see, Richard is frantic. The *Titanic* show, it just about hangs on Gerald working with Richard. I told them yesterday I wanted out, but then I could see Richard was absolutely wild to do it, so I said I'd help offstage and that I'd find Gerald early this morning so the two could work all day on the horrible thing. But I couldn't find Gerald, and Richard said to keep looking, and when I bumped into Julia Clancy and she told me—"

"I know," said Sarah with a grimace, "that I live to meddle in other people's lives."

"She didn't say meddle. Not exactly. But do you? I mean are you a private investigator or something in real life? Like Kinsey Millhone or Carlotta Carlyle?"

Sarah stood up and faced Deedee. "In real life I teach English. Julia only means that sometimes I've been around when something's happened, or Alex has—he's one of the county's medical examiners—and, I may add, Julia has. But I *will* come up on deck and see if we can find what's left of Gerald Hofstra. And then we can all have breakfast if you're not feeling seasick or anything."

"That's the least of my worries. I've got a good stomach."

"What's up with you, Deedee?" It was Alex, a large white

bath towel with *Victoria* in purple wrapped firmly around his middle.

Deedee, now rather shamefaced, described her search for the errant Mr. Hofstra. "Sarah's coming on deck to show me where he spent the night in a deck chair."

"And if he's not there," said Sarah, "he's probably back in his stateroom or having breakfast."

"If he's not throwing up somewhere, poor miserable thing," said Deedee of the soft heart.

"I'm going to take a quick turn on deck, and then I'll see you in the cafeteria," said Alex. "If I bump into Mr. Hofstra, sick or well, I'll tell him to report."

But Gerald Hofstra was not huddled on his deck chair. Unfortunately, Sarah was not able to identify the exact spot where she had spoken to him, since in deference to the rolling ship and the sea-splashed deck one of the ship's crew had stacked the deck chairs and chained them together.

"Oh, dear," said Deedee, peering over the expanse of the after section of the Quarter Deck, where a few hardy souls were half jogging, half lurching, dodging behind the covered swimming pool, and circling the volleyball court—its net now furled and tied.

Sarah shrugged. "I'd be surprised if he spent the whole night out here. He'd have been soaked even in a blanket. Why not go up to the Boat Deck where there's more shelter?"

But the Boat Deck, although somewhat more populated with wan-looking passengers and lovers of the rolling sea doing their laps, was empty of Mr. Gerald Hofstra.

"Look," said Sarah, seeing Deedee's face beginning to crumple, "let's have breakfast, next check his stateroom, and then we can cover all the decks. And ask the ship's crew to help."

"No." Deedee almost yelled it and shook her head. "Richard is adamant. No negative publicity. But I agree to looking. We'll go after breakfast."

"We'll eat together," said Sarah. "And we can compromise. We won't ask for official help but we can use friends. Aunt Julia, Alex. Sam Greenbank. And Liza Baum, she's very sharp. And

Teddy. Even Teddy can be useful. And Julia's friend, Erik Anderson."

Deedee brightened. "And Aubrey Smith. Such a nice man. I'll ask him and his cousin and their southern friend, you know, Margaret."

Sarah hesitated, but what the hell. If her own interest in those three revived—and she hoped it wouldn't—well, it might be interesting to see if they threw themselves into the search or simply evaporated to meet in odd places about the ship. "Okay," she said. "And we could ask Aunt Julia's stewardess, Mary Malone, who is apparently Mother Macree in person. She might even open up Gerald's stateroom if he's still a no-show by noon."

Deedee bit her lip and then nodded. "Mary's a nice person. She might be willing. I met her because she's a friend of our Irish stewardess, Annie Maxie."

And so it was that the morning's activities for a certain number of passengers on a stormy Saturday were set. Julia, who disliked Gerald, announced that her needlepoint bag was missing and she would be looking for it so she might as well keep an eye out for the wretched man. And so could Erik and his grandchildren. Brian and Kirsten were running wild all over the ship as it was. Alex and Cousin Vivian said they would check out the midship passageways, the Chapel, and the Computer Center; Aubrey and Margaret the lower decks and the Wellington Spa; Teddy and Liza the Seaview Staterooms, the Peter Pan Nursery, and the Battledore Game Room; Richard and Deedee the upper deck rooms, restaurants, and theater; which left Sarah free to again circle the Quarter Deck and Shopping Gallery, although she could not picture Gerald Hofstra lurking among the evening dresses and perfumeries.

By noon, meeting by agreement in the Pickwick Grill—now sadly emptied of hearty eaters—some of the searchers had to admit defeat. "Not defeat," said Sarah. "We're working against all those hordes of people aboard." She shook her head at the remaining team members, Sam Greenbank, Deedee, Alex, and Richard. The Aubrey Smith trio had pleaded luncheon engagements, Julia was off with Erik Anderson, but everyone promised to keep looking.

"I've got to find him," insisted Richard, who was red in the face, irritable with futile searching, and likely, Sarah thought, to be suffering from nerves without his manager to support him.

"Lunch," said Alex. "Then we try the ship's personnel. As we should have from the beginning."

"No," said Deedee. "Mary Malone. I saw her a little while ago and she's agreed to help. See if he's . . ." She faltered.

"He's likely hiding out in his stateroom," said Sam Greenbank. "Hanging over a basin, and if he's that sick I don't blame him for not answering the phone or opening the door."

Lunch over, the searchers repaired to One Deck and found Mary Malone with a mound of linen and a collection of trays featuring half-filled teacups and partially bitten toast.

"I've been run off my feet," said Mary. "All those poor people who can't keep food on their stomachs and are too proud to ask for pills or don't believe in them."

But Deedee and Richard had no time to spare for the victims of the sea, and both reminded Mary Malone of her promised help.

"I shouldn't be doing this," said Mary. "A proper job it is for Security."

"Mr. Hofstra's my partner," said Richard. "He'd want me to come in. To check on him."

"Oh, please, Mary," said Deedee. "Just open the door. You needn't go in and we'll take every bit of blame."

And Mary, pursing her lips in disapproval, selected a key from a small collection in her uniform pocket, inserted it in the lock, turned the handle, pushed the door of number 1061 inward, backed away, and retreated down the passageway.

And Sarah, standing at the door, saw the blue and gold "Victoria Daily Programme" for Saturday, July first, together with the "Morning News" sheet just beyond the threshold, saw the empty cabin, the bed made, the blue counterpane pulled tight, its flowered eiderdown folded at the foot. Fresh towels laid out on the chair.

And saw the bathroom door that was open giving a full view of a muddled, towel-strewn interior.

16

RICHARD strode into the stateroom calling out, "Gerald, Gerald?" He was followed by Deedee and Sarah and Alex, the latter having been dragooned into what he referred to as a "break-in" because of the possibility that Gerald might have been rendered senseless by seasickness and would need emergency aid.

It didn't take more than a few seconds for each visitor to discover that the stateroom proper was empty, that Gerald Hofstra was not in the clothes locker nor had crammed himself under the bed. The bathroom, always a suspicious place with its electric outlets, running water, and toilet-kit collection of medicines and poisons, proved to be uninhabited. But in great disarray. Wet and crumpled towels lay underfoot, a tap dripped, a bottle of tablets labeled "For Motion Sickness" stood uncapped on a shelf, and an unpleasant mixed odor of vomit and mint mouthwash hung in the air.

One look inside the bathroom was quite enough. The group retreated to the healthier atmosphere of the stateroom, and Richard turned to Sarah accusingly. "You said you ran into Gerald and he meant to spend the night on deck."

Sarah shrugged. "He said so, but then I left, so he may have decided later to try bed. Those deck chairs are pretty hard, and if you're going to be sick anyway, why not be comfortable?"

Alex walked over to the telephone, consulted a plastic sheet of telephone numbers, lifted the receiver, punched in a number, and asked if a Mr. Gerald Hofstra had visited the clinic in the last twelve hours. "It's time," said Alex, putting his hand over the receiver and addressing the waiting group, "to do something by the book. I'm calling ship's clinic. Sarah"—here Alex fixed Sarah with a severe eye—"likes to look into things without being handicapped by protocol."

Sarah tried to think of a retort, a difficult task because, of course, Alex was right; none of them had any business in Gerald Hofstra's stateroom. But before she could speak Alex had turned back to the telephone.

"Yes, I see," he said. "What time was that? No, I'm not family, but his business partner is worried. They have to give a show tonight. Yes, the *Titanic*. Yes, I'm sure you're looking forward to it, but right now his partner, Mr. Herrick, wants to get in touch with him. Yes, Mr. Herrick is wonderful, but what time? Yes, you do that." Here Alex rolled his eyes at Sarah. "I've hooked a fan. The nurse has seen both shows and she can hardly wait." Then listened, nodding and tapping his foot impatiently.

"Yes. Okay, I've got that. No, you don't have to explain about the medication. I do understand. But not later than two-thirty. Did he say what he was going to do then? I see. Well, thanks very much. Good-bye."

Alex put down the receiver and faced Richard. "There you are. Gerald Hofstra went down to the clinic just before two-thirty A.M. He told the nurse that the medication he was taking for seasickness wasn't working, that he'd been trying to sleep out on deck and he needed something stronger. The nurse wouldn't tell me what the clinic people did or said—patient confidentiality and so forth—but I'd guess they tested his vital signs, pronounced him living, and sent him away. Perhaps gave him those tablets we saw in the bathroom. The nurse thought he said he was going out on deck again, but she wasn't sure because he also mentioned throwing up in his stateroom. End of story, but I think Richard and Deedee should hit the decks again. Gerald must be out there somewhere."

"But he was at the clinic in the middle of the night," exclaimed Deedee. "We've found him."

"We've found him at two-thirty A.M." said Richard in a discouraged voice. "Lot of good that does us."

"Can't we find out more of what happened in the clinic?" wailed Deedee. "He might be seriously ill."

"If he was," said Alex, "they would have kept him in the hospital."

"But you're a doctor," said Deedee. "Can't you go on down and find out what went on?"

Alex shook his head. "I have absolutely no authority to do anything of the sort."

"But how about your friend, Sam Greenberg or Greenbank? He knows the ship's surgeon, doesn't he?"

Alex sighed. "Okay. I'll look up Sam and see what I can find out. I'll get back to you if there's anything to report. Where will you be?"

"Deedee and I will be be searching all over the ship for him," said Richard firmly. "If he's on the ship we'll find him. And we hope Sarah here and those friends of hers will still be keeping their eyes open. If you want me I'll be in the Prince Albert Lecture Hall. We're using that instead of the Pinafore Theatre because it's bigger and we expect a crowd because, you know—"

But Alex cut what was undoubtedly going to be another rave review of the "Ships in Peril" programs. "See you later," he said and in five quick steps was out of the stateroom and hiking down the corridor.

And was immediately replaced by Mary Malone, standing in the doorway, a stack of fresh towels in her arms. "The regular stewardess, that's Annie Maxie, is a little under the weather," she explained. "Not seasick, something she ate, so I told her I'd fill in for her today since it's easier to tidy an empty cabin." She paused and looked in at the others. "He isn't here, is he? You didn't find him, did you?"

188

"No," said Richard shortly. "The stateroom is all yours. But if he turns up, please tell him I'm looking for him. The Prince Albert Lecture Hall. That it's getting late and I need him."

"Yes, Mr. Herrick," said Mary. "I'll keep it in mind." She stepped past him and pushed into the bathroom. And returned immediately. "It's a mop and pail and disinfectant I'll be needing," she said reprovingly. "This storm is ruining all the bathrooms and the beds, too."

"You mean," said Sarah, "it's ruining the passengers."

"That's what I said," returned Mary, banging out of the cabin and stamping down the hall.

"Okay," said Sarah. "Deedee, I'm going out on deck and look at the waves, and if I see Mr. Hofstra I'll rope and tie him for you."

With an eye to exploration in stormy weather, Sarah stopped in at their stateroom, noted that Alex had not returned, picked up her windbreaker and a head scarf, climbed the carpeted stairway—where two maids were at work with mops and pails—and walked unsteadily in an aft direction, occasionally reaching for the backs of chairs, through the Pickwick Grill, the Snuggery, past the library, on through the Osborne Cafeteria noting as she went the scarcity of passengers and the pallid faces of some of those present. She emerged outside beside the now-covered Quarter Deck pool and took up her station at the rail, the wind ballooning her jacket, snatching at her head scarf, flecks of ocean spray salting her face. She needed to think. And remember.

There was absolutely no point in reminding herself that she had sworn off any interest in shipboard affairs as lately as the previous evening. It was easier to give in to what amounted to an obsession than to go blithely about the ship as if God was in His heaven and all was right with the world. Well, He might be in His heaven for all she knew, but something was out of tune.

Mary Malone. Why did she seem sure Gerald Hofstra was not in his stateroom? She had told Annie Maxie that it was easier to tidy up when the passenger was absent. But until

Mary's key opened the stateroom door, no one knew if the manager was in. And Mary hadn't waited around to find out; she had scooted away down the hall as soon as the door was unlocked.

Sarah forced herself to open a Mary Malone file. What else do I know? she asked herself. Well, there was the woman's voice—or a countertenor male's—that she had heard outside of the utility closet. A voice with an Irish or Highland Scot's singsong. The pitch, she thought, was something the same as Mary's.

"Sarah. That's where you are. I've been looking for you. A good idea to be out here on deck. Out in the wind. Shows that going to sea isn't all crumpets and cream, as my mother used to say."

Sarah whirled around. Aunt Julia. Julia zipped into a bright green windbreaker, a white scarf snapping like a tiny flag at her throat. Julia's face was flushed, her steel-wool hair whipped into bunches of gray. But somehow she looked uncommonly pleased with life. But Sarah at that moment could have wished her dear aunt back in her cabin suffering ever so slightly with mal de mer.

"Hello, Aunt Julia," she said without enthusiasm.

"Well, it's obvious you haven't been pining for me. But I am glad to see you. I like to share a stormy day. Half the ship's company is flat on its back or bending over a basin. But Tom and I used to hang over the rail and shout into the wind. You ought to feel you're on an ocean, not just putt-putting along in a resort hotel. And have you found my needlepoint bag?"

"No, I haven't, and a lot of passengers wouldn't agree with you about loving the storm. But I do like to see everything whipped into a froth." She turned and studied her aunt and considered. Julia was observant. Julia could tell a hawk from a handsaw and often had done just that in a tight situation. In short, when the chips were down and Julia was focused, she could be damned useful.

Sarah took a deep breath and began. "Aunt Julia, please, don't go on about my sticking my nose in where it doesn't belong, but listen. For starters, it's about Mary Malone and Gerald Hofstra."

Julia gripped the rail and stuck her chin in the air, looking more than ever, Sarah thought, like an angry terrier. "I cannot abide that man," she said loudly. "He's what's wrong with the world. The so-called entertainment world, as they call it. And he dares to use the word 'theater.' Titillation from violence, that's what it is. The fact is he's making a fortune out of tragedies, so I hope no one has found him."

"Well, they haven't. Right now forget about the shipwreck programs and listen for one minute without saying a word. Some things don't add up, and Gerald Hofstra may be part of the puzzle. If it is a puzzle. First, I talked to him last night and he isn't quite as bad as you think. He just has a second-class dream of glory and it's probably not as sickening as half the movies or TV shows we all feed on."

"I don't feed on them," snapped Julia.

"Hush!" Sarah shouted into the wind. "Listen, we can't talk out here. Come on down to the Pickwick Grill." And, grasping her aunt by the arm, Sarah propelled her off the Quarter Deck and down the passageway to the Grill where she found a table with a splendid view of the roiled ocean. Settled there together, Sarah told her story.

And Julia listened. Sometimes Julia, who was fond of her niece, did listen, and now she leaned forward and paid attention as Sarah reviewed the case of Mary Malone's conviction of Gerald Hofstra's absence and then filled her in on the conversation overheard from the utility closet.

Here Julia exploded. "You spent the whole afternoon locked in a closet and didn't tell anyone?"

Sarah signaled silence. "First there was a man's voice with the sort of accent you hear in Cornwall. Or on *Poldark*. And our good waiter Frederick is from Cornwall, as we found out last night. I didn't hear that voice again but one like Mary Malone's. And the name Clancy was tossed in. There"—seeing the Clancy eyebrows lift—"I thought that might grab you. And maybe, although it's hard to hear through a door, the name Hogarth."

"I expect there are quite a few people on board from Cornwall just as there are other Clancys and Smiths, and besides, what does Frederick have to do with Mary Malone?"

"I suppose," Sarah said, "the crew members all know each other. Waiters and stewards and the maids probably all bunk down together in the crew quarters. Like one big family."

"You're right except for one thing. This is the *Vicky*'s maiden voyage. A lot of these crew people are meeting each other for the first time."

Sarah pursed her lips. Then shook her head. "Maybe they're old shipmates from some other boat. Anyway, there was a third voice. An American accent. Just a standard eastern U.S.A. voice. Nothing remarkable. Except this voice was the boss voice. He swore and told them they weren't supposed to be standing around."

"Well, if it was Mary Malone or Frederick, I suppose they weren't."

"You make it sound normal, but it wasn't. More as if the American voice was scolding someone and saying that 'they,' whoever they were, would be after someone. But the Irish voice wasn't disturbed and said no one was around, everyone was off having tea."

"I think," said Julia slowly, "that you're making a whole cake out of very little flour."

Sarah saw a waiter approaching—or rather teetering his way across the moving floor of the grill room. "Let's have something warm," she suggested. "Besides, it will keep the waiter from hovering."

Settled back with hot cups of spiced tea—a departure from the usual Darjeeling in deference to the weather—Sarah zeroed in on the matter at hand.

"Putting aside the idea that someone might have actually locked me in that closet, I'd like to review any little scenes you've had with Mary. Any American crew member you've run into."

And now it was Julia's turn. It meant a certain amount of data shuffling, but on the third long sip of tea and the first bite of a digestive biscuit, she nodded. "The red and green stickers on the cabin doorframes," she said. "Only three of them. Green to clean, and red, it has been cleaned."

"What!"

Julia explained. "Mary told me. They put a little sticker on the doorframe to show which staterooms haven't been cleaned. Not just tidied with clean towels, but a thorough cleaning. They do it twice a week at least. Mine had a red sticker because apparently it had been cleaned, but yours—the one that Hogarth boy had—had a green one, which meant it needed cleaning. But then a red one later which meant the cleaning was finished. General Gordon's had a green sticker because, of course, after what happened it would need a good scrubbing. It all seemed a bit odd so I did a little looking. Decks One, Two, and Three. Port and starboard. It was exhausting because I almost ran. But no other red and green stickers. I decided it must be a system only Mary Malone and some other maintenance people use and that it didn't mean very much."

Sarah looked doubtful. "It's odd only because I wouldn't think the *Vicky* people would want stickers on doors where they could be seen."

"Hardly seen," Julia corrected her. "Just tiny strips."

"Anything else?"

"Well, there was that chaplain's assistant I found in my cabin. An American who lives in England. He was going around handing out pamphlets. He seemed to know Mary. At least they were talking away when I walked in. I asked him what he thought he was doing."

Sarah grinned at her aunt. "A scene I can imagine."

"Yes, well, you know me. I don't like my home turf invaded. Especially by the pseudo-religious."

"What makes you think he was pseudo?"

"He was running around the ship passing out pamphlets of comfort and joy. Spreading the word. Not typically Episcopal."

"A lot of Episcopalians are evangelical these days," Sarah reminded her. "It's quite the thing. But I have met the real chaplain and he was more of the antique variety."

"I sent this specimen on his way. After all, this isn't a Bible ship or a missionary cruise."

"I don't think that his American accent and knowing Mary is really unusual. Assistant chaplains probably get around."

"Here I give you all these tidbits and you shoot them down."

Sarah put down her cup of tea. "I'm not shooting but I don't want to jump because I don't know what to jump at. Here we are setting up more suspects. But suspects of what? It's like Aubrey Smith and Cousin Vivian and friend Margaret. I simply suspect. Aubrey seems to have a key to General Gordon's cabin, did I tell you that? And he may have seen me watching him go in and so he may have locked me in the utility closet. And he warned me last night—in a fake humorous way—not to go prowling the deck at night. And to add to the mix, Vivian lies, and dear Margaret is not a belle of the Old South."

"My God, she's right off the plantation."

"She may have lived on the plantation, but she's also spent a fair piece of time in Britain. Yet Aubrey told us that she's on her way home from her first trip ever to the U.K.—or anywhere abroad. Just a little old homebody from Charleston."

"How on earth . . . ?"

"The fine-tuned ear of the English teacher. I bumped into her on deck last night. She was collapsed on a deck chair feeling worse for wear. Very seasick. Anyway, we had a conversation of sorts and she was very southern. All we needed were minstrels and corn pone and Robert E. Lee riding up on Traveller."

"So she was feeling sick and reverting to the Deep South."

"I think she was acting a part and because she was sick she was overacting. But the crux of the matter was that she referred to runs in her stockings as 'ladders,' said Vivian thought she should be in hospital, not in *the* hospital, and said something wouldn't be fair *on* me. Three goofs in two sentences."

"You're not making sense."

"Americans, as far as I know, say something isn't fair *to* them. Not fair *on* them. 'On them' is British usage. I remember that T. S. Eliot in *The Cocktail Party*, which is veddy veddy British, said 'fair to you' because he was American. It's not anything so noticeable as 'ladder' or being 'in hospital' but it's one of those little flags."

"A different word and two little prepositions and you think she's a spy."

"That's how spies give themselves away."

"But spying what? Spying on whom? And what has this woman to do with Mary Malone and Frederick our waiter and that chaplain's assistant?"

Sarah stood up. "Right now, that's what I'd give our Balmoral class stateroom to know. Maybe I'll try Margaret again. See how she reacts to questions about Fort Sumter and the Citadel. It might have something to do with Gerald Hofstra."

"And with General Gordon and the green sticker on his door?"

"Maybe. Even connected with that poor man—Lyman-Smith—run over in front of the Savoy."

"Random acts," announced Julia. But she didn't sound her usual confident self.

"And how about that little fainting spell of yours when you felt you were falling over the rail—or were being helped over? When you first came aboard."

"Vertigo. As Mary Malone said, I was excited by the trip."

"And you believed Mary? You've made dozens of trips across the ocean without having the vapors."

"But I'm older now. Not in such good shape, not so steady on my feet." But again, Julia, even to her own ears, didn't sound sure.

"Well, chew on all the things we've been saying. I think you've added a few pieces to our puzzle—"

"If it is a puzzle."

"Yes, if it is. We have to figure out how the Aubrey Clyde Smith team fits into any of this. And you'll keep an eye out for Gerald Hofstra? Maybe ask your friend Erik Anderson to help. I think if Gerald doesn't show by, say, teatime—or cocktail hour—Alex will put the squeeze on Deedee and Richard about going straight to the purser's office and, to borrow a phrase, make some waves. It's crazy having all these civilians looking around for the man when the crew could search much more efficiently."

"My friend, Erik," said Julia with a certain satisfaction, "is not the sailor he claimed to be. I've given him pills and ginger and said I'd join him for drinks before dinner if he felt up to it. He'll have to pull himself together and keep an eye on those grandchildren of his, Brian and Kirsten, who are raging around the boat with a couple of friends. Playing some kind of pirate game."

"But you like Erik? You enjoy his company?"

"I've decided that for now he's a fine shipboard friend who can talk horse. Are you concerned that Auntie might fall victim to someone who has designs on her farm and her animals?"

Sarah gave her aunt a knowing smile. "Maybe I thought so at first, but now I'm beginning to think it's more likely to be the other way round. That you'll euchre poor Erik out of some wonderful sixteen-hand competition beast and he won't know what hit him."

"It's an idea," said Julia. "But to be serious, what's next?"

"Maybe I'll pay the Chapel a visit and listen to the voice of this assistant and ask about pamphlet distribution. And flaunt the name of Mary Malone and see if he says he's never heard of her and has never consorted with a stewardess. And you?"

"I'll think about hunting up a few more stewardesses to discuss the use of stickers on cabins that need cleaning. And let me find Margaret Lee and have a chat about southern ways. I've spent a lot of time doing the southern equestrian circuit, and if Margaret's a fraud maybe she'll give herself away."

"I wish," said Sarah as she turned to leave, "that we'd tried to put some of this together before."

"If you'd be more careful and not get yourself shut up in utility closets, we might have," retorted Julia.

Sarah's trip to the Chapel bore small fruit. Only Father Peter Bottomley was in residence, and he was in his shirtsleeves, on hands and knees between pews. Confronted, he scrambled to his feet and dusted off his trousers. "I'm hunting for hymnals," he said. "We were to have a shipment of new ones for the maiden voyage, but no one can find the package. It's probably down in the hospital labeled intravenous fluid. So I was trying to see if a few of the old hymnals—some we got from a defunct cruise ship—had slipped down under the pews. You see, a late afternoon service has become quite the thing, especially after the ocean has started to act up. Passengers seem to feel that if they come to vespers they can run riot afterwards. We've been seeing people with bad hangovers. Very repentant they are."

It was the perfect opening.

"Goodness," exclaimed Sarah, restraining any more colorful expressions, "you can't take care of everyone on shipboard who needs"—she searched for the word and found it—"needs consolation. I heard that you have an assistant, an American. Doesn't he deal with hangovers and things like that?"

Father Bottomley nodded. "Yes, that's Amory Frye. He's been very useful, but after all, some people want, shall we say . . ."

"The real thing," put in Sarah.

"I suppose you could put it that way. Amory is interested in going to theological school and seems quite eager to help."

Another opening. Sarah stepped in. "All those pamphlets, you mean. His distributing them all over the ship."

Father Bottomley's eyebrows shot up. "Pamphlets? Distributing? Whatever do you mean?"

Sarah was pleased to explain and ended by saying that her Aunt Julia, although Anglican by persuasion, was not happy to find someone in her stateroom passing out pamphlets.

"Good Lord," said Peter Bottomley, looking shocked. "I should think not. We try for a low profile. We're here if we're needed, we go if we're called, but we don't go bustling around with religious tracts. And," he added sternly, "we do not go pushing ourselves into staterooms."

"Perhaps," murmured Sarah, "Mr. Frye saw Aunt Julia when she was being difficult"—an understatement if there ever was one, Sarah thought—"and he decided she needed guidance."

"No, no," insisted Father Bottomley. "Or at least, no for my part. I will have to find Amory at once and have this out."

"Or perhaps," suggested Sarah, "our stewardess, Mary Malone, is a friend of his. Aunt Julia said they were talking together when she walked into the cabin. Maybe Mr. Frye was trying to have a social moment and used the pamphlets as an excuse."

"That's even worse. That makes Amory Frye a liar."

"But the pamphlets are real?"

"Yes. We do have a number of brochures on different subjects, but they stay in my office or on the table in the back of the Chapel. They're part of a reach-out program for travelers. Nothing confrontational, commonplace stuff, really. Anglican missions in the Sudan, the place of the Dead Sea Scrolls in the liturgy, hunger relief, fellowship with other Christian denominations."

Sarah had heard enough. "Please don't mention my visit to Mr. Frye. It's not important and if I see him I'd have to say I'm sorry for my aunt's biting his head off."

Father Bottomley gave a short laugh. "I'd say he deserved what he got."

And Sarah departed, thinking to find a quiet nook in which to digest the possibility that Father Peter Bottomley was sheltering a questionable assistant. But as she stepped into the passageway she walked directly into a man who, head down, was aiming at the open chapel door. And as they both straightened and Sarah heard the accents of her native land in apology, saw the sober gray trousers and the navy blazer, she knew she was in luck.

"Oh, Mr. Frye," she said, holding out her hand. "I've heard about you. From my Aunt Julia. She met you talking to her stewardess, Mary Malone, who's a friend of yours. You were handing out pamphlets, but Father Bottomley says you don't usually. Hand out pamphlets, I mean." And Sarah with effort smiled the smile of a naive and interested visitor.

Amory Frye, suitably flustered, confused at the presence of an unknown female who seemed to know him, could only gabble incoherently something about not knowing the household staff personally, so many of them, and making calls "to let people know what services are available." And then, gathering steam, he added that he and Father Bottomley tried to be there for everyone aboard. "Not just Anglicans, Episcopalians, but every passenger who needs to talk."

Sarah, listening to the pitch of the voice, its intonation, nodded without taking in anything the man said. She had heard enough. "A wonderful day, isn't it, Mr. Frye," she said. "I do love a big storm, don't you?" And, before he could speak again, she was gone, walking with determination as far away as she could get.

By the time Sarah had found her way back up to One Deck and her own corridor she had put everything in a neat basket. Mr. Frye and Mary Malone not only knew each other and met for conversation (with or without pamphlets), but one of them at least had briefly joined in talk with Frederick of the Windsor Castle Dining Room—Frederick late of Cornwall. Now she needed to find out whether Aubrey Clyde Smith et al. had ties to any of the above. Three questionable employees of the good ship *Victoria*; three dubious passengers.

Walking slowly down the corridor on One Deck, mulling the possibility that there were six people on board who might, each in his or her own way, be up to no good, Sarah was stopped cold by a heavy hand on her shoulder.

She whirled. Liza Baum.

"Hey, hold up," said Liza. "Listen, are you all still looking for Gerald what's-his-name?"

Sarah gaped at her. "You haven't found him?"

"Yes. Just now. After all this commotion and everyone racing around. I found out the number of his stateroom. It's ten-sixty-one."

"But where is he?"

"Where he should be if he's feeling lousy. In the stateroom."

"You *saw* him!"

"No, not exactly. But there's a 'Don't Disturb' sign on the door and the stewardess, Mary somebody—she was doing up another room—said he must have come back because the sign wasn't there earlier when she cleaned his stateroom. Come on and see for yourself."

They did. Cabin 1061. And there it was. In black and white. A DO NOT DISTURB sign hanging at a slight angle from the polished metal doorknob.

17

FOR a minute both women stared at the sign, then Sarah shook her head. "I don't know if seeing is believing. Let me try to find Mary Malone. She's the stewardess who's filling in for someone else. You hang in here and if Gerald Hofstra makes a bolt for it, knock him down and sit on him."

"Gladly," said Liza. "I can use the exercise."

Sarah disappeared down the passageway and returned almost immediately. "Mary Malone is down the line in another stateroom. She says she heard from a steward on a different corridor that Gerald Hofstra said he felt awful and was going into his cabin and wanted to be left alone."

"You believe this?" asked Liza.

"It sounds reasonable. In keeping with Gerald's routine. You know, sit on deck, go to cabin, throw up, go to clinic, throw up, go back on deck again. I don't think we have to break into the stateroom just to prove the man is there hanging over a basin."

"It's all very boring," said Liza. "I can think of a dozen more interesting solutions to this. Like finding Gerald decapitated in the Snuggery or in a hypnotic trance trying to balance on the Boat Deck railing."

Sarah grimaced. "Let's just stick to boring. Your friend Lyman-Smith and General Gordon being dead is enough for one trip."

"Amen," said Liza. Then, "So that's that. The hunt's over."

"Right," said Sarah. "And we should tell Deedee. She and Richard have been running around like rabbits with their heads chopped off."

"I thought it was chickens."

"Chickens, hens, rabbits. Anyway, they'll be happy. At least Richard will be. I don't think he likes the idea of going solo without Gerald's theatrical razzle-dazzle. But I'd say Deedee wouldn't have minded if their manager had vanished into thin air."

Liza looked at her watch. "It's past four. How about going up on deck and lash ourselves to the mast and have tea or drinks or something bracing? I told Teddy I'd meet him on Quarter Deck. I gave him a few hours to resist temptation all by himself. I can't hound him forever. If he's still sober when we hit New York we might see each other around town. But I'm not holding my breath."

"But so far, so good."

"Yeah. He's looking a little more wholesome. His face was the color of blue cheese when we left Southampton. Now it's more like cheddar."

"All right," said Sarah. "I could use some deck time. I've been indoors mostly, scooting around looking for Gerald."

"Okay," said Liza cheerfully. "Come on, we'll find Deedee and Richard and spread the good word."

"That Gerald is in his cabin?"

"He may be in his cabin," said Liza, "but he may also be a very sick no-show item tonight."

"We," said Sarah, "have done our bit. Now it's up to the Herricks and maybe the doctor if they want to revive him."

Deedee Herrick was discovered on Stair C looking pale and generally tumbled. She was hanging on to the banister for balance and working her way up, peering at passengers as if she expected Gerald Hofstra to be in some sort of exotic disguise.

Sarah gave her the glad news—if a sequestered and nonresponsive Gerald could be so described. But Deedee brightened, clasped her hands together, and made a little chirping sound.

"Don't get your hopes up," said Liza. "He may stay in his cabin until we hit New York."

"Never mind," said Deedee. "Now that we know where he is, Richard will ferret him out. Richard can be very determined."

Deedee's prediction was accurate. Richard was found in the empty Prince Albert Lecture Hall checking sound cues.

"I'll go right now," said Richard. "He has to get up."

"He won't answer," Sarah warned. "And he's hung a 'Don't Disturb' sign on his door."

Richard paused in midstride. "I'll phone," he announced. "Tell him he's got to be down here by six at the latest." And Richard flung open one of the lecture hall's big double doors and disappeared. And reappeared in seven minutes' time. "He sounds sick as the devil," said Richard. "I could hardly make out what he was saying. Something about not to worry. To go on ahead as he might not make it. But I'm calling again at five-thirty."

"And we," said Liza, "are going topside. Deedee, do you want to join us? Teddy Hogarth, Sarah, and me. Tea on the rolling brine"

Richard looked up. "I need Deedee. I can't do this alone. Deedee, I really need you."

And from the almost proud expression on Deedee's face, Sarah guessed that Richard had not used those words since Gerald Hofstra had taken up the reins of management. Liza and Sarah left the two together and made for the after Quarter Deck.

There they found Teddy Hogarth in the possession of several deck chairs pushed into a sheltered corner together with a pile of blankets, trays of tea with a quantity of scones, slices of Dundee cake, brandy snaps, tightly rolled little mushroom and watercress sandwiches, triangles of shortbread, and several slabs of a dark and sinister plum cake.

"We can eat here," said Teddy, "and we won't have to shout at each other. The waiter who brought the trays almost threw up looking at all this stuff."

"My God," said Liza, "are you trying to kill us?"

"It's a funny thing about alcohol—not having it, I mean—I'm ready to eat an ox. And I'm not seasick, which is a little odd except I've been gobbling up wads of ginger."

"It all looks marvelous," said Sarah, folding herself into her blanket and trying to keep a steady hand for the teacup; the ship seemed to have added a fore-and-aft pitching to a now augmented side-to-side movement. She looked around the deck and viewed the scene by the covered swimming pool. Only a few hardy souls sat hunched in chairs.

"They're falling one by one," said Liza. "I'm glad we're not going around the Horn because that might really get to me."

"Pass the scones," said Teddy. "My addictive personality needs to be fed."

"It's no joke," said Liza, scowling at him.

Sarah let the two of them get on with it. She sipped her tea, chewed her way through mushroom and watercress, and ended with a divinely crumbling piece of shortbread, and then closed her eyes and allowed the cradle of the deep to take hold.

She woke some time later, aware of a scuffling by her side. Liza and Teddy were throwing off what the Elizabethans called "lendings"—blankets, jackets, coats, and shoes.

She sat up blinking. "What on earth are you doing?"

Liza grinned. "We have this little idea. Everybody's gone in from around the swimming pool. We thought we'd take a little dip. Work off some of the food."

"But," said Sarah, "the swimming pool's closed. They've drained it, haven't they? And it's covered."

"No," said Teddy. "I looked. It's half full."

"Half full," said Liza with a mischievous look, "is enough."

Sarah shook her head. "You are both crazy and you'll both be nailed to the mast." She looked at her watch. "Oh, God, it's almost six-thirty. I can't be late again for dinner. Okay, enjoy. Me, I'm settling for a hot bath. Teddy, thanks for the tea. It was lovely."

But Teddy was already letting his trousers slide down to his ankles, revealing a pair of boxer shorts made out of a Union Jack. "Wait up," he called. "Take this to Gerald. Or to Deedee and Richard." He held up a bright blue nylon windbreaker and with his thumb indicated a heavily inked *"Hofstra"* inside the collar. "I found it earlier behind our deck chairs. Gerald must have left it here on one of his deck visits."

Sarah accepted the jacket, holding it gingerly by thumb and forefinger. Who knew what Gerald had in it, or had done on it? "Okay," she said, "I'll drop it off. He was sitting about here last night. He must have been too sick to notice he'd left it."

But Sarah, yearning for a bathtub foaming with Vitabath, found it was not to be. At least not yet. First, there was the jacket, received gratefully by Richard—further proof to them that somewhere there really was a Gerald Hofstra. And second, she was stopped by, of all people, her favorite object of speculation, Aubrey Clyde Smith.

"Aha," said Mr. Smith, confronting Sarah at the door of the Disraeli Library. "Just the person. We need to talk."

Sarah bit her lip. Aubrey Smith was not on her present agenda. And if he was to be on it later she wanted to be prepared and perhaps accompanied.

"Sorry, Mr. Smith, I mean Aubrey, but I'm off to our stateroom. Alex expects me and I'm already late." It was time, she thought, to emphasize the joint nature of her life aboard ship. She hoped that Aubrey would think that this reference might mean that Alex would spring into action the second he decided she was not where she should be.

Aubrey indicated the library. "Call and say you'll be a few minutes late. There's a telephone on the desk."

"I'm afraid . . ." Sarah began.

"I'm afraid," said Aubrey, "that I must insist. It's quite important. And I know just the place to talk." Here Aubrey fastened his hand firmly around Sarah's upper arm and before she could dig in her heels had rotated her half a circle. "Not the Snuggery. We can go to the Harrods shop. It's closed now. And even if you don't want to call Alex, I need to make a call. Don't leave," he said in such a voice of command that Sarah, who had been planning a twisting escape motion and a flight in another direction, paused. And reconsidered. By offering to let her call Alex he had defused the idea that she was about to be kidnapped. And a man who could command entrance to Harrods after hours must have some connection with officialdom. Or, and this was a chilling thought, did he have a collection of master keys? First General Gordon's room and now Harrods. These conflicting ideas, to which were added a sense that here at last might be the answer to some of the shipboard puzzles, left Sarah standing uneasily just inside the library door.

"That's that," said Aubrey Smith. "It's arranged. And I left a message for Alex saying you'd be along soon. Now, please, come with me. The Harrods shop will be just the thing. Nothing in there but a lot of silent tweeds and woollies. And several comfortable chairs. I've used them while Vivian was busy trying on gloves."

And Sarah allowed herself to be led down Stairway E from the Quarter Deck to the Harrods shop where, not entirely to her surprise, Aubrey produced a key. Either Aubrey really had friends in high shipboard places or he had a number of accomplices. But at that thought, Sarah remembered Margaret Lee, shivered slightly, and to be safe, made a note that the Princess Alice Lounge that lay forward of Harrods might prove a haven in case of the need to escape. She would keep the shop's exit door in sight, be ready to run for it, ready to scream her head off.

Aubrey Smith, however, made no attempt to herd Sarah into a place of isolation. He merely switched on the overhead light and drew two green leather chairs together.

"Now," he said, "all we need is a pint of bitters and a good piece of Stilton."

"What we need," said Sarah with asperity, "is for you to tell me what this is all about."

Aubrey leaned back in his chair and folded his hands across his slightly rounded stomach. He was wearing, under his worn tweed jacket, one of those buff-colored wool waistcoats that reminded Sarah strongly of nineteenth-century home comfort. Now he regarded her for what seemed like several minutes and then shook his head.

"I had no intention of bringing you—or any passenger— into this. But I've learned from a few chats with your Aunt

Julia—and a few grumblings from your husband Alex—that you have a propensity for walking a slippery plank. No." Aubrey raised his hand for silence. "Let me talk. Then it's your turn. First, I did notice your interest in the Chapel when I and my friends were there, and yes, I did see you peering at me when I was visiting the hospital, and I must say you have a talent for turning up in every nook and cranny aboard ship. I play bridge and you're there, I am part of a jolly dinner group and I see you watching me. In fact, you positively make my flesh crawl, especially when I see you hovering at the end of the passageway as I am entering General Gordon's stateroom, and then, to cap it all, you vanish into a utility locker. From which you do not emerge. So I assume you ducked in there voluntarily since here you are, out of it. But if you were locked in and later released I'd like to hear the story. I did try, you know, to keep the locker in view, but finally other duties called me elsewhere."

Sarah fastened on the tag end of Aubrey's speech. "Duties? You have duties? Aboard ship? I thought you said . . ."

"That this was a pleasure trip with my dear long-lost cousin, Vivian, and her friend Margaret from South Carolina."

"Margaret," said Sarah resentfully, "is not from South Carolina."

Aubrey shook what could only be called a reproachful finger at her. "Oh, but she is. She has a house—a condo, I think she calls it—near Charleston. At the Kiawah Resort. Margaret is an ardent golfer and the place has a number of golf courses, all of which are, I believe, entirely surrounded by golf-ball-eating alligators."

But Sarah was not to be humored. She leaned forward in her chair and glowered at Aubrey Smith. "I don't care where Margaret spends her vacations, but the woman isn't a southerner. She grew up or she's spent a lot of time in Britain."

Aubrey opened his eyes slightly wider and unlaced his hands. "What makes you think that?"

"She overdoes the southern act and she uses British expressions. When she was feeling seasick she slathered on the accent so that she sounded like a southern caricature, plus she slipped up on word usage. U.K. expressions, a preposition."

"You would hang a woman because she misplaces a preposition?"

"No, but—"

Aubrey looked at his watch. "Time is slipping away. Put Margaret and Vivian aside for the time being. Here's what I have to say. I do have duties. I have been asked by certain parties to keep an eye out for untoward activities. A year or so ago several advertisements appeared in British newspapers, and one or two in American and European ones. The person or persons who placed the ads wanted to get in touch with anyone who felt that their families had been injured or had their lives adversely affected by a passenger ship mishap. As you know, survivors from various disasters have formed reunion groups; this is the reverse. Not reunion meetings but meetings for the purpose of taking some sort of arcane revenge. Revenge for injuries done to families many, many years ago. Injuries that were the direct result of some maritime disaster. Recently British newspapers have received some garbled messages to the effect that 'revenge is coming.' We have had a suspicion that *Victoria* may be a 'target ship' for this sort of action. And that some persons aboard may have actually come together as a result of these newspaper notices and now have something very nasty in mind."

Sarah shook her head in disbelief. "Are you saying these are terrorists? And what sort of revenge? For what sort of injuries?"

"We don't know if these are terrorists in the political sense or persons acting from a feeling of personal injury. And we don't know what these people intend. We—my superiors—are guessing the threats relate to one or more ocean disasters in the last eighty or so years. Domestic disasters, not war ones. I can't imagine that these go back more than three generations, four at the most."

"You mean like the *Titanic*? People who lost family members?"

"That's a possibility. Or the *Lusitania*. The *Andrea Doria*."

"But that's an Italian liner."

"*Andrea Doria* is an outside guess. Most possibly an English ship was the culprit, though it may not matter what company owned the ships. *Lusitania* was Cunard but *Titanic* was the White Star Line, and that's defunct."

"But you mean random acts against random people."

"We're not sure the choice of victims is entirely random. It's just possible that the threats—despite the newspaper notices—have nothing to do with a maritime disaster. It could be the IRA aiming at a British ship, British citizens. They make just as good a target on board a ship, I suppose, as if they were in the middle of Piccadilly. Or queuing up for boarding passes at Heathrow."

"How about Libya, the Arabs, the Israelis? The Basques?"

"We think not. The newspaper notices gave a sense that British ships or British passengers would be the focus of an attack."

Sarah was silent and then turned on Aubrey. "Just tell me why I should believe any of this?"

"I refer you to Captain Mitchie. Would you like to make a call to the bridge? There's a phone over there on the counter."

Sarah hesitated. Calling the master of the *Victoria* seemed a rather drastic move. Besides, she wanted to hear more.

"I'm not allowed," Aubrey went on smoothly, "to go into details. Our contacts have suggested that these persons might plan to pick off several people—the number three was mentioned—each time this ship—or any British ship—crosses the ocean."

"But you called the *Victoria* the target ship," Sarah said.

"It's an informed guess. We think a *Titanic* link to the *Victoria* might make sense. Both on their maiden voyages."

"Has any of this been confirmed?"

"We have reason to believe that Donald Lyman-Smith was deliberately run over in London just before we sailed."

"But that was in London," Sarah objected.

"Donald Lyman-Smith and General Gordon had tickets for first-class—Balmoral class—passage on *Queen Victoria*'s maiden voyage. There was a wave of hard feeling after *Titanic* went down that first-class passengers survived at the expense of third class. And it's believed by the ship's medical people—

as well as by your friend, Sam Greenbank, who was called in—that some of the general's cranial injuries are not explained by a fall into a doorframe."

"But the two men don't have anything in common, do they?" And then Sarah remembered. "Yes, they do. The trade commission."

"We think that's a red herring or a coincidence. The trade commission is of very small consequence. I don't see any terrorist or revenge group worth its salt bothering with it."

"But I told you Teddy Hogarth's stateroom was entered in the middle of the night. Someone with a Harrods bag. But you see, Alex and I had traded cabins. And Teddy is on the trade commission. Of course, you asked for the Harrods bag so for all I know you were the one who entered the stateroom and you were retrieving damaging evidence." And Sarah gave Aubrey a tight little smile.

And Aubrey returned it. "Now that is an interesting idea. I'll have to think about how to answer you. In the meanwhile we've been asking ourselves what else besides the trade commission do General Gordon and Mr. Lyman-Smith have in common."

"Besides being Anglo-Saxon males with first-class tickets?"

"Consider the names Smith and Gordon. Captain Smith was the captain of *Titanic* and there have always been questions about his performance that night. And Sir Cosmo Duff Gordon was one of the men who did manage to find a place in a lifeboat."

"I think," said Sarah slowly, "that it's all very far-fetched. After all, as you said, there are a multitude of Smiths aboard and probably a few Gordons."

"We have to start somewhere," said Aubrey quietly. "If revenge for a catastrophe plays a part, we can't leave *Titanic* or its crew or passengers out of it. We have people watching other British ships, of course, and aboard the *Vicky* we've started a background check on personnel and some of the passengers, trying to go back several generations to see if we can find a common thread."

"But my God, that will take years."

"It isn't easy, but we have computer searches going and

undercover people aboard whose specific job is to meet passengers and drag out life stories. If the revenge seekers—that sounds like a boy's adventure book—if these people really feel aggrieved they may say too much. Boast. Tell the sad story."

Sarah nodded. "You mean, I'm a penniless orphan because Great-grandfather was lost on the *R.M.S. Bathsheba* and me mum had to go and work as a charwoman instead of me dad inheriting the title and me being Lady Slopover."

Aubrey's mouth widened into the first genuine expression of pleasure Sarah had seen on his face since the so-called conversation had begun. "Your Aunt Julia said you dabbled in fiction. Well, this whole business has fictional qualities. Unlikely as it all sounds, stranger things have happened for stranger reasons. Two men are dead, and now this Gerald Hofstra is missing. He's a first-class passenger and he's doing a show on the *Titanic* sinking. The security people don't know officially that he's missing, but they know unofficially and they're looking around. We had his cabin searched very early this morning but he wasn't there. And we haven't found him anywhere else."

"Relax on that score," Sarah told him. "He's back in his bunk with a 'Don't Disturb' sign on his door."

Aubrey shook his head. "Anyone can have a sign on his door and be at the bottom of the ocean."

"Richard Herrick called the cabin and Gerald answered. Said he was too sick to function now but would try to make the show."

Aubrey pushed back his chair and stood up. "Well, good. That's that. At least for now. But if Hofstra doesn't turn up by show time I will arrange to have his cabin entered and searched." Here Aubrey took hold of Sarah's arm as she rose to her feet, kept his hand firmly in place, and looked Sarah directly in the eye. "Please do not discuss what I've been saying. With anyone."

Sarah shook free from Aubrey's grasp and moved behind the leather armchair, her eye on the doorway. "Do you want to tell me about Margaret Lee and your cousin, Vivian? Are they working out of MI6, or is it the CIA? Or are they ship's officers in drag?"

Aubrey Smith extended his hand, reached for Sarah's, and shook it firmly. "We're agreed, yes? So let's leave those two ladies out of this. And do be careful walking on a rolling ship. A woman from Pennsylvania lost her balance this afternoon and broke her arm in two places. And thanks so much for your help . . ."

"I only listened and I didn't help," she said with some irritation.

"To some advantage, I hope. To help you be a little cautious and cease from trailing after me. Or after Gerald for that matter. He may be bad news. What's the expression, an attractive nuisance? And tell me, I am burning with curiosity. Were you locked in the utility room or was that part of a surveillance scheme of yours?"

Sarah hesitated and then decided that an honest answer would not be dangerous. "I honestly don't know. I didn't want you to see me watching you so I slipped inside. I thought at first I was locked in, but maybe I snapped the lock when I closed the door. Later, I fell asleep, and when I woke up, the door was open."

"And you saw nothing, heard nothing?"

"Voices," she admitted. "But I'm not sure I could identify them again." I'm not going to give this man everything, Sarah told herself. At least not now. Aloud she added, "One man with an English accent, maybe one Irishwoman. One American."

"That's not too useful. Plenty of English and Irish aboard, crew and passengers. And Americans are as common as cockroaches."

"What a nice expression," said Sarah. "Why don't you try it on Aunt Julia."

"Speaking of Mrs. Clancy—a woman I admire with caution—we may have to put her on the Gerald Hofstra suspect list if he doesn't turn up. She is almost rabid on the subject of *Titanic* movies and shows because her family apparently lost an uncle when *Titanic* sank. She's certainly made her opinion of Mr. Hofstra very clear. I heard her myself say that she hoped he'd be washed overboard."

"I know," said Sarah. "If Julia gets an idea in her head, it isn't easy to dislodge."

"Of such material are terrorists made. And she fits the profile."

"Not Aunt Julia," protested Sarah. "She's all growl and snap. She hardly ever bites anyone."

"How reassuring," said Aubrey, and together they left the Harrods shop, probably the only two passengers who, after spending more than half an hour surrounded by high-class luxury merchandise, had not had the slightest urge to make a purchase.

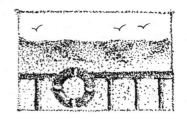

18

THE closer Sarah's steps brought her to the stateroom and the longed-for bath, the less confident she became of Aubrey Smith's story. Why had he taken the Harrods bag? And had he made any attempt to validate himself? Show an ID, a scrap of paper with an official seal or signature? A little note from MI6 or whatever secret intelligence outfit it was that Kim Philby and his buddies had bamboozled? Or at least a chit from the *Victoria*'s captain stating that "this identifies Aubrey Clyde Smith as one of our faithful investigators of suspicious persons"?

Sarah slowed her steps in the passageway. It should be easy enough to verify Aubrey's position. After all, Aubrey had said she could call the captain, and certainly he wouldn't have suggested it if he had qualms about being supported. Could it be that Aubrey had fooled the entire complement of ship's officers, he and his so-called cousin and her so-called friend?

Or perhaps he made the suggestion to phone because he was pretty damn sure she would be reluctant to drag the captain away from his duties on the bridge to ask if Mr. Aubrey Smith was all that he claimed to be. Wouldn't the captain be busy not only with a substantial storm on his hands but, since this was the fourth day out, wouldn't there be a possibility of icebergs?

When did icebergs show up, anyway? Everyone knew that icebergs were still a very real hazard in the North Atlantic. And, as the captain's column in the "Victoria Daily Programme" had noted, icebergs, the wonders of electronics notwithstanding, are watched for by men with binoculars and given respect as well as a wide berth.

No, Sarah would not call the captain. He had better things to do. However, she would keep a sharp eye on Aubrey and his two cohorts, because what would be a better ploy than pretending to hunt down these shapeless, shadowy revenge seekers while all the time you are working on your own little destructive scheme? Perhaps Aubrey himself was a grandson of a *Titanic* or *Lusitania* victim and his two lady friends were of the same ilk. Or, more frightening, members of some genuine terrorist organization.

Arrived at her stateroom, Sarah thrust her key into the lock and entered. If Alex is in, she decided, I'll tell him the whole thing even if I'm not supposed to. Find out if he's seen through Aubrey Smith. The trouble was that Alex was something of a straight arrow as far as people went. He tended to believe that what you saw was what you got. That was a doctor for you. Doctors—other than psychiatrists, of course—usually thought in terms of demonstrable pathology, what the lab and the EKG and the MRI showed, and had little truck with the sort of symptoms that attracted Sarah. Even Aubrey's visit to General Gordon's cabin wouldn't have turned Alex into a bloodhound. He would have said that the cleaned room was now available, and perhaps Vivian and Aubrey had thought of it for Margaret and had wanted to check it out. As for Margaret using British expressions, Alex would laugh and point out that certain British words like "loo," "telly," and "fridge" had long ago embedded themselves in the speech of many Americans.

So perhaps it was just as well, Sarah thought, that Alex was not in their cabin and therefore not available to make remarks about her overheated brain. A scribbled note lying on his bed announced that cocktails had been set for seven o'clock in the Balmoral Lounge and to practice her French—an unlikely request that left Sarah exactly where it found her.

The Balmoral Lounge, usually teeming with predinner jollity and bustle, was almost empty. The heaving and rolling ship had continued to exact its toll, and Sarah found that with the exception of a few groups, pale of face but still bravely dressed in evening splendor, the huge tartan-draped lounge with its separate clusters of tartan-covered sofas and chairs offered a degree of privacy. She hesitated at the open doors of the lounge, trying to pick out Alex and Aunt Julia and speculating on why the cocktail hour required a knowledge of French. And, ah, there was Julia. Or rather Julia plus Erik Anderson, who must have recovered his sea legs. The two were sitting on the port side of the room, leaning over a small curly-legged table, and doing something with glasses, sandwiches, and small plates. Both were in animated talk and Julia was gesturing.

Then across the room she spied Alex and discovered his drinking companions to be none other than Sam Greenbank—which was to be expected—but also their dinner companions, the cheerful Charles and the almost recumbent form of a ghost-like Marci, but, wonder of wonders, also the unfriendly Charlotte and Adèle. Was their appearance the reason she'd been told to practice her French? Sarah paused in the act of traversing the room—a long rope had been extended down the center of the room as an aid to navigation—and gaped. Was Alex out of his mind? Who wanted to spend even a minute more in the company of those two females? Certainly not she, Sarah. Was it too late to retreat? Yes, Alex had raised a hand in salutation and Sam was beckoning.

She would, with reluctant feet, join them because it was always possible that Charlotte and Adèle had had a personality transplant since last night's dinner. But she would join the party by way of Julia and Erik and so get a fix en route on that couple. She grasped the back of a chair as the great ship gave an extra shudder and roll and then cautiously found her way over to her aunt and her companion.

Julia was in her familiar crimson paisley, to which a black scarf and a pearl pin had been added, her hair was brushed, and she gave off a faint scent of Shalimar; Erik was in a white dinner jacket, a maroon tie and cummerbund, with a white carnation as a boutonnière. Both were rather red in the face, possibly the result of drink combined with heated conversation. They reminded Sarah of a cairn terrier seated next to an amiable and well-dressed bull.

Julia waved a hand. "There you are. What have you been up to all day? Nosing about and making false accusations, I suppose. Have you seen what Alex has picked up? The sisters from hell. I think he must be out of his mind, but he's got them laughing and chatting, although they're probably about to put cyanide in his whiskey. Thank heavens for Erik. He was going to join in but I dragged him over here."

"I'm always willing to be dragged," said Erik affably. "Besides, your aunt has got me jumping over the hoops. Literally."

Julia indicated a ballpoint pen lying next to the stem of a wineglass. "I'm showing him how to improve his cross-country course. He's got too many tight fences and the water jump comes much too early. He needs to move it far over here to the left." Here Julia indicated three crackers laden with slivers of salmon.

"But I think," said Erik, "that the novice riders like to get the water obstacles over early on. It builds confidence."

"Wrong," said Julia, reaching for a small paper napkin in the Royal Stuart tartan and rolling it into a log and placing it beyond the ballpoint pen. "If you arrange for a brush and an easy oxer at the very start . . ."

Sarah gave up. Even Adèle and Charlotte might be preferable to time spent with these two arguing over fences. She waved good-bye and after a treacherous lurch into a small sofa, she sat down at the edge of an animated group where Alex, with paper and pencil in hand, was making little track marks on a piece of paper. Charlotte and Adèle, in floral prints under their usual silk vests, sat each on a side, Adèle clutching a book, heads bent over Alex's artistic efforts. Sarah, as she sat down and nodded at Sam Greenbank, Charles, and the languid, white-faced Marci, could only wonder if Alex had suddenly found a talent for sketching or, more likely, was explaining the niceties of some medical horror like a malignancy of the lungs or a closure of some vital duct.

The conversation, lively and bilingual, left Sarah for the first few moments in a state of confusion. Alex was expounding in a bastard mix of French and English, emphasizing his words with his pen, and the sisters were bobbing their heads and saying things like, *"Ah, je comprends. Mais non, c'est incroyable. Mais où se trouve le grand puffin de l'Atlantique?"*

Alex reached for Adèle's book, and Sarah saw that it was a French-language bird book, the *Guide des Oiseaux d'Amerique du Nord.* He ruffled the pages and pointed with his pen. "The greater shearwater, *Puffinus gravis,*" he said.

And Sarah saw light. Alex was doing his bird thing. Somehow he must have discovered that the sisters were bird-watchers and in need of ornithological guidance and so had moved in to fill the void. Aubrey Smith faded in interest and Sarah turned to Sam Greenbank for enlightenment.

"Good old Alex. He found them on deck trying to spot sea-birds, but the boat was pitching and their binoculars were covered with spray and the light was awful, so he told them that he'd help them make a list of North American birds they would be likely to see. They're going to New York, Boston, and then on to Quebec and Nova Scotia. They're both mad about theater and birds."

Marci lifted her head from the back of the chair. She was dressed in a gold and white shift that did nothing for her sallow complexion. "I thought they were just a rude pair of nasty French ladies, but maybe I'm wrong. Maybe I'm not thinking positively because I'm not a bit well. I'm drugged up to my eyes, so everything seems peculiar."

Charles took possession of Marci's limp hand and stroked it. "She'll feel better any minute. She's going to try broth and a few crackers and maybe a Jell-O, aren't you, hon?"

Hon let her head fall back on the tartan-covered chair back, drew a filmy mauve shawl over her shoulders, and smiled weakly. "Whatever you say, Charlie."

"You need something in your stomach and then you'll be

able to stay up for the *Titanic* show. It's supposed to be the feature attraction of the trip," he informed Sarah.

"Yes," agreed Sarah. "That's what I've been told."

Sam looked up from contemplation of a short goblet filled with darkest amber. In defiance of the ship's suggestion that gentlemen wear evening dress or a dark suit, Sam was decked out in white flannels and a natty double-breasted bottle-green blazer with a yellow bow tie. "I understand," he said, "that Gerald Hofstra is still a man of mystery. That he's locked himself in his stateroom and does not wish to be disturbed."

"That's what I hear," said Sarah cautiously.

"You mean," said Marci with slightly more energy, "that he might not be there to run those special effects we've heard about?"

"Time," said Sam, "will tell."

"I've seen the movie and read all about the *Titanic*," began Charles. "The whole thing is absolutely incredible . . ."

Sarah turned back to Alex and the sisters, who had moved on from the greater shearwater to the possibility of seeing one of the larger owls. Charlotte, it appeared, was lusting after the *grand-duc d'Amerique* or great horned owl. Charlotte and Adèle had obviously accepted Alex as someone who, if not exactly a candidate for friendship, was at least a holder of useful information, and as far as their personalities would allow, they were in a state of semiaffability, a fact Sarah thought boded well for the dinnertime atmosphere.

Which it did. The eight o'clock seating in the Windsor Dining Room was at less than half strength, and Sarah, as she was pushed gently into her chair by Frederick, was able to imagine passengers by the hundreds supine on their berths, sipping seltzer water and perhaps trying a few spoonfuls of consommé.

The bird theme continued through the dinner; Sam, in his high school French, proved himself knowledgeable and was able to contribute with the help of the bird guide the fact that the common flicker—the *pic flamboyant*—could be seen easily but that the *pic à bec ivoire*—the ivory-billed woodpecker—was, *"hélas, en voie d'extinction."* Charles allowed that at one time he'd had a barn owl as a pet and had raised baby crows.

Marci stirred her soup and crumbled her bread and tried to take deep breaths, and so dinner went, if not on its merry way, at least greatly improved in bare civility.

Sarah had decided that in the matter of food, caution was the way to go, and had opted for the clear soup and an omelet without additives, topped off with baked apple—these items taken from the children's menu. Ignoring the bird conversation, her thoughts returned briefly to Aubrey and his team of spies, but then she was distracted in the middle of her baked apple by the remarkable way that Frederick and the other waiters managed to cross the rising and falling dining floor while carrying huge trays of food and then somehow distribute dishes to the appropriate diners without dribbling gravy or slopping food on shoulders and heads. Sarah had read about dining at sea and expected to see little fences circling the tables, but the white tablecloths had been made damp with water and this somehow kept the dinner plates from skidding about. She supposed the waiters had undergone special training for the serving of meals in heaving and rolling ships, training akin to the weightless practice given astronauts before they launch into space. Sarah put down her spoon and imagined a dining room capsule filled with waiter trainees being heaved and rotated by some exterior engine. She swiveled around to watch a waiter at a nearby table dealing with a flaming dessert and became aware of two figures at the dining room entrance.

Two figures making small beckoning gestures in her direction. Two familiar figures. Liza Baum and Teddy Hogarth. Sarah faced them, moved her head slowly from side to side, and mouthed "No," but with that Liza stepped just inside the open double doors and drew her open hand swiftly across her throat.

Sarah turned to Sam. "I've forgotten my . . ." she fumbled, "my, my, uh, pills. I have to take them after dinner."

"You're sick?" said Sam with interest. "Like seasick?"

"Oh, no, it's just a regular thing I take. Like vitamins."

"You can't wait until dinner's finished to take a vitamin?"

But Sarah had risen, shook her head at Sam, frowned in Alex's direction, and started off across the dining room. Unfortunately, Sarah had not worked out in a waiter's training capsule, and she ricocheted first into an elderly woman in blue satin, causing her laden fork to slip into her lap, and then full tilt into Frederick, bearing coffee and brandy. Frederick had time to steady his tray and reach out for Sarah, but she had lurched past him and into Liza Baum's arms.

Liza grabbed Sarah by her waist and pushed her to the door, where Teddy seized her wrist and propelled her into the anteroom that opened onto the Boat Deck. "Let's get out of here," he said.

But Sarah shook off Liza, pulled loose from Teddy, and grabbed the back of a bench. "What in hell do you think you're doing?" she yelled.

"Keep it down," said Liza.

"Out on deck," ordered Teddy.

"The hell I will," said Sarah. "And Alex and Sam and God knows who else will be after me in a minute. So out with it."

"On deck," repeated Teddy.

"Is this a joke? Are you both drunk?" said Sarah angrily.

"No such luck," said Teddy.

"We've found something you should see and then we'll tell the security people," added Liza. "Or maybe not. But we need another opinion. I mean you're mixed up in this in a major way." And she grasped Sarah's sleeve and began to pull.

And Sarah, ever the victim of her own curiosity, yielded.

They stepped out onto the Boat Deck. Although there were, as on all outside decks, a number of lights fixed into the bulkheads, the area was a mixture of dark and darker shadows. A number of deck chairs had been folded and chained together in a rack, a series of ropes had been fixed from bow to stern, and an illuminated sign informed them that the deck was slippery when wet and to use all caution.

To steady herself Sarah planted herself against the deck chairs and folded her arms. "Okay, this had better be good."

Teddy hooked himself to a stanchion, Liza next to him, her feet apart for balance, one hand on Teddy's elbow, her face somber, showing nothing of her usual challenging and impish expression.

"We did go swimming," she announced.

"So?" said Sarah.

"We found a crew member, a young guy," Liza went on. "We talked him into turning on the swimming pool lights. He said he shouldn't but he did."

"Get on with it," said Sarah, feeling anger rising.

"The fact is," said Teddy, "that we found things in the pool."

"What sort of things?" demanded Sarah, her teeth clenched, for suddenly she had a picture of Gerald Hofstra as a dark and bloated presence at the bottom of the pool.

"No, not a body," said Liza hastily. "Some coins, about ten or so at the bottom."

Sarah relaxed. "People always throw coins into pools."

"That's not all," said Teddy. "A ballpoint pen, an expensive one. And a shoe."

"A sort of loafer with one tie," put in Liza. "Brown leather. We want you to look at it."

Sarah stared at her, unbelieving. "You mean you didn't tell the crew member, the one that turned on the lights?"

"Oh, he was gone," said Liza. "Said he didn't want to have anything to do with us. But you saw a lot of Gerald, talked with him, stuff like that."

"I didn't look at his feet."

"Never mind," said Teddy impatiently. "Come on down to the Quarter Deck Pool and have a look. If all the things we found look like the normal debris people toss into swimming pools, we'll jolly well wash our hands of the lot."

"And," added Liza, "we'll stop worrying about whether Gerald Hofstra's body has been stashed in a lifeboat or that he's gone berserk and jumped overboard."

So Sarah, with unsteady feet, found herself following the two aft through the labyrinth of stairs and lifts, past the library, the Scepter Room, hanging on to ropes and steadying herself on banisters, and finally out through the Osborne Cafeteria to the windswept and spray-lashed Quarter Deck with its covered swimming pool.

"Okay," said Sarah. "Do I have to get in the pool?"

"Of course not," said Liza. "We've got the stuff behind that rack of deck chairs. Come on."

And Sarah found herself crouching behind the chairs and staring at a collection of coins, a sodden brown leather shoe, and a black ballpoint pen.

"We didn't bring up all the coins," said Teddy. "They were scattered all over the bottom and the light was too dim."

Sarah, putting aside the shoe inspection until last, forced herself to look at the coins. Two quarters, a dime, a nickel, all U.S., a fifty-pence piece, three ten-pence pieces, plus two French five-franc pieces and a twenty-centime coin.

"I suppose that's the usual collection of someone who's been to the U.K. and the States," said Teddy, bending over Sarah's back.

"And a side trip to France," said Sarah.

"The pen is expensive," said Liza. "Mount Blanc."

Sarah moved her attention to the shoe. "That shoe wasn't cheap," she said. And then, poking at the object with her finger, she gave an involuntary shudder. "The heel's built up. It has some sort of a lift built in."

"And?" said Liza.

"I don't know what it adds up to."

"Remember I found Gerald Hofstra's jacket here," Teddy said.

"He wore a tie with the Eiffel Tower on it," said Sarah. "So maybe he went to France, though I suppose half the passengers aboard did, too." She straightened and backed away from the collection. "I guess you'd better bundle up the stuff—not touching anything more than you've already done—and take it to the Purser's Office. Or to some official somewhere."

"Or go on looking for the other shoe," said Liza. "See if it has a foot in it."

Sarah bit her lip. "This isn't Cinderella. I think we'd all better return to civilian life and play by the rules."

"But my God," exclaimed Liza. "Everyone has been busting his ass over this guy Hofstra and no one's actually seen him. He answered the telephone, but has he turned up in the Prince Albert Lecture Hall? I say let's get on down there, and if he's a no-show we'll ask Richard Herrick if he wore a lift in his shoe."

"And if he did wear one," said Sarah slowly, "why is it in the pool and his jacket left on the deck?" She paused and then, grimacing, "Are you both absolutely sure there isn't something else down in the pool?"

"No!" shouted Liza. "No body. No corpse."

"To the Albert Hall," said Teddy. "Right now. On the double."

"Christ," said Liza. "I knew if you got sober you'd turn into your father and be impossible. It's that British military DNA."

"Both of you shut up," said Sarah. "Let's get this settled. If it's Gerald's shoe we go straight to the Security Office."

"And it'll be your fault if they arrest us for swimming without permission," said Liza, and she took off at a run.

The Prince Albert Lecture Hall was almost in darkness. Only the stage and the first few seats had been illuminated by the side wall lights, and what with the gloomy presence of Richard standing by a lectern and slowly turning over the pages of a script, and Deedee slumped in a front-row seat, the whole scene smacked more of a wake than of a prelude to a stirring presentation of one of the world's most infamous sea disasters.

As the three came through the doors Sarah saw Richard's head lift expectantly, his expression suddenly transformed to one of hope. And as suddenly collapsing into despair. He turned back to his script without even glancing at the persons bearing their swimming pool trophies so that it was Deedee who pushed herself out of her seat and confronted the three.

"Richard can't be disturbed," she said almost angrily. "He has the whole show on his back because Gerald hasn't come. So please leave. We can't answer questions."

Sarah extended the sodden shoe. "Only one question. It may be about Gerald. Do you know if he wore a shoe lift?"

"Oh, for heaven's sake," exclaimed Deedee. "I never looked at Gerald's feet. We don't want his shoes, we want him. And if you don't know where he is, go away and find him."

"Have you tried his stateroom again?" queried Liza. "I mean that's something you should keep checking."

"I know, I know," said Deedee impatiently. "Our show goes

on at nine and it's almost eight-thirty and at eight forty-five someone from Security has promised to open his stateroom door—it's still locked—and see what's happened to him."

"But why not sooner?" said Teddy. "He might be dead in there. Or," he added in a voice of understanding, "dead drunk."

"Oh, the officer I spoke to said something about a passenger's right to privacy or his having his civil rights. Some nonsense like that. Because, you see, it's not like he hasn't communicated. The 'Don't Disturb' sign is up and he told Richard on the telephone that he wanted to be left alone. And a little later one of the ship's officers called the stateroom and got the same answer."

"Let's get back to this shoe," said Sarah.

And Deedee, rising on the balls of her feet, almost shouted, "Get out of here and leave us! We have a show to put on."

Liza nudged Sarah. "I think we'd better go. Try another idea."

But Richard had at some point looked up from the script, seen the shoe, and now descended the narrow steps on the side of the stage. "Let me see that thing," he demanded.

Sarah passed it over and Richard turned it in his hand, inspected its interior, and then nodded. "Gerald Hofstra," he said, "had one leg shorter than the other. I noticed a slight limp once and asked him. He told me he had something wrong with his back, his spine. Scoliosis, something like that."

"So this could be his shoe," Sarah persisted.

"Not only could be, but I think it is," said Richard. "He said he buys shoes from New York with a special insert. Where did you find it?"

And then, the implications of a shoe without a foot becoming only too clear, Deedee put her hand over her mouth to stifle a scream.

19

AFTER the implications of the single shoe had been digested, Deedee heaved a trembling sigh and Richard sat down heavily on one of the theater seats.

"Where was it? Where did you find it?"

"Quarter Deck," said Liza. "In the swimming pool. But," she hastened on, seeing both Herricks gaping with wide eyes, "he wasn't in it. Just some coins. U.S., French, and English. And a Mont Blanc pen, but a lot of people have those. And the shoe. Of course, his jacket turned up earlier—the one we took to you."

"We'll take the shoe and the other things over to the Security Office," said Sarah. "And it's about time for them to open up Mr. Hofstra's stateroom, so you'll find out if he's really there."

"And if he is, what sort of shape he's in," added Liza.

But the Herricks, with the failure of the manager to appear, seemed to have lost interest in Gerald Hofstra. It was almost show time and he had become a nonperson. Someone in whom they no longer had trust, no longer awaited.

"The show," said Deedee in a weak voice.

"You could put up a canceled notice if he doesn't turn up in the next ten minutes," said Sarah.

"No," said Richard. He stood up, inhaled, squared his shoulders, thrust his chin out, and flung out a hand, indicating the stage with so theatrical a gesture that Sarah expected him to shout "The show must go on." But Richard simply dropped his hand. "But I will post a sign saying there will be a fifteen-minute delay. That gives me time to get my head together. Then I'll go ahead, climb on that stage and tell the *Titanic* story."

"But," protested Deedee, "the lights, the simulation sequences. The animations Gerald put together. You know, the ship sinking with all the lights blazing and the lifeboats around. I can't handle that stuff, and even if I could, I don't want to."

Richard, who had started back to the stage, turned back to his wife. "Please, Deedee, don't say anything. I've got to think."

"Now," Sarah said, "we've got to get over to Security." And without further attention from the Herricks the three left the lecture hall.

Outside, Liza pulled at Sarah's arm. "You go on to Security. Me, I'm going back to the Quarter Deck and have another search. Teddy, go down and hover about Gerald Hofstra's room and report what happens there when they open the cabin."

"I thought I'd go back on the Quarter Deck with you," said Teddy. "That's where the action is."

"You, Edward Hogarth, are being given a job of great responsibility for which you're not suited. Get the hell over to Hofstra's cabin. We've got about fifteen minutes."

"Talk about military genes," muttered Teddy. "Where did you come from, Liza Baum? West Point? And where do we meet later?"

"Prince Albert Lecture Hall, back row," said Liza. "By that time Gerald will have turned up or be officially listed as missing and the ship's crew can hunt him down." And Liza took off toward the stairway while Teddy swung himself through the lecture hall doors and headed toward the lift to One Deck.

Sarah, rather annoyed at having the action initiative snatched by a mere snit of a girl—Liza must have been at least three years younger—started for Two Deck and the Security

Office. There the clerk in charge—a broad-shouldered female whose voice bespoke a life in Liverpool and who could have probably earned her living throwing steers—expressed only mild interest in Sarah's evidence. "Coins," she said, "are always in the bottom of the swimming pool. People do it for luck, you know. They make a wish and toss in money. We have a charity fund, see, and we'll be donating what the pool cleaning people find."

"But the pen, the shoe. Mr. Hofstra's shoe. We've all been looking for him."

"Yes, I've a note about that and I'll tell the security officer. He's not here at the moment. But pens, why, now, everyone loses pens. You should see what's come in to our Lost and Found in only a few days. Pens by the dozens, and very expensive they are and simply dropped or thrown away. Watches, you'd be amazed. Not so many shoes, but we have trainers—sneakers to you—by the dozen."

With that Sarah had to be content. She looked at her watch. Five minutes of nine, and the delayed *Titanic* show would begin at nine-fifteen. She would just have time to make it to Gerald Hofstra's stateroom for . . . well, for what? The unveiling? The unmasking? Somehow in Sarah's mind the unlocking of the cabin had begun to take on the significance of the opening of an Egyptian tomb.

She found Teddy Hogarth at the end of the passageway leaning against a wall. "I've been watching Hofstra's stateroom," he said. "The 'Do Not Disturb' sign is still up but I feel like a damn fool. I'll probably be arrested for loitering. These passageways are impossible. There's nothing to do in them and no chairs. A steward has been going by and giving me a very fishy look."

"We can walk to the end together, slowly and deliberately, and then turn around," said Sarah. "Like a loving couple. Look like we're going somewhere and then come back as if we've forgotten something."

"How many times can we look as if we've forgotten something?" complained Teddy.

"Quiet," said Sarah suddenly. "Someone's coming. Actually,

three someones. Let's move along, get to the end, turn, and go right past Hofstra's cabin."

It was all over in a matter of minutes. A uniformed officer, a steward, and a square-faced man in a dinner jacket approached the door. The steward knocked, waited, knocked again. The officer called out, "Mr. Hofstra, are you there?" The steward knocked again. The officer nodded at the steward, who inserted a key, turned it. The door opened; the officer and the square-faced man went in; the steward waited outside. Five minutes passed and the two men returned, the door was re-locked, and the steward departed in a direction toward the bow. The other two men, walking quickly, ducked down a connecting passageway and were gone.

Sarah turned on her heel, shoved Teddy aside, and fluttered up to the steward, who was proceeding more deliberately.

"Oh, excuse me," she said, "but is Mr. Hofstra still ill? I'm asking because his partners are in a state. Having a fit. Because he's supposed to be helping with the *Titanic* show."

The steward, a tall and imposing presence who reminded Sarah of an infinite number of butlers of the silver screen, said that he was not at liberty to discuss Mr. Hofstra.

"Well, then," said Sarah, raising her voice to a sort of soprano squeal, "I'll just have to stand outside his door and call and call until I'm blue in the face. And my friend here, Lord Hogarth, will help me knock on the door. We'll drive Mr. Hofstra crazy and he will have to open up."

That was apparently enough for the steward. "Mr. Hofstra is not in his cabin. Perhaps you could telephone him at a later time."

That was all Sarah needed. She grabbed Teddy by his jacket and propelled him ahead of her, down the passage and out.

"Hey, let go," yelled Teddy. "You women. No wonder men drink. Push, pull, yank all day long. And 'Lord' Hogarth. I like that. No one is impressed by a title these days."

"Don't bet on it," said Sarah. "I saw that steward's eyes open a little wider. Okay, now that's that. Security has the ball. Let them find Gerald Hofstra. Come on, we're supposed to be meeting Liza at the lecture hall."

But Liza was not there. Sarah slipped in ahead of Teddy into the last row on the left aisle. The Prince Albert Lecture Hall was elegant in its mix of pseudo-Victorian, pseudo-classical plushness, the red brocade walls covered with elaborate gilt-framed panels showing pastoral scenes of shepherds and nymphs, its ceiling decorated with cherubs frolicking among pink and saffron clouds, the stage hung in heavy crimson velvet draperies. Sarah, looking about, could see that the hall was only three-quarters filled and decided that the unruly ocean was still taking its toll, and it behooved even the best stomachs to beware and stay put. She reached into the pocket of her black skirt and came up with a wad of ginger pieces and put one between her teeth.

"Have some ginger and keep your voice down," she said to Teddy. She would have to fight this young man later for his remark about women, but now was not the time.

"Ginger, why not? Maybe it'll settle my head. I may have to take up smoking. I need one good vice. And where the hell is Liza? This is her plan. Damn, here go the house lights, so we won't even be able to find her if she does come."

"Shhh. Richard Herrick's coming on stage. God, he looks like he's been up for thirty days and thirty nights."

"No makeup," said Teddy. "And no costume."

Richard Herrick walked slowly, deliberately, to center stage and nodded into the middle distance. Even at her remove from the stage, Sarah thought the man looked shadow-eyed and haggard. And he was certainly not in costume. Hadn't Deedee mentioned that he would begin his narration in the uniform of a wireless operator and then add and subtract coats, life belts, and finally, as the ship began to go down, put on Captain Smith's jacket and cap? But Richard had simply changed from his dinner jacket and now wore a dark gray business suit, a white shirt, and a navy tie with small dots. His appearance, his general bearing, suggested more the chairman of a small corporation than the player of many parts.

"Good evening," said Richard in a modulated voice. His own voice, Sarah noted. "Although we have advertised a showing of the tragedy of the *Titanic* as a spectacle of sound and sight, we are not able to bring you the show in the promised format. Instead I will simply"—Richard raised his shoulders and then swallowed hard—"tell you the story as it has been told by many of the survivors of the sinking. Anyone who feels that this is not what they came to see and hear, you are most welcome to leave. We, my wife and I, will understand, since the last thing we wish is to be presenting a program under false colors."

Here Richard paused and looked expectantly at the audience, watched as here and there a few couples, a straggling band of teenagers, and several singles rose and worked their way to the exit. Then he moved to the lectern, picked up a notebook, turned a page, pushed his glasses back on his nose, and said, "The weather on the Sunday evening of April fourteen, 1912, was, from all accounts, cold, clear, and remarkably calm. Just before nine o'clock the commander of the White Star Line's newest ship, Captain Edward J. Smith, had left a party of first-class passengers and gone to the bridge. Iceberg warnings had been coming into the radio room at irregular intervals for the last two days, and that very evening the junior wireless operator, Harold Bride, had intercepted a message from the steamer *California* on the sighting of three large bergs."

Here Richard paused, turned over a paper, and, keeping his voice quiet and without inflection, went on. "Captain Smith, arriving on the bridge, was told that the temperature was close to freezing. Although the crew had been told to watch for ice, they as well as the passengers had the utmost confidence in the new ship . . ."

And Sarah found that as Richard Herrick spoke, her own brain, stimulated by her own reading, her own experience with the many movies and documentaries she had seen, plus the actual fact of the *Vicky*'s slow but relentless rolling and pitching, filled in the background, the sights and sounds of the doomed *Titanic*. She felt the jolt of the collision, the scraping of the iceberg, heard in her ears the rush of water, the sounds of slipping footsteps on the deck, saw lifeboats lowering, felt the tilt of the deck and then . . .

Then she felt a clutch of her shoulder, felt a face next to

her ear and Liza's voice. "Sarah, for God's sake pull yourself together. Wake up. I've found him. You've got to come."

Sarah started from her seat. "What? Who? Where's Teddy gone? What are you talking about?"

"Gerald Hofstra, who do you think? Come on. You must have been asleep. I've got Teddy waiting outside the lecture hall. Don't make any noise."

The theater doors closed behind them, Sarah shook herself free of Liza's hand. "What do you mean? Gerald wasn't in his stateroom."

"Well, how could he be," said Liza, "because he's in the equipment locker or whatever it's called. On the Quarter Deck. Where I was. Come on, we've got to hurry."

"The Security Office," began Sarah.

"You have the Security Office on the brain."

"Is he . . ."

"No, he's not dead. At least he's making noises. It's really weird, he's rolled up in some kind of net."

"A what?"

"Let's get up there," said Teddy, stepping forward, "and stop all this stupid arguing. If he's alive we'll call for help. If he's dead . . ."

"We'll call for help," said Sarah, but she turned and headed for the Quarter Deck doors.

"You can't climb down to the next deck," said Liza. "They've closed off the outside stairways because of the storm. Take the elevator or the inside stairs down."

But Sarah, followed by Teddy and Liza, was already in motion and led the other two down through an almost deserted Card Room, around the Pinafore Theatre, and on to the Osborne Cafeteria and out to the Quarter Deck. And from there to a small door opening behind the pool and close to the food bar.

"In here," said Liza. And she twisted a handle, pulled open the door, closed the door behind them, and at the same time pushed a wall switch that turned on a small overhead light. "I know my way around here because they keep the sports and deck tennis stuff here." And pointing to a cylindrical bundle in the corner, "There he is. He's got a gag in his mouth and a bump on his head, but he certainly seems alive. I didn't dare touch him. And I thought—"

"You thought wrong," said Sarah. "Teddy, go now and find the first crew person you can lay your hands on and tell him to find a doctor and some officer in a hurry."

"But I don't think—" Teddy began.

"Teddy Hogarth," yelled Liza. "You heard the lady. She's right. I should have done it myself but I didn't think straight."

And Teddy, looking as rebellious as a mule, took one step toward Liza, thought better of it, and retreated to the deck and disappeared. And Sarah knelt down by the bundle. A bundle made up of netting, which was now twitching and turning, the eyes of the net-wrapped head rolling frantically. The netting—it looked like volleyball or badminton netting—had been apparently cut from its supports and had been used to wrap Gerald Hofstra tightly round and round, head and body, as if he had been some sort of sausage.

Gerald was certainly alive. But the gag, a piece of striped material tied around his mouth, was obstructing speech and not helping his breathing, which was coming in snorts quite audible even against the gale blowing outside on deck. But if color was any guide, the man was not cold, which was understandable since the equipment locker, despite the turmoil outside, was stuffy and warm. And shirt and trousers, which should have been wet if he had indeed spent time in the swimming pool, appeared to have almost dried.

"Help me unwrap him," Sarah ordered.

"Should we touch him?" asked Liza in a worried voice. "I mean the police or the security people or someone might . . ."

"For God's sake, take the gag out and take the net away from his face. Let him breathe properly. We won't move him, because I think he was banged on the head."

And Sarah began pulling at the netting around Gerald's head and finally managed to loosen the gag and pull it free. She was rewarded by Gerald letting out a breath and then raising his head, opening his mouth, and giving out with a string of four-letter words. Gratified, Sarah leaned over to loosen another layer of netting from around the man's neck and shoulders.

And the light went out.

For a moment Sarah and Liza stayed absolutely still and stared at the figure—a black shape only against the dimly lit deck. And the figure stood at the same time as still as the two women. Then it whirled, shot away from the doorway, and disappeared.

Sarah, without thinking of what or why, yelled at Liza to stay with Gerald, jumped up and took off down the deck.

And ran into a trio of hastening crew members led by an officer, his white uniform acting as a beacon. But the figure—it was a man, Sarah decided, a tall and most agile man—twisted past the approaching party and ran full tilt through the door to the stairway inside and, still running, began the descent. Sarah, not as nimble, found a long arm reaching for her. She pushed free, and, stumbling, fighting for her balance, hurled herself at the stairway, plunging down two steps at a time. Then, racing down the long blue and red carpeted corridor, heard steps behind her.

Yes, someone, another man, must have detached himself from the rescue party and was after both of them. But there was not time to check to see if he was a helper or an aider and abettor of the rolling up of Gerald Hofstra.

The man ahead was putting almost a deck between them, while behind her Sarah had the sense that she was being overtaken. Even with the thumping of their feet she heard a choking, panting breathing—the person behind was not used to fast pursuit. Then suddenly, the man ahead, now taking the stairs two at a time, turned into the passageway at Two Deck and lost himself in a group of passengers who were walking unsteadily in the opposite direction. And then he was free, past the Purser's Office, the Security Office, the Money Exchange booths, and directly through the double oak doors of the little Chapel.

And Sarah, rising on her toes, grateful that the heavy carpeting absorbed some of the sound of her feet, found herself in a darkened chapel with only the dim light from the narrow stained-glass windows shedding a soft glow. Then as she stood hesitating at the last of the row of pews, she was once more seized by the shoulder and flung down on the aisle, then pushed and almost hoisted into the narrow space between the pew seat and the row of kneeling stools.

"Stay down, you fool," said a voice in her ear. And before she could struggle around and force herself loose, the first figure heaved himself upon her attacker and began what sounded like a vigorous strangling.

Sarah, no longer the object of the action, rolled free, wiggled out into the aisle, and, without any sense of who was the attacker, who the attackee, who was friend, who was foe, stood up, reached across the pew, grabbed a hymnal, and slammed it down on the nearest head. For a moment there was a pause in the throttling noise coming from the throat of the man on the bottom.

Sarah tried it again, this time taking a tighter grip on the book, and bang, bang, bang, repeatedly thumped the head and neck of the topmost man. This time with the admirable result that her victim reared up, gave Sarah a hefty shove so that she tottered backwards against a pew back, and left the chapel on a run, pulling the double oak doors closed behind him.

And the underneath man sat up slowly with what appeared to be a great and painful effort. And swore. A string of oaths with a heavy naval flavor, oaths that had probably been sworn by His or Her Britannic Majesty's sailors since time began. And then he rose and limped over to the chapel wall and leaned heavily against it and looked directly at Sarah, who in her turn was struggling to her feet and looking about for another more satisfactory weapon than a Church of England hymnal.

"I don't know whether to shoot you on the spot for doing whatever you thought you were doing," said an all-too-familiar voice, "or to thank you for saving my life—or at least my throat."

"Oh, my goodness! Good God! What on earth is going on here?"

Another quarter heard from. An angry quarter, if Sarah could judge from the tone of voice. But the anonymity did not last. The chapel was suddenly flooded with light from the two hanging chandeliers and the room regained its common and unthreatening aspect with its priest standing at the altar side, his hand still on the light switch.

"What is going on?" repeated Father Peter Bottomley. Then, with a puzzled look at Sarah, he returned to the man against the wall, and shook his head. "I told you, Aubrey," he said reproachfully, "that this would get out of hand. You and your cohorts. And using the Chapel, too. I can't allow it, I simply can't." He took a step forward and faced Sarah. "I think I've met you, haven't I? We had a little talk about, what was it, group counseling, I think."

"Yes," said Sarah, "we did. But since then some pretty awful things have been happening and—"

"She's right," said Aubrey. "Let me use your phone, Peter. I've got to touch base and call the ship's hospital. I had a message that Gerald Hofstra's been found, and then I chased Miss Deane here and another man. A man who just might be your assistant, Mr. Frye. Or might not. It's a guess. And," called Aubrey over his shoulder as he headed toward the Chapel office, "keep Miss Deane here. By force if you have to."

"Oh no you don't," said Sarah, starting for the door. But Father Bottomley was quicker. Looking like a black beetle in his cassock, he fairly flew down the aisle and blocked the doors, his arms outspread like wings.

"I'm afraid," he said apologetically, "that you really must stay. I'm sure Mr. Smith can explain."

Sarah, temper rising, said with clenched teeth that nothing Mr. Smith could say could explain holding her in the chapel. "Have you considered," she went on, "that Mr. Smith isn't exactly what he says he is? That he's not Mr. Law and Order and Mr. Security rolled into one? That he just might be working with some sort of gang?"

Peter Bottomley looked truly shocked. "You can't mean gang in the criminal sense. Mr. Smith's friends, the people with whom he is traveling—"

Sarah cut him off. "If you mean his cousin, Vivian Smith, or his cousin's friend, Margaret, I wouldn't trust them an inch.

They are both fakes, and as for Mr. Frye and his pamphlets, I'd bet they're all in it together."

"My dear young woman," began Peter Bottomley.

"And I'm not your dear young woman, and for all I know you're in it up to your—what's that thing you're wearing, a cassock or a soutane or an alb—well, up to your knees in it yourself."

Peter Bottomley gave her the sort of patient look that Sarah had seen on the faces of doctors confronting irascible patients. "You say 'in it'? In what? To what do you refer? And Mr. Smith is a personal friend of the captain."

"I don't care if he's the personal friend of the Archangel Gabriel, I don't trust him. What's he doing chasing after me all the way to the Chapel?"

"Sarah," said Aubrey, who, apparently walking on velvet feet, reappeared suddenly. "I was not chasing you. I was chasing after the man who is very possibly responsible for rolling Gerald Hofstra in a net. Preparatory, I would guess, to rolling him right over the rail, never to be seen again. You just happened to be in the middle of the chase, and I must say although my chasing days are over I find I still have a fair burst of speed."

Sarah eyed Aubrey Smith with distrust and then gave Peter Bottomley a long hard look. The idea of that man as yet another member of a conspiracy was almost more than she could swallow. However, she reminded herself, either gentleman might be a source of some up-to-date news—if they could be trusted to repeat it accurately. "Does anyone know how Mr. Hofstra is?" she asked.

"A sensible and compassionate question," said Aubrey. He walked over to the last row of pews, sat down, and turned to face Sarah. "Gerald Hofstra has been, what's the old term, illused. Very ill-used. But he's a very tough bird. Whatever else has happened to him, it's made him forget about his stomach problems. The doctors will keep him in the hospital overnight and watch him for general shock and bruising. Also he has a nice bump on the head, so mild concussion is a possibility. He tells us he was jumped by two people when he was on his way out of his cabin in the early morning hours, taken with a gun at his back to the Quarter Deck sports area. Quite deserted at four in the morning. He tells us that he was blindfolded, gagged, and shoved down into the swimming pool apparently with the intent of drowning him, but the water was partially drained so he could touch in most places, and fortunately there was an air layer between the water and the canvas cover. So, failing to cooperate and drown, he was fished out by these two characters and wrapped up in the badminton net. Put on hold until this evening in the sports equipment locker. After all, with this storm no one was going to play shuffleboard or badminton. He thinks that they—whoever they are, Mr. Frye at least is one we believe—"

"And I *cannot* believe—" interrupted Peter Bottomley.

"We shall see," said Aubrey. "But Hofstra thinks that the plan was to send him overboard in the middle of the *Titanic* show, the idea being with the combination of the rough weather and a drawing card like the Herricks' program, few people if any would be on deck."

"What about the surveillance cameras?" asked Father Bottomley. "The ship is bristling with them."

"I suppose they found an area which wasn't covered," said Aubrey. "Or the cameras were disabled. After all, we're guessing that the people in question—"

"You mean the so-called terrorists?" asked Sarah, still in a state of skepticism—Aubrey was so damn smooth and plausible.

"Call them what you want, the revenge team, Murder Limited. They, some members anyway, must be part of the crew. As such they had access to staterooms, equipment lockers, security plans."

"I can't believe," said Sarah, glaring at Aubrey and then at Peter Bottomley, "that we're having this cozy little chat about terrorist or revenge teams on an ocean liner when one of the terrorists—unless he's really one of you in disguise—is right now running around loose."

"One of my calls was to Security," said Aubrey, "and they've put out an alert for Amory Frye in particular and anyone else acting in the least suspiciously. And, for good measure, I'm sorry to tell you, they have taken your aunt, Mrs. Clancy, into custody."

"They have WHAT!"

"Well, not exactly custody. But they are detaining her in the Security Office in order to ask a few questions. Clear up some things she's been saying. And doing. As I told you before she fits our profile of persons who had lost family members on *Titanic*. And you know yourself that for some time she has been extremely negative on the subject of the *Titanic* show and said abusive things about Mr. Hofstra, including a wish that he either drop dead or be swept overboard."

You Have Till

ten to-Night

20

BUT," Sarah spluttered, "that's just Julia. That's the way she is. She doesn't *do* anything, not really. Sometimes she goes around biting heads off and sometimes she's wonderful, a very generous, kind person. She takes terrific care of her animals. Her dogs and horses."

"A genuine heart of gold," said Aubrey, smiling. "My mother has a cousin exactly like her, so I'm sure it's all a misunderstanding."

"You mean like my misunderstanding of what your cousin Vivian is up to? And her friend, Scarlet O'Hara?"

"Sarah, if I may still call you by your first name, I think your Aunt Julia would be very glad to see you right now, so why don't you go and comfort her. I'll pledge myself into the care of Father Bottomley, whom you cannot suspect of anything untoward."

"I suspect everyone," said Sarah crisply. "Mr. Frye, whom you *do* suspect, is Father Bottomley's right-hand man." And she turned on her heel and hurried toward the door, and Peter Bottomley, shaking his head, let her go.

Julia Clancy was the sole occupant of the small waiting area of the Security Office, a not surprising fact considering the late evening hour—it was almost eleven P.M. Looking strangely diminished, small and gray, she sat hunched in an office chair, her hands folded over her quilted bag of needlepoint—the one, Sarah knew, that she had been searching for all day. A woman in a navy-blue dress sat with her, both women entirely silent.

"Aunt Julia," exclaimed Sarah, rushing up to her aunt. "Are you all right? What on earth's going on?"

"I think," said the woman in an icy voice, "that everything has been cleared up to our satisfaction."

Julia looked up, her face haggard. "Not to my satisfaction." But a trembling of her lip belied her words. She looked, Sarah thought, every bit her seventy years and then some.

"Let's get you back to your stateroom," said Sarah, and she leaned down and pulled her aunt to her feet. "And you can tell me all about it. You need something hot to drink. You look done in."

"I am done in," said Julia. "Thanks to these people."

The woman rose and bent her lips upward. "We must do our job, you know. And Mrs. Clancy, please be careful about leaving your needlepoint bag around in odd places."

"Why is she talking about your needlepoint bag? Did she find it?" asked Sarah as she steered her aunt toward the lift to One Deck.

"Oh, Lord," said Julia. "It's all part of the same thing. Those security people are off base. Out to lunch. Crazy as loons. Just wait until I get back to my room and I'll tell you."

Fifteen minutes later, Julia sat in an armchair in her stateroom nursing a hot cup of spiced tea. She had dismissed Mary Malone, who showed a tendency to hover solicitiously, and now was ready to tell her story. It was a simple tale. Any odd package, bag, or container left around the ship was always picked up by one of the security patrols or crew members and brought to the attention of the ship's authorities. "Bombs," said Julia. "They're scared to death of bombs. That's how bombs are left. Briefcases, knitting bags, backpacks. There was a warning in our welcome packet about leaving things around. I must have left my needlepoint bag in the Balmoral Room, and it had scissors, extra needles, some postcards, and a tape measure. But

240

wouldn't you know, in it was this black circle of paper and the message on the other side about having until ten tonight. I thought it was a children's joke—Erik Anderson got one and so did one of those French sisters, and she said it was from '*quelques méchants enfants.*' But judging from the fuss the security people made, some other people have had them. To top it off some spy told the Thought Police that I'd been threatening Gerald Hofstra. Hoping he'd get lost, fall in the ocean. And now I'm listed as some sort of undesirable."

"You did make it pretty clear what you thought of Gerald," Sarah reminded her.

"I mentioned to a few people, you, Alex, Erik Anderson, Sam Greenbank, that I hated the idea of any more *Titanic* shows and how I couldn't abide a publicity hound like Gerald Hofstra who was milking a poor tired tragedy for all it was worth. And because of a few harmless remarks those people have had the gall to question me. Oh, Sarah, I am so tired but I am also so . . ." Here Julia faltered.

"Pissed," suggested Sarah.

"Yes, yes I am. Thoroughly pissed. Just because this man Hofstra has disappeared or reappeared or whatever he's done, innocent people like me are picked up and grilled."

"Not really grilled," said Sarah.

"Not with a spotlight and no one pulled my fingernails out, but it was not nice. No one was very pleasant."

"I don't suppose being pleasant is part of the job description," Sarah pointed out. "Anyway, Gerald Hofstra, should you care, was grabbed, dumped in the swimming pool, tied up, but is now in the ship's hospital and doing pretty well."

"And you're mixed up in it, I suppose," said Julia accusingly.

"Liza Baum and her pal Teddy found him in a sports equipment locker and alerted the ship's people."

"They were looking for Hofstra in a sports equipment locker?"

Sarah sighed. Really, the whole business made less and less sense. And when one added the people together, Amory Frye and whomever he was working with, plus Aubrey and *his* women and possibly Peter Bottomley and the Church of England, well, it was a nightmare that didn't bear thinking about. She sat down on the edge of Julia's bed, looked over her exhausted aunt, and decided to make it short. "A few of Gerald Hofstra's personal things turned up near the locker, so it was a logical place to look. And now, I think . . ."

"Yes, it's bedtime, I know, but where, my dear untrustworthy niece, do you fit in? And where, by the way, is Alex?"

"I don't know where Alex is because I've been busy. Well, if you must know, I chased someone who turned up at the sports locker, and Aubrey Smith chased me, and we ended in the chapel, and there was a sort of wrestling match, but the man I chased got away. Although," she added wearily, "I suppose someone has caught up with him by now."

"No, dear," said a soft voice. And Mary Malone came soundlessly into the cabin and now stood looming over both women.

"Mrs. Clancy," said Mary, addressing Julia, "I hope you're feeling better because I want to use this stateroom for a bit. Now don't be refusing me, I have no choice. In fact both of you, please stay right where you are. No, Mrs. Clancy"—this as Julia started to rise—"don't try to get up. You've had enough excitement for today. Thank you. Mr. Frye—you've both met Mr. Frye, haven't you, now—quite anxious he is and he needs a place that's perfectly safe and he's asked for my help." Mary turned slightly, leaving her listeners wide-eyed and unbelieving, and said quietly over her shoulder, "It's all right, Amory. Come out of the bathroom."

She smiled and addressed Julia again. "You see, I put him in the shower with the curtain drawn, because I didn't think the security people would go as far as to search your room, Mrs. Clancy. They only wanted to talk to you about the things you've been saying about Mr. Hofstra. Word gets about, you see, and not too much goes by the house staff. We all talk to each other. And I wouldn't have let you try to use the shower or tub tonight. Isn't that so, Amory?"

Amory Frye quietly closed the bathroom door and came up and stood next to Mary Malone, so that the effect of the two sturdy, tall persons was to shrink both Sarah and Julia to almost child size. Amory was wearing a black turtleneck, dark gray trousers; his face was red, perhaps from his recent exertions in the chase. In his hand he held a small revolver.

Which he pointed first at Julia's head and then moved to aim at Sarah's right ear—Sarah sitting sideways on Julia's bed—and then returned to point again at Julia.

"All right, Mary," he said. "I'm in charge now. You stand by Mrs. Clancy where you can watch her, and I'll keep an eye on this one. Later on, we'll watch them in shifts."

"What in God's name—" began Julia.

But Mary put a heavy hand on her shoulder. "No talking, Mrs. Clancy, please. I've tried to keep you out of this ever since I found where your sympathies lay, but you've made it so hard on us, calling attention to Mr. Hofstra the way you have."

"But what do you think—" began Julia, trying again to stand up. She was shoved down none too gently by Mary.

"We didn't want a scene like this, but all the meddling that's been going on has been a real bother. I'm sure, Mrs. Clancy, if you'd known that we planned all along to take care of Mr. Hofstra, you wouldn't have gone about denouncing the man, now would you?"

"Mary," said Amory, "there's no point in rehashing this. It's enough to say to these two as I tell everyone who asks for counseling"—here Amory gave a small chuckle—"that the wages of sin are despair and destruction, and no matter how long the tide takes, yet it comes in, the Lord willing, and do not ask for whom the bell tolls." And he chuckled again more loudly, apparently pleased with his wit.

"You," said Julia stoutly, "are an evil man and you are the one who should go overboard." Julia's fatigue seemed to have left her, and Sarah, watching her almost visibly bristle, decided that what Julia always needed, when exhausted, was the adrenaline roused by a good fight. However, there was no need to encourage this aspect of her aunt's personality. She would try sympathy.

"Poor Aunt Julia has had a horrible day. She needs to rest, to go to bed. And so do I. We aren't enemies. We're perfectly ordinary passengers. So why don't you both go and find another cabin—or a utility closet—to hide in, and we won't say a word."

This was so patent a lie that Amory looked at her in disbelief and drew his weapon across her chin. "You started this sneaking about, bringing that Baum woman and her drunken friend into it. Now you pay for it. The wages of, shall we say, not sin, but nosiness." Again the small chuckle. Then, becoming practical, he added, "If the telephone rings, Mrs. Clancy will answer and say she's gone to bed, and if someone asks for this Sarah person, she's here because she's worried about her dear old aunt."

"You can't possibly think we're going to stay here for the next two days," said Sarah.

"There's a nasty storm out there," said Mary. "A lot of passengers have taken to their bunks and can't keep a single thing on their stomachs. We'll pass it about that Mrs. Clancy has been overcome with seasickness and her niece is staying to help take care of her."

"We'll let you sleep here," said Amory. "Which is very thoughtful of us. We're not sure what's to be done with you. You weren't on our program."

"Tell us about your program," said Sarah in what she hoped was an encouraging voice.

Amory hesitated, looked over at Mary, who moved her head slightly from side to side.

And the telephone rang. Once, twice, three times.

And Mary picked up the receiver and handed it to Julia.

Julia grasped the receiver, said hello in a hollow voice, and then said, "I'm all right. Just a little seasick. No, nothing serious. I just need rest. Sarah? Oh, Sarah's right here. Taking care of me. Yes, I'm sure. Yes, yes, I'll tell her. No, no don't come. I'll be fine. Yes, good-bye." She hung up the receiver. "That was Alex," Julia said unnecessarily. "I told him not to but I think he's coming anyway."

Amory frowned and then waved the gun at Sarah. "Call him back and tell him you're spending the night and not to come. Right now."

Sarah reluctantly reached for the telephone and obeyed.

"Hello, Alex. Yes, I'm with Aunt Julia. Please don't bother. Everything's fine. I'll see you in the morning. If she's better. No, don't come. I mean it. No, please. You know how Julia is when she's ill. Falls apart, always has to have someone with her. Yes, I'm sure. Good night." Sarah handed the receiver over to Amory and said to herself, I'll be damned if Alex buys the crap about Julia falling apart, so maybe we'll get some action. But as the nature of the "action" began to make itself clear, Sarah allowed herself a shiver of apprehension.

"What's wrong!" demanded an alert Amory Frye, frowning at her. Not for nothing was he put to counseling the disturbed passenger, Sarah told herself.

"Nothing," said Sarah. Then, facing him, "No, as a matter of fact, plenty is wrong. We're trapped in here with a gun at our heads. Wouldn't you feel a little out of sorts? A little nervous?"

Amory shrugged, subsided, reached behind him for a small straight-back chair, sat down, and retrained his revolver on Julia's throat. And silence prevailed.

"Julia is apparently sick," said Alex to Sam Greenbank, who had stopped off at their stateroom to talk about the management of a light concussion as it applied to Gerald Hofstra, who seemed to be anxious to leave the ship's hospital and go to his own stateroom.

"Apparently?" said Sam, his eyebrows rising.

"Apparently. But not actually. Julia, to my perfect knowledge, does not want anyone hanging around when she's under the weather. Sarah says she's spending the night with her at Julia's behest. And Sarah also says, and I quote, 'Everything's just fine.' "

"So you smell a rat."

"A familiar rat. But I'm not sure what to do about it. I think the idea is not to go charging down to Julia's stateroom with a machete and a fire extinguisher. Nor come with the police or whatever they call themselves aboard ship."

"Shore patrol," suggested Sam. "Or marines? The old frigates and ships of the line carried marines."

"Shut up and let me think," said Alex. "Let me imagine a worst-case scenario and work from there."

"Well, Sarah's alive," said Sam. "And so, I'd say, is Julia. That's in their favor."

Alex, who had begun walking back and forth in the cabin, halted by the telephone. "I'll call again and let her know I know something's haywire."

"Things might go more haywire if you do," observed Sam.

"One call, and then action stations." Alex picked up the telephone and tapped in Julia's cabin number. "Hello, Julia. Yes, it's Alex again. Just another message for Sarah. Can you put her on? Hello, Sarah. I just remembered to tell you that Big Daddy can smell mendacity even over the telephone. I see. No I wouldn't dream of it. And a good night to you."

"So," demanded Sam. "How is a smart-ass remark like that going to clear up anything?"

"It did what it's supposed to do. Sarah knows we know."

"Yeah, great. Super. Now can I call the marines?"

Alex ignored him. "I'm guessing Sarah and Julia have unwelcome company. And that the company is—or are—the same birds who trussed up Gerald Hofstra. And that Sarah's long nose has landed them into Julia's cabin. The thing to do is how to break the women loose without a full SWAT team going into action and killing one of them. Or both."

"How about the person-to-person approach? Send Father Bottomley."

"Good Christ, no!" exclaimed Alex. "Father Bottomley would try to turn his other cheek and probably have it blown off."

"So what about the SWAT team? Or maybe the *Vicky*'s people have some more subtle approach up their sleeves."

"Let me think," growled Alex. And he flung himself down in the armchair and put his head in his hands.

Julia had been allowed to move to her bed, where she now sat propped by pillows. She sat scowling, her hands rubbing ceaselessly together, trying frantically to think of a way out. Out of the mess, out of the stateroom, out of danger.

Sarah had been ushered to the chair vacated by Julia and

was now prey to many regrets. The foremost of these was that she had told Alex absolutely nothing about Aubrey Smith's warning—if it had been that—of a group of revenge seekers threatening the peace of the *Vicky*'s maiden voyage. She had been warned by the dubious Aubrey not to share this information, and because she hadn't trusted the messenger, she had not done so at first. Then, when she felt like unburdening herself, Alex had been absent. But now the only person or persons with whom she had really been open were Liza Baum and Teddy Hogarth, and even they knew only the half of it. Oh, God. She squeezed her eyes shut and tried—as her husband Alex was at that very moment doing—to think her way if not to a happy ending, at least to personal freedom. A freedom that included Julia. Which was the rub. One person might cause a distraction and slip out the door, but that might spell the certain death or destruction of the other. So damnation.

Sarah opened her eyes and looked across at Amory Frye. He was slumped against the wall of the stateroom, one of Julia's bed pillows under his head, his long legs stretched out in front of him. He was sound asleep, lips blubbing out with each exhale. This was apparently part of their plan. Mary Malone was to keep watch, keep the weapon at the ready for three hours, and then would trade places around three A.M. with Amory, after which time Mary would rest. Thus they would be bright-eyed and bushy-tailed for whatever complicated, crazy disposal plan was in the works for Julia and Sarah.

Mary, however, might be the easier mark for distraction, even if right now she sat over them in an almost military posture, reminding them both in a sharp voice to sit still, stay still, and be quiet. And her very assured handling of the revolver— obviously not an unfamiliar object—was disturbing.

On the other hand, Sarah told herself, Mary must be tired. Physically tired. She'd been coping with bed making, stateroom cleaning, seasick passengers, basins and tea trays, from dawn to dusk. Amory would be much fresher, what with merely trotting about the ship with messages and offers of friendship and consolation plus assisting in a minor way at Father Bottomley's vespers service. Therefore, Mary was the more vulnerable of the two. And one hour of Mary's watch had already gone by. It was now a little past midnight. The witching hour.

Forget Alex, Sarah told herself. Or at least count on him not to come raging in like an angry bull. Nor to be at the head of a ship's security raiding party. Alex had sense and a lively feel for what was not appropriate. And he weighed options and was very patient. Ideal qualities for a practitioner of internal medicine. Unless he lost his temper. But those times were rare and had been associated with a direct physical challenge and the desperate need for action. Now she could picture him silently patrolling Julia's corridor, perhaps with Sam. Low key, wait 'em out. That was Alex.

But time was a-wasting. And some tiny thread of her thoughts had attached itself to her brain and wouldn't let go. Some name. Something that had happened before. She began reviewing her experience in boats. Small boats, skiffs, rowboats. Canoes, sailboats. Cruising ships. The *Vicky*. Her brother, Tony, her companion on assorted adolescent adventures. A recent cruise with Tony and a doubtful skipper. That time when they had to jump ship and get to shore in an inflatable rubber Avon raft. Was that useful? Hardly. She and Julia could hardly jump ship into a chilled Atlantic Ocean and swim to—what? An iceberg? But still the memory nagged at her. She and Tony escaped from the boat—an eighty-foot sloop—because they had been able to start a process of sinking the ship by the simple method of leaving the sea cock of the toilet open and flooding the cabin and the lower deck.

But they could hardly flood the *Victoria*. But? But there was a small space under the stateroom door. The cabins were not airtight, not watertight. So what if she let enough water out of the cabin to create the look of a flood? Of a leak? Or if not a leak, the appearance of something amiss? Even with all the hundreds of safeguards aboard, the safety systems, the alarm units, surely even today, almost eighty-eight years after the sinking of the *Titanic*—not to mention other unhappy marine events—the untoward appearance of water might cause a stir. Alex, if he was outside, would call someone. Or act. There would be a knock on the door which, if unanswered, would be followed by a forced entry. Men and maids with mops and wrenches. Maybe. Maybe not. But surely, Amory and/or Mary wouldn't put a bullet into Julia and herself in the full view or hearing of others. The whole idea wasn't one of the great plans of the western world; in fact it probably rated a D-minus. But what the hell. It was worth a try.

"Mary," said Sarah softly. And then louder, "Mary, Mary Malone." And Mary, Sarah was pleased to see, reacted slowly. She had now slipped down in her chair. She *was* tired. Even sleepy. Good.

"Mary, I have to use the bathroom," said Sarah.

"Oh, but you can't," said Mary, pulling herself erect.

"I have to," repeated Sarah quietly. Not the time to challenge. Just the small voice of reason.

"I'm afraid not," said Mary. "Please, just . . ." She paused and then added, "Hold yourself together."

"You see," said Sarah, "I've had diarrhea all day. It won't be very nice in here if I have an accident."

And Sarah saw Mary hesitate. Mary was a tidy person. One whose trade was cleanliness and order. She nodded. "All right. But don't be taking too long about it."

Sarah rose and then saw Julia alert. She would have to take a chance that her aunt would not, to borrow a phrase, upset the boat. Balancing herself on the moving floor, she walked carefully to the bathroom, a room most happily located by the entrance to the cabin.

Okay, she told herself in the bathroom, the door closed, this has got to work. She turned to the sink and closed the sink stopper and shoved a washcloth into the overflow drain, then a hand towel at the bottom of the sink to cut down on noise. Then she eased on the cold water. First to a small drip, then a steadier flow. Next, Sarah heaped up two of the large, fluffy white towels with the handsome embroidered *QV* and rolled them into a loose bundle under the sink. Then, as the water rose to the brim of the sink, Sarah turned the flush handle of the toilet, the swoosh of which most beautifully coincided with the small waterfall that poured down almost silently onto the bath towels. Next, Sarah took the rubber bath mat and the shower curtain and rolled them tight to form a small breakwater at one side of the bathroom and so send the stream toward the stateroom door, not into the stateroom itself. Of course the rolling ship might upset these plans and send the water into the cabin proper, but with luck the pitch and toss could just as well accelerate the departure of what she hoped would be a small Niagara into the passageway of the starboard side of One Deck.

Sarah opened the door, stepped out and closed the door behind her. Then, forcing herself not to look at the first small saturated area appearing on the carpet by the bottom of the bathroom door, she returned to her chair and gave Julia the very slightest of what she hoped was a meaningful look.

Julia, however, had resources of her own. In one hand she held a small glass, in the other her traveling companion of many years, a small flask which usually held ten ounces of the best whiskey.

"I've told Mary," she said, "that I always have a nightcap and that she should have one, too. After all," Julia added with a benign look at the woman, "she's taken very good care of me since I've come aboard, and I'm sure this is a misunderstanding, and we'll get through the night better with something warm on our stomachs."

Sarah began to protest; she wanted Mary to be stupefied with fatigue, not excited by whiskey. On the other hand, in the matters of drink, Julia sometimes knew best. She closed her mouth.

"And," continued Julia, "I think a television program. Something very soothing, not loud enough to wake Mr. Frye, would be good for all of us. We do have to get through the night somehow."

With this idea, Sarah heartily agreed. A low-key, low-sound television program would go far to mask any splashing from the direction of the bathroom. And it might keep Mary Malone's attention away from the stateroom door.

"Well, all right," said Mary, accepting three inches of neat whiskey from Julia with one hand and keeping her weapon pointed with the other. "There are some good late-night shows."

"You choose," said Julia. "Whatever you want to watch."

"After all," said Sarah sweetly, "you're the boss now."

And Mary turned to the television set and after a certain amount of channel switching chose a folksinging group from the Emerald Isle and settled down with an almost contented look on her broad face.

And Sarah, moving her head a few inches to the right, watched with satisfaction the spreading of the dark stain on the carpet as it inched its way toward the cabin door.

21

ALEX, after much thought and argument with Sam, had reached the conclusion Sarah had expected. No raids, no mustering of the ship's forces, no strong-arm stuff. He had for a brief moment considered an all-ship alarm, something that called for a lifeboat drill, but Sam had pointed out that the probable result would be a trip to the ship's brig or to an available psychiatrist because after the *Titanic* lecture, the crew would be alert for jokers. Or some unstable fool losing his head, imagining disaster.

"Okay," said Alex after more pacing and another period of thought. "Let's go over to the stateroom. Get on site."

"Lurk?" suggested Sam. "Or blow nerve gas under the door?"

"I'll think of something. Something simple. Like a steward with a message. Have flowers delivered. Or champagne. A late dinner. There's a menu for people who crave food at two A.M."

"You call that simple?" demanded Sam. "Why not dancing girls and trained dogs?"

"This is damned serious," said Alex angrily.

"I never said it wasn't," retorted Sam.

"Go back to the steward idea. Stewards aren't threatening and it's natural for them to knock on doors with messages."

"And it's natural for them not to be let into staterooms in the middle of the night."

Alex turned and strode to the door. "Arguing isn't getting us anywhere. We've wasted almost an hour doing absolutely nothing. Let's get ourselves to Julia's stateroom and take it from there."

"Do you have weapons in mind?" called Sam, hurrying after Alex as he started down the corridor.

"My brain," retorted Alex. "And common sense."

"Lot of good that's going to do if you're looking down the barrel of a gun. How about at least one ship's officer?"

"He'll want to go official. Call Security, a backup. Sound an alert. All the things we don't want to happen. Now keep quiet. There's Julia's door. Number ten-forty-five."

Together the two men approached the stateroom door. Then stopped. Listened.

"Something's making a little noise. Maybe the television's on," said Sam.

"That and something else," added Alex, who had acute hearing.

"Like what?"

Alex-looked puzzled. "I don't know. Just a very soft sound."

"TV sound effects," said Sam. Then, "Get away from the door or we'll be accused of voyeurism. A couple of Peeping Toms."

"Who have nothing to peep at," complained Alex. "Keyholes aren't what they used to be." Then, shifting his feet, he looked down. "Hello. Someone's spilled something. On the corridor carpet."

Sam inspected the carpet in his turn. "Not spilled. Coming out from Mrs. Clancy's stateroom. A sort of ooze."

Alex bent over, reached out and ran a finger across the surface of the carpet, brought his hand back to his nose, and sniffed cautiously. "Water," he announced. "For a god-awful minute all I could think of was blood. The wet looks dark because they don't light the damn passageways properly."

"They dim 'em down a little at night," said Sam. Then he, too, leaned down and touched the carpet and followed Alex's testing procedure. "Yeah, you're right. Seems to be water. So now what? Has the stateroom sprung a leak or have Sarah and Julia drowned someone in the bathtub? Or been drowned? Just kidding, just kidding," said Sam, backing away from Alex.

"Don't even think about making a joke," growled Alex. He reached for the doorknob and turned it gently. "Locked," he added. "Naturally. I think we'd better get ready to go in there pretty damn quick."

"You're the one who didn't want to cause a shoot-out."

"Water leaking from the cabin makes a difference. There's a legitimate reason for going in. Better than champagne and a midnight snack. I'm going to find a steward. Or anyone with a uniform. You stay here."

"Don't forget, easy does it," Sam called softly after him.

In a matter of minutes Alex came back, followed by a white-coated steward and a man in a coverall with the words "Victoria Maintenance" in script on the breast pocket.

"They were working on the elevator," explained Alex. "I drafted them." He turned to the steward. "Look at the water coming out of that cabin. I think you'd better find out what's going on. My wife is in there with her aunt. They may be having trouble with the plumbing."

The steward in his turn bent down and felt the carpet. "It's wet through," he announced. "That shouldn't happen. I'll get on to it right away. I'll call Maintenance."

"You have Maintenance standing next to you," Alex said.

"But I usually don't do plumbing," said the man. "I'm assigned to the electrical system. The lifts."

"For Christ's sake, man, don't quibble," said Sam. He turned to the steward. "Unlock the door," he commanded.

"Do it," said Alex. "Knock once, then open the door or we won't be responsible."

And the steward, with a gusty sigh, reached into his trousers and produced a set of keys on a ring, shook one loose, looked again at the soaked carpet, and inserted the key.

Mary Malone was approaching meltdown. Going to pieces. Disintegrating. Whether it was the second glass of whiskey, her fatigue, the television program of songs by a green-clad quartet singing of cockles and mussels and the minstrel boy who to the war had gone, Sarah only knew the combination had brought their watcher to a sorry state. Mary was now slumped tearfully in her chair, her gun-holding hand wavering back and forth, her face resembling nothing so much as a large candle that had begun to soften and lose shape in the heat. Sarah and Julia, for once in tune with each other, made sympathetic noises, nodded, and encouraged Mary to let it all out, they were friends, weren't they? She was much too good a person for this sort of thing. After all, Julia pointed out, Mary was Irish. And this Amory Frye—Julia waved at the sleeping man—he was just an American living in London and so probably English in origin. She, Julia, had no patience with the English. A bad lot they were—Julia's accent had now taken on a slight Hibernian lilt. Her husband, Tom Clancy, had wanted to be buried on Irish soil. "And more's the pity it is the poor old man is not in his native ground," finished Julia as Sarah listened to her aunt in wonder and admiration.

And Mary, as Al Capone might have put it, spilled the beans. She had answered a newspaper ad for families who had lost someone in a shipwreck, and sure it was that she, Mary Malone, fitted the description. She was a fourth-generation survivor of the *Titanic* sinking. Her great-grandmother and great-grandfather and their two little boys and one girl—"she that was my grandmother," Mary told them tearfully—they were all on their way to New York. A new life, a job promised. All but her grandmother were lost, crowded out by those people in first class. Not a sign of them left, as if they'd never been alive at all. It was only by the great mercy of heaven that her grandmother alone, a girl then she was, had been tossed into a lifeboat. She'd been sent back to Ireland and lived with this relative and that one, hand to mouth, sometimes begging. Working for other people. "And it's been like that ever since for the lot of us," said Mary, her face now red as a raspberry. She stopped and gave a great snuffle, and then, prompted by Julia, went on with her tale.

Amory had said that it was time to take revenge; wasn't it time to get their own back? His great-grandparents had all been lost in the sinking, and his grandfather had gone to an orphanage in Brooklyn, turned into a drunk, and his own father and mother had never had a chance. Their lives had been ruined, their futures gone sour, changed forever for the worst. He, on a scholarship, had managed to go through a community college, and then he came to England on a steamer, but his life was nothing but so much—he'd used a word Mary hadn't liked, and it stood for garbage. Amory's life was garbage.

"Oh, that was true for me, too," said Mary, reaching for her apron and smearing a streak of wet from her cheek. "So Amory had this plan. He'd choose some rotten rich people crossing the Atlantic and we'd have our revenge. We'd begin on the *Victoria*'s maiden voyage because it would be making our point ever so much clearer. And we wouldn't take more than three people on every trip. We would only be taking the first-class passengers, the sort that were saved in those lifeboats. Amory, he'd been doing odd jobs in London and then he found a place as a volunteer in the chapel on the *Victoria*. Father Bottomley—he that calls himself a priest—is that simpleminded and he took Amory on. And being the chapel assistant, it meant that Amory went all over the ship and no one to ask questions of him at all."

Here Mary paused and took a deep breath—a second wind, Sarah thought. "As for me, why, I had no trouble at all finding work aboard. I've been a maid ever so long it is, one cruise line or another, and I was hired right away for the *Vicky*'s maiden voyage because of my experience. The other persons on this crossing—now I can't be telling you their names because they put the fear of the Almighty Lord into me—so dangerous they are. But this Amory," here Mary bent a look of pure hate at the sleeping man, "is in a fair way to being a snake in the grass. He doesn't follow the rules he himself made. Why, he tried to kill you first thing after boarding, Mrs. Clancy. Just because you'd booked first-class passage and you being an old woman who looked like an easy target."

Julia's eyes widened. "He what!"

"Ah, a pity it was the way he went after you and you just out for a bit of air on the very day of sailing and we supposed to be choosing people, some first-class passengers, or some terrible foul persons who wouldn't be missed."

"Like General Gordon," said Sarah in a soft voice.

"Yes. A very useless man and very cruel to his servant. I heard the general berate the poor man when they were settling their luggage. No one will miss the general. And indeed the name was right. There was a Sir Cosmo Duff Gordon who saved himself in a lifeboat. But I said to Amory, I said, you've made a fair mess of it this time when you tried to drop that poor woman overboard and she married to a Clancy, an Irishman. I stopped him in time, caught him in the very act, and he let go of you."

Julia with a visible effort controlled the muscles of her face and stilled the hands which convulsively gripped the comforter. "Well, thank you very much, Mary Malone. I've been troubled by that and been thinking I was having dizzy spells and hallucinations. But what about Mr. Lyman-Smith? Was he one of your . . . your targets?"

"Oh, that was Amory again. Too quick by half. Jumped the gun he did. Because of the name Smith, and we all know Captain Smith was partly responsible for the sinking. But I knew no harm of Mr. Lyman-Smith, and Amory doing it before we even sailed wasn't the plan. Amory was in London that night and going down to Southampton in the motorcoach in the morning. Helping the passengers he was supposed to be doing. But we'd never agreed to attack Mr. Lyman-Smith. That sort of thing was to be decided by everyone."

"Teddy Hogarth," said Sarah. "When someone entered our cabin which had been Teddy's. Was Teddy on your list?"

"Ah, what a mix-up that was," exclaimed Mary so loudly that Amory Frye snorted, half-opened his eyes, and then fell back in sleep. "Who was to know that worthless boy would give up a first-class cabin and move down to Five Deck." Mary wiped her eyes again and said, in a choked voice, "We never meant to be taking passengers like you hostage in a stateroom. And Amory didn't take proper care of that Mr. Hofstra the way we planned. Trying to drown him in the swimming pool, and we having to pull him out again. And leaving him tied up for anyone to find. And then there's Amory having to hide out in Mr. Hofstra's cabin and answering the telephone while all the time Mr. Hofstra's in the equipment locker. And both of us worrying about someone from Security breaking into his cabin or the equipment locker looking for him. Oh, such a muddle Amory made of it, Mr. Hofstra being found like that and Amory having to escape."

"What were you going to do with Mr. Hofstra after he was tied up?" asked Sarah.

Mary shook her head. "Oh, we were going to wait for almost the end of the *Titanic* show, and in the middle of the storm with no one on deck we'd slip him over the rail, and good riddance to the man." Here Mary reached for her glass and drained the last inch of whiskey. And Sarah with a side glance at Julia's travel clock that sat on her bedside table saw that the time for the changing of the guard was almost at hand. Unless. Unless they could further distract Mary, who slumped in her chair, looked like a talking doll whose machinery had wound down. Whose hand wandered back and forth waving its pistol first at one head, an ear, sometimes at knees and then back to point at a chest, a neck, a throat.

"Mary," said Sarah, still keeping her voice low, "I'm so happy you saved Aunt Julia."

"Ah, yes. Well, Amory wasn't so well pleased. Claimed she reminded him of his aunt and a terrible woman she was, he said. Used to beat the boy senseless."

"I'm sorry," said Sarah for lack of anything else to say. Then, thinking to move the conversation to safer shores, asked, "Mary, do you have any family at all now? In Ireland, I mean?"

But what the answer would be, Julia and Sarah never knew.

It all happened at once. The knock on the door. The small click of a key in the stateroom door lock. A man's voice calling, saying, Maintenance, that there was a leak and he was coming in. Another voice saying Steward here, that there was an emergency, he was coming in. Then Alex's voice, demanding that everyone stay exactly as they were. No one would be hurt.

And Amory Frye, jerking up to his knees, to his feet like a disheveled puppet hoisted by his strings, reaching for Mary and Mary's gun. And Mary shrinking back from him, standing up, pushing back her chair.

And the door opening and four men one after the other walking into the stateroom. And Amory lunging at Mary. Mary, taking her pistol in both hands, taking a wobbling aim, shooting. And shooting again. And again. Pumping three bullets straight into Amory Frye.

And Amory, a look of astonishment on his face staggering back, sliding in slow motion down the wall to the carpet, leaving a long red smear on the white paint to mark his descent. A puddle of blood marking Amory's resting place; a puddle that began to widen and would soon threaten to debase the water that flowed steadily under the bathroom floor.

Sarah, even if she had been placed in a court of law and made to swear to the truth, the whole truth, and nothing but the truth, would have failed. After the entrance of the four men—Alex, Sam, and the two crew members—and Mary Malone's shooting of Amory Frye, the whole stateroom scene fractured itself, turned itself into a kaleidoscope of shifting and arriving persons, persons in uniform, in states of undress, furniture being shoved aside, lights being turned on; a cacophony of voices, sobbing (Mary), swearing (Sam), remonstrating and exclaiming (the steward), demanding (Alex), finally, ordering, commanding (officers and crew). The end being that Mary Malone, divested of her weapon, was led off in a tearful and trembling state for parts unknown while Sarah and Julia were both firmly escorted, together with the necessaries of Julia's wardrobe, to Sarah's stateroom, after which Julia crawled thankfully into Alex's bed. Alex himself followed Sam, and the stretcher-borne Amory Frye to the ship's hospital, either to assist in assessing damage or to join with colleagues in declaring the man dead.

Sarah, finding sleep the furthest thing from her mind, listened to Julia's somewhat incoherent recounting of what she had thought of as a moment of hallucination on that first day aboard ship but had become—Julia was now speaking in caps—a Sinister Attack. This tale was in turn followed by an angry rehash of what Julia called the Arrest and Interrogation by the ship's security officers, and next by a less than lucid assessment of Mary Malone and her role in the night's events. But finally, with an assist from another jolt of whiskey and with the perception that the storm seemed to be abating and the rolling of the great ship had lessened, Julia wound down, mumbled to a stop, slipped down on her pillow, and was asleep.

Leaving Sarah to toss and wrestle with bedclothes and finally fall asleep at the dawn of Sunday morning, July the second.

It was well past ten when first Julia, and then Sarah by reason of Julia's noisy bathroom splashing, woke. Woke to a gleam of sunshine outside the porthole and the sense that the ship had improved vastly in steadiness. Both ladies, none too chipper, dressed quickly and were about to take stock of what the day might hold when a knock sounded, Alex's voice was heard, the key turned, and he entered. Looking as unhealthy as the ladies in his party.

"A shower," he said. "Then breakfast and I'll tell you what I can."

"No you don't," said Sarah. "Tell us right now what's happened. To Amory Frye. I mean is he alive?"

Alex nodded. "Just. Lost a lot of blood. Two shots went through his chest and grazed his lung, the third ruptured his spleen. The hospital is set up for most emergencies, but this one is quite a challenge."

"Were you up all night?" asked Julia, who was struggling into a light cotton jacket, a choice dictated by the idea of a smoother sea and a lesser breeze.

"Not all of it. I helped a little in an advisory capacity to stabilize the patient as far as possible. Then I crashed in Sam's stateroom, which has two beds."

"And Mary Malone?" queried Julia. "I do feel sorry for her."

"I'd say it's damn lucky she felt sorry for you," said Sarah crisply, "or you might be quite dead by now."

Alex nodded. "I think that's right on the money. Mary, before they took her away, said she'd left a red tab on Julia's door as a sign that Julia was off limits. The green on General Gordon's door meant that he was a chosen one. Same with our cabin—formerly Teddy Hogarth's. Later when we moved in, a red tab exchanged for green. We were protected by being related to Julia. It was a pretty simple-minded scheme, but then Mary Malone isn't exactly a professional terrorist. Now let's save the rest of it. After breakfast we can let it all hang out on the line. And I'll just bet Sarah has some dirty laundry to air. This Gerald Hofstra business, for one. Liza Baum and that Teddy Hogarth seem to have been in on it, not old faithful dog Alex."

Breakfast in the Osborne Cafeteria over, the three travelers repaired to a quiet nest of deck chairs somewhere near the bow on Boat Deck. "After all," Sarah pointed out, "everyone is back on the Quarter Deck playing games and swimming and telling each other how much they loved the rough weather. We can be exclusive."

"I wish you'd say 'aft,' not 'back,' " said Alex. "Otherwise, love of my life, you are perfect."

"Not quite perfect," said Sarah, settling down in her chair. "I haven't exactly—as you suggested—been open about what I was up to. Of course, from time to time you were both busy doing your thing, Julia off with Erik Anderson and Alex with Sam Greenbank."

"To continue the dirty laundry analogy, that excuse will not wash," said Alex.

"I," said Julia, "am always available. But I do try to give the younger generation some space."

"Okay, okay," said Sarah. "I kept some things to myself because everyone always thinks I'm—"

"No excuses," said Julia. "Out with it."

And Sarah, drawing a deep breath, began. She skipped much of her afternoon in the utility closet because, after all, she had told Julia much of what she had overheard. As for the search for Gerald Hofstra, as she reminded them, they had all been involved in that. "But I do owe you a summary of how I found out about Gerald's things being in the swimming pool and how Liza discovered him wrapped in a badminton net.

"You see, if we believe Mary Malone, Gerald Hofstra was to be the third victim. Amory had run over Donald Lyman-Smith in London—ahead of schedule and not even aboard the *Vicky*— then he tried to dump Aunt Julia over the rail as victim number two, but he was stopped by Mary Malone. Then General Gordon was taken care of—I have no idea how, but maybe Mary will explain. Probably one good hard push. Julia must have been a random first-class passenger choice, but the general and Donald Lyman-Smith, both first-class passengers, were loosely linked to the *Titanic* by their names."

"And Hofstra was a natural because he was such a *Titanic* enthusiast," said Julia.

"He had plenty of company in that," said Alex. "We've all been caught up in a *Titanic* epidemic. My God, over two hundred million spent on that movie."

"Then why did Amory Frye and company get worked up about Richard Herrick and Hofstra's production?" demanded Sarah. "I mean if it was such an everyday event, *Titanic* shows all over the map."

"Not 'everyday,' " said Alex. "It was to be a dramatic program about a very famous British ship sinking on her maiden voyage to New York. And this show was taking place on *another* British ship on *her* maiden voyage to New York and fairly close to the same latitude where the *Titanic* went down. Come on, that is an attention getter."

"Now comes the real confession," Sarah admitted. "Remember I've been queasy about Aubrey Smith and his lady friends. I don't know if I've told you, but I've caught the ladies lying in their teeth. I don't suppose they're connected with Mary Malone and Amory Frye and the other mystery people, but who knows? What are they hiding? Aubrey took me aside in Harrods after hours and went on about how he was hired—by either the shipping company's people or British intelligence, he was very mysterious about it all—to track down some threats to the *Vicky*, some crazy revenge plot, he said. One that might be connected to the *Titanic*. Or the *Lusitania*, the *Andrea Doria*— you name it. He claimed that any British passenger ship might be in danger. And to be wary and to steer clear of Gerald Hofstra, who might be, in his words, an 'attractive nuisance.' I thought that was a little sinister."

"Well, he's right," observed Alex. "Hofstra is, was, and may still be an attractive nuisance."

"I asked Aubrey about his two girlfriends and he wouldn't answer. Dodged a question about taking the Harrods bag and told me not to mention the conversation to anyone. He complained that I kept turning up where I shouldn't and I was to cease and desist. Anyway, I didn't tell either of you, and now I guess I was wrong."

"All things considered, you most certainly should have told us," said Julia. She had taken out her hunting-scene needlepoint and was busy working the legs of a foxhound.

"One more thing and I'm finished," said Sarah. "I'll leave out my suspicion that Father Peter Bottomley is in cahoots with our friend Aubrey Smith—offering him his Chapel office, things like that. But I've had this crazy idea that Aubrey Clyde Smith is a pseudonym. Borrowed from C. Aubrey Smith, the old movie actor with the bushy eyebrows."

"Come off it," said Alex. "Common names all of them. Hundreds of British Aubreys, Clydes, and millions of Smiths worldwide. And I don't remember a C. Aubrey Smith."

Julia put down her needle. "Freddie Bartholomew's grandfather in *Little Lord Fauntleroy*. Now wait a minute. Hold it. Don't say a word. I have an idea as crazy as Sarah's. C. Aubrey Smith, Aubrey Clyde Smith. And he has a cousin, Vivian Smith."

"Yes," said Sarah impatiently.

"Be quiet. I think I have it. Cousins," observed Julia, who was enjoying herself, "often have the same last name. Since they're related."

Sarah reached over and gave Julia a little poke. "Stop it and put us out of our misery."

"Shh," hissed Julia. "Let me think. Vivian Smith has a dear

friend from South Carolina, Margaret Lee. A good southern name."

"Who is not entirely from South Carolina," Sarah put in.

"And," continued Julia, "I ask you what are some nick-names for Margaret? Shall I run down them? Peggy, Peg, Margie, among others. And Maggie."

Sarah raised her head. "Maggie Lee? So?" But then she stopped and a wide grin spread over her face. "You're right. Aunt Julia, you're a genius. It's a switcheroo. Maggie goes with Smith. Maggie Smith. Starred in *The Prime of Miss Jean Brodie*. They show it once a year on the movie channels."

"By George," said Alex, "I think you've got it."

"And," finished Sarah triumphantly, "if we have Maggie Smith, then we have Vivian Lee or, properly spelled, L-E-I-G-H. Our southern belle. We've been making remarks about Scarlett O'Hara and there it was, smack in our face. A movie actor scam. But, dammit, why?"

Julia took up her needlepoint again. "I've done my work," she said complacently. "You come up with the other answers."

"But now it seems so easy," Sarah protested. "I said Aunt Julia was a genius but really, anybody could guess it."

"But we didn't," Alex pointed out. "It took three of us almost five days and a raft of disturbing events, and Sarah prowling around after Aubrey Smith and company, to come up with all this. And," he added, "it may just be a coincidence, these names. Perfectly ordinary names."

"I don't think so." Sarah almost shouted it.

"What don't you think?" said a voice.

It was Aubrey Clyde Smith. He stood over them, and for the first time since their acquaintance, Sarah saw that he was not his usual well-kept, clear-eyed, urbane self. Fatigue was written all over his face, his posture; his eyes were circled and his shirt was so rumpled that it suggested a night spent outside of his bunk.

Julia thrust her needle into her canvas and sat up, Alex cleared his throat and opened his mouth, but Sarah beat him to it.

"What," she demanded, "is your real name?"

264

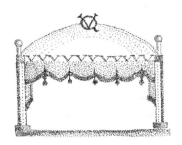

22

AUBREY Smith, ignoring Sarah, gave the party a general nod, reached for a nearby deck chair, and drew it close to Julia's elbow. "I may sit down, may I not?" he said and sank with a sigh of relief onto the seat. "I don't thrive on one hour's sleep," he added. "But the ocean has quieted down and some control has been established below deck, so I expect to be able to take a nap this afternoon."

"But you can answer our question, can't you?" asked Sarah.

"Our question? Do you all have the same question? Or a battery of questions all of which I probably can't answer?"

"We would," said Alex, speaking as to a patient who was not cooperating with his medication schedule, "like to hear about what Sarah calls the Gang of Three. A gang she claims has been sailing under false colors."

"And false names," said Sarah. "So let's start with you."

"Oh, dear," said Aubrey. "My first name is Aubrey, my middle name is Clyde."

"And Smith?" asked Julia.

"Smith is such a popular name," said Aubrey. "I thought it would fit in with the other two."

"Did you think of C. Aubrey Smith, the actor?" asked Sarah.

Aubrey shook his head. "I rue the day I spoke to you and Alex in the Snuggery. I suppose you, Sarah, despite my request to keep quite quiet about plots and threats and my job on the ship, have now spread the word. Would it help if I told you again that the master of the *Victoria*, Captain Mitchie, knows why I am aboard? And that the chief of Security is also aware of me?"

"I didn't think I could bother the captain in the middle of a major storm to ask if this Aubrey Smith is who he says he is."

"I took a chance you wouldn't. And Captain Mitchie would deny me as an investigator. He would identify me as someone interested in security systems—electronic monitors, concealed cameras, things like that. Which I am, of course, but not directly on this trip."

"So how can we trust you?" asked Sarah sharply.

"The Security Office will admit—if they are backed up against the wall—that I am helping with certain personnel problems. Do you want to go over right now and have a chat with them? I'll come with you, even though I'd much rather stay here with my feet up and my eyes closed."

"Alex can go along?" Sarah had visions of another tryst in Harrods or, worse, in the utility closet.

"Yes."

Sarah hesitated, looked over at Alex, who lifted his eyebrows in a noncommittal gesture. She looked down the long deck, where singles and couples had begun to walk vigorously or jog; looked out to sea and saw the now diminished waves had settled into engaging patterns of moving shadow and sun.

"I don't know what I think," she said uncertainly.

"You could," returned Aubrey, "simply trust me. What does that man—was it Kierkegaard?—call it, a leap of faith?"

"The man," said Julia, who sometimes revealed a knowledge beyond the care of horses, "was not talking about people traveling under false pretenses aboard a ship; he was talking about God."

Sarah took a deep breath, saw Alex lift his eyebrows in an encouraging manner, and said, "Okay. Okay. We'll trust you. Though we might . . . what's the expression . . ."

"Curse the day," suggested Aubrey.

"Kick ourselves," said Julia, returning to a horse metaphor.

"But then *you* have to trust *us*," insisted Sarah. "What about your name? And Margaret Lee and your so-called cousin, Vivian Smith? All of you British actors?"

"Would that we were. It would be a lot more fun," said Aubrey. "I won't tell you our real names. That, as our onetime enemy says, is verboten. But you've sniffed it out. You see, we didn't have much time to put a surveillance team together. The direct threats to *Victoria* came in less than a week before sailing to the shipping company, and they passed the information along to our people."

"But who is 'our people' "? demanded Julia.

"Mrs. Clancy, we're going in for trust. My employers are a low-profile lot, so let me finish without every detail in place. We had to scramble to find out who was available to make the trip. Put together a persona for each of us. We grabbed at theatrical names we could remember. C. Aubrey Smith, Maggie Smith, and Vivian Leigh. With a little changing about we turned into the people you, Sarah, have been trailing for the last few days. The woman you know as Margaret Lee has indeed spent time in the southern U.S. I told you she has a place in South Carolina. And she has done a good bit of acting at one time, is an excellent mimic, and we thought she'd do well working with a southern accent and making friends on that basis. Just another friendly American who talks to everyone."

"But she blew it."

"She knows that. It was being seasick. We hadn't considered what a storm can do to one's concentration. She said she just reverted to a British vocabulary. A few times, not often."

" 'Ladder' for a run in the stocking, for instance," Sarah said.

"Not fatal but awkward," said Aubrey. "We used the name Smith hoping we'd attract this revenge group, that the name of *Titanic*'s captain would be a focus, and perhaps Vivian Smith or I would, as they say, draw the fire."

"You mean," said Julia, "you were ready to be pushed overboard or banged on the head."

"Or nailed by a car in front of the Savoy, though we never thought it would begin before sailing. But Amory Frye is a hothead. Among other things. But yes, we were ready to be targets. It's part of the job, and lest you think we're being overly brave, all three of us have been quite nervy over the whole business."

"You never really stayed together," Alex reminded him.

"As a matter of fact," said Aubrey, "we did." He indicated his hearing aid. "I'm not really hard of hearing. Neither is Margaret, but we can communicate. And Vivian has a very useful watch. Our modus operandi was to mix in with as many passengers as possible, eat often in separate dining rooms, sign up for as many activities as we could fit in, and so get a sense of the passengers and their interactions with crew."

"You were the weirdest group I'd ever seen," said Sarah. "I wondered why so-called friends were never together and why on earth you were all frantically chatting it up with anyone who came along. And those programs, Vivian signing up for a fat suction clinic. You at beginners' bridge. Are you a beginner?"

"I am," said Aubrey with a modest smile, "a life master. That class was torture. In general, Margaret was to keep an eye on the Four and Five Decks and the social activities people. Vivian and I concentrated on the Balmoral or first-class passengers—the most likely targets. But we all intermixed with both groups."

"Did you watch stewards and crew members?" asked Julia.

"Yes, particularly after General Gordon's death, which we're almost sure was due to an assault. We became convinced that at least one of the revenge team was part of the crew—a maintenance person, a steward—someone who could open cabins and go about the ship without any questions."

"Well, well, well," said a voice. "What evil lurks in the hearts of men?" It was Liza Baum. And Teddy behind her. Both looking well rested.

"Ah," said Aubrey, looking up. "The rest of the Unholy Alliance. I had rather hoped you both would have found something else to do other than playing games in the swimming pool. That Ted here might have decided to read over his trade commission briefs."

"You're not a plant here sent by my father?" demanded Teddy.

"Thank heavens I am not," said Aubrey. "But I spoke to your father the other night, and he hopes you're—"

"Being a good little boy," said Teddy. "Depends what you mean by that. Besides, someone should be grateful we found Gerald Hofstra rolled up in that net."

"I think," said Aubrey dryly, "he is adequately grateful. And he's doing very well. Back to his stateroom, I believe."

"Under guard, I hope," said Liza.

Aubrey nodded. "As you say." He hesitated, turned his attention to a couple who were walking in an entwined condition down the deck. "Ah, young love . . . or young glands. Anyway, friends, if I may call you so, I'm about to take another 'leap of faith' and admit you two into the charmed circle. Liza I've had checked out, and although she's a little on the wayward side, she can be trusted. As for Teddy, if he stays away from the temptations of the bar, well, I think we can trust him, too. I've known his father from the year one and Teddy since he was in his pram."

"So what are you talking about?" asked Liza suspiciously.

"Only that it would be helpful if you two continue to keep yourselves alert. We are worried that Mr. Hofstra will remain a target since he escaped—through your help—what was planned for him. I'd like to talk to you all later this afternoon. Sketch in a few more details and tell you what's happened so far. I think you all deserve this, even if we haven't been exactly grateful for your activities up to now. How about around teatime? Don't come in a bunch; we don't want to attract any more attention than has already been done."

"Come where?" said Alex, lowering his binoculars; his attention had been partly directed at some passing gulls.

"My friend, Father Bottomley, has, with a little extra persuasion, allowed us to use his study again. The one with the wooden panels in which Sarah has shown such interest."

Julia stared at him. "Don't tell me," she said, "that you've roped the poor chaplain into your affairs."

"I was at school with Peter. He was in the lower fourth when I was in the upper fifth. Things like that have great weight.

And I'd like to have someone else join us. Someone who has been marginally involved in what we've been trying to do. Erik Anderson is an old friend and he's been helpful. Mrs. Clancy, I believe you know Mr. Anderson?"

And Julia, sitting bolt upright, eyes flashing, nodded without speaking.

Sarah, thinking to change the subject—Julia looked ready to explode—looked over in a seaward direction. "Don't look now, but another couple seem interested in our group. Our French dinner buddies, or I should say, Alex's bird students. Adèle and Charlotte." She tilted her head toward the rail and there, true enough, stood the two sisters under the shadow of a lifeboat, looking rather like two crows in their matching long navy skirts and black long-sleeved shirts.

Aubrey studied the pair, who, on being examined, swiveled about and looked toward the horizon. He frowned at Sarah. "Do they fit in any way into any scenario you've been hatching, Sarah?"

Sarah hesitated. "No," she said finally. "I did hear people speaking French when I was in my utility closet, but they went away down the corridor. Then the Frederick voice. And Mary and Amory."

"Were you going to suggest that those two women were trying just now to listen in on our conversation?" persisted Aubrey.

Sarah shook her head. "No. But I caught sight of them a few seconds ago looking at us. Besides, I think they only speak French."

"Don't be too sure of that," said Liza unexpectedly. "The French make a point of only speaking French even if they can speak five other languages."

Aubrey looked at his watch. "Time for me to have another word with Mary Malone. This whole business isn't finished by a long shot. And I need my nap. Until four-fifteen, then."

"I," announced Julia, beginning the struggle to get out of her deck chair, "am going to have a word with Mr. Erik Anderson."

"One more thing, Mrs. Clancy," said Aubrey, reaching out

a hand to help her to her feet. "Where did you get that black round piece of paper that was found in your needlepoint bag with the message about ten o'clock? Some passengers have had others like it and turned them in. None of the ship's people have the least idea where they've been coming from."

"I don't know," said Julia, looking displeased. "I gave mine over to Security and told them it had turned up in my needlepoint bag. Sarah found one, too. In a rubbish bin."

"So did I," added Liza. "It's just a stupid joke."

"All right," said Aubrey. "If anyone hears of any more black paper disks let me or the Security Office know."

"If I find out," said Julia crossly, "who put the thing in my bag, I will wring his neck."

"Or her neck," said Alex, putting his binoculars aside and reaching for his bird guide. Something atypical about that gull with the wide wing span.

"This black circle business," said Julia, "to be sexist about it, is, I'd say, a typical male trick."

At that the group broke up and went their way: Teddy and Liza to the gym, Liza prodding Teddy in the small of his back; Julia to find Erik Anderson to discuss his concealed relationship with Aubrey Smith, which Julia had begun to think was based on some questionable level of intelligence gathering; and last Alex and Sarah, both heavy-eyed from lack of sleep, to make several slow circuits around the deck—all of them, as Sarah remarked, like endangered animals in a very large ark.

But before they had gone more than fifteen steps in an aft direction Sarah suddenly halted, turned, and walked up to Adèle and Charlotte, who had not moved from their station under the lifeboat.

"*Bon jour,*" said Sarah in a pleasant voice, and then in the same level tone she said, "I'm so sorry, Adèle, but I have to tell you there is a large spider crawling up the side of your neck."

The results were gratifying, and Sarah left Adèle wrenching at her blouse and brushing wildly at her neck.

"That," she told Alex with satisfaction, "is that. Another pair of frauds in our midst."

"Of course," Alex reminded her, "We should have known

they spoke English. Remember how all that talk about black mambas and scalps and pieces of liver disgusted the ladies and they mentioned getting another table. Liza is right; those two prefer speaking French but their comprehension of other languages is in good working order."

"So, tell me," said Sarah, "does it mean anything? Anything important?"

But Alex gave a weary shake of his head. "I think, my love, we have merely stumbled on a well-known behavior pattern of the French."

Sarah, feeling a strong sense of déjà vu, walked with Alex past the small row of deserted pews, slipped behind the altar and through the oak door marked with a brass plate proclaiming CHAPLAIN QUEEN VICTORIA, and into Father Peter Bottomley's private sanctum.

Julia was in place, having snagged Father Bottomley's desk chair, and Alex and Sarah settled themselves on two leather-covered side chairs. Again Sarah found herself examining the painted wooden panels of the saints whose existence had first revealed that Vivian Smith was not a teller of truth. The air in the office was warm, and while she waited Sarah found herself drifting into a reverie about the painted panels, imagining Saint George and his dragon in conversation with Saint David about the edibility of leeks and chatting with Saint Patrick on how to tell a venomous asp from a common garden snake. Saint Andrew she pictured lurking behind a rowan tree, wearing a kilt, and ready to spring forth with a claymore—to do what, she hadn't decided.

From these imaginings she was jolted by the arrival of Erik Anderson, who, dwarfing the room by his height and bulk, walked in, waved in a cheery way to the company, and sat down on the long cushioned bench under the porthole. Julia, looking up at the same time as Sarah, frowned, picked up her needlepoint, and jabbed a threaded needle hard into the fabric. Teddy and Liza came next, not exactly as a happy couple, Sarah decided. Teddy appeared to be simmering about something and Liza's entrance suggested a cat ready to scratch.

Teddy, looking about for a chair, found a folding metal number and drew it up to Sarah. "We've had a fight," he informed her.

"Sorry to hear it," said Sarah, who really did not want to be drawn into whatever was going on between the two.

"Fact is," said Teddy, leaning forward in a confidential way, "I told her I really had to spend time with my briefing papers and couldn't play all day until we disembark. She wants to have fun. After all, her job is done; she's on vacation."

"Oh?" answered Sarah.

"I think she wants me as some sort of Teddy bear, to push about and order around, and I don't fill—"

"Good afternoon, all," said a quiet voice. Aubrey Smith had arrived, Teddy subsided, and the rest looked up expectantly, while Sarah filed away the fact that Teddy and Liza were in a two-way snit and that Julia looked ready to run Erik Anderson through with her tapestry needle.

"Let's start with Mr. Hofstra," began Aubrey. "He is a matter of great concern. He represents unfinished business. From what we've understood of this team's plan, he should have been disposed of by now. But now, I suppose to their chagrin, he's back in his own stateroom, well guarded, I may add. We are worried that Mr. Hofstra will remain a target since he escaped—through your help—what was planned for him."

Sarah looked up, alarmed. "Do you mean to say that you're going to allow Gerald Hofstra to go roaming around the deck and eat dinner and just act like an ordinary passenger?"

"We can hardly put him in irons. He's furious, wants action, and, showman that he is, wants to go ahead with the *Titanic* program. I've tried to talk him out of the idea, but he's . . ."

"Got the bit in his teeth," put in Julia.

"Exactly. And since the *Vicky*'s social director contracted for such a show, I suppose he will be allowed to go ahead."

"Richard Herrick wants to do it again!" exclaimed Liza.

"No. He says he's done his part and it's over. At least for this trip. But Gerald is a stubborn man. After all, he's a man who wouldn't let himself be drowned so he can—"

"Hang tough about this," finished Sarah.

"Correct. The trouble is that Mr. Hofstra's enthusiasm for staging a *Titanic* extravaganza made him an excellent target. And now he's planning on doing the show as originally planned. We hope and pray that the removal of Mary Malone and Amory Frye from the scene will forestall any more attacks. And that there's a limit to the number of people trying to do in Balmoral-class passengers. The two that we have in custody have been remarkably clumsy. If anyone else is involved, let's hope he or she is just as stupid. Unfortunately we can't learn anything from Amory Frye because he's unconscious, and Mary Malone is too frightened and upset to cooperate."

"She cooperated last night," Julia pointed out. "She told us all about it. How it began and how Amory had bungled everything."

"But you had the advantage of Mary being in an emotional state and half drunk with whiskey. We can hardly pour alcohol down her throat, and since the days of the rack are behind us, we have to count her out as a source of information."

Sarah, becoming more and more impatient, waved a hand for Aubrey's attention. "What," she called out, "about the other person? What about my hearing Frederick's voice? With Mary and Amory. He's our waiter in the Windsor Castle Dining Room and he probably has access to all sorts of places and people on the ship."

Aubrey nodded. "Yes, we have your description of hearing a voice with possibly a south of England accent, but the ship's roster shows about twenty crew members who have lived for a time in Cornwall, Devon, Somerset, and thereabouts. One of them is the waiter, Frederick. And yes, we plan to keep an eye on him."

"You mean," Sarah objected, "you'll let poor Gerald Hofstra go into the dining room tonight, and if you're not on your toes Frederick might take a carving knife to the guy. Finish the job."

"I don't like the man," said Julia sharply, "but I'm not sure he should be allowed to float around like some balloon ready to be punctured. I would think . . ."

Aubrey raised the palm of his hand in an arresting motion and Julia subsided. "Mr. Hofstra is as mad as a hornet about what he rightly considers an attempt to kill him, and he assures us that he won't go anywhere alone. We will have a man watching him at all times, and several of the waiters in the Windsor Castle Dining Room belong to the ship's security team. To repeat, he's adamant about staging the *Titanic* show—a true son of the theater."

"A sitting duck for anyone with a stiletto tucked up his sleeve," put in Teddy.

"You, Ted, and the others are only being asked to be alert. That's why I asked you here. We don't want any more dramatic moments. And you should know that Gerald wants this last night to be a happy one. He's asked that all the people he's met and who have been helpful—you, Teddy, and Liza and Sarah, for instance—eat dinner at adjoining tables. I think he wants to end the trip with a flourish—toasts, wine, champagne."

"But," said Sarah again, "you really will watch Frederick, won't you? I'm sorry to keep talking about him, but it's a little scary thinking of him passing food and carving meat next to Gerald's table. Couldn't all of us try to surround Gerald, protect him somehow?"

Aubrey tipped back in his chair, folded his hands over his stomach, and smiled at Sarah—the sort of forbearing smile she associated with her father when she had produced some wild idea that, if carried out, would bring ruin on her family.

"Sarah, everyone, believe me, our people and the ship's security personnel are taking care of it. Now, please, go along and keep everything I've said to yourselves. Thanks for your support and I'll see you at dinner."

Julia was the first to leave. Vespers was just over, the tiny organ was playing "Eternal Father Strong to Save," and as she joined the small stream of passengers up the Chapel aisle, she brooded not about the safety of Gerald Hofstra, but about questionable Erik Anderson. She, Julia, had been open in all things with this man. She had talked about her life, her husband, Tom, her farm, her family. She had been very tolerant of Brian and Kirsten, his racketing grandchildren. And now she had found out that Anderson had been working undercover for Aubrey Smith and not saying a word about it. Well! So much for mutual confidence. Unfortunately, Gerald Hofstra's idea of a festive farewell gathering meant that Erik would be around at dinnertime, so some appearance of civility must be kept up. But after tonight, Julia would go her own solitary, independent way. To borrow a phrase from the late Thomas O'Sullivan Clancy, bad cess to Mr. Anderson.

Alex and Sarah followed Julia out of the Chapel and turned their steps toward the stairway C Lift, both too tired to climb even one flight of stairs.

"So the *Titanic* show is on again," said Sarah as she and Alex reached their stateroom. "Poor Richard Herrick, he's certainly done his bit. Anyway, it's all a bit much but I'm too tired to care."

"Care about what?"

"You know," said Sarah as they reached their stateroom, "to care who does what to who."

"To whom."

"What I'm saying is to hell with the whole damn business." And Sarah opened the door and flopped fully dressed on the bed.

"So," said Sarah, that evening as the two climbed the stairs which led to the Boat Deck and the Windsor Castle Dining Room, "what's this party idea of Gerald's? Are we eating with our usual group?"

"Who knows?" said Alex. "Gerald may be trying for the Hollywood touch. Or Deedee may want to mix us up. But stop stewing over Gerald's safety. After all, Aubrey told you that a number of waiters will actually be security people on the prowl."

"Won't Frederick, if it is Frederick, be suspicious if a bunch of new waiters turn up?"

"I gather the security people have been acting as waiters off and on for the entire trip. Frederick's cowaiter, name of Colleen, is one hefty lady, in case you haven't noticed. I'll bet she's under cover."

"You mean with an AK-forty-seven in under her apron."

"You've got it." Alex paused at the dining room entrance. "That's a pretty snazzy outfit you're wearing."

Sarah gave Alex a look of exasperation. "It's Aunt Julia's present and the same black skirt and blouse with a different scarf added that I've worn every night. I'm trying for a presence, which is pretty hard when you're built like a lesser praying mantis."

"And here we are," said Alex in an unnaturally loud and cheerful voice as the maître d' bowed them into the dining room, and with a good deal of nodding and bowing Sarah and Alex were put in Frederick's charge.

"It's Mr. Hofstra," the waiter explained. "He feels ever so much better after his seasickness, and since it's the last night at sea he wants it to be special. So all his friends are sitting at different tables. If you have no objection. A real party Mr. Hofstra wants it, with champagne all round. Now, Miss Deane will be with Mr. and Mrs. Herrick, and Dr. McKenzie will be at Mr. Hofstra's table."

"Oh, Sarah," exclaimed Deedee, who was glistening in a sequined blue number with a challenging neckline, "it's such fun, mixing us all up like this. Sitting in different places. Sometimes Gerald has good ideas. Saying good-bye to all the people we've met."

"I think," said Richard, whose expression was a dour one, "we've met enough people to last us a lifetime."

"I'm sorry I couldn't stay for all of it, but I hear that your *Titanic* lecture was a great success," said Sarah. "Even without Gerald and his magic tricks."

Richard shrugged. "I played the hand as it was dealt. A pretty plain hand. But people were kind. And now, if you can believe it, Gerald is just fine and putting on this dinner affair. And he says we'll be doing the whole damned show over tonight at ten. Doing it properly, he says. Tonight! I said no, but he was adamant. Said people are really into it. That my little talk last evening—those were his words—was a warm-up. And I still don't know why he was hiding out. He talks about being a little out of his head and forgetting where he was."

"I liked Richard up on stage by himself being dignified and just telling the story," said Deedee. "I was proud of him. It's the way we started. A simple story and some slides."

"We didn't even have slides last night," said Richard. He scowled and turned his attention to the menu, and Sarah, finding Teddy Hogarth on her other side, allowed herself to relax; Richard's ill humor left a sour feeling. Teddy, however, seemed entirely sober, and Sarah realized this was one of the few times she had seen him as a person, not as an object of Liza's solicitude, her proddings and pokings. He was neatly put together, dinner jacket, black tie and cummerbund, hair slicked, looking like an ad for conservative young men's apparel. Teddy, Sarah decided, might turn out to be just another rather ordinary government appendage, albeit one with an ambiguous past.

"Here's to our last night," said Teddy to Sarah. "Although I don't remember the first night and was sick as a cat the second."

"How is life without the cocktail hour?" asked Sarah. Teddy might not be her first choice for a dinner partner on the last night aboard, but he was a vast improvement over Richard Herrick.

"I miss that first glorious buzz when number-one drink slips down my throat, and I can't say much for lemonade or carrot juice or even Coca-Cola. But spicy hors d'oeuvres keep me going, which probably means I'll have ulcers by the time I leave New York."

"And what did you think about our lecture this afternoon?" said Sarah, lowering her voice and giving Teddy a meaningful look.

"You mean do I think the butler or the waiter did it? Or was the—what's the term—the mastermind?" asked Teddy. "Don't answer that. However, I intend watching your suspect, Frederick, especially if he's using sharp instruments, although frankly I don't think anything is going to happen in a great big lighted dining room."

"Well," said Sarah lightly, "let's just keep our fingers crossed."

23

SARAH picked up her menu and made a show of puzzling over the evening's choices. The last night aboard ship often featured, she had been told, a dazzling selection of culinary items, so that the *Vicky*'s passengers would be left, literally, with a good taste in their mouths. And because the ocean was fast settling into a beneficent mood, the chances were excellent that most diners would be taking advantage of the augmented menu.

Holding the big royal-blue and gold-tasseled menu in front of her, Sarah spent the moments before ordering to look around. Get a fix on everyone and try to get a sense of this odd sort of gala of Gerald Hofstra's. Looking about the dining room, she thought she sensed a heightened gaiety. Although evening dress was not required on this the last night, many women passengers wore their finery, white dinner jackets were in evidence, and the talk from all directions buzzed louder than on previous nights. All in all there was a sense of an ending, that in less than twenty-four hours the coach would turn to a pumpkin and real life would engulf them all.

Where, thought Sarah, had Alex ended up? Ah, there he was, at one of the tables within the orbit managed by Frederick and the waitress Colleen. Colleen, Sarah decided, while probably not a linebacker, could undoubtedly wreck havoc on any person she chose. The woman as Alex had noted was built like an off-the-road vehicle. Had she gotten her job through a skill in gracefully tossing a salad, or was she one of Aubrey & Co.'s minions? Craning her neck toward Gerald Hofstra's table, she saw Cousin Vivian next to Alex with Sam Greenbank on her other side, then Aubrey Smith, Gerald, and on Gerald's other flank an unknown young gentleman of strong jaw and generous proportions.

Gerald himself, Sarah decided, was playing the part of the jolly host to the hilt. He snapped his fingers at the wine steward; he turned and waved at guests at surrounding tables; he gestured grandly toward the piano player, who was working his way through a Gershwin medley, calling out loudly for the theme from the *Titanic* movie. Sarah, seeing Gerald's flushed face, his brown eyes like rolling brown marbles, decided he looked like someone hoisted out of bed too soon.

Julia Clancy's table, just behind the Hofstra table, seemed to Sarah a pool of dull tranquillity. Marci and Charlie, shoulders touching, sat, goggling—there was no other word for it—at each other. Next to Charles came Margaret Lee, who, judging from audible scraps of conversation, was keeping up the charade of the southern belle, and then Julia, her fingers drumming on her menu, had a place by Erik Anderson. Erik, ever affable even in the face of a frosty Julia, spoke loudly and cheerfully in a mix of French and English. Sarah, listening, judged that he alone at the table was endeavoring to keep the social amenities afloat. The French sisters, however, seemed not to be buying into any idea of a festivity. They sat in their dark silk vests and black beads, heads bent over small plates of hors d'oeuvres. In fact, Sarah would have thought them objects created by a taxidermist if every so often Adèle or Charlotte had not lifted her head and swept the room with the gaze of a basilisk.

"Madam would care to order?" It was Colleen, bending over Sarah's shoulder.

"You first," Sarah told Teddy. She had not even focused on the evening's possibilities.

Teddy went for the *salade Nicoise, soupe à l'oignon,* and

châteaubriand béarnaise along with a bottle of Vichy water, and said he would choose the dessert later. Sarah, who wanted to keep her mind uncluttered with choices, said she'd have the same.

"Even the Vichy water?" said Teddy. "Do you have a drinking problem, too?"

"I want," said Sarah, "to have my wits about me. And here's a tidbit for you. Our French sisters over there speak English."

"I told you they did," said Liza, appearing suddenly and slipping into place next to Richard Herrick. "Sorry to be late. I found an absolutely fabulous collection of nineteenth-century theater magazines in the Snuggery. Stuff I can use for background research. Anyway, French people are like that. They have this compulsive thing about their own language. And just look at the two of them." Liza flicked a slim finger in the sisters' direction. "Like visiting buzzards, glowering and hovering over their plates."

Sarah decided that the expression "absolutely fabulous" described Liza to a T, and thought again, sadly, of her missed appointment at the Lily Langtry Beauty Salon. Liza was hung in strips of deep green silk that layered themselves on her perfect body almost like feathers. Her cheeks, her eyes, all of her simply glowed. And Teddy, who earlier had declared himself a free man, ignored his newly arrived *salade Nicoise* and stared.

"Now isn't this festive?" It was Deedee addressing the whole table. "And the roses for our tables. Gerald ordered them. Did you know there was a florist aboard? Talk about glamorous." Here Deedee paused and pushed a hand through her tight red curls—curls that seemed to be newly sheared like topiary, Sarah thought.

"Anyway," Deedee sighed, "I think it's a perfect last night if we just didn't have Gerald trying to revive his *Titanic* show."

Richard glanced up briefly from the shreds of a smoked salmon. "Right, Deedee. For once we agree on this. Enough is enough."

And so the dinner went, talk less than sparkling perhaps at Sarah's table, Richard's discontent oppressive, Deedee's enthusiasm flagging, Teddy and Liza eating hungrily. As for Sarah, she might have been dining on moist sawdust. Forced to seem calm, inside she was in a high state of apprehension. She had Frederick too much on her mind. Handsome devil that he was, tall, black-browed, agile, he seemed quite capable of overwhelming Gerald with his bare hands, and perhaps taking one or two diners along with him—Alex and Aubrey Smith for starters. She had reached the anxious point of trying to decide whether it would be assault by carving knife—several nearby diners had gone for prime roast beef—or poisoned wine. How easy, as Frederick filled the wineglasses, to drop a little strychnine into the Haut Brion Blanc or the Pouilly Fuissé when he decanted the wine. Or slip a lethal but soluble powder into the bubbling glasses of champagne that had begun to sprout on all the tables.

"Madam would care to select a dessert?"

Sarah shook herself and stared at her cleaned plate. She had finished the entreé without knowing it. She looked up and saw Frederick. In person. He must be taking dessert orders from their table, because now she saw Colleen attending to Alex's table. Waiters must have a trade-off system. Perhaps Colleen would deliver dessert and Frederick would handle the coffee.

"We have something quite special tonight," said Frederick. "It's our special Pudding Flambé Victoria. All the waiters carry it in together and we make a parade."

"Stolen right from the QE2's baked Alaska scene," said Liza. "That's what they do. It's quite fetching."

Deedee said something about imitation and flattery, and Richard said he didn't care, why not. Liza said sure, what were a few more calories, Teddy said he hoped there'd be a least a smell of brandy, and Sarah said she'd go along with the crowd.

"Pudding Flambé Victoria for everyone, then?" said Frederick, seeming pleased and reaching for the dinner dishes.

Honestly, Sarah scolded herself. Relax. What harm can come to Gerald Hofstra if Frederick is marching around the room carrying a great flaming pudding? She was beginning to wonder whether she really had overheard a voice like Frederick's. Somehow she didn't want the dinner scene to end with the man being dragged out of the room in chains. On the other hand, she didn't want Gerald to be attacked, didn't want any more blood shed, didn't want anyone she knew hurt. It was a no-win situation, and the best she could hope for was that Frederick was innocent and, if there truly was a "mastermind," as Teddy called it, running the whole business, he—they—or she—had long since jumped over the rail and ended it all.

Then Sarah stiffened. Saw Liza across the table stiffen and look up. Felt Teddy begin to rise from his chair and then sit down, his head tilted as if listening.

Because the lights had gone dim, dim, and dimmer so that the entire Windsor Castle Dining Room had become an enormous cavern of dark shadows, only the cloths of the dinner tables showing as indistinct, blurred circles of white. Then, erupting from the double serving doors, as the last lights went low, came a corps of marching waiters streaming into the room, holding aloft blazing platters.

"Good Christ," muttered Teddy into Sarah's ear. "What a setup!"

Sarah grimaced, but there was nothing to do but await the Pudding Flambé and hope that Gerald's fellow diners had ordered some less spectacular dessert—a dessert that would follow this procession and be delivered into a fully illuminated dining room.

Their pudding arrived, borne by Colleen, and was placed triumphantly on a nearby serving table. It looked, Sarah thought, rather like a pallid version of the head of John the Baptist, the beard being provided by greenery wreathing the inflated, oval-shaped object.

The parade came to an end, the lights came up, Colleen served the pudding in molten slabs to the waiting diners. Then, throughout the room, other waiters, including Frederick, began to arrive with the usual selection of desserts, and Sarah found herself slowly letting out her breath. Nothing had happened. Nothing was going to happen, and they could look forward— depressing thought—to the presentation of the original *Titanic* show. Sarah lifted her dessert fork and poked it into the soft underbelly of the Pudding Flambé Victoria. And as she lifted the lump toward her mouth, a high shiver of a scream rose from Aunt Julia's table. A scream that held its high note, and then cascaded down the scale and ended in a wild sob.

It was Marci, standing up, pointing over to Alex's table. Pointing to the back of Gerald Hofstra, who, head slightly bent forward, sat rigid in his chair, a small dark stream of red running down the side of the white tablecloth.

And for the fraction of a second, time and motion ceased: lifted glasses, raised spoons and forks held still, waiters holding dishes and wine bottles, standing like statues, heads turned and frozen, a husband assisting his wife to rise pausing, his helping hand extended in midair. And then the moment shattered and all was bustle and alarm and a disembodied voice from some sound system warned the diners to "Please stay where you are. Do not leave the dining room. Remain at your table. Repeat, please stay exactly where you are."

Sarah, half out of her chair, was stopped in midmotion by a push from Teddy. "They're taking care of it. Sit still. And keep your eyes open. Because I don't think it was Frederick."

Sarah's brain tried to adjust to this statement but failed. Instead, unable to see through the knot of people now surrounding Gerald Hofstra's table, she searched for Frederick. Had someone caught him, stopped him, held him? Yes, there he was, just in front of the small serving table, Colleen on one side and a man in an officer's uniform on the other. He stood with a look of almost foolish puzzlement on his face, one hand holding a plate on which sat a fluted glass of ice cream, the other hand, even as Sarah watched, being captured and held behind his back—Sarah saw the metallic gleam of handcuffs.

Liza leaned across the bosom of Deedee, who sat mouth open, making little moaning noises. "What do you mean, not Frederick?"

"I was looking at him," said Teddy simply. "He'd just brought in a tray. A whole tray of dishes."

"Plenty of time to slip a knife into Gerald," insisted Liza. "Or shoot him. And, my God, where were all those security people Aubrey was going on about?"

But before anyone had a chance to reply, Deedee Herrick,

with a kind of squeak, announced the arrival of the rescue team, the gurney, the ominous wheeled boxes, the IV apparatus, the scrub-suited attendants, all of whom joined the cluster around what must be either the living or the dying—or even the expired—Gerald Hofstra. Sarah could make out Alex's back; he was on his knees, bent over something, while Sam Greenbank, standing, pushed chairs aside to make room for the emergency team.

When the whole scene, from the dimming of the lights to the arrival of the blazing puddings to Marci's scream, was reviewed, it was found that each assigned watcher remembered in vivid detail three or four useful facts: the movements of Frederick; the excited behavior of Gerald, giving toast after toast; and, most importantly, how the darkening of the dining room acted to disorient. How even the fellow diners at one's own table faded into silhouettes, how waitresses and waiters disappeared, how the bright sparking lights of the procession of Puddings Flambés Victoria confused and distorted vision.

But everyone for tables around remembered the performance of one Julia Clancy. When Marci's scream died away after her companion, Charlie, placed a large hand over her mouth, and as Sam Greenbank and Alex jumped from their chairs and descended upon the white-faced Gerald, who had begun to list slowly toward a horror-stricken Aubrey Smith, Julia reared up from her own table, twisted her head, scanned the dining room, and then demanded in a piercing voice that overtopped the anxious cries of nearby diners, "Where are they? Where are those Frenchwomen? Where have Adèle and Charlotte gone?"

And everyone remembered with the greatest clarity how Aubrey Smith freed himself from the collapsing body of Gerald Hofstra, pushed back his chair, and ran like a man possessed by demons through the broken field of tables and chairs toward the open doors that led to the deck, calling for help as he ran, shouting orders, pointing at exit stations, and finally disappearing into the night.

"Julia, sit down. We have to be quiet." It was Erik Anderson taking charge—or trying to do so. But Julia, pausing only to scowl at him, turned on her fellow diners. "When did Adèle and Charlotte leave? How long have they been gone?" Then, seeing a uniformed ship's officer approaching their table, Julia sat down and beckoned him over. "You'd better find those two women," she said. "One minute they were sitting here talking to themselves before those damned puddings came in, and when the lights came back on they were gone. Just like that."

"No," interrupted Marci, who seemed to have pulled herself together. "Adèle and Charlotte planned to leave the table. They told me they didn't want to have dessert, they didn't like sweets, and would slip out and not bother anybody. I'm glad they missed seeing Gerald being wounded. They're probably sensitive. The French are supposed to be, aren't they?"

"Back up there, Marci. How do you know what they said?" demanded Charlie. "You don't speak French and they don't speak English."

"Oh, but they do," said Marci. "It was very good English. They were perfectly easy to understand. I guess they just don't want to. Maybe they're shy about it. I'm shy about trying to speak French."

"Those two," said Julia, "are about as shy as a pair of barracudas."

And then the officer, pulling up a chair, opened a notebook and began asking for names, stateroom numbers, regular table assignments, and a sort of dreary quiet descended on the group—on the whole dining room—as other men with notebooks, a man with a camera, began taking over the Windsor Castle dining room. Gerald Hofstra, bundled, blanketed, was wheeled away followed by the two ship's physicians, by Sam Greenbank and Alex. And Frederick, relieved of the tall parfait glass of melting ice cream, was led away, handcuffed, in another direction.

By eleven o'clock, two hours after the arrival of the fiery puddings, a sort of order had been restored and passengers were instructed to quietly return to their staterooms, thank you. This order, Sarah construed to mean that as long as no one lingered in passageways it didn't matter into what stateroom one settled. Julia's for instance.

In the passageway to the lifts outside the dining room Sarah and Julia said good night to Deedee Herrick—who, always the soul of ready sympathy, was literally wringing her hands over Gerald—and to Richard, who appeared delighted not to be forced into a second *Titanic* show and showed little regard for the events that caused the cancellation. It was an odd switch, Sarah thought. Deedee being kind about Gerald; Richard casting him off.

Taking hold of her aunt, she steered her toward the elevator—no stairway exercise for them tonight. Arriving at stateroom 1045, Sarah found that Liza and Teddy had beaten them to it and stood waiting outside Julia's door.

"We need to reconstruct," said Liza. "I can't believe it's those two witches. Those two little Frenchwomen."

"Who are going to the States for bird-watching and the theater," finished Teddy.

Julia opened the door and to Sarah's surprise did not banish Liza and Teddy to their proper place on Five Deck. Perhaps Julia was still keyed up, needed the excitement, even the aggravation of other people around. "Do you think it's really not Frederick?" asked Julia as she perched herself on the edge of her bed.

"He didn't have time, he was bringing in a big tray," said Teddy. He pulled up a straight chair from the dressing table and straddled it. "I was watching him."

"The idea is," said Liza, "to find those two females."

"I suppose," said Julia, sitting up straight on the bed, "that the entire ship's complement is doing just that. Lifeboats, staterooms, engine room, the Chapel, the gym, the theaters. It might take days."

"Plus," said Liza, "there are all the laundries, the cleaning supply and utility closets on every deck."

Sarah stared at her. Utility closets. Her utility closet. Those French-speaking voices. One of the sets of voices she had heard that long Friday afternoon. Not just the voices of Frederick,

Mary Malone, and Amory Frye, but before those, women's voices. Whispery voices speaking French. Were they Adèle and Charlotte walking along the passageway? *Patrolling* the passageway? The reference to "they." "They'll be after you," Amory's voice had said. And then Mary's fearful refusal—after the shooting of Amory—to say anything about the other unknown assassins. Oh, God.

A knock at the door. Aubrey Smith. A tousled, disheveled, red-faced Aubrey. "Just to let you know that Gerald's still alive—the man has more lives than a cat. Lost a lot of blood, but he's stabilized and they're transfusing him now. Stab wound under the arm, may have nicked a lung. A dagger, a carving knife. Something like that and probably forty fathoms deep by now. We opened Adèle and Charlotte's stateroom and found a blouse with a bloody sleeve stuffed into their toilet but not successfully flushed. They're quick, those two. Got up from the table in the dark, everyone looking at those damned puddings, slipped the knife in from the back—lucky thing it *was* dark, otherwise Gerald would be dead. And scooted to their stateroom, shed any bloody clothes, and took off."

"And you haven't found them?" put in Liza.

Aubrey shook his head. "No. But we will. It's a matter of time. And Sarah, your Frederick . . ."

"Not," said Sarah, "my Frederick, but I'm very sorry I gave you a wrong steer about him, and now I've caused him a lot of grief."

"It's all right. Frederick's in the clear and we need him— and the other waiters. They may be able to help us tell when Gerald was attacked, because there's a good chance that one of them saw one of the French sisters where she shouldn't be and we'd have a witness. Now I'm off to help out with the search. I've got two men waiting outside."

Sarah jumped to her feet. "Wait up. I have this crazy idea."

"We do not," said Aubrey, "need a crazy idea."

"Listen, it can't hurt. It's just that I might have been locked in that utility room by one of those two women. They may have gotten a key from Mary Malone. They could have used the room as a bolt-hole before and after doing in old General Gordon. Or they supervised the attack on him. It's a reasonable guess, any-way."

"A guess, but I'm not sure how reasonable," said Aubrey.

"But you haven't searched this corridor yet, have you? No? Then, please, get your men. Let me show you because the room's right down the hall."

Aubrey rubbed his head, frowning. "I think I know where the room is. Near General Gordon's. So you stay put."

"You need me if you don't really know where it is," said Sarah. "I won't get in the way. I promise. No, Aunt Julia, you can't come. Teddy, Liza, sit on Julia. Let's go, Aubrey." And Sarah ran to the stateroom door, opened it, and then, followed by a dubious Aubrey and two men who had waited for him, walked past the line of doors until she came to the unnumbered, almost invisible closet entrance. "There," she said almost in a whisper. "But watch out. Those two may be sitting in there with hand grenades."

Aubrey pushed Sarah behind him, beckoned to one of the men, who silently produced a key, inserted it into the lock, backed himself out of range, and kicked it open. The second man, holding a large flashlight over his head, shot the beam into the opening.

And there they were. Huddled against the familiar mop and ironing board, peering, blinking into the light. They were, thought Sarah, taking a sneak look over Aubrey's shoulder, like two crones whose potions and tricks have failed and now awaited the wrath of heaven—or, more likely, the wrath of hell.

"You both come out with your hands on top of your head," shouted the first man, whom Sarah now recognized as the large-jawed one who had supposedly guarded Gerald during dinner. He repeated the command in French, adding, *"Vite, vite."*

And they came. Wearing matching plum-colored raincoats, heads high, chins out, narrow shoulders braced, mouths pinched closed in a tight grimace. And dark brown eyes bright with hate.

Afterword

MONDAY morning, July the third, presented passengers aboard the *Queen Victoria* with almost calm seas, a brilliant sun, and a soft southern breeze. Sarah and Alex, packed and ready by dawn, joined Julia Clancy in the Osborne Cafeteria for a last splendid breakfast before the ship docked in New York. They were joined briefly at the buffet table by Deedee and Richard Herrick. Deedee seemed buoyant. The "Ships in Peril" series was now history and Gerald Hofstra, no longer a problem, had become an object of her pity and concern.

"I visited him in the hospital this morning," announced Deedee as she helped herself to an oversize waffle, "and he says he's going to rethink his career. That perhaps working with amateurs like us is not something he's suited for. He said something about us not getting the big picture."

"I think," said Richard gruffly, "that Gerald was damn lucky to have latched on to us. As far as Hollywood or the theater goes, I'd say he's pretty much over the hill."

"And I," said Deedee, "am trying to be charitable." And the two Herricks stepped away toward a distant table.

The next disturbers of their peace—as Julia termed it—

were Teddy Hogarth, combed and almost healthy looking in a gray business suit and carrying a briefcase, and Liza, in yellow slacks and a red striped shirt, her fair hair bound in a red leather band.

"We've agreed to disagree," said Liza. "Ted will try life without me and keep his nose to the trade commission grindstone, and then at the end of two weeks we might fly out to LA and see my family."

"Liza lives to push people around. Especially drunks like me," said Teddy cheerfully. "So we'll try the separation route for a bit. She may really hate me sober. In fact, I'm beginning to bore myself. The corporate kid, the Circumlocution Office's junior clerk."

"I hope," said Julia as the two departed, "that we can now eat without any more reunions. We have a long day ahead. Make out our customs slip, pick up the rental car, get to Maine."

"And make depositions about last night's goings-on," Alex reminded them.

"Oh, but that can be long distance with a local attorney," Sarah said. "I saw Aubrey on the way in and he told me. And he wants to meet us after breakfast. A last debriefing. Guess where?"

"The Snuggery," exclaimed Julia and Alex in one voice.

"The chaplain's office. Our other favorite trysting spot."

"Speaking of 'spot,' " boomed a voice, "I have a confession. May I join you?"

"The more," said Julia in a sour voice—she had not forgiven Erik Anderson—"does not mean the merrier."

Erik balancing a platter of poached eggs and bacon with muffins on the side, pulled up a chair next to her and heaved a deep breath. "Actually," he said, "I have two confessions. The first is about my grandchildren. Brian and Kirsten."

"You mean they're not really your grandchildren?" said Julia, speaking in the same unfriendly tone.

"I almost wish they weren't. You see, they've had this game going. With a couple of other kids. They worked it up after they saw the movie. *Treasure Island.*"

"And what does that have to do with us?" snapped Julia.

"Aunt Julia, hush," Sarah threatened. "We want to hear. I love *Treasure Island*."

Erik shook his head. "I got it out of the kids this morning. Caught 'em in the act. Cutting up paper into circles, coloring one side black, and printing on the other side, 'You have till ten tonight.' Printed it just the way it is in the book."

Sarah's eyes widened. "Yes! Yes! Of course. The Black Spot. The Admiral Benbow Inn. Billy Bones drinking rum and getting the Black Spot from Blind Pew. And Billy dropping dead from apoplexy."

"Right!" said Erik in admiration. "You've got it. It was all a game. Without my knowing a thing about it, these kids have been sneaking Black Spots into people's staterooms—under the doors—or leaving them—"

"In needlepoint bags!" exclaimed Julia. "Well, I'll be damned."

"I think you were," said Erik gently. "I felt I had to tell Security about you having received one. And now here's my second confession. I had promised my old friend Aubrey to keep an ear out for any . . . well, call them expressions of hate. Particularly having to do with the *Titanic* show. And Julia, I'm afraid I was a real snitch. You were so vehement about Gerald Hofstra and how you hated his exploiting the tragedy—and how your mother had lost an uncle on the *Titanic*—well, I felt I had to share the information. I'm very sorry about your trip to the Security Office, and I know what I'm telling you is upsetting."

Julia glared at him, eyes blazing. "Upsetting! How . . . how could you? How on earth could you? Go away. Just go away. I hope I never see you again and I hope . . ."

Sarah put her hand gently on her aunt's arm. "Easy, Auntie. He's trying to apologize. And you *were* pretty outspoken."

Julia shook Sarah off, sputtered, opened her mouth to speak, and then turned away, and Sarah saw a tear about to brim over from one eye. And Erik Anderson pushed back his chair and, carrying his plate, left the table.

Alex, entirely silent during this exchange, shook his head. "Let's eat up and get down to the Chapel. Finish this thing. I promised to look in on Gerald and Amory this morning before we disembark. They'll be taking them off to the hospital, and the medical staff wants to make sure they can be transferred safely."

The meeting in the chapel office was short, not sweet, but to the point. Once again Sarah found the four saints looking down at her, their expressions enigmatic, indifferent to the ills of the world. Aubrey, now rested and in a lightweight summer suit and striped tie—his old regiment? Sarah wondered, but then remembered. Aubrey came from the world of the Royal Navy. And right now he was conducting the briefing exactly like some executive naval officer.

"First," said Aubrey, "I want to thank you for your assistance. Alex for lending us his medical expertise; Sarah for her meddling, which was nicely balanced by her concern and her alertness; Julia for her forbearance and with apologies for her encounter with the Security Office. I am to blame for putting pressure on Erik Anderson, and he was, needless to say, unhappy about his role in the matter."

"But what," interrupted Sarah, trying to steer the conversation away from Erik, "about Adèle and Charlotte?"

"Yes," said Aubrey. "Well, as you must guess we couldn't run a check on every passenger aboard the *Victoria*. There may well be others aboard whose great-grandparents, great-aunts, great-uncles had friends or family members who took passage on *Titanic* and were lost. With the result that orphans were left, hope of a future in the New World gone and their life turned into a bitter and unforgiving struggle. But it took a peculiar paranoia—I'm using the word loosely—mixed with a vengeful nature to produce these four people and bring them together. They all had two things in common."

"They lost key members of an earlier generation," put in Aunt Julia. "Like my mother's Aunt Harriet."

"Exactly. Mary Malone you know about. I've found out that she's an absolute encyclopedia of *Titanic* information, especially the statistics about third-class passenger loss. Amory Frye, I've told you, was, through his great-grandfather's death and his family's subsequent poverty, directly affected by the sinking. And Adèle and Charlotte are the third generation of a family cut to pieces by the loss of their great-grandfather and great-grandmother. Their grandmothers—children then—were from a French family who had promises of a new life in Quebec, but had to turn around and live and struggle in France as *enfants trouvées*—orphans."

"But how did they all finally get together?" asked Sarah, puzzled. "How did Adèle and Charlotte recruit Mary and Amory? Such different people. Did those newspaper ads do it?"

"Yes, that was the start. Certainly they are very different people, but they have two things in common. One, as you know, is the *Titanic* experience. The second, a pure and lively hatred of all things English. Mary is Irish—enough said; Amory, an expatriate American living in England but with a mighty chip on his shoulder about a country he decided was at the bottom of his family's troubles. Adèle and Charlotte shared with some of their countrymen the ancient suspicion and dislike of the English—in their case fueled and fanned by their family's *Titanic* experience. It was the perfect quartet for a clandestine operation: a stewardess with keys to staterooms who had free hours during the day, a chaplain's assistant who went everywhere with few questions."

"Until I caught him with Mary in my stateroom," put in Julia.

"Right," said Aubrey. "Then add Adèle and Charlotte, two Balmoral-class—or first-class—passengers who could direct the goings-on without getting their hands dirty."

What," asked Sarah, who liked conclusions, "is going to happen to them all?"

"Adèle and Charlotte? It will take time. Right now they are angrily demanding to see the French consul when we hit New York. Much talk about their rights as French citizens. Amory, when he recovers, will return to face the music—the British judicial system. And Mary will join him in the dock."

"Is Mary up for attempted murder?" asked Julia. "You know, I really liked that woman. And she saved my life."

Aubrey rose from his chair and faced Julia. "Then, Mrs. Clancy, you may be called on by Mary's counsel for some sort of statement having to do with mitigating circumstances. And so good bye, all." He extended his hand to Julia, to Alex, and then to Sarah, on whom he bestowed a wry smile. "I have to thank you again for the useful Harrods bag. You were right, it *was* evidence and we *were* interested in fingerprints. Amory Frye's to be exact. And Sarah, when next I go out into the world I hope not to meet with you—or if I do, to have chosen a better nom de plume. And Margaret Lee says to tell you that she is giving up her southern alias and looking for a persona that won't make you suspicious. A well digger from Tasmania, perhaps."

Alex and Sarah and Julia stood at the foot of the gangplank, pausing for a minute before braving the customs declaration line. And as they hesitated, behind them came a small procession of men, some holding aloft IV bags, others carrying two stretchers, one after the other and followed by a watchful ship's medical officer. And as the second stretcher came abreast of the three, a weak voice called out. It was Gerald Hofstra, wrapped like a mummy with only his pale gargoyle face showing. He rolled his eyes at Sarah. "I'm switching gears, babe," he said. "No more of this amateur stuff. I'll be doing a big-time film script. World class. Been thinking about it all night. Ready-made plot."

"Really," said Sarah, smiling down at him. "What's it going to be called?"

"*A Voyage to Remember.* You like? Yeah, I know it's sort of a spin-off from that other book by what's-his-name, Walter Lord, but then it takes off like gangbusters on its own. I think it'll be a real smash." And Gerald extricated a hand from his blanket and gave a feeble wave and was borne out of sight.

"Good God," said Alex with feeling. Then, "Okay, let's get a move on. There's our customs section ahead. We can get through in nothing flat. After all, no one bought much."

"We were all too busy chasing after liars and terrorists and people wrapped in badminton nets to do any real shopping," Sarah reminded him. She turned to look behind her. "Now where on earth has Aunt Julia gone?"

Alex nudged her and pointed ahead. Erik Anderson stood in a line of passengers, a small canvas bag at his feet. And in front of him, head tilted up, her face flushed, and her hand extended in what appeared to be a gesture of greeting, was Julia Clancy.

"A farewell scene," said Alex.

"I think," said Sarah, inspecting the two, "I hear the sound of the hunting horn and the thunder of hooves. And see two riders galloping off together into the sunset."

"Or if not together," said Alex, "at least one after the other."

"Yes," agreed Sarah. "And Julia is ahead by a neck."